PASIPHAË

Jane Dougherty

The Book Social, 51 Gower Street, London, WC1E 6HJ
info@thebooksocial.co.uk | www.thebooksocial.co.uk

Contents © Jane Dougherty 2026
The right of the above author to be identified as the author of this work has been asserted in accordance with the Copyright, Designs and Patents Act 1988. British Library Cataloguing in Publication Data available.

Print ISBN 978-1-91716-329-3
Ebook ISBN 978-1-91716-330-9
Set in Times.

Cover design by Rose Cooper | www.rosecooper.com

All characters, other than those clearly in the public domain, and place names, other than those well-established such as towns and cities, are fictitious and any resemblance is purely coincidental.

All rights reserved. No part of this publication may be reproduced, stored in or introduced into a retrieval system, or transmitted, in any form, or by any means electronic, mechanical, photocopying, recording or otherwise, without the prior permission of the publisher. Any person who commits any unauthorised act in relation to this publication may be liable to criminal prosecution and civil claims for damages.

Jane Dougherty is of Irish origin, and was brought up in Yorkshire. She studied Early European Medieval History and Literature at Manchester University. Her first job with a London wine merchant, sent her to Paris where she settled down and worked until her fourth child was born and the family moved to Laon, a medieval town in the Aisne. She worked as a freelance translator and voice actress in Laon, where her fifth child was born, and began writing short stories and a YA series for her teenage children. She carried on translating and recording voice-overs for short films after the family moved south to Bordeaux. Her first novel was published by an American publisher Musa in 2014, then a YA series by Finch Books in 2016. Since moving to the countryside of the Lot-et-Garonne in 2017, Jane has written several novels. Her poetry and short stories have been published online and in anthologies and magazines. She has been nominated twice for the Pushcart Prize and has published three poetry pamphlets.

This book is dedicated to my parents, grandparents and all the grandparents before them, for giving me a history and teaching me its importance. They gave me both the passion for unravelling a story until I hold the threads of a truth, and the tools to create something new with them.

PART ONE

The far-shining girl

Pasiphaë, Moon Princess of Kolchis, was wife of one star and mother of another. Her story began, to all intents and purposes, at the first full moon after the spring equinox of her fifteenth year. It began as the story of the second daughter of the royal house of a not very important country, and it grew and swelled, like a child growing in its mother's belly. It became the story of a woman who rose to the summit of the greatest power in the world. She was given two stars to hold, and when they fell, the world fell too.

1

Kolchis

The touch of a hand on her shoulder dragged Pasiphaë from the blinding blue of sea and sky, dissipated the scents of honey and thyme on hilltops baking in searing dry heat, the taste of roses. The roaring of lions faded. Wolves were howling their eerie songs on the mountain, and all that remained of the dream was a pang of longing and loneliness.

'Princess, your mother wants you.'

The young pine marten curled up on the pillow woke too, opened amber eyes, unwound her supple body and stretched. With a sigh, Pasiphaë swung her legs out of bed. The servant didn't bother to explain, and she didn't ask. These midnight summonses happened often enough. She slipped her feet into her sandals, and the girl handed her a warm cloak. Together they pattered across stone pavements through the sleeping house. The marten followed.

The royal house of Aea was old, perched on a hill among tall trees, lush and evergreen. It was spring, it had been raining, and the night air was sweet, salty and flowery. Pasiphaë tried to recapture the dream, the taste of roses, but curiosity about what her mother wanted swept it away definitively. She followed the servant through the house, the empty central courtyard where the sacred basin lay still and silvery in the silence. This wasn't an official ritual then, with fierce priestesses and the wild weaving of sacred dances. This was special, secret, and they left the courtyard and the house behind, taking the path through the night garden.

In a clearing among the dark trees was Perseis's private stone basin, and Pasiphaë entered the grove of fig, plum and oak alone. The spot was sheltered by a dark flank of the hills, clad in a thick pelt of pine forest. Dawn broke late here, but evening lingered in the scented faces of roses, the pale blooms of rhododendrons. Through their wild vegetation, she saw the light of flames flickering on water.

Night spread stars overhead between the passing clouds, and below, fire blazed bright. In and out of the firelight, shadows moved – Perseis, her mother, and Circe, her older sister. Dark hair glittering with gemstones was caught up in golden fillets; dark eyes flashed in the flame light. Her mother and sister had dressed as carefully for this ritual as they would have done for a public one.

'Mamá, what's all this about?' Excitement chopped the words small, nostrils quivered at the smell of herbs in the tripod over the fire, pine smoke, the sharp pinch of juniper. The moon sailed between the clouds, revealing the broad smile on her sister Circe's face.

'We're going to find you a husband.'

Perseis hushed her. 'We're going to *look* and hope that we find.'

Circe shrugged. 'Why wouldn't we? The world's full of men.'

Perseis shot Circe a reproachful look. 'Exactly. Too full. The world's getting smaller, louder. Even the sea creeps now with warships full of men looking for adventure, booty, people to enslave. Remember those brutes washed ashore this spring? Thinking they'd find golden sheep grazing in the fields with only a few girls to protect them?' She sighed one of her theatrical sighs. 'We will have to cast our nets wide to find a suitable husband for you, Pasiphaë.'

Perseis made it sound like a hardship, but Pasiphaë knew there was nothing her mother loved more than disappearing into the sea. She practised water magic, and some claimed she wasn't a woman at all but a nymph. Sometimes she thought her mother was neither woman nor nymph, that her true nature was wave. When she talked about her countless sisters, Pasiphaë saw them as the rippling surface of the sea. She was never invited when Perseis took Circe to visit these famous aunts, to swim with dolphins and women as supple as seals. She had no sea blood, they said. She was the Moon Princess, a daughter of the sky and the air. Pasiphaë hated the sea.

'Where? How far?'

Perseis sprinkled a pinch of something pungent into the bronze bowl from a jar placed on the parapet of the water basin, and sparks spat, green and blue. 'Patience.'

Pasiphaë settled her skirts about her and perched on the edge of the basin. The marten sprang onto her lap, then her shoulder, and peered through the smoke into the pool from beneath her ear. From another jar, with a polished wooden spoon, Perseis took some of the thick, sticky potion that she called *fruits of the earth*, a mess of dried and ground leaves and berries, mushrooms and bark. There was blood in it too, and beetles' wings. The mess was full of magic and visions, and Pasiphaë watched with a slight shudder as her mother's teeth parted, her tongue darted, almost as red as her painted lips. The dark, heavy-smelling stuff disappeared and her jaw worked, chewing. With a gesture of studied indifference, Circe helped herself to a spoonful and drifted off, chewing abstractedly, to sit at the pool's edge.

Perseis swallowed, licked her lips and looked down into the pool where petals floated, broad and pale in the moonlight – rhododendrons. The water was misty, but not with cloud reflections. Circe played a tune in honour of the Mistresses on a syrinx. The reeds fluttered softly like small birds, and Pasiphaë hummed then took up the words of the song, a song of life and love and death.

Her mother swept the surface of the basin with a bundle of oak leaves, her movements as graceful and fluid as waves, murmuring an incantation, too low for Pasiphaë to catch the words. Pasiphaë watched, singing and rocking to and fro, waiting for the water to clear. The water would clear for her mother; it always did. Circe would claim she saw the vision too. Maybe she would; her eyes were certainly sharp enough. Pasiphaë expected simply to be told what the vision showed.

Circe's tune changed tempo and volume, loud now as the fluting of an owl, and she watched, almost as intently as Pasiphaë, the story that was beginning to unfold on the pool's surface. Circe knew her destiny. As the elder, she would rule in Aea after Perseis, but beyond Kolchis, who knew how many peoples respected the ways of the Mistresses? Did anyone? Pasiphaë understood why Circe would be pleased to have a sister in a strong place to keep back the wave of bronze blades that was sweeping the world.

'Stop fidgeting. It's a bad habit.' Circe frowned at her from beneath the dark cloud of her curls. 'And that creature in your hair,' she wrinkled her nose, 'it's disgusting.'

Pasiphaë placed a protective hand on the small animal peeping through her sleep-loosened tresses and glared at her sister. Perseis paid no attention. She rarely noticed fidgety or untidy behaviour. Her thoughts rolled with the tides, and she moved with them, in waves of graceful gestures, at one with the water, her thoughts woven into the unseen currents. Suddenly, her pose tensed. Circe's mockery stopped abruptly, forgotten, as she too peered into the pool.

'Pasiphaë, shut up.'

'I didn't say anything!'

'Mamá, is that Knossos?'

'Such a big house, immense, gallery after gallery, tier upon tier…' Perseis's voice was distant, a song at the bottom of the pool. Pasiphaë listened. 'Paintings, blue and red, golden dancers, lilies, bulls. Where else can it be?'

'It seems empty. There's something missing. I don't feel any…'

'In the dark room, do you see, Circe? On the bed? The girl in red, pale as death.'

'Is she dead, Mamá? She looks it. Laid out all in red, like a blown poppy, and such a weight of gold at her neck…'

'It's a serpent. She was a High Priestess. Princess.'

Pasiphaë saw nothing, just water lilies and reflections of the stars. She glanced at her mother, waited for her glazed eyes to focus again, for her to explain.

'Europa is dead, but I knew that, and she must have been forty when she died. This dead Princess isn't Europa.'

'So, who is she?' Pasiphaë found some interest, if only morbid, in the fate of a girl who looked much the same age as herself.

'I'd say it's Kriti, the child Europa had with Asterius of Knossos. Her only daughter. She must be ten or eleven years old now, and they say she is sickly. This dead poppy girl looks rather older.' Perseis glanced at Pasiphaë. 'About fourteen, maybe fifteen. The seeing must be showing the future. Kriti might not be dead yet, but it looks as though she soon will be.' Perseis frowned, considering the future and how she and hers fitted into it. 'Of course, the seeing might be wrong, but if, when Kriti dies…'

'If Kriti dies, one of those half-brothers of hers will demand the throne.' Circe's eyes had narrowed, staring into a bloody, violent future.

Perseis was barely listening, deep in thought, picking shreds of scrying potion from between her teeth. The bitter mixture sharpened her sight, she said. It certainly made her see some very funny things. Circe used it too. Pasiphaë had tried the foul-tasting stuff once and had had to go and lie down for the rest of the day, her head full of flashing lights, burning clouds, trees that grew limbs and leapt like dolphins into the sea. Perseis had not proposed it again.

'So, suppose Kriti dies, who does that leave?' Perseis asked herself thoughtfully.

'Europa hasn't got any nieces?' Pasiphaë asked, more to

show that she was following the conversation than out of any real interest.

'Oh, pay attention, Pasiphaë,' Circe snapped. 'Haven't you followed anything? Europa doesn't count, she's foreign, and not of the bloodline, so where do her nieces come into it?'

'Why was she Queen then?'

It was true that Pasiphaë hadn't ever followed talk about family histories. They were all so complicated. Her mother, possibly deciding it was time that Pasiphaë knew a little about the unlucky fortunes of the royal house of Knossos, took her hands and looked sternly into her eyes. A signal to Pasiphaë that she was to listen carefully.

'Years ago, Knossos had a Queen named Keraso, and she chose Lycastus for her King. Well, her last King. She'd had several, but never any children. When Keraso died, it was decided to find the old King Lycastus another Queen, and the one the families of Knossos chose was Europa of Tyre.'

'Tyre? Why—'

'That's another story. All that concerns us is that Europa produced only males for Lycastus, so when he died, they found her another husband from the same royal house as Keraso.'

'Asterius?'

Perseis nodded and smiled. 'Asterius. And she finally produced a daughter, Kriti, who will be Queen when she is old enough, and if she is still alive. Understand now?'

'And apart from Kriti,' Circe grinned, showing small white teeth, 'there's no one left of the old Queen Keraso's bloodline, except Karpasia, of course.'

Perseis looked thoughtful. 'I'd almost forgotten about her.'

'Who's Karpasia?'

'A niece, grand-niece maybe,' Perseis replied in a faraway voice.

'Well then—'

'Be quiet, Pasiphaë. Karpasia has a cleft lip and doesn't want to be Queen. Mind you, they say Minos has been pushing her claim anyway.'

'Who's Minos?' Pasiphaë asked, but her mother wasn't listening.

Perseis frowned. 'I heard he is even offering to organise the choice of her King. I wonder whose name the divination would come up with?'

'At a guess, I'd say Minos. On the other hand, it could be Minos. Unless it was Minos of course,' Circe said laconically. 'And I don't suppose he's particularly interested in what her face looks like. He'd marry her if she had cow's hooves and brayed like a donkey, to get his backside on the throne.'

'That would be disastrous. I imagine Asterius feels the same way. I wonder what he'll do?'

*

Pasiphaë let her mother and sister's voices fade out, weighing the possibility of this, the unlikelihood of that. She had lost interest in the plot, the windings of a family tree of a distant royal house. Men didn't rule; they didn't decide anything. She dropped a flower petal in the water, blew on it. A tiny boat, drifting. She sighed heavily. As if remembering her second daughter was still there, Perseis turned and looked at her with the pride of a potter in a well-made jar.

'This one was not named far-shining for nothing. She'll keep the light of the Mistresses alive. Knossos will be safe with our little Pasiphaë on the throne.'

This time, it was a pebble Pasiphaë dropped in the water. 'Me? You said yourself, this Princess Kriti isn't dead yet, that the seeing only shows what might happen. If she doesn't die, she'll be Queen as soon as she's old enough. What's all this story of sons and cleft lips and thrones got to do with who I'm to marry?'

Perseis exchanged a quick glance with Circe and smiled indulgently at her younger daughter. 'Of course, Pasiphaë, you're quite right. Kriti is the heiress and will inherit the throne of Knossos. But Knossos needs a Queen now, a regent, if only for a few years, to keep the throne safe for her. It would be a shame if, because of some palace intrigue, she were to find someone else was sitting on her throne when she comes of age. So unfair.'

'Until then, as the wife of Asterius, you'll rule in her place,' Circe said, and snapped her fingers. 'Simple.'

'Has anyone told Asterius? What if he doesn't want to marry me?'

'He will. There must be a Queen at Knossos, and you'll do very nicely.'

Perseis beamed, but Pasiphaë could not rid herself of the image of a fearsome, vengeful woman with a cleft lip. 'He should marry whatshername, whatever she looks like.'

'Don't be silly.' Circe was already sweeping up her skirts as if everything was settled. 'He can't. He's Karpasia's uncle. Or perhaps she's his aunt, I'd have to work it out. They're far too close anyway.'

Pasiphaë was lost, but she had grasped the gist. The last of the female line of Knossos was Princess Kriti, who was a child and might or might not die young. If she did, Knossos would need a Queen quickly, before someone decided a King would be more appropriate. It was an extraordinary idea, and it only made Pasiphaë even more apprehensive.

'Do the Mistresses not counsel them then? Don't they listen to what custom tells them?'

Perseis read her daughter's fear, and in a rare show of affection, put an arm around her and kissed her on the brow. She smiled. 'Of course they do. Knossos holds the Mistresses in the highest esteem, and you, Pasiphaë, as Moon Princess and High Priestess of Potnia Theron, Mistress of Animals, will be especially beloved. As adept of Theron, you will make sure that custom is followed, and the throne is kept safe for the Queen.'

Pasiphaë flinched at the recitation of her titles. The burden weighed heavy sometimes, and she noticed Perseis didn't say the throne was to be kept *for Princess Kriti.* The unseen image of the girl who would soon be dead, if the seeing was correct, floated behind her eyes, like a blood-red water lily on the pool.

Perseis decided the convocation was over and rose with a satisfied sigh. The marten on Pasiphaë's shoulder stared at her, unblinking, but shrank away when she tried to stroke her head.

'She's timid, Mamá,' Pasiphaë said in excuse.

'Wild,' Perseis corrected. 'Animals obey their own rules and only Potnia Theron and her favourite adepts understand them.' She smiled again and stroked her daughter's cheek instead. 'The Bull will dance for you, and you will hold the end of the string. Tight.'

*

The night was full of scent. Floral and spiced, with the tang of the not distant sea. Pasiphaë lay awake, waiting for the moon to fill the window space with serenity. She was to marry Asterius and keep Crete within the arms of the Mistresses, but her thoughts ran on after Kriti's death, as she knew her mother's and Circe's did. Whatever they pretended, she knew they expected her to be Queen, and her daughter after her, in the dead girl's place.

Circe had gone off into one of her regal harangues about the responsibility of incarnating the power of the Mistresses and preventing their cult being watered down by foreign gods. Circe was so much better suited to the job than Pasiphaë. She would have enjoyed it. What a shame she was already married.

Pasiphaë wondered if marrying a Bull King would be the same as marrying the Sun King. The Cretan custom was different, but was it only a superficial difference? Would the Bull be as yielding in the end as the Sun? She knew she wasn't as strong as Circe, and she feared that she would have no more power over the bull than the heifers he covered. She was disturbed by the idea that Minos had designs on the throne.

She knew what happened to women in the places where men ruled, and she didn't want to be a slave. In the morning, she would visit her father. He would explain truths that Perseis would gloss over as if they didn't matter.

The pine marten crept onto her pillow and chittered softly in her ear. She was frightened too.

2

Aloeus

Circe flounced into Pasiphaë's room, and the pine marten dashed across Pasiphaë's bed and out of the door. Circe shrieked as the small animal brushed past her. 'You'll have to behave more like an adult, you know, when you're at Knossos. Sleeping with that animal is disgusting.'

'Why don't you talk to me like an adult then?'

'Because I can't take you seriously. Make an effort! You're supposed to be High Priestess.'

'Of Potnia Theron. Mistress of Animals. Remember?'

'There's more to creation than fluffy little animals, you know. And the High Priestess isn't expected to spend all her time playing with them. You'll be a married woman soon, and a Queen. Managing a husband and a country isn't like training a pine marten. Mother behaves as if every man just does as he's told, but he won't unless you spell things out to him.'

Pasiphaë looked up at the ceiling. She hated it when Circe lectured her about being a woman, a priestess, a credit, a Queen. She only did it to frighten her, to make her dread everything that happened to her.

'Anyway, I just wanted to tell you, in case you needed either of us, that Mamá and I are going to the island house today.'

'And I'm not invited.'

Circe rolled her eyes theatrically. 'We thought it would be better that you didn't put yourself in danger, not when we're so close to finding you a husband. You know that you and the sea don't get on.'

'I suppose you'll be taking Medea with you,' Pasiphaë said darkly.

Circe smiled broadly before replying. 'Of course. The child must be trained. A talent like hers could be dangerous for everyone if it isn't taken in hand now.'

Medea was a niece, their older brother Aeëtes's nine-year-old daughter, and Pasiphaë considered her a brat. She was no judge of magical skills, but she did know that Circe was quite capable of exaggerating Medea's talent just to hurt her. She had a cruel streak, like their other brother, Perses, but Perses had only his fists to give it expression. Circe had magic.

Circe waited with a smile to see how her announcement was received. Pasiphaë had no doubt that she expected an outburst of petulant outrage. She shrugged. 'Well, don't worry about me. I don't want to drown myself either. Go play at being dolphins together. I shall visit my father. There are things I want to talk to him about.'

Circe's lip curled in a sneer. 'Have you got a question about foot rot in the sheep, or a new kind of scabies in the cattle?'

Pasiphaë swung her legs over the side of the bed and stood up. She was as tall as Circe and looked her directly in the eyes. 'I enjoy his company. Father doesn't use conversation to belittle or to score points.'

'The question doesn't arise when the conversations are with farm animals. But do give Aloeus my respects all the same. I'll think of you both, talking to the pigs while I am teaching Medea how to call up a storm from a high tide.'

Circe turned on her heels and left. A trail of some strange musky perfume lingered in her wake. She was angry, had never forgiven her stepfather for trying to curb what she saw as her right to terrorise. She would be Queen, and he had no authority over her. He wasn't even her father. Even so, Pasiphaë saw that it saddened him that he meant so little to Perseis's other children. Circe disliked him, and neither Aeëtes nor Perses looked up to him, or turned to him for guidance. Pasiphaë was his daughter, though, his only child, and the only one of Perseis's children to visit him at the house where he had lived in quiet seclusion since he was retired from his functions as King.

Aea had no palace. The royal house rarely received visitors, and those who did venture to cross the Inhospitable Sea were commercial traders, not noble heads of state. Kolchis was wealthy enough, but sheepskins did not have the same attraction as precious metals or ceramics. Aea was quiet, and Pasiphaë thought nobody would have noticed if the old King still lived in the royal house, but Perseis had insisted that she couldn't allow Aloeus what had been denied her two previous Kings, so he had moved into his hilltop solitude.

Pasiphaë regretted it, but Aloeus counted himself lucky. Custom had it that a Queen took a King for seven years. When his time was up, his life was ended in the oak grove, and the Queen took another King. That was the old custom, though, and these days not all Kings ended up hanging from an oak tree. Perseis had decided not to replace Aloeus, but to let him live out his life in half-forgotten seclusion. Aloeus had built his retreat on a sunny hillside looking down on the sea, the mountains and forests thick and green at its back. Pasiphaë felt as at home there as in in the royal house at Aea.

*

The path to the house wound through green pastures edged with oak. The orchard produced plums and peaches, and Aloeus kept bees. He tended his flocks and herds himself, with the help of a few herdsmen and women who made sure there was always cheese to eat with his honey. He had never wanted more than this quiet life, and of all the royal children, Pasiphaë was the one who understood why, the one who could sit with him in silence, watching the sun set across the great grey sea, listening to nightingales filling the dusk with their interminable songs.

The house was small, undistinguished. Pasiphaë took off her sandals, threw them into a corner behind the door and pattered barefoot to where she knew she would find her father. He had everything he needed in the room that looked down on the sea, with its terrace for the spring and autumn days, its hearth for the winter. She opened the door without knocking. She had retained a childish delight in catching her father unawares. Observing him sitting in the light, absorbed in some task, filled her with affection.

Aloeus wasn't old. Pasiphaë didn't think so anyway. There was silver in his hair, but the black still dominated, and he had a soft voice. His movements were measured; he took his time. He took the time to explain things too, and to tell his stories. Aloeus had lots of stories, the stories the country people told, about sheep and cows, giant fish and forest spirits. He knew about the heart of things. Perseis knew about administration, the value of crops, the exchange of sheepskins and barley. She knew about lineage, who was related to whom, the different High Priestesses, Queens and heirs. She told Pasiphaë only what she considered she needed to know.

'It's complicated, sweetheart,' she'd say, 'and it's really not your problem. You already have so much to learn, and you want Potnia Theron to be pleased with her High Priestess, don't you?'

Of course Pasiphaë did, and sometimes she felt she would never be capable of learning all the rituals, but she did want to know whom she was to marry. Asterius sounded harmless enough, but there was all the business about Europa that she wanted to understand. She would be living with Europa's sons too, and from what Circe said, at least one of them had strange notions about who should inherit the throne now that his mother was dead. Her father would know, and he would explain.

She stood in the doorway of the little room with the big window full of light, her eyes drawn as ever to the painted frieze of goats and sheep in a field, at the musical instruments propped against the wall beneath it. Her gaze lingered fondly on her father, waiting for him to realise she was there. He had a sheepskin over his shoulders despite the warm sun, and the cups and dishes of his last meal, the same dented and worn cups and dishes of her earliest memories, were still on the table. His head was bent over the piece of wood he was carving, absorbed in some detail, and it was the dogs who welcomed her first. They raised their heads and thumped their tails on the floor. Pasiphaë thought it would be more respectful on their part if they had at least got to their feet, but they were old country dogs and didn't know any better.

Aloeus too raised his head, his hand with the small knife poised over the creature he was carving. 'Pasiphaë! I was thinking of you. Look.' He held up the piece of olive wood, showed her the sinuous form of a running long-tailed animal. 'What do you think? Is it like?'

Pasiphaë's face broke into a broad smile and she took the carving from him, running a finger along the marten's silky back. 'It's perfect. Just like her.'

'It will be. She's not finished yet. Her face needs making and her toes. Soon though. So, what brings you up here? Has your mother magicked up a husband for you?'

'She has. That's what I wanted to talk to you about. It's Asterius of Knossos.'

Aloeus raised an eyebrow, waited.

'Mamá won't tell me much about him, or the rest of them.'

'Your mother is a wise woman. Asterius is a good choice. From what I've heard, he is a fine man. Respectful and wise. You won't have any difficulty with him.'

'But it's not just him, is it? There are his sons and he has a daughter who will be Queen, and nobody wants to explain what will happen to me then!'

Aloeus placed the carved marten on a table next to his chair and stretched out his legs. 'I imagine your mother told you about how the continuation of the royal line rests on Princess Kriti?'

'Whether she'll live to be Queen? That's the point. Mother

doesn't say what will happen to me if she does, and I'm no longer needed, or what will happen if she dies and the noble families choose a new Queen.'

Aloeus smiled. 'In either case, I expect you and Asterius will retire to live in Knossan luxury in the royal palace. They're not barbarians, you know.'

'You say that! But even the barbarians know that only a Queen can rule. Mamá says that Minos, one of Europa's sons, thinks he ought to rule as King. How is that civilised?'

Aloeus threw back his head and laughed. His eyes disappeared into billows of wrinkles in his ageing, outdoor face, but his teeth were white and strong, and there was no malice in the sound of his laughter. 'Spoken like a true daughter of the Mistresses. It's what passes for civilised with the Greeks.'

Pasiphaë didn't see what the Greeks had to do with anything. Aloeus glanced at the furrows forming on her brow and anticipated the unspoken question.

'Europa, the wife they found for Lycastus, was Greek, from Tyre, an economic arrangement.'

'Mamá said. Was she very rich?'

'Extremely. And it stopped the bickering that had started about which family should provide the next Queen. So, they brought over this Europa, and she produced three sons.'

'But no daughters.'

'No. And then Lycastus died, leaving Europa – who was foreign, Greek and wouldn't accept to rule even if she'd been asked – and her three sons.'

Pasiphaë shuffled on her stool. This was the part that seemed most ominously important. 'And Europa thought one of her sons should rule instead. But that doesn't happen, except among the Greeks. And she wasn't among the Greeks.'

Aloeus nodded. 'Unfortunately, she had brought her sons up with Greek ideas about succession, even whispering to them that their father wasn't the Bull King, Lycastus, but the Greeks' chief god, Zeus, in the form of a bull.' Pasiphaë grimaced in disgust. 'I know, Europa seems to have been rather simple-minded. The two elder boys refused to be manipulated by Athenian politics, but the youngest—'

'Minos?'

He nodded. 'Minos. He got it bad. It still rankles with him that the Cretans persisted in treating his mother as Queen, and gave her another husband—'

'Asterius.'

'—to finally get this elusive female heir. Asterius was a not very important or rich or influential noble but respected for being unassuming and a competent and just administrator. And, of course, he had some of the old Queen Keraso's blood, being a nephew, or grand-nephew, I forget. The rest you know. Europa produced a daughter, Kriti, before she died, but Kriti isn't old enough to rule, so Knossos needs a Queen to keep the throne for her until she is.'

'Otherwise, Minos will sit on it. I understand.'

She did, sort of, but the idea was so preposterous it refused to materialise as a distinct possibility. What she could quite imagine, though, was a bull-headed man who felt slighted and had let the slight poison his life. Aloeus put his arm around her shoulders and together they walked out onto the terrace. It was shady beneath the big pine tree, but the wind was warm, full of the twittering of birds. The sea stretched dark blue and calm, and in the distance the sun caught the cliffs of the island where Perseis had a house, where she swam with the dolphins and her many sisters. Pasiphaë sighed, wishing she had their gift, but the seawater always found its way into her mouth, her throat, and she would have to be hauled out of the waves to her great shame and Circe's merriment.

'Your mother wouldn't have proposed this marriage if she thought there was the remotest chance that Minos would cause problems. He is a small-minded man, spoilt by his mother, with a great sense of grievance, but he is just a man. Knossos is greater than Minos and the men whose loyalty he has bought.'

'Knossos is great because of the Mistresses. The Cretans would never turn away from them, would they?'

She wanted to hope, needed someone who she trusted more than her mother to tell her she was right. Aloeus would never pretend just to make her feel better. He was her father after all. Perhaps because his role had not been to provide for the material well-being of the royal children, he had always been attentive to their happiness. As much as had been allowed anyway. If her father said that Asterius would make her a good husband, she would believe him. She laid her head on his shoulder, waiting for a reply that would give her hope.

'The Cretans are not fools, and Asterius is a good man. That is worth more than palaces and wealth.'

She looked up into his face, the wrinkles that deepened when he smiled, and was comforted.

'Come. There's something I wanted to show you and ask Potnia Theron for her blessing. But put something on your feet first.'

The big barn was at the side of the house. Close enough to hear if one of the cows was in distress. Aloeus led Pasiphaë to a stall where a white cow was licking a new calf: a white heifer with a black saddle and red ears.

'She was born last night,' Aloeus said.

'Oh! She's beautiful,' Pasiphaë whispered. 'Theron has marked her. We should make an offering right away.'

'It's a sign, don't you think?'

Her father would never dream of *telling* a priestess of Potnia Theron what the goddess' intentions were, but they both knew that the birth of the special heifer could be taken as a blessing on Pasiphaë's marriage. She would hang on to the image of the white cow and her calf for the weeks that followed, when the doubts clamoured to be heard, and she feared that the light in her mother's eyes signified triumph more than affection.

3

Aea

Looking back through the memories of her short life, Pasiphaë found few instances of her mother's affection. It had always been her father who comforted her when she was upset, when the others wouldn't let her play, when Circe brushed her hair for her and made her cry, when she was left behind when the aunts carried Circe off with them on their secret watery excursions. She looked back on the time when Aloeus had lived with them in the royal house as a happy, safe time, when the melancholy of a small child without friends was softened by the presence of a father who always had time to listen. No court function was ever more important to him than comforting a tearful child.

And Pasiphaë was often reduced to tears when she was small, until she learned to find comfort in the aspect of the world ordered by Potnia Theron. The boys were too old and no company for a small girl, and Circe, with the pretext of taking her education in hand, teased and humiliated her. Aloeus had shown her the beauty that surrounded her, the world of the Mistress of Animals.

'They'll tell you that there are other Potniai more important than Theron, but what would this world be without birds and animals? You are their protector, Pasiphaë. You speak the words of the Mistress, and the wild things speak through you.'

On summer evenings, he took her on walks to listen to the

nightingales singing in the woods, taught her the names of the trees and how to hear the voices of the goddesses in the wind and rain. Without his gentle explanations and encouragement, her childhood would have been unhappy as well as solitary.

Aloeus was always gentle and quietly spoken. Later, Perses, when the first fluff he called *beard* appeared on his chin, had mocked Pasiphaë's father for his quiet nature. 'If a man is to make his mark on this world, he has to make himself heard. Especially if he is a King and wants to remain one.'

'If you think you can box your way to a kingdom, go ahead,' Circe had replied. 'The boys are outside in the training courtyard now. I can hear them. Why don't you join in? Show them what manly stuff you're made of.'

'One day, sister, when those boys are men, I might just lead them to conquer a kingdom. And mine will be a kingdom where the King rules, not just hangs on his wife's arm.'

Perses was athletic, at least in build. He refused to follow any serious training though, not seeing the point since he was generally allowed to win whatever contest he competed in. Circe despised sports and the boys whose brains were in their fists, and Perses was slightly afraid of his sister because she didn't need fists. She would be Queen after their mother, and she wielded the magic of a High Priestess, the secret women's magic. Fear and contempt made them enemies, and they sparred constantly. The only time Pasiphaë had ever seen her father white with anger had been because of them.

It had been when Aloeus still lived with them in the royal house. She, Pasiphaë, had been playing with her wooden animals; Circe and Perses were playing a board game. Aeëtes would have been already married at that time. Pasiphaë didn't see how it had begun, when the squirrel, leaping through the branches of the pine outside the window, had misjudged the strength of a branch and ended up on the terrace. Perses had pounced, his foot pinning down the long red tail.

'Quick! Fetch me a jar with a lid to put it in,' he shouted at Circe. 'Go on, quick!'

'Don't you dare!' Little Pasiphaë leapt to her feet, scattering her toys. 'The goddess will be angry, and it's cruel. Let it go!'

Perses laughed. 'It's only a squirrel. I'll make it do tricks, and if it doesn't learn, I'll roast it. Circe! That jar!'

'Let it go, Perses, or you'll regret it.'

Circe's voice was low and venomous. For a moment, Perses looked frightened, but his honour was at stake now. The squirrel wriggled and screamed angrily.

'Let it go,' Circe repeated.

Perses hesitated. Perhaps it was a shift in the pressure of his sandal on the creature's tail that allowed the squirrel to grab the fleshy part of his big toe and bite it. Perses flew into a rage and shrieked, 'It bit me, the little bastard! I'll bash its bastardy little brains out for that!'

Perses grabbed a stone oil lamp from its niche and raised it, his teeth bared.

'You asked for it, brother.' Circe grinned and leapt at him, her arms raised above her head, in a swirl of skirts. Pasiphaë watched in terror, sensing her sister's excitement, but she had not been quick enough to see – or the swirl of Circe's skirts had hidden – how Perses's nose came to pour blood.

The squirrel scampered away over the edge of the terrace and Aloeus appeared in the doorway, drawn by Perses's squealing. Before the swirl of her skirts could settle, he had grabbed Circe by the arm. He bellowed over his shoulder for someone to fetch one of their women, his voice strained as he struggled to contain his anger. Circe's eyes flashed, and Pasiphaë remembered feeling numbed with fear that she would throw a curse at her father.

'I will not have you using such violence in this house,' he muttered, almost in a whisper.

'Perses deserved it! He was going to hurt a small animal!'

'And you love small animals so much you rushed to its defence? Is that it? Answer honestly.'

Circe was silent. She tried to wrench her arm out of Aloeus' grasp, but he held her tight.

'You learned a new trick today, didn't you? A little bit of magic that you couldn't resist trying out.'

'Perses deserved it,' she hissed between her teeth.

'That is not why you hurt him, though, and all the difference is there. The idea of justice never entered your head. Remember, stepdaughter, the women's strength you have inherited is not to be used like the brute strength which is all your brother has. If you cast your magic, hurt or enchant for your own amusement, you are no better than the men who brawl in their cups and throw punches to prove a point. Remember who and why you are, who taught you, and be worthy of the honour.' He let Circe go and turned to Perses. 'And you will go to the temple immediately. Make a suitable offering to Potnia Theron and beg her forgiveness.'

Perses whimpered as the nurse bathed his nose with cold water and plastered it with sage. Circe flounced out of the room, but the image that remained with Pasiphaë was of the look her sister shot her as she turned in the doorway. She had been terrified of the hatred in it and had not understood what it meant until much later. Circe wanted power, and she despised all those who had the possibility of wielding it and chose not to.

*

The royal house gradually emptied of its menfolk. Not surprisingly, Aeëtes rarely visited after his marriage. Perseis had never had much time for him, pronouncing him dull and lazy, and influenced by the last person who spoke to him. Aloeus retired, and Perses grew up wild and arrogant, until their mother, weary of his constant warring with Circe, married him off when he was sixteen to the Queen of a country of barbarian horse-folk.

Circe had married shortly afterwards. Given how much she despised and disliked Perses, her choice of a husband had been a surprise, to Pasiphaë at any rate. Agrius was like

Perses's twin, sharing his love of horse riding, boxing and wild company. She also saw the same fleeting light of fear in his eyes when Circe shot him an unexpected sharp glance.

'What do you see in him?' she had asked.

'You saw how he danced the Sun Dance, the way his muscles slid, those arms and thighs. You must have noticed how he's built like a prize stallion. He'll be fun for a few years, then we'll see.'

Pasiphaë had wrinkled her nose in disgust, but disbelief was the stronger impression. 'You really think it will be so easy to get rid of him?'

Circe had laughed, showing all her very white teeth. 'Agrius will do exactly as he's told. He knows his place, and besides, he's terrified of me.'

Pasiphaë was sceptical. Her sister's loud-voiced, brash husband did not seem like the type who was used to doing *as he was told* at all. She doubted he would go willingly to the oak grove when Circe decided his time was up. And there was something besides fear that Pasiphaë had seen in Agrius' eyes, that she had never seen in a man's eyes before. She knew it for desire, and it gave her the same sick feeling in the pit of her stomach that tasting her mother's *fruits of the earth* had given her, the one time she had tried it.

The first time Agrius had looked at her like that had been around the same time that her first bleeding had come. Circe had accompanied her to the ritual bath to let her blood join the blood of the priestesses. At Kolchis, there were few set-piece ceremonies. Mostly the rituals were performed in small shrines inside the royal house. The people made their offerings where and as they thought fit. Sometimes, one or other would come to ask for a special blessing, or to ask a special favour of one of the Mistresses. Circe and Perseis dealt with most of those. Potnia Theron was solicited so often for lambing, cows in calf, crop blight, sicknesses and to celebrate multiple births in the livestock that the farmers had their own shrines in the fields and forest. They rarely bothered asking a priestess to officiate.

Pasiphaë had let herself be prepared, her face painted, the red skirts arranged. She had said nothing, frozen with fear and disgust. She had a horror of blood, and the idea of seeing a whole basin of it was unbearable. That she should enter the basin and watch as the water turned a darker shade of red filled her with horror. But she bit her lip. What could she have said anyway? It was the custom, a show of respect to the Mistresses.

'Better that than carving up one of your little furry friends, hey, Pasiphaë?' Circe had joked. For her, blood wasn't a problem. Nor was suffering or fear.

As Pasiphaë was her High Priestess, they went to the lustral basin in the shrine dedicated to Potnia Theron. Of the many shrines in the royal house, Potnia Theron's was the oldest and darkest, and Pasiphaë knew that it was the least respected. Theron had her place in things, but she was not the Mistress of the World, not the great Potnia Athana who was the head, the wisdom and the firm hand that guided all things.

The shrine with the lustral basin was dark and cool. Pasiphaë tried to focus on the painted figures that trooped across one wall, until a line of priestesses entered and obscured them. They wore bright colours, scarlet and crimson dominating, and intense orange, and their lips and the contours of their eyes were painted a dark ox-blood red. Handbells shaken by a child gave the rhythm to their low chanting.

Pasiphaë stood at the edge of the stone pool as two priestesses helped her out of her white skirts, staring into the limpid water, clear and still, at the irregularities of the stone beneath. She was the first to enter, hers the first blood to tinge the water the holy colour. It would be pale, barely visible in the penumbra, but once the last of the women had offered her blood in the monthly ritual, the water would be dark, clouded, the heavy smell would weigh on the squirming in her stomach, and she would have to concentrate with all her strength on not being sick.

She let the rhythm enter her, occupying the space where her fear lay, and she gave in to the flow, the ripples washing higher and faster as more women stepped into the water. She was not required to speak, just give the tribute of her blood, and gradually the nausea recoiled. The presence of the other women, knowing that she was now one of them, the same, filled her with a feeling of peace. She stepped out of the pool, was dried, perfumed, dressed, her hair coiled and decorated with flowers. When she led the procession out into the sunlight, she felt like a Princess, almost like a Queen.

Circe and her mother were waiting in the big internal courtyard with their followers, priestesses and members of the household. Among them was Agrius. She felt his eyes upon her, but when she tried to meet them, to stare at him with all the disdain of the goddess, she found that they were fixed on her young girl's breasts, and she turned away, her face hot with shame.

*

Pasiphaë avoided Agrius, discovering something important that needed her attention whenever he paid the royal house a visit. He had his own house and household, on his mother's lands a half-day's ride away from Aea. Circe had insisted on it.

'Agrius is useful for one thing, and he's good at it. Doesn't mean I want him under my feet, or anywhere else for that matter, during the day as well.'

She laughed at Pasiphaë's agitation when she heard his voice bellowing at the servants to look after his horse. She mocked the way she fled at the sound of his boots pounding through the house.

'You'll have to get used to having a man around, you

know. Agrius isn't some kind of unnatural demon. They all like to throw their weight about, shout, boast.'

'Father doesn't.'

Circe snorted. 'Maybe he's the reason you're so terrified of everything. Maybe if he was more assertive, you'd have turned out more queenlike.' Her face had darkened as it did when she was thinking of something unpleasant. 'This world needs strong hands to guide it. Men will grab the reins from our hands if we show weakness. They are pushing all the time. The Mycenaean rot is spreading. We'll see it here before too long, you mark my words.'

*

It was in the spring, while they were waiting to hear the Cretan response to the proposed marriage of Pasiphaë and Asterius, that Circe's prediction came true. Some of the local women with sons of marriageable age had been asking for advice on the most propitious day for a wedding ceremony. Perseis had been discussing it with her daughters and Medea, who seemed to be invited everywhere, and it had been decided that the marriage ceremony would be combined with the spring sacrifice to Potnia Theron. This was the high point of the religious year for Theron's priestesses, when they made offerings for the safety of the lambing ewes, for the richness of their milk and the health of the lambs. As High Priestess, it ought to have been Pasiphaë's big day. Circe watched her to see if she registered the slight, but Pasiphaë was secretly pleased not to be the focus of the ceremony. Circe would have to find another way to irritate her.

Pasiphaë disliked these little meetings, which made her feel odd, out of place and unnecessary. Circe used every occasion, from the choice of her clothes, the way she dressed her hair, the way she ate her fruit, to compare her unfavourably to the little pest, Medea. And Medea lapped it all up, her bright black eyes shining with malicious pleasure when her Aunt Circe ridiculed her Aunt Pasiphaë. The pest always seemed to be at Aea, at home among the many shrines, the dark, sombre places, where prayers and invocations were murmured. When Pasiphaë ventured that they weren't places suitable for a child, Circe retorted that Medea was a natural High Priestess of the serpent goddess. She was the one who looked after the house snake in the shrine.

'It always comes out for her. She likes to feed it. It's not as though you've ever got on with it. You're more one for the sweet, fluffy animals.'

Pasiphaë could imagine the bright black eyes lighting up when the snake took a live, wriggling mouse from her fingers. Her sister was right though. She didn't like the snake. It made her feel uneasy, the way it was never in its place when she went to look for it, always hidden somewhere so she didn't know where to put the offering to tempt it. The snake mocked her just like the others.

Circe was pointing out a drip of peach juice on Pasiphaë's bodice, when a servant clattered into the room.

'Greek sailors, Mistress, washed up down below Tiduni's place. Athamas has brought 'em over to the harbour, while you decide what to do with 'em.'

Perseis frowned in irritation, but both Circe's and Medea's eyes glittered with excitement. Circe dropped an uneaten fig onto her plate and wiped her hands. 'Well, Mother? What are we waiting for?'

It was only a short walk from Aea down to the harbour. Perseis strode ahead, followed closely by Circe, Medea by her side, skipping to keep up. Pasiphaë trailed behind, unsure that she even wanted to see these sailors. She was pleased to see Athamas, though. Her mother had a small palace guard, and Athamas was their captain, a big man with shiny dark skin and hair that he wore in dozens of tightly tressed braids, held back from his face by a band of coloured leather. He was a reassuring presence, comfortably solid in his strength, in her small world where power was wielded by the unseen or the half-seen, veiled and obscured in mists of scent and smoke.

'These are the men, Mistress.'

He waved his arm towards a huddled group, hands tied behind their backs. Pasiphaë thought they looked miserable but not threatening. She couldn't see what the fuss was about.

'Greeks. From Iolchos. They said they were after fleeces. They'd been told we had flocks of golden sheep guarded by a bunch of girls.'

'They're cowards and idiots as well as thieves then,' Perseis sniffed.

'Get up,' Athamas barked, and one of his men kicked the nearest sailor. The huddle moved and the men got to their feet slowly, their sullen expressions growing murderous. They wore ragged tunics, belted at the waist, and though their skin was tanned by the sun and the wind, it had not the rich colour of the men of Kolchis. They were sinewy and finely muscled, and Pasiphaë wondered at the courage or folly that had driven them to sail so far from home.

Perseis asked them their names. None replied until Athamas dealt a few blows to the head of the nearest men. They muttered their replies.

'Note down their names and send a message with the next cargo to the Middle Sea. If their families want them back enough to pay for their crime, they'll know where to find them. Otherwise, they stay here as slaves.'

She turned away, judging the situation dealt with. Circe, too, had looked the men over and found nothing in them to excite her interest. Medea, though, hung back, absorbed in the strangers, eyes bright, her lips slightly parted. The eyes of one of the men slid over the child and settled on Pasiphaë. She was horrified to see his lips curl in a leer that had not a featherweight of respect in it. Angrily, she grabbed Medea by the shoulder.

'Come away. There's nothing to see here but a bunch of slaves.'

Medea shrugged her hand away. 'They sailed the Inhospitable Sea until their ship was wrecked, but they didn't drown. They must be heroes.'

'Well, now they're slaves,' Pasiphaë snapped. 'Come!'

Medea glared up at her, her bright black eyes full of intense dislike, and Pasiphaë shivered. She had seen that same look in Circe's eyes, and once again she felt excluded from something she was not sure she even wanted to be part of.

4

Marriage promises

'It's arranged,' Perseis said, one bright morning in May. 'You'll marry Asterius. His adopted sons are restless, or at least one of them is. Minos has fought with the other two. Rhadamanthus has fled, and Sarpedon has moved his household to Malia along the coast, out of the way.'

'What about Kriti?' Pasiphaë asked hopefully.

'Also keeping out of his way. Asterius keeps her close. He knows his stepson.'

'Minos?' She already associated the name with dark ambition.

'Don't worry about him. As I said, Asterius knows how to handle Europa's son. He'll keep him in his place.'

Her mother's teeth shone strong and white in the shiny dark bronze of her face. Her teeth were all that Pasiphaë noticed. Her eyes were as black as sloes and conveyed nothing. She didn't like to look too deeply. There were shadows in their depths that moved like waves, or people drowning. The lips smiled again, cool, a smile for a vision, not a flesh-and-blood daughter.

'The moon will be full this year at the summer solstice. A good day for a wedding.'

Pasiphaë shivered as if the wind had blown cold. She bowed her head. What else could she do? Perseis took her face, her round, girlish cheeks, in her hands, and pressed her lips to her daughter's forehead. Pasiphaë was fifteen years old and knew that it was time, but marriage was still a fear that haunted her nights. Of course, she knew the custom, knew the dance, but she feared that when it came to the wedding day, she would lead the dance only if Asterius was willing. Did the Cretans know that this was how it should be? Crete was a long way away. How could they know the same things?

'When must I go?'

She was aware that she was full of questions, always asking others what was intended for her. She had imagined she would be allowed to choose whom she danced the marriage dance with, and that her husband would live with her in the house at Aea. But instead of protesting, she found herself simply asking, when?

'As soon as you're ready. The journey's a long one. Asterius is sending one of his elegant ships for you. I won't send a daughter of mine to be married in one of our smelly tubs. And there are your wedding gifts to be prepared. Asterius is rich, like his island, but I've never yet met a King who thought he was rich enough.'

'He's heard about the gold and the fleeces too then.' Pasiphaë surprised herself at her cynicism.

Perseis was oblivious. 'Of course, the gold makes you a very attractive proposition.' She gave her daughter a critical look, an inspection, brief, superficial. 'You'll make a delightful bride. Are you pleased?'

Pleased at what? To be leaving my home, to be married to a man I've never met, to play mother to his sickly daughter and share a house with his son who has delusions of divinity?

That was what she thought, but obviously not what she replied. She looked at the ground, at the grass spotted with white flowers. Bees drifted in a noisy cloud. Birds chattered. She wasn't pleased. The word had no sense in the context. She was resigned.

'You won't have to live with him, you know,' Perseis said gently. 'Circe doesn't live with Agrius, does she? He's happy enough to be known as Prince of Kolchis and never interferes in Circe's work.'

'But Agrius is Kolchian. He understands how the world functions.'

'And you think Asterius doesn't? Crete is rich, powerful. His are the only people to have mastered the art of shipbuilding to control their islands, their trade and to protect their wealth. Why would he reject the protection of the Great Mother when she has been so generous?'

But what if his people don't know it's the Mistresses who count? The Great Mother sleeps now, unless something upsets her and she blows up a fire mountain or shakes the sea out of its bed. She protects nothing. The Mistresses protect us from her foul moods.

Pasiphaë couldn't answer her mother, but she looked at her critically, for the first time doubting her judgement. Perseis was a creature of the sea, not of the earth. She was High Priestess of Potnia Athana, but the earth was not her element. What did she know of men who trod the earth and only the earth, who never touched the sky or mastered the waves? Kolchis was held in Mistress Athana's cupped hands, between sea and mountain, but the world was huge.

Perseis patted her arm. 'Don't worry. Asterius is kind and wise and knows that daughter follows mother. Sons are good, but not as rulers, not alone. Look at Perses. He tries to keep order among the tribes of his wife's people and only succeeds in giving them more excuses to fight. I think he enjoys stirring them up. It's in the nature of some men to fight and brag about their prowess. Since Europa died, Knossos has been without a Queen. Asterius needs a wife who will provide that stability, and a daughter for the succession.'

'But he *has* a daughter,' Pasiphaë said obstinately, her head down, brow furrowed like a calf. 'Why do you and Circe make it sound as though the throne of Knossos is my responsibility?'

'Kriti might die. Then you will be Queen.'

'No, I won't! Crete is run like a commercial operation. You told me that yourself. All the ruling families are business partners, all connected by marriage. They'll choose another family if Keraso's has run dry.'

Perseis looked at her sharply. She probably hadn't been expecting little Pasiphaë to have even been listening to that particular conversation. 'They tried that after Keraso died, but the choosing went round and round in circles. Each family reckoned it was their turn. That's why Europa seemed like a good idea. Not only did she bring her wealth, but the Greeks agreed to stop threatening Knossos with war in return for a reduction in their tributes.'

Pasiphaë laughed. One other political fact she had learned – no one challenged the might of the Cretan navy. 'Threaten Knossos? They wouldn't dare!'

Perseis shrugged. 'Apparently, they shouted enough to get the Cretans worried. But,' she patted Pasiphaë's hand, 'that's all sorted out now. And it has set a precedent. If Lycastus could marry a Tyrian, Asterius can marry a Kolchian, especially as it won't affect the inheritance. As you keep reminding me, there's Kriti.'

Pasiphaë saw glittering Greek cities, ships full of treasure, a stately Queen in a warship from Tyre with an army of bristling bronze spears at her back. Then she saw the undistinguished, rather shabby house at Aea, forests full of birds, hilltops, sheep, a girl running barefoot with untidy hair, and she couldn't see where she or Kolchis fitted into the picture.

'They're really scraping the bottom of the barrel with me.'

Perseis didn't heave another dramatic sigh. The light in her eyes changed, softened. For a few moments she stopped being a ruler and became just a mother. 'What matters is that you are a daughter of the Mistresses, and that is what Knossos needs. Minos *owns* almost every powerful family in Crete. None of them dares to oppose him. Whichever girl was proposed as Queen, from whichever family, she'd only ever have one candidate to be King.'

So, it was a case of any foreign wife would do, even insignificant little Pasiphaë. Before ever setting foot in Crete, before meeting the King, Pasiphaë understood that the most important force in the world that was shaping around her was Minos.

'And what about me? You're sure he won't... do anything?'

Pasiphaë wasn't sure what he *could* do, but a man who believed a King could rule instead of a Queen was capable of anything.

'Of course not.' Perseis smiled with her teeth, and Pasiphaë didn't believe her. 'Oh, he'll stamp around like a frustrated bull, but he has no claim, no matter what idiocies Europa used to whisper to him about Zeus and gods and ruling after her when she died. That was before she had Kriti.' The smile flashed again.

Pasiphaë frowned. 'Until she dies.'

'Unless. She might not. The seeing could be wrong.' She patted Pasiphaë's hand again. 'Stop worrying! You're marrying Asterius not Minos. You'll make his home yours, and you'll rule in it.'

'And if the seeing was right?'

Perseis the ruler, the maker of Queens, was back. Her eyes had lost their sympathetic softness. 'Then Knossos will need a new Queen. If that is to be you, the people must see you, know you and love you. That part of the arrangement, daughter, is entirely in your hands.'

Perhaps the people would love her by then. Perhaps she would have a daughter to give them. It would be up to her. Perseis's indulgent smile had grown calculating. She was incapable of feeling empathy for anything, not in a meaningful way. She was never cruel, but the lives of everyone and everything else scarcely touched her. Pasiphaë thought with bitterness that it might really be easier to be loved by thousands of unknowns than by her own mother.

5

Voyage

The port of Aea was crowded to see the Moon Princess leave. She had performed her last ritual as High Priestess of Potnia Theron, an offering to the goddess for the safety and health of the animals that would be travelling in the ship's hold, to the animals of the sea to let their ship pass safely. She had poured the oil and wine for the last time, burned a pot of grain on the altar and, at Perseis's insistence, sacrificed two doves. Then she had handed over the key to the shrine to her successor, Ino. She was in limbo, still Moon Princess, but her authority was no longer the same. She hoped it didn't show in her face.

She wondered why leave-taking was such a popular entertainment, but then ships were entertainment in themselves, great painted wooden bowls, with their glorious sails. And this Cretan vessel had a splendid, curved prow with a red-horned bull's head, and its oars bristled like fish bones, sparkling with the splashing of blue water. The crowd looked happy. Pasiphaë tried not to take it personally. They would have waved and carried on for any ship decked out like this, even one carrying a cargo of cattle.

The harbour wall was strung with the bright gems of festive dresses, the tressed clouds of elaborate hairstyles, the glitter of gold on bare necks and arms. There were flowers too, and she imagined she could smell their perfume though most of the showy blooms had no scent, and they were already too far away.

She picked out Perseis and Circe. Her brother, Perses, wouldn't be there; his wife's barbaric little country kept him far too occupied. Circe's hand rested on Medea's shoulder. *Circe's got what she wanted*, Pasiphaë thought, with a hint of bitterness, *an apprentice High Priestess, replacement Queen if one is ever needed.* A band of royal children waved green boughs, and musicians played. She heard gales of laughter and singing.

Her gaze glanced over the faces of the noisy crowd, the waving arms, until she found Aloeus at the far end of the quay. It wouldn't have been seemly for him to have stood with Perseis and the royal family. He raised his hand in farewell and the sun caught the gold pin of his cloak. It shone out like a star. Smoke rose from the offerings to the sea, stinging her eyes. The ashes washed in the ship's wake, grey and dirty.

Was she sorry to be leaving them, or simply afraid of where she was going? The green boughs waved like seaweed. They would wave and sing until the ship was out of the harbour, her prow pointed to the vast emptiness of the sea, then they would go back to their occupations. And they would forget about her. They would forget about Pasiphaë but not about the kingdom she was being sent to rule. There would be trade with Crete because of her marriage, and there would be ships to protect their coastline. Nothing was ever for nothing; nothing was wasted.

*

The young marten stirred in her nest of plaited grass that smelled of home, and Pasiphaë settled down next to her beneath her canopy in the stern. She, too, was hardly out of childhood. The Cretan servant, a parting gift from Perseis, hurried to make room for her. Dark, chestnut-haired and slender-boned, she tucked her feet beneath her, taking up barely more room than the marten's basket.

'Eritha will help you with the language,' Perseis had said. 'The Cretans speak Greek, but the common people don't. It's always best to know what the servants are saying behind your back. And she knows the art of bringing women safely through childbirth.' Her teeth had shone white in her dark face. 'She'll bring you luck.'

Pasiphaë thought she needed a sight more than luck, but the woman was gentle and had a way with animals too. It was she who had calmed the fretful pine marten and settled her in her basket. The emblem of the Cretans' protector of women in childbirth was a marten and the marten's cousins. Pasiphaë knew things like that. Animals interested her, and not just because she was Potnia Theron's High Priestess. She scratched the little animal between the ears. Her thoughts were far away, not in the future and the perils of pregnancy, but in the past, childhood, so close yet lost forever. Even though the sun was hot, she pulled her wool cloak about her shoulders. It, too, smelled of home, of cedar wood and the oily perfumes she wore, bergamot and pine.

The thought of her room with the window full of the moon, the boughs of the larch tree swaying in the wind, night pressing over the sill, soft and comforting, brought a tightening in her throat. Her bone earrings and necklaces clinked, reminding her of her status. She was the face of Potnia Theron and must be dignified, show no emotion before the crew and the servants, though she felt like weeping.

The motion of the ship was beginning to change, to plunge with the regular rhythm of a running horse. She thought she heard the uneasy snorting of the white bull hobbled below in the hold with the cargo of wedding gifts. The bucking of the sea was already making her feel queasy, and they were barely out of sight of the harbour. Barely out of mind. She stroked the marten, and its amber eyes blinked.

*

The voyage was long, and although the ship was luxurious compared with Kolchian vessels, Pasiphaë was cramped and sick and bored. After the first few days, when she stopped being sick, she was just cramped and bored. She had nothing to do but listen to her serving women bickering.

'Shove over, Semele, will you?'

'Over where? I'm nearly in the sea as it is!'

'It's your fat arse. It takes up more than its fair share.'

'Ah, stop whinging, Eune. If you don't like the company ask him if you can sit on his lap.'

The oarsman who had been listening with a broad grin on his face laughed. Eune snapped, 'Haven't you got any rowin' to do?'

The oarsman pumped with his arms, in out, in out. Arete mimed hitching her skirts up. 'You want me to show you how women do it?'

Tyro, the other brawny-armed country girl, roared with laughter. 'Give over! They need all their strength for rowin'.'

Pasiphaë sighed. They were all older than she was. She oughtn't to have to tell them how to behave. Did it matter though? She wasn't their mother. And they weren't at Aea any longer either. Their world was the ship now, narrow and low-keeled, pointy and masculine. Even the sail had a bull's head painted in the middle of it. Fifty oars at two men to each oar – that made a hundred men. Nothing existed now but the ship, its ways a foreign country to her women. Let them shout. The men wouldn't take any harm from being reminded they were still only men.

She studied the oarsmen with curiosity, looking for similarities with her own folk and seeing mainly differences. They were shorter, she judged, mostly dark-haired, and they chattered like jackdaws. Their skin was tanned bronze, but none shone with the rich colour of forest earth like the skin of Kolchians. She compared them with Athamas, whom Perseis had sent to be her personal guard. Athamas was Pasiphaë's idea of what a man should look like, heavily muscled, thick black hair and brows, skin dark as polished oak. He was dressed as a soldier, leather kilt and broad belt, his calf muscles bound by red leather bootstraps. She expected that Asterius would look nothing like Athamas.

The oarsmen were laughing and nudging one another, and Pasiphaë caught the expression of contempt that flitted across her guard's face before courtesy smoothed it away. Athamas despised the Cretans already. She wondered if he would despise her too for marrying one, even if it made her Queen of all the Cretans. It was difficult to know what men thought. They had their role to play in the organisation of a realm and they stuck to it. Theirs was not to judge, but to carry out the wishes of the Mistresses through their Queen. Yet they must have their own ideas, and sometimes Pasiphaë looked at the bulging muscles of the palace guards and wondered what it would take to make them flex those muscles, as they said the Hellenes did, and turn the world upside down.

*

The voyage was slow, as the master kept within sight of the shore, avoiding inshore reefs, but not venturing into deeper waters for fear of the currents and sudden storms. The Cretans were the world's best sailors, but they had the good sense not to pit themselves against the Inhospitable Sea. The coastline was monotonous, bare and glittering with white stone piled in heaps amid scrubby vegetation where the most exciting activity was the leaping of wild goats.

A week passed before the ship entered the straits and the horizon narrowed. There were hills now on either side, never distant. The women's eyes darted about nervously, looking for titans and other monsters. The dolphins that had followed them since leaving Aea laughed at their fears. Once the ship had breached the second straits and hit the open sea, the women had something different to worry about. For the first time, they were out of sight of land. The waves rose higher than in the Inhospitable Sea, and there seemed to be no end to them.

Pasiphaë and her women huddled together, and the marten curled with her tail over her nose, refusing to believe in this world of water. They kept the curtains pulled around the canopy to shut it out. The smell of six women, with only buckets of seawater to keep themselves and their clothes clean, huddled with them like a seventh woman, large, sweaty and bloody. Pasiphaë gritted her teeth and stared through a crack in the curtains at the line of the horizon, fighting back her fear of the emptiness.

On the second day of open water, the lookout spied land, and Athamas turned to Pasiphaë, bellowing as if he had been in the exercise yard back in the palace at Aea. 'Land! Lemnos ahead, Princess, look!'

Following Athamas's pointing finger, Pasiphaë saw a faint low line like a pile of grey clouds. She almost laughed aloud. Lemnos was the first sign of civilisation since the voyage began, and it meant that, very soon, it would be over.

*

The Moon Princess was expected, and the mole of the harbour was already thronged with curious onlookers. Pasiphaë let Eune and Semele manoeuvre her into a suitably impressive dress, with skirts stiff with gold, a bodice that covered shoulders and upper arms in the Kolchian style. She held her breath as Eritha, the smallest and deftest of the women, painted her eyes and lips, and hung silver horses from her ears in honour of the horse cult of Lemnos.

The women clucked and fussed around her, slapping one another's hands out of the way, tugging here and straightening there. When the complicated styling of her hair was complete to their satisfaction, spangled with gold ornaments, ears and neck heavy with them, they stood back proudly, as if Pasiphaë was an egg they had laid jointly. Potnia Theron, Mistress of

Animals, was not such a fearsome deity, comforting even in this unfamiliar environment, but this was the first time Pasiphaë had appeared alone, in the role of her High Priestess. And she had never had to represent the far more important Potnia Athana before. Perseis was her High Priestess, but now Perseis was far away. Pasiphaë's eyes must have betrayed her fear and timidity, for the large, moon-faced Semele took her hands as a mother might have done.

'You're the goddess for these folk, Princess. She shines in your face. You don't need a pair o' lions to prove it.'

The gentle pressure of the servant's fingers was comforting, reminding Pasiphaë that her mother would probably not have even noticed her secret terror. She smiled her gratitude and drew a deep breath. 'Draw back the curtains then.'

The women pulled back the drapes, pushing cushions to one side. Semele clapped her hands and shouted at the men to get their arses out of the way. The little pine marten whimpered.

'Take her, Eritha. A marten is beautiful in the eyes of Potnia Theron, but she's no substitute for a lion.'

She turned her eyes to the crowd gathered in welcome. It had swelled, much the same as the crowd at her departure from Kolchis. People were more or less the same everywhere, she decided. Anything out of the ordinary captured their attention, any excuse was a good one for a party. They waved branches and coloured scarves, and small fishing craft bobbed away from the shore to escort the great ship. Women threw flowers, and the oarsmen leaned over the side, laughing, to catch them.

Music from pipes and trumpets made an enthusiastic din, and men hurried about with ropes and boarding ramps as the helmsman manoeuvred the shallow-draughted ship close to the harbour wall. The sail was furled, the mooring stones dropped, oars raised. Hooks and ropes secured the ship. It felt like a homecoming, and Pasiphaë listened for a sign. In the slap of waves on the harbour wall, she heard Athana, the Mistress of the World, whisper that land, any land, was home.

6

Lemnos

There were three impressions that Pasiphaë took with her from Lemnos. The first was that first sight of the glorious, ethereal grace of the palace. It seemed to hang, as if by some enchantment, between heaven and earth, suspended between blue-painted columns, behind it only the blue of the sky. The roof was weighted down with blue, and sunlight poured from the gold of the decorations that ran around the pale stone of the walls.

Used to the cool secrecy of the house at Aea, with its shade trees, low ceilings and bright frescoes that soaked up the light, leaving coloured shadows, she found the Lemnos house strangely bright and naked. Its colours were sun colours, brilliant and sharp. The polished floors were like mirrors, and there were no dark corners anywhere. She wondered if the royal house at Knossos would be the same, flung open to the sky and the sun, with nowhere to hide.

The second impression was of the torchlight procession in her honour, dedicated to the horse god Sabazios. Procession! She had been expecting something stately and vaguely boring. The wild exuberance of the race across the dark hills by torchlight was a spectacle she could never have imagined.

Torches led the way to the high place above the town where the procession would start. Lit like a star, the terrace vibrated with excited laughter and the high, chattering voices that made Pasiphaë think of goldfinches twittering in a summer tree. Chairs painted in blue and red had been set out, and Queen Theodora and Gordianos, her King, were already seated. A flock of brightly clothed nobles flitted around them with cups of spiced wine, their fingers sticky and scented with sweetmeats. The fine lines of Theodora's face creased into a hundred wrinkles of unconcealed excitement. She patted the seat next to her.

'This is where you'll see some real fun.'

'Not a ritual then?'

'A ritual? A race across the plains, Princess, torches streaming through the night, horses and riders falling, dozens more racing back to the town. Excitement, Princess. Action-packed fun!'

After the libations and the blessing, the horses shook their heads and bounded away to wild applause. Torch flames bounced into the night sky, weaving streamers of light over the hillside and back down into the town.

'Listen to the roaring of Cybele's lions!'

Theodora clapped her hands in time to the beat of the drums, and Pasiphaë grinned like the child she still felt herself to be. Cybele and Potnia Theron, both goddesses, flanked by lions, watched and approved. The braying of bronze salpinges made its way up from the port, following the torch streamers of the horsemen. The crowd surged after them to the high ground, to get a good view as they raced into the dark. There was a smell of horses and pine resin and the sound of singing, a wild song that evoked geese flying to their summer home, eagles soaring above mountain crags, echoing the galloping of horses across a vast ancestral eastern plain. Pasiphaë perched on the edge of her seat, gripped the stiff fabric of her dress in tight fists.

The third impression was the one that lingered longest, eclipsing the brilliance of Sabazios' procession, like a cloud of madder colouring a vat of clear water. Pasiphaë had been so absorbed in the spectacle, clapping her hands to the rhythm and stamping her feet with the enthusiastic crowd, that she hadn't noticed the dark, stocky man who had taken a seat behind her until he leaned forwards. His perfume, heavier and muskier than the other perfumes that already drifted in the night air, wafted over her shoulder, and she felt his breath on the back of her neck. There was a scraping noise as he pulled his chair closer.

'So, this is the little goddess Asterius is taking into his bed.'

The man's speech was slightly slurred. She smelled the wine on his breath, sweet and sickly. His rudeness confused her and she fumbled for the right angry words.

'Not *goddess*. I am Pasiphaë of Kolchis. Moon Princess and High Priestess of Potnia Theron.'

'*High Priestess!*' He spat on the ground, his drunken smile suddenly gone. 'All that claptrap. The Mothers and their bloody tribute was supposed to have ended. It was part of the contract – Europa and the goodwill of the Greeks in return for Europa's sons on the throne of Knossos.'

That, she knew, was a lie. 'There was no such contract, and Europa's sons will never sit on the throne of Knossos.'

'Because Cretans are oath-breakers! Even after Zeus did the business because Lycastus couldn't, and got three sons on Europa, Knossos still prefers a sickly girl child.'

A woman would have known the words to put him in his place, to have stopped the tirade that was offensive and disrespectful, but Pasiphaë was not a woman, not yet, and she was alone.

'Crete will always be ruled by a Queen, obeying custom and the Mistresses. No man has ever ruled, nor ever will.'

He ignored her, listening only to the sound of his own voice. 'Minos at least won't let a girl steal his throne. No man, once he has had power within his grasp, will let it go without a fight. And that goes for any man.'

He turned his head, looking meaningfully in the direction of Gordianos, where he stood with his Queen. Suddenly, as if ravelling up his anger, his expression changed, and he looked at Pasiphaë with different eyes, a gaze that crawled over her flesh.

'Meanwhile, Asterius thinks he can breed a more useful heir on you. Can't say I blame him for trying.'

She had never seen cold desire before, except perhaps in Agrius's eyes when Circe wasn't present. She stifled the shiver of fear, of change, and tried to think of the kind of answer her sister would have given. But Circe would have cursed him, and she didn't know how.

Theodora returned to her seat and he got to his feet. 'I'll join the men now, if you don't mind.'

The Greek left behind him the brooding sense of a coming storm. If he was to be believed, the world was fracturing. Traditions could be chipped away and new ones substituted as easily as mending a broken pot or bribing a serving girl to carry a love note to a suitor. Her eyes must have betrayed her trouble, because Theodora patted her hand.

'Don't take any notice of Butes. He's a boor at the best of times, like all the Pallantides, but he's angry because I have refused his business proposition.'

'He dared to claim that Minos was the rightful heir to Knossos. And he said that no man would refuse a kingship if it were offered him.'

Theodora's lips pouted, reminding Pasiphaë of a gesture of Circe's when she was about to say something dismissive. 'He's right. Toss a crown into a crowd of men and they'll squabble over it like dogs over a bone. Mycenae and Athens and a few other barbaric holes are dismantling the old ways, but they've nothing to replace them with except war. They've turned their backs on the Mother, replaced order with chaos. No civilised society will let that happen. Knossos is true to the Mother and always will be.'

Pasiphaë knew she was being weighed up, and fumbled for the kind of reply her mother would have given. 'The Mistresses have given me a part to play, and I intend to do my duty. I will keep Knossos safe for them and for Princess Kriti.'

She wanted to believe her own words. Knossos was her future, and she must embrace it in both arms. Kolchis was a memory, and she knew she would never see it again.

Theodora pointed down the hill towards the first houses of the port, where the water of the harbour came into sight, heaving and glittering with torchlight. A great yell went up, and scores of musical instruments began their unmelodious racket.

'They're coming!'

The courtiers leapt to their feet. The sound of dry grass crackling beneath their sandals recalled to Pasiphaë the sound of her feet pattering through the fallen leaves around her mother's basin beneath the trees, crisp winter air nipping her nostrils, her breath steaming like a horse's. The memory brought a pang of unhappiness. Like all of Kolchis, it had slipped into the past. She wondered if there would be a place to run in the palace of Knossos, to stir up shadows and memories. Would she feel as joined there to the earth, her fears and desires, as the child in the royal house of Aea had been?

Then, looking down beyond an olive tree that bent its back to the wind from the sea, she saw the sudden flare as torchlight caught the silvery leaves. The silent darkness became a raging river of light and noise, and riders streamed past, roaring and yelling, their horses' hooves thundering down the stony path. She winced at the piercing horse cries of terror when they lost their footing in the curve into the town and rolled, wreathed in spinning torchlight and dry dust.

Among the houses, light clotted and leapt. Cheers rose, and the bullroarers mimicked a pride of lions. Pasiphaë heard Potnia Theron and shouted in reply.

*

Later, in the apartment reserved for royal guests, Pasiphaë lay in her bed and mulled over the tumultuous events of the day, the most momentous since leaving Aea. The most momentous ever, if she was being honest. She wanted to remember it all. All except the Athenian.

The day birds had settled down for the night, and the call of an owl, the wild voice of Potnia Theron, drifted across the terrace. Pasiphaë *thought* she heard the Mistress, but she couldn't be sure. Sometimes, in Aea, she said that the Mistress was speaking in the wind through pine boughs, sometimes in the jays' laughter, and often, at night, in the soft call of the owls.

Perhaps she was, but she found it hard to believe the Mistress would be speaking to *her*. Circe's mocking voice murmured in her ear, *High Priestess of Little Furry Things.* Was that all she was? All Potnia Theron was? She wanted to call out to her, but what if she didn't answer? If the Mistresses didn't listen to her, there was no one in this strange, bright world who would. On the distant mountain, a wolf howled, and the little pine marten chattered in response. Pasiphaë decided it was a sign, an answer to the prayer she had not dared say. Sleep soothed her fears, as dusk smothers distance with soft grey shadow.

7

Knossos

Flames and the pounding of horses' hooves filled her dreams that night. When she woke, blinking in the light that fell through the high window, the pine marten curled on her pillow also woke and sniffed the air. She raised a hand and stroked the small head with her forefinger. 'More ships. More sea. Then we'll be home.'

She whispered the words aloud, as much for her own benefit as the marten's. Home. Would it be? She had no choice in the matter anyway. She would have to make it home. She refused to even consider the question that bobbed in the back of her thoughts like a child hopping from foot to foot, hoping to be noticed by her mother – would she be happy? There were no divinations for happiness. It wasn't important enough.

The pine marten curled around herself, then got up and repeated the process in the other direction. She fretted. With a sigh, Pasiphaë left her couch and called for her women. She would make herself splendid for her parting appearance, a foretaste of Pasiphaë of Knossos.

*

Gulls screamed and the mole rippled with movement, the glitter of gold and shiny gewgaws. On the steep hillside behind the port, the grubby white shapes of sheep moved slowly, all in the same direction. Children scampered and Pasiphaë heard their shrill whistling. On the flat lap of the hill the royal house glinted in the sun, light and airy, blue and gold as the sky. Beyond the houses of the port, on the plain, horses would be grazing with the cattle, a link with the past, the people who left the vast steppes of the east, driven by snow and ice, and found themselves on a drop of the moon in the sky of the Middle Sea.

The wind struck the sail and it flapped taut. The oarsmen turned to Pasiphaë and cheered as if she had been responsible. She couldn't let her face betray her surprise. The priestess of the Mistresses was never surprised, and she took the credit though the gulls laughed at her and a pair of seals barked in amusement.

'Two more nights, Princess, before we reach Knossos. The master says the wind is fair, there should be no storm, and we will make good time.'

Athamas beamed from his dark face, his body glistening with oil. His hair smelled of exotic flowers and he wore a chain Pasiphaë hadn't noticed before. She guessed how he'd been amusing himself. He was also slipping into familiarity.

'I know the ways of the Mistress who calls up the winds better than a Cretan ship's master, Athamas.'

'That was never in doubt, Princess. What I meant was that the signs are so clear, even a ship's master can see them.'

Was he being sincere, apologetic, or was it flattery she saw in his eyes, humouring his little charge? Athamas made his way between the rows of oarsmen to join the master, slapping backs and tossing comments to one or other of the crew. He and the master had dropped their attitude of mutual contempt and struck up a friendship, cemented in some joint excursion the previous night. The Cretan, like all ship's masters, would have known the best stews in the port. Men lived in their own world, she thought, and instead of condescension, she felt the stirrings of unease.

Arete and Tyro also followed the two men with their eyes and nudged one another. Pasiphaë heard their suppressed laughter. So did the oarsmen. The two last banks turned, and Eune fixed one man in the eye then leaned over and whispered something to Eritha. One of the oarsmen tossed her a question that made the Cretan girl blush.

'What's he say?' Eune asked.

'Wants to know do we like the merchandise.'

'We haven't seen it yet!'

His oar mate chattered something accompanied with an unequivocal gesture.

'And he's offering you a private demonstration.'

'Cheeky devil!'

Semele hooted. 'Keep that kind of offer for your wives, pair of sluts!'

Pasiphaë listened to their laughter and would have joined in if she hadn't been a Princess and almost a Queen. But the Athenian's ugly face broke into the picture, with his expression that meant, *You are not worth the piece of rag I wipe my arse with.* She caught herself wondering what thoughts passed through the heads of the men on the ship. The women were like birds, the men like big cats. It would be so easy for the cats to snatch the birds. How could they defend themselves out on this sea where all the rules were changed, where a drunken merchant could insult a Princess? She wondered if she was a bird too. She wanted to make a show, to call up a storm and quell it, to throw lightning across the waves and make the crew cringe beneath the rowing benches.

Circe could do that. Pasiphaë had seen her, once, when she was in a fury. She could do other cruel things too. Pasiphaë remembered the time when her sister had seen the bath servants helping themselves from the dishes set out for her in the next room. The following day she made a potion, invoked Potnia Theron, and sprinkled it on the meat left on the table. Then she went back to her bath. Pasiphaë was watching from behind the pillars of the terrace, and saw the servants scuttle away into the forest, bent over and running on all fours like animals. Circe too watched, smelling of honeysuckle and lavender oil, draped in a linen robe. 'Swine,' she roared after them. 'Go eat acorns! You'll not eat at my expense again.'

Pasiphaë knew the trick of it, Circe had shown her, but she couldn't do it in a ship on the sea. Who would man the oars if she turned the men into beasts, and where would they run? She shivered at the idea that they might simply turn on the women rather than leap into the waves.

Lying back among the cushions beneath the awning, she twisted the fringe of a wool blanket between her fingers. She had made a vow to uphold the rule of the Mistresses, but without the magic and menace of her mother or Circe, how was she to do it? Men like Pallantides the Athenian had no respect for the *Mistress of Little Furry Things*.

*

As Potnia Athana had promised, the ship met no bad weather, the wind held strong and fair, and early on the afternoon of the third day out from Lemnos, the lookout hanging from one of the horns of the bull-headed prow figure called out, 'Land ahead! Knossos! I see the golden cliffs with the sun on them!'

The crew chattered, there were bursts of laughter, the oars rose and dipped faster, pulling with the wind in the sail, and the ship sped like a swallow or a dolphin over the shining waves. A knot tightened in Pasiphaë's stomach, and she felt the fluttering of anxiety, like when the house snake refuses to unwind and leave its home. It wasn't just marriage that filled her with apprehension. She knew perfectly well what men and women did together in the marriage bed after all. It was the enormity of the role that awaited her, to be held at arm's length and revered or perhaps feared and hated or, worse, to be mocked. However ambiguous her position as stepmother to the next Queen, she would always be High Priestess, always know the mysteries of the Mistresses and obey them in all their bloody imperatives. In this, she would be alone.

'Princess?' Eritha was watching as though she heard her fears and sympathised. 'We ought to be getting you ready. The King will be there to greet you.'

If she had touched her, Pasiphaë would have screamed, or cracked into brittle pieces. She felt cold and fragile, despite the sun that beat down on the awning. Fish, disturbed by the oars, flashed past on silver wings until Arete drew the curtain, shutting out the world. Eritha was holding up the dress she would wear to meet the King, her bridegroom. It was a dress fit for a goddess, and it was almost more than she could bear.

'I won't have to dance for Asterius, will I? Not straight away?' She knew it sounded pathetic, heard the whining of a terrified child in the question, but it was all she could do to keep her voice from trembling.

'Not today. You won't be dancing the Bull Dance straight off the ship. There'll be all sorts of ceremonies first. Today will be feasts and suchlike.'

Eritha held up the dress again, like a mother, insisting now that she had given her reasons. Like a good child, Pasiphaë obeyed, let the women undress her of her ordinary clothes. She held up her arms and was buried beneath the billows of the goddess robes, their gold and silver, scents and textures both familiar and alarming. When all was settled and the flounces straightened, pinched, crimped or patted into place, Eune brought the casket of jewels. Pasiphaë lifted the lid, and the scent of cedar wood chased away all the other smells. She knew these pendants and necklaces, their histories and their properties. They spoke to her as they had done since she was a child, in her mother's voice, brisk and firm. She listened for Perseis now, to tell her which to wear.

For her hair she chose a diadem of moonstones that matched her silver earrings. Then she lifted out the heavy gold chain with the pendant of Potnia Theron, curved, full-bellied and resplendent as the moon, her hands resting on the heads of two lionesses. She hung it around her neck, felt the wide, cold arms of it embrace her throat above the swell of her breasts. The cold burned. It was a sign. Above the sound of the waves, she heard the roaring of lions, the goddess speaking to her High Priestess.

'Coil my hair in serpents and egret necks, streams, rivers

and waterfalls. At my waist I'll wear my belt of Kolchian gold and on my feet sandals strapped with Kolchian doeskin. Make me Kolchis.'

When Eritha had transformed her face into an image of the goddess, Pasiphaë called for her pots of herbs and dried bark, strips of meat hard as wood, bones and feathers, and had a brazier lit to make offerings to Cybele. Through teeth gritted to keep her voice firm, she repeated the rites Circe had taught her to make her husband respectful and obedient if he didn't want to end up like Attis – minus his manly parts. She would take a pinch of the ashes and mix it with scented oils and place it in a leather pouch hung on a leather thong, and she would place it around Asterius's neck. He would wear it as a gauge of the respect he owed her.

The ritual gave her comfort. She took deep breaths of the scents, letting them fill her head with visions. She saw the labyrinth of the dancing floor and the bull-headed King, the dance steps she would weave about his, and the thread binding them both that she held in her hand. But the smoke made her eyes smart, and instead of feeling the hardening of resolve, she shook away tears.

*

When all was ready, she had the curtains of the awning tied back. As the long, rocky coastline of Crete rose up in cliffs burning orange in the afternoon sun, and the helmsman had the sail trimmed to navigate the entrance to the port of Amnisos, she left her women in the stern. She stood at the prow, with one hand on the neck of the figurehead, to be the one the waiting crowd would see first.

The crew shouted and whistled as the ship advanced along the mole, where all other vessels had been cleared away to the seaward side, leaving open blue water for the ship bearing the Moon Princess. The women were silent at first, awestruck by the huge crowd that made the gathering on Lemnos look like a village wedding festival. But awe soon gave way to curiosity. Arete and Tyro, leaning their strong brown arms on the ship's rail, chattered and pointed, admiring dresses and the bare-chested men. Eune had to drag them away.

'This stuff won't pack itself up, you slack pair of heifers!'

Pasiphaë's eyes, though, were on the city that climbed the hillside behind the port. Its walls were pure decoration, ornament, covered in friezes in blue and every red the earth possessed. The defence of Knossos was the sea.

The master of the ship pointed to a long wall that dominated the western side of the hill, and the broad staircase that climbed up to it. The stair led to a great terrace, a portico and the bronze glitter of huge doors. Above the door were what looked like gold-painted bull's horns.

'See that, Princess? We call that the Barley Court, biggest court in the palace. Beyond the wall's where the bull-leapers dance.'

The word *palace* echoed like the notes of the koudounia. She stopped herself staring and swallowed the question. She had taken the piled majesty of the buildings for a town, and a prosperous one. Was it possible that all of this was the royal house? She followed the long wall of the bull-dancing court to a lower terrace where the sunlight glinted on running water. From there, she let her gaze rise with the columns that surmounted it, holding up roofs that held up more roofs. She would come to know that dazzling geometry as dwellings, shrines, storerooms and theatres, a maze of galleries and terraces where flowers spilled over from terracotta pots and jars. But then, that first impression was simply of walls and roofs borne up by columns of fluted wood, more and more roofs that rose, tier upon painted tier, into the unmarked blue of the sky.

She had never seen anything more breathtakingly wonderful but retained her poised indifference. The goddess is never surprised. How can she be when she knows everything? She stood at the prow, hand resting on the figurehead, as the port enveloped the ship in the arms of the mole, and she sailed smooth as oil into the belly of Amnisos. The towering, many-eyed palace of Knossos on the hills behind returned her gaze.

She saw Asterius immediately, and immediately the waving, cheering, bird-bright crowd receded. He stood with empty space around him. No courtiers hovered at his elbow; no slaves scuttled about his feet with stools, cups of wine, the small delicacies Kings usually expect at their fingertips. All kept their distance. Respect or fear?

Pasiphaë observed the man in the empty frame. He was not so tall as Athamas, athletic in build, but not as broad in the shoulder or as well-muscled. He was not young but not as old as Aloeus, dark hair pulled back from a narrow brow, black-bearded, bronze-skinned. He wore no tunic but a dark pleated kilt to his calves, and over his bare chest a short cloak, purple, gold-bordered, pinned on one shoulder. She stared, but what was she looking for? The mark of a hero, an omen? She stared, but no eagle appeared to circle over his head; listened, but no wild beast roared in approval. He remained just a man.

The ship's master credited her with enough intelligence to have worked out for herself which was the King and busied himself with issuing orders to the crew. The sail was furled and taken down, the ship manoeuvred to its berth, the oars raised and the anchor stones heaved overboard. Workers hurried to tie up and bring boarding ramps. Pasiphaë made a silence in her head, put the women, her boxes and caskets, Kolchis itself, out of her mind. There would be time for souvenirs later.

Athamas shouted to the men heaving on the mooring ropes to be quick, waved on the slaves with the ramp, and when it clattered into place, had two men hold it steady. Then he stood back. The moment had come. Pasiphaë stepped onto the boards that led to the shore, to Crete, and to the man whose Queen she would be. She wrapped herself in silence, hearing only the rustle of her dress, the patter of her feet, the slap of water between the hull of the ship and the wall. She heard no calling, no cheering. For the Moon Princess there was nothing in the round of her world now but the King.

Asterius held out his hands as she stepped ashore. *Welcome, Princess Pasiphaë.* His lips moved but had she heard a voice? She let his strong fingers fold around her palm. If she had been expecting the sharp jolt of magic, she was disappointed. She felt nothing, no leap of the heart, unless it was that making the blood pound in her ears. She saw nothing but his face, eyes dark-lashed, thick as a girl's. Were they the eyes of a god? A fitting consort for the Moon Princess?

Silently, she called upon Potnia Theron. In the space of a withheld breath, she heard the bellow of the white bull as he was led from the hold. The sound broke on her ears, broke the silence of the world, and it was filled with cheering. She took it for a good omen. Asterius's face broke into a smile.

'The white bull knows his home!'

This time, she heard. The crowd roared and clapped their hands. The white bull snorted and shook his head, pleased to be beneath the sun again. She wanted to put her arms around his neck and whisper *Kolchis* to him, breathe in his bull-smell of familiar pastures. But Asterius claimed her and drew her about to face the people.

'The Moon Princess of Kolchis is come to be the Queen of the Cretan Bull, and I, Asterius of Knossos, ask her to accept the seat by my side.'

Immediately, before she could reply, the music began, women beating tympana, salpinges braying their brazen call, and the rumble of bullroarers. Asterius led her to a chair to be carried up the steep road to the palace. The air shivered with noise so loud it seemed as though it must break. She spoke polite words of greeting, but the sound was so small, she wondered if even Asterius heard. He had *asked* her but hadn't waited to hear if she *accepted* him as her King. The most sacred aspect seemed not to matter to the cheering crowd. And now she was to be paraded like the bull for their entertainment. The child sought her mother's hand but found only the hard grasp of a King's.

She fought back whatever it was trying to force tears from her eyes – disappointment perhaps, or a longing for something she had never had – and shrugged off the hand helping her into the chair. Taking a deep breath, she turned to face the faceless, unknown people and raised her arms like a goddess statue. Curiosity perhaps silenced their excited voices.

'I, Pasiphaë of Kolchis, Moon Princess and High Priestess of Potnia Theron, thank Asterius of Knossos for his graciousness, and accept to take him for her King, to sit at his side as his Queen.'

Perseis had taught her the words of acceptance, and she was damned if she wasn't going to speak them. Her voice was light, childlike, she knew, and probably only a handful had heard what she said, even fewer understood it, but that was enough. She had made her point. She didn't dare look at any of the faces, not individually, afraid that her gaze would fall on some old crone who disapproved or some man who sniggered. Then the silence broke.

'Pasiphaë! Pasiphaë! Pasiphaë!'

She let her eyes slip out of focus, let the middle distance become a sea of mingled colour and movement, her ears fill with the pounding of the tympana, the pounding of her heart and the chanting of her name. A voice close to her ear, warm and soft, nonetheless pierced the din.

'It was well said, Princess. The goddess heard and she is with you.'

It was a warm voice, gentle. She forgot her irritation. 'With us both, I hope.'

He smiled, white teeth in a tanned face, and the creases around his eyes deepened. She guessed he was a man who found laughter easy. She smiled back, and this time gave him her hand. He turned the hand palm up and kissed it. The crowd roared. His smile broadened.

'There. That was her answer.'

He stepped away from the litter chair, slaves lifted it, and Pasiphaë began the last part of her journey to the palace of Knossos. Carried like a Queen, her feet didn't even touch her new land.

PART TWO

The first star

Pasiphaë arrived in Knossos, a child with a sense of duty and dignity. Her mother had never shown her what it was to be loved or even valued for herself. She was useful, and she was used. Perseis probably didn't mean to be unfeeling – it was simply not in her nature to empathise with anything. She was a wave on the sea, a breath of wind. Mothers made their requests and the Mistresses chose their sons' wives, their daughters' husbands. Mother, Mistress – they were almost interchangeable.

Asterius didn't question the choice of the Mistresses either; Kolchis was rich enough after all. He had been chosen, and desire played no part in the destiny of a King. Neither he nor Pasiphaë expected more than mutual tolerance from this marriage. Nothing had prepared them for the Mistresses' gift.

1

The first dance

Asterius watched the docking manoeuvres with curiosity. He had watched Europa with the same curiosity as she walked across the shining stones of the great entrance to greet him, her young suitor. His Aunt Keraso had walked the same stones when she came to greet Lycastus. This time, the positions were reversed, and it was the King who would walk across the stones to greet his bride. For the people, she was no more than that, but for Asterius, she was the way out of a delicate situation.

He had only ever been the King, had no real claim to hang on to his position once Europa was dead. He had been saved only because he was the father of the next Queen, and she was too young yet to rule. Minos had tried to demand that Karpasia be named instead, but the people seemed prepared to wait until Kriti was old enough. In any case, Karpasia had no interest in being Queen, even less in being *his* Queen, and had told Minos in no uncertain terms to go fuck himself.

Yet the shadow of Minos and his ambitions hung heavy, reminding Asterius of the vulnerability of his position as a King without a Queen, and he watched the ship with a sense of relief more than anything else. He stood in a circle of empty space, like a leper. The taint of death, of superfluity, was on him, even though the bright, carefree crowds along the mole had not done away with their outdated Kings for generations.

Minos would have introduced the ways of the mainland if he could. It was no secret that the Kings of the mainland stepped aside for their sons, and if they didn't, they were pushed.

Putting aside the thought of Europa's favourite son, he watched the young woman at the prow of the great ship, one hand around a curved horn of the figurehead. He wondered afterwards if he had known then, in that first sight, that she would be more to him than any Queen. The people had seen how she clasped the bull's horn and interpreted it as he expected. They cheered with delight. Flowers made coloured arcs of sweet scent as they flew towards her. The bullroarers roared and the air vibrated with cries of *Pasiphaë! Pasiphaë!* The oppression cast by Minos's shadow dissipated in the general expression of joy.

Then the girl in white, the Moon Princess, stepped from the ship. Curiosity became a pounding in his chest, focused on a face, a woman, not an idea or an imposition. The voice of the crowd rolled back and forth in his head like the tide, and she walked through it, her feet wading through the shallows strewn with flowers. A great white bull stamped onto the boarding ramp behind her and let out a majestic bellow. At the sound, the woman half turned and smiled. The crowd clapped and cheered, and something changed in the quality of the light.

*

'I hope the chair doesn't remind you too much of the rolling of your ship, Princess.'

Asterius walked by her side, attentive. Pasiphaë would have liked to say, yes, it did, and she would much rather have walked, but that would not have been gracious.

'I think I'll feel waves rolling beneath my feet for years to come.'

The road from Amnisos wound in gentle meanders between majestic houses, any one of which could have been a royal house, and Asterius pointed them out, naming each family who lived there. He also pointed out olive groves and cattle in pasture, as if she might not have known what a cow was. She hoped he was just making conversation.

Faces bobbed in and out of her vision, like birds after a feast of seeds, but she couldn't stare. Her eyes darted from one woman brilliant as a sunrise to another, their tight-waisted dresses hooped around the hips, bare legs that flashed through splits in the skirts. Men and women glittered with jewellery, and the fabrics, patterned in strange geometric designs, sparkled with sequins. The impression formed at Lemnos returned, of a flock of brightly coloured birds, swift in movement, chattering and almost childlike. Some of them even carried birds, or led animals on leashes, like martens but larger and spotted or mottled, monkeys that gazed at her with their big man-like eyes.

Her women followed the litter. She could hear Tyro and Arete making critical comments about the herds.

'Funny-coloured cows they've got here. Pretty though.'

'Skinny. There's no eating in this grass, it's parched, clapped out. Like that excuse for a bull over there.'

'Wait till he sees our Snowy.'

'He'll show him what's what. Show them cows an' all.'

'They won't know what's hit 'em.'

Eune and Semele were making similar comments about the people.

'Did you see the state of that one?'

'Her with the hoops in her ears and her tits hanging out?'

'Don't leave much to the imagination, do they?'

'Mine's working overtime. Get an eyeful of that fella over there.'

'I wouldn't mind seeing what he's got under his kilt.'

'You going to ask him or will I?'

Their laughter, loud and unabashed, made Pasiphaë smile. She hoped it wouldn't look rude, but the sound was so reassuring she didn't much care. White clouds shoaled above the palace, softening the almost brazen brilliance of the sky, like great pelican birds, and with a suddenness that brought tears to her eyes, she was reminded of home.

The bearers stopped, and Asterius waited, one foot set on the lowest step. Pasiphaë stared up at the great white staircase. She had been expecting walls, fortifications, but saw only a monumental assembly of piled boxes, windows, terraces and flowers. Beyond, she saw only blue sky, white clouds and the circling dance of white seabirds. Asterius held out his hand in a courteous gesture, and she joined him on the glittering stone to climb by his side. Hundreds of people pressed behind, but she didn't look back. She climbed with the blue above and white stone beneath her feet, the Moon Princess climbing to her place in the sky. But when she placed her foot on the last step, the Moon Princess struggled to maintain her bland, unimpressed expression.

Before them stretched a sea of stone, dazzlingly smooth, to the columned portico of the royal entrance. In the shadow, through the tree columns, stood the great door bound with bronze, and on the roof above it, the symbol of Knossos: bull's horns, red-painted and banded in gold. The sun beat down remorselessly, and everything seemed too white, too bright, too gold-glittering. Pasiphaë walked without breaking step with Asterius, towards the shade between the columns where more people were gathered, more brilliant costumes and bejewelled courtiers. The journey and the light began to seem like unbearable burdens.

The crowd followed like the tide rising on their heels, fringed with the froth of fabrics and the glitter of gold, washing up to the shade beneath the portico. As Pasiphaë and Asterius drew closer, the froth parted at either side of a lone girl, her slender frame lost in the billowing mass of her scarlet skirts. She was painted like a priestess, her tiny mouth a violent red, eyes encircled with black, casting their light into shadow. She stood in isolation, a lonely reed bending beneath the weight of a diadem of moons and stars, where her tightly braided hair coiled like miniature serpents.

Asterius turned to Pasiphaë and murmured, 'My daughter, Kriti.'

She cast her mind back to what her mother had said about the heiress. How old? She hadn't said, just not old enough to be Queen. Ten years? Eleven, perhaps? Though she was not yet a woman, Kriti was dressed as a goddess; the bodice would have exposed her breasts if she'd had any. *She won't live long enough to marry.* Pasiphaë wondered if her father had asked for a seeing, been shown the signs. Had anyone told the girl she was just a tiny backwater that would never see the ocean? Her mother was dead, so perhaps there was no one to tell her such a thing, no one to hold her tight to stop the fear of death swallowing her before her time.

And if she did live? Pasiphaë's words of acceptance echoed, hollow and insubstantial. She was the Queen of the Bull King, but no more than that. She was to marry the King, but Kriti would be Queen of Knossos. She would be the regent until Kriti became a woman. Had the girl been trotted out just to remind her that she was no more than a seat warmer? Pasiphaë glanced at Asterius's face and saw only compassion. She remembered that he was the girl's father, and she imagined Aloeus, how he would have wept to see his daughter painted and paraded, a feeble echo of a goddess.

Pasiphaë had never thought of the Mistresses as cruel, and the idea shifted the ground treacherously beneath her feet. She tried to read in Kriti's dark eyes that she knew she was going to die, but the woman painted onto her child's face hid almost all humanity. She wondered if her own timidity was so well hidden.

Kriti's steps halted, the tip of a pink tongue shone pale against the red lips, and the dark eyes flicked to Asterius, where perhaps she found the courage to speak. 'Welcome to the house of Knossos, Moon Princess of Kolchis, High Priestess of Potnia Theron, Face of the Mistresses.'

The short speech tumbled out, rapid and clear as stream water. The corners of Asterius's eyes creased in a brief smile, and the girl sighed in relief. A woman, an old nurse possibly, hurried out of the shadows, put an arm around Kriti's shoulders and guided her back to anonymity like a mother hen. Anger flickered in Asterius's eyes, but he forced a laugh.

'She forgot the part where she should have introduced herself. Too quick to fly away.'

He hesitated, watching as his daughter was enfolded by priestesses and other high-ranking women, and Pasiphaë saw pity and helpless concern watering the dark anger in his expression. When he turned to her, he had composed his features, master of himself again. But before the cortège reached the great doors, there was a stir among the watchers beneath the sun on the square behind. The wave of bright garments and jewels retreated, making a space around a heavyset young man with a broken nose and dark hair that curled to his shoulders.

'Welcome, Moon Princess.'

Out of the corner of her eye, Pasiphaë saw Asterius's jaw clench. The young man stared at her and she was reminded of Butes Pallantides, the Athenian from Lemnos, the same blend of contempt and desire. She guessed who he must be before he opened his mouth to introduce himself, placing his right hand on his breast in a dramatic pose that could only be in mockery.

'Minos. Son of the woman you are replacing in Asterius's bed. He has chosen a ravishing bride for his final years.'

The voice grated. Not the sound, which was perfectly poised – Minos had been taught public speaking after all – but the words themselves scraped like blades against a whetstone. Pasiphaë felt the intentional nicks in her flesh but didn't lower her gaze.

'The Mistresses chose his bride, sir, as is the custom.'

'Then I hope the Mistresses know what pleases a man who may not have long to enjoy his pleasures.'

Minos looked about him and his followers sniggered. He stood taller, knowing he was not alone, and the gold around his neck and his waist glittered. His eyes were dark, and all they reflected was bitterness at a promise made and broken.

'May my final years be far away, Minos,' Asterius said. 'The Mistresses know which is our path and when it will end. They are our mothers, and we are in their hands.'

'*My* mother was a Phoenician Princess. Her blood was Argive, a daughter of gods. But I would never deny your right to follow your own fantasies, Asterius. Send me word when the sacrifice begins. The bull the Kolchians sent will make a fine spectacle in his death throes.'

Pasiphaë hadn't given much thought to what would happen to the white bull. He was a gift, and if Asterius had wanted to sacrifice him, she wouldn't have opposed his decision. Even if she considered that Potnia Theron would have preferred that his seed be used to improve the royal herds. In the mouth of Minos, the word *sacrifice* had a foul taste. She looked quickly at Asterius and saw anger in his eyes.

'The white bull is a gift, and a precious one. I see no reason to make a sacrifice of him. The Princess will find a suitable offering from among my herds to give thanks for her safe arrival.'

Asterius held Minos's angry glare in his own calm gaze, refusing to let any emotion disturb the placidity of his features. Pasiphaë, though, felt the animosity like a living thing that fluttered between the two men, black and chaotic. Minos pointed an accusatory finger.

'The white bull from across the sea is the only suitable sacrifice for Poteidan. The sea god demands it! You have, so far, kept me, the son of a god, from his birthright, but to deprive the gods themselves of their due is to court disaster. Far be it from me, though, to offer advice to the *King*.'

Satisfied with his threat, Minos turned, and the backcloth of courtiers parted to let him pass then flowed back behind him, some laughing, some casting backward glances at the Princess who thought that by marrying a King she would be Queen.

Pasiphaë felt the chill of winter beneath the Cretan summer

sun. This was the fracture that Circe had spoken of, the fault in the glaze that ran through the bowl of the Middle Sea and was spreading, like crow's feet from the corner of an ageing eye, to the rest of the world. She felt like a small bright beetle caught in a spider's web and only terror of ridicule held her motionless on the smooth pavement. Where would she run, anyway? Perseis would have turned her straight back to face her fate.

She glanced at the face of the man who was to be her husband and saw that he was no freer than she was. Circe's fracture was real, and although she and Asterius were on the same side, Pasiphaë had no way of knowing which side held the balance. She watched Minos disappear, the crowd at the edge of the square surging back to fill the space left by him and his followers. The darkness lifted as the music began, and the laughter that rang out was unequivocal – innocent anticipation of entertainment. Asterius offered her his arm and she took it, willingly this time, and let herself be escorted into the palace.

*

The double doors opened onto a long, wide hall. Just inside was a guardroom with racks of spears against the wall. Beyond, curious faces filled innumerable doorways, administrators in their sober tunics, artisans in leather aprons, tools and pieces of work in their hands. There was a buzz of excited talk, and Pasiphaë held her head high, pretending to be unmoved and unimpressed.

The crowd that had followed the royal couple from the port was still close on their heels, their voices like the swell of the sea, ringing out louder as they poured into the enclosed space of the palace. The tide rolled along a gallery and into a vast court full of sunlight – the Barley Court, Asterius said. He pointed out the three circular doors let into the stone pavement.

'Granaries. The wealth of Knossos, some of it at least, is stored down there. There is never want here.'

By Knossos, he meant the rambling palace and the thousands it employed, housed and fed. The surrounding farmland too. He spoke like a man proud of his land, proud of its abundance, perhaps also like a man explaining a legacy.

'The Barley Court is the people's court,' he said. 'Beyond,' he pointed to the far wall pierced with wide, high openings, 'is the Court of Ceremonies and the labyrinth.'

He led the way along another gallery to the smaller courtyard. A flock of servants, plain sparrows these compared with the courtiers, were fluttering away after arranging cushioned seats on a raised dais at the shaded eastern end, and Pasiphaë seated herself gratefully. The rolling motion of the ship was still in her blood, and the firm earth bucked beneath her feet.

A small number of courtiers had followed, and they took up their seats behind the royal couple, but the bulk of the crowd had been left behind in the Barley Court. They thronged the window openings, though, some sitting on the sills, their lags dangling over the side. A quick, darting movement caught Pasiphaë's eye – Princess Kriti escaping from her nurse to slip down to the front of the dais. She sat, her toes just scraping the edge of the dancing floor, without a backward glance for the old woman obliged to remain among the servants. Asterius had seen too, and a smile flickered across his lips.

More palace intrigue, Pasiphaë thought, and sank into the cushions, letting the world of waves and the inhospitable comportment of Minos slip away. What she looked down on was a dancing floor with coloured stones set among the white flags to create a complicated path, the path the dancers would follow. That she would follow.

'You know the labyrinth dances?' Asterius asked.

'We have a labyrinth and dances.' Her gaze followed the winding paths to admire the beauty of the polished stone and how the red veining glittered in the westering sun. 'Though our dancing floor isn't so large or so beautiful.'

Asterius smiled with genuine pleasure. 'There'll be

dancing in your honour this evening, and tomorrow, we'll dance here together, you and I.'

Trepidation stirred the fearful animal in her stomach again. 'I know the Sun Dance when the Queen chooses her King.' She left the rest unsaid.

'Our dance will be the same. The Bull King will bend his steps to those of the Moon Princess. He will become the Sun to her Moon.' His voice was gentle. She smiled quickly in gratitude, and the fearful animal was still, curled back into sleep. He touched her arm. 'The dancers are arriving.'

Women drifted through the crowd, stepped onto the pavement, their boldly patterned dresses flashing with gold and silver discs. They wore no bodices, and their skirts split to the waist displayed long brown limbs. In their hair they wore the long white and grey tail feathers of cranes. High-stepping, dainty as birds, they took up position on the red path of the dance and the music began. First came the soft beating of a dozen tympana, taken up by the low fluting call of the aulos, and the birds fluttered into their dance to the trembling strumming of the kitharai. Headdresses bent and bowed, and the crane women swept along the meandering path to the outer edge of the labyrinth before swooping back to gather in the centre.

The music swelled louder, and from the edge of the swaying crowd that clapped hands and tapped feet to the rhythm, male dancers moved onto the maze, their slim bodies oiled and glinting in the sun. Unadorned and naked except for a loincloth, they moved cautiously around the glittering women, each putting an individual stamp on his dance steps, to draw attention to his prowess. The crowd cheered the acrobatic leaps and figures, and the women dancers replied in kind, their skirts swirling and feathers sweeping the ground.

This was more flamboyant than the spring bird dance of Kolchis, and wilder. The crowd encouraged the dancers with gestures verging on the obscene, and Pasiphaë watched, entranced. The end came when the courting birds leapt one last time into the air, vaulting and springing to hands to feet and back again, and each broad-skirted woman wrapped her wing arms around the man who had pleased her most. Kriti bounced up and down, clapping wildly, and the courtiers smiled indulgently at their little Princess.

*

When each couple had danced their way out of the labyrinth and through the applauding crowd, Asterius placed a hand on the armrest of Pasiphaë's chair.
'Tomorrow, they'll cheer for us and the beginning of our dance together.'

He looked into the eyes of the girl he was to marry. Everything about her was unknown and he had no idea what she saw. They had only exchanged a handful of words; how could she have any idea what he thought of her? He didn't even know himself. She didn't *look* afraid of him, nor did she sound it. Her voice was firm, eager even.

'I will dance the Moon steps in our Sun Dance. All you'll have to do is follow me. Your Bull steps are probably not very different to the Sun's.'

He nodded. It was her place to lead, and he accepted it. They had struck a bargain at least. He had seen no fear in his bride's eyes, but his own fear that gnawed at his bones had never really gone away. The relief he had felt when he clasped the hand of the woman who would represent the Queen was ephemeral. The dull, nagging fear was Minos and his followers, the men who looked at him with their eyes of hungry panthers. With an effort, he put it aside.

'Tomorrow will be a day of celebration and feasting. Tomorrow you'll marry the King, but today you're his guest. It's time for me to show you the hospitality of a host.'

He rose and held out his hand and felt an unexpected shiver of pleasure, hope perhaps, as Pasiphaë accepted his invitation with a smile. Her fingers closed around his with confidence as they were swallowed up by the echoing immensity of the royal house of Knossos.

*

Later, Pasiphaë stood at the heart of the palace, at a window of the Queen's apartment that they called the Dolphin Chamber. The window looked out onto the great staircase that flowed down to the lower levels from the Court of Ceremonies and climbed behind her line of vision to yet more regal apartments above. It looked across to the Great Shrine with its three faces, red and gold, of painted stone and wood, and everywhere, beneath the eaves, on the altar set in full view in front of the shrine, was the sign of the bull, curved and pointed.

The sun had set and its light had faded. The sky had deepened to turquoise at the western horizon, and soon the first stars would prick the blue with white light. The air was filled with the smell of the sea and the scents of unfamiliar shrubs and flowers. She took a deep breath. This view would grow as familiar as the dappled movement of her moon-filled window at Kolchis, but for now she was enchanted by its magic.

A faint rustle made her turn. Eritha stood in the doorway, framed by the silver and blue of painted dolphins, the pine marten in her arms. She set the marten on the ground and the little animal bounded across the pavement to her mistress. Pasiphaë scooped her up and buried her nose in the silky fur that smelled hot and musky and as familiar as her mother's scent.

'Will you be wanting any of us this evening, Princess?'

Pasiphaë shook her head. 'Just leave my creams and a basin of water and you can all go off to bed. I'll want you with me early tomorrow.'

She could think no further ahead than that. Another deep breath that might have been a sigh, might have been the drawing up of courage, and she gave a last circular glance across the rooftops. Her gaze lingered on the western hills beyond, the deep cleft where the last of the light lay, until it was drawn to an unexpected movement. A single figure was climbing the great staircase. The animal in her belly squirmed, and she peered down into the gathering shadows. A face turned up to hers, unsmiling. Minos.

2

The would-be King

Since his mother's death, Minos had mostly kept away from Knossos, but when he was in residence, it was his habit to roam the palace at night. Only at night, when it was emptied of what he recognised as idle flattery and self-interest, rivalries expressed in costly fabrics and exotic pets, was he able to fill the echoing palace rooms with his presence. Knossos was his, promised to him by his mother. Since he had been old enough to listen and understand, Europa had told him he was the son of a god, and he was the son his father had chosen to succeed her.

He despised his brothers and refused to believe that they, too, had been sired by Zeus, the father god he invoked when he worshipped at Poteidan's shrine. Sarpedon and Rhadamanthus were content with their flocks and their olive groves, their festivals and full bellies. He, Minos, would be content when he had the whole of Crete in his hands, when his ships inspired fear throughout the Cyclades, and when he had an army that could crush the brawling bands of the mainland. It was time to end the rule of women and for Knossos to become the heart of an empire. It was not enough to be the richest merchant in a league of merchants, and if Crete didn't pick up the spear and claim the Middle Sea, there were plenty of rising stars among the brawlers of Peloponnesus who would attempt it.

It was ambition, not filial respect, that had brought him

back to Knossos, to pace what he considered his birthright. His steps brought him to the glorious central staircase, the artery that flowed through the layers of riches, like the lifeblood pumped from the original power source from which all of the present magnificence had sprung. He felt the ancient magic still, though the Mother who birthed it was long dead, no matter what the credulous people thought. Her son lived, though, and he, Minos, was his incarnation.

He stopped at the level of the Court of Ceremonies, silent and glittering silver beneath the moon. Asterius imagined he could prolong his life of idle leisure by passing off his new wife as a provisional Queen. In a few years, Kriti would be Queen, and her husband would be King. There would be no place for the old King, and the ancient custom would have Asterius lying in his larnax with a spear hole in his throat. But the old ways had slipped, and Asterius thought he could hang on to his throne, his easy, idle life.

Minos raised his face, knew she would be there, the pebble in his sandal. He sensed her presence, her foreign scents and perfumes on the night air. She was dark. Too dark to see much in her features, her hair a thick cloud about her shoulders. Night. Asterius thought he could cling to life, presiding over the slow death of Cretan power. It was time to end all that. It was time for the sons of the father god to rule.

Pasiphaë's face hung in the sky, blushed a dull silver by the low moon. He felt the cold that emanated from her, the cold of the priestesses and their exclusive cults, their rituals that denied the true source of life, the seed only men produced. The world of women was ruled by blood, moon-blood and birth-blood, to fertilise the earth. Theirs were small ambitions, like the slow death of flowers, barely raising their heads before sinking back into the darkness. He would bring his world back into the light, raise it from the sea into the glitter of the sun, and he would fence in its horizons with a wall of spears.

'Make the most of the stars, Lady Pasiphaë. The night won't last forever.'

She didn't reply. What could she say? He wasn't really addressing her anyway. She was no more than a symbol, a ploy. She would be swept away like the bloody darkness, with no more weight in the world than a dry stalk.

3

The Bull Dance

Pasiphaë had seen the labyrinth and knew the dance. One labyrinth is much like another after all; the essential thing is to know the steps. She had been taught the Sun Dance as soon as she could raise one foot without falling over. It was at the heart of all the dances, its steps interwoven with the pattern of every other. She had danced it as an infant with a servant girl for a partner and had seen it danced in all its glorious ritual when Circe took Agrius for her King. Circe would be dancing it again in a few years when his time was up and the oak grove claimed him. Pasiphaë had not imagined it would feel so different to be dancing it herself to bind her own King. Different and momentous.

The sun was barely risen, but already she was dressed and prepared. She wouldn't eat. Hunger sharpened the wits, and she would want to hear the words the Mistresses whispered. She would drink only clear, cold water, let it cool the fire in her belly, dampen the fumes that rose to her head. The marten slept calmly, a good sign, and a flock of egrets had flown past the open terrace into the dawn, the sun golden on their white wings. Another good omen. Yet still she was gripped by apprehension. She had been taught to be a Princess, a High Priestess, but never what it felt like to be just a girl on the day of her wedding.

The serving women had been awake since before dawn,

and they drifted in the shadows of the room sleepily, stifling yawns. She was aware of Eune's familiar morning irritation as she organised the tidying away of her belongings, sorting which would be removed to the royal apartment she would share with Asterius. Tyro and Arete, as usual, had been given the heavy jobs. Eune wrestled her into the bridal dress, Semele placed the headdress of the Moon Princess over her piled hair. She became a work of art. Everything – hair, throat and arms, ears and fingers – glittered with gold and polished stones. When she moved, she jingled. Eritha had painted her eyes, lips and the tips of her breasts in the Cretan style. When she looked in the mirror she wondered where Pasiphaë was hiding.

Perhaps it was this strangeness that made her so anxious, being turned into an object, a spectacle, someone she didn't recognise. The face she would present to the crowd today was not the face of Pasiphaë, the girl who had grown to be a woman in the woods of Kolchis above the Inhospitable Sea. The thought made her heart ache. She wished that Asterius had known her then, known the girl before the Princess.

She gazed out over the tiered rooftops of Knossos, to the distant hillside, pale green with olive groves, just brushed with the first gold of the rising of the sun, listening for the voices of the Mistresses. Turtle doves roo-coo-cooed somewhere above her head, speaking of peace and order. The proper rites would be accomplished, the words said, and blood, wine and water would flow. Nothing would perturb the pattern. So, why did her heart still pound?

*

Athamas, resplendent in his lion-skin kilt, a fleece flecked in Kolchian gold over his shoulder and his leather casque plumed with egret feathers, waited in the doorway with an escort of ten guardsmen. The serving women would follow, their chattering hushed to a whisper by the unfamiliarity of the palace. Pasiphaë touched the pendant of Potnia Theron at her neck and joined Athamas. She walked in a cloak of silence, barefoot, so not even the patter of sandals disturbed the quiet. She emptied her mind of her fears, paid no heed to the innumerable stairs and terraces, the friezes and coloured columns that opened out to reveal the Great Shrine, the bull-horned altar, the basins and the ranks of priestesses dedicated to the Mistresses.

For this first part of the ceremony, the men left her at the foot of the steps, and she climbed them alone, beneath the burnished sky, too bright, too metallic to be blue, enclosed by baked bricks. There was barely a green stalk to carry the whispering of the Mistresses, only the plants on a balcony spilling over from their jars. She was glad at least that there were no watching crowds, and at the altar, she was alone except for the priestesses led by the Key-Bearer, an intimidating woman of her mother's age whose name she didn't yet know. Labrys and spear blade glittered and sun glinted on the water in the basin. The occasion was too important for an offering of grain and oil. For this, there would be blood. The light drove needles into her skull.

Acolytes brought up the sacrifice, twin bull calves, white with black markings and dabs of red on their faces. They looked about them and blinked, unsteady on their legs after the long walk from the fields. Pasiphaë fought the sharp sunlight and the feeling that something was wrong and spoke the words to the sky, calling on the Potniai to hear. She placed a hand on each of the curly heads where the buds of horns lay. The calves skittered, fear replacing unease. The acolytes tethered them to the iron rings set in the altar stone.

She took up the spear, felt its weight, the thin sharpness of the blade, raised it above her head.

'In thanks for your daughter's safe deliverance from the sea, and for your gift of a King, accept these offerings, Mistresses of the Earth, the sky and all creation, the ones who made the arc of the heavens and the great bowl of the sea.'

The acolyte led the first calf forward and pulled back his

head over the flat rim of the basin. She watched life throbbing in the white-haired neck, and her own heart beat to its pulse. She plunged the spear into the life river. The animal struggled, his eyes rolled, starting in pain and surprise then clouding over. Blood flowed, more water. The acolytes untied the carcass and moved it to one side. The blood continued to flow then drip into the basin below. Pasiphaë turned to receive the second calf, met his eyes, so dark and so full of fear and questioning. As she hesitated, the calf lifted his head and bawled, again and again.

The acolyte dragged him to the basin, small hooves scuffling on the slippery stone, his nostrils full of the smell of his brother's blood, and through the hot, still air came an answering cry, full of distress. The priestesses shuffled restlessly as the cow in the distant field called to her calf. Pasiphaë would not look at any of them. Her head split with the light and the sound of weeping, and she cried out.

'No! The Mistress says, *no more*. She is life-giver too, and she returns the calf to its mother.'

The acolyte still held the calf, looked from Pasiphaë to the Key-Bearer. No one spoke. The air vibrated with pain and she wanted to close her eyes and sleep, to wake among cool leaves.

'Potnia Theron is content with her offering. She will not take the cow's second calf. Let it be taken back to its mother.' No one moved. 'The Mistress has spoken!' Her voice rose shrill and imperious and on the point of breaking. Still, no one moved, as if the unexpected order was inappropriate or improper.

'You heard the Princess. Take the calf away.'

The voice, Asterius's, came from the foot of the steps before the shrine where the men waited. The words were sharp, but not as sharp as the sunlight. There was understanding in them too; the sharpness was only for the acolyte.

*

Pasiphaë's servants were waiting in the shrine's bathing room for the ritual cleansing and to change her dress. It was a brief respite before the marriage dance. That was what the people came to see, not the death of a calf. The sweet scent of hot oils drove the cloying blood and animal smells from her head, swept away some of the jagged light into cool darkness. She breathed easier.

There were flecks of blood on the skirts. Tyro was already scrubbing at the stains. Pasiphaë turned away, but the sound of the mother calling for her baby echoed, filling her with unaccountable sadness. She had never felt such compassion for a beast marked for sacrifice before. It was unnatural, yet she was sure that it had been the wish of the Mistress to spare the calf.

All mothers are the same. Even Perseis wept when her last child was born dead.

The women watched her, concern in their faces. It was Semele who spoke. 'You did right, Princess. One child is enough for any mother to lose.'

Semele, she knew, had lost both of hers. She forced a smile. Of all her servants, only Semele had been married, glad to see the back of her husband though. Pasiphaë hoped she would find a better one in her new life.

The smell of the sacrifice had gone, the traces cleansed away. Only thoughts of death and sorrow remained and would not be shifted. She was to be married, to sit in the Queen's seat, save Crete for the Potniai. She would become a mother too. Pasiphaë had gone, replaced by a symbol of power. She wondered if it was possible for a symbol to live, and if it did, could it still be a girl, a woman?

Her thoughts returned to the cow and her grieving. Perhaps grief was weakness, and the women like Perseis, who put duty before affection, had surpassed such a failing. She looked at her hands, the fingers laden with rings, the arm rings and bracelets. They were symbols too, the gold and the polished stones, but the fingers were the slender fingers of a girl.

Lodged beneath the skin at their tips she still felt the curly head of the calf. She wanted to weep, to run beneath tall forest trees, to be alone with her thoughts, to be with a mother who would let her weep.

'Princess, the overskirt. Is it tight enough?'

Eritha's voice broke gently into her thoughts. Perseis was far away and would have been of no help anyway. She felt the belt that held up the heavy skirts. She could get one finger behind it, no more.

'It'll do.'

She held out her hand for the mirror, looked at the face in the polished silver and judged it as she would a vase or a painting. Black eyes, red lips, symmetrical earrings, diadem on her brow and pendant on her breast. Nothing was marred. She was a pool reflecting moonlight. In the pool, a girl danced, but no one could see her. She pushed the mirror away.

'I'm ready.'

*

While Pasiphaë was preparing herself to dance with her King, the people were being allowed into the Court, pushing to get the best view. Men and women streamed along the walls, rolled up like a tide to the pavement's edge where they clung, jostling to stay in the front ranks. Hundreds of them, like a flock of gaudy starlings. The raised platform was set with cushioned seats as the day before, and the important people were already installed, but this time the crowds were not kept back. The openings in the walls that surrounded the court were filled with onlookers who vied with the wall paintings in vibrancy and colour. The smell of perfumed hair and bodies hung in the air as heavy as the earthy miasma above a forest swamp.

Labyrinths all followed the same pattern, as did the steps of the dances. Pasiphaë would bind Asterius and become the Queen. Asterius would be reinstated as King. Kriti, with her unhappy destiny, would not cast a shadow on the festivities, a vague memory that sank like a stone into a deep pool, leaving only ripples.

The sun was almost overhead and the red stones of the pavement glowed like the stones of an oven. It stretched, broad as the sea, to where Asterius stood, the Bull King with his golden horned mask. He wore only a black loincloth and his skin glittered with gold dust. Bull or Sun, it made no difference. Pasiphaë was the Moon, and he would follow. As she took her first steps on the white path through the labyrinth, a tympanum began its steady beat, matching the rhythm set by her feet. Asterius stepped onto the red path, his movements supple, a dancer's. She wondered how old he was. Nobody had thought to tell her.

More tympana took up the beat, turned it into a more complicated rhythm, and the Bull reached the centre of the labyrinth where the Moon wove her moon dance. Her heart fluttered and she fumbled for the ball of thread at her belt, the thread of Kolchian wool, glittering with powdered gold like the fleece of Athamas's cloak. This was how the Moon drew the Sun to her in Kolchis, and she would bind the Bull with it in Crete.

Asterius was so close that she could smell his sweat, close enough to have felt the pulse of his heart had she placed a hand on his chest. Instead, she handed him the thread, wrapped it twice around his open palm, closed his fingers on it. Then she spun away, the red-painted soles of her bare feet matching the red path, letting the thread unwind, then doubling back, spinning a web that bound Asterius in its centre. He understood the pattern, kept hold of the thread and let the Moon wind him about in gold. He twisted too, stepped high and proud as a bull, lowered his head and shook his horns from side to side. Pasiphaë parted her lips in a smile of triumph. He was caught; the path of the labyrinth always brought him back to her. She danced around him, brushing him with her hand. He opened his mouth to speak, but she twisted away.

*

Words welled up in Asterius's throat, tripping over his tongue, but he was slow, slower than she was. She had danced away, a bird, before he could ask her, was her anger gone? He had never seen a sacrifice stopped halfway through, never seen such looks of incomprehension on the Key-Bearer's face. The High Priestess of the sanctuary who knew every law, every ritual, who could read the clouds, the flight of birds, knew the language of the waves, had been without words. He had been afraid that Pasiphaë's defiance of custom would bring down the wrath of the Mistresses.

He looked at her face, wild with the dance, and tried to measure whether it was anger or abandon. She seemed as entranced as Kriti had been when she was allowed to dance, before her nurse whispered to her that dancing was immodest and unsuitable for a girl destined to be the voice of the Great Mother. He smiled to himself. It looked as though nobody had told Pasiphaë such stories.

*

The ball of thread was almost done. Pasiphaë ran, an egret along the edge of a pool, until the ball trickled out, and she held the end, slender and gold-dusted in hot fingers. This was where she drew in her catch, where the moon's mesh caught the sun. But as she moved back to Asterius, winding the thread back around her hand, he did the same. Pacing in time to the beat of the tympana, his horned head held high, his steps high and proud, the Bull came to meet her, and their hands, full of golden thread, clasped.

A sigh, like a great wave, rose from the crowd, and Asterius with his free hand removed his mask. Reverently, he placed it on the pavement where it rolled, empty and silent on its eyeless face, and placed his arm about his bride, drawing her to him gently, his eyes full of concern.

'It seems that the Mistresses are smiling after all. They have given you wings.'

Through her excitement, the realisation struck Pasiphaë that Asterius had been afraid for her, afraid that the Mistresses might have been offended by her outburst at the sacrifice. The thought filled her heart with such tenderness that she let herself go, uplifted by the wave and Potnia Theron's arms to Asterius's lips in an embrace as abandoned as the dance had been. The crowd applauded wildly, the music soared, and in the distance, rolling in echoing waves among the hills, she heard the roaring of a lion.

'Was it well done?' Asterius asked in a breathless whisper when their lips parted. 'Did the Bull dance well for the Moon?'

The taste of his mouth filled her, coating the words. What could she do but nod in agreement? 'We have done what the Mistresses commanded.' Then she smiled, unable to keep back the great relief that the thing was done and she was still Pasiphaë, and she could feel a small stone stuck to the sole of her left foot. 'And it was well done.'

Together, they rewound the ball of thread, Pasiphaë dancing around Asterius while he turned slowly and the tympana beat. A chorus of voices joined the bird-like tune of the auloi and the chords of the kitharai picked it up until the whole world seemed to be singing to the sky to commemorate the rite. The world sang, but she was barely conscious of it. When all the thread was wound, she took her knife and cut off a short length.

'So you won't ever forget,' she said, and slipped the thread around Asterius's wrist, tying it into a loose bracelet. He looked surprised, having nothing to give in return, and for a second, Pasiphaë thought his hesitation meant refusal. He touched the thread as if it was spun gold.

'This thread is more precious than any jewel in the treasury, or I would offer you a bracelet in return.'

'You have made me a Queen,' she replied, and found that she was smiling. 'I'll make do with that.'

4

Bull-leaping

Asterius touched the strange bracelet that he understood would bind him more surely than any chain. The light was so intense, the edge of every object sharp enough to cut flesh, and he felt more alive than he had done since he was a boy. The world was singing on the other side of consciousness, like a place in a dream, and he almost touched hope, happiness. But suddenly, the sense of unreality fled. A voice spoke, breaking into the flow of the glittering river of celebration, dashing him with cold water.

'A pretty performance, Asterius. And so... original.'

Minos strode into focus, backed by a shimmering curtain of followers. His gestures were respectful, but the slight smile that curled the corners of his mouth said mockery. Asterius clenched his jaw on his irritation.

'The Bull may dance as the Sun when his partner is the Moon. The intention is the same.'

From Asterius, Minos looked to Pasiphaë, the sneer open. 'A web. And the Lady Pasiphaë wove it with more grace than any spider.'

Asterius almost heard the anger coursing through Pasiphaë's veins again, mounting to her head where the Mistress sat. With a short command, Asterius silenced him. 'That's enough, Minos. You're being offensive to the Lady Pasiphaë and the Mistresses.'

Minos gave a silent laugh. 'Far be it from me to upset the Mistresses. If they were to sleep for eternity, it wouldn't be too long as far as I'm concerned. But if the Lady is upset, I beg her forgiveness.'

He made Pasiphaë a slight bow and melted away into the crowd of his followers. There was blasphemy in his words, and hidden barbs she didn't understand, but she remembered what Perseis had told her and vowed she would watch Minos as the sparrow watches the hawk.

*

After the wedding rites were over, the doves released and the holy fire lit, food was carried out to a shady terrace for the royal couple and their guests. Acrobats and dancers performed, and the tense atmosphere created by Minos's outburst relaxed. He seemed not to be present, but Kriti, relieved of her goddess panoply, sat with Pasiphaë and her father, the same old woman in black dancing attendance behind her. Asterius pointed out his most important advisors, the big landowners and rich traders. Pasiphaë saw only gracious smiles; it was too soon for friendship, welcome.

There were exceptions, though. One group in particular she remembered with gratitude: a woman, pale-skinned and auburn-haired; a tall, intelligent-looking man with an iron-grey beard; and a boy of her own age with the same bright hair as his mother, who stared at her with unabashed curiosity. She could have taken offence, but his expression was so open and admiring that she simply smiled back. Asterius followed her gaze.

'They are a wealthy family from Malia.'

'But not just wealthy?' She had felt a warmth in their expressions.

Asterius smiled. 'They are good people. Kerameia manages her vineyards well, and Antanor has five fine ships that trade all around the Middle Sea. Their son Kesandros will make a fine King. The divinations say that the Mistresses will choose him for Kriti.'

Pasiphaë looked at the boy with renewed interest and saw that she was not the only one. It seemed as though Kriti approved of her father's candidate for her husband and shot Kesandros sidelong looks from beneath her lashes. Pasiphaë couldn't blame her. With his fine features and long, clean limbs, he was worth looking at. He had the same quick intelligence as his parents in his eyes too. She decided Asterius had made a good choice.

Kriti picked at her food. The boy's presence perhaps disturbed her, and she quickly left her seat to sit at the edge of the dancing floor, absorbed by the rapid movement of the dancers that mimicked the flight of birds. Perhaps she envied them, their fierce wings, untrammelled by any destiny except flight. She looked timidly over her shoulder at the group from Malia, but her eye was inexorably drawn back to the shadows with the watchful presence of the woman in black.

Asterius smiled indulgently. 'Kriti used to enjoy dancing.'

'Used to?'

'It's not... seemly for a Princess.'

'Who is the woman who hovers at her elbow, pressing her to eat and fussing with her to move into the shade?'

Asterius's face clouded. The woman had turned and was staring boldly at the royal couple. 'Ananke, her nurse. She was nurse to all of Europa's children. When Europa died, Kriti clung to her. It seemed cruel to break the only link she had to her mother.'

The woman had not lowered her gaze. Behind the buzzing of voices and the bursts of applause for the acrobats, Pasiphaë heard the muttering of deeper voices, the growl of felines. She heard, too, the unspoken regret that Ananke had not been replaced. She thought the Mistress tongued a warning, felt the prickle of danger, but the thread was frayed, dangled untied.

Asterius's voice broke into her thoughts. 'As soon as

you're ready, we'll move to the Barley Court. You've heard of the dance of the bull-leapers?'

'Bull-leapers?' Something stirred in her memory.

'The most exciting entertainment in the world.' He placed a hand on hers. 'We two have the pleasure of knowing we have served the Mistresses well. The people deserve their pleasure too.'

Pleasure. Entertainment. Pasiphaë was already beginning to see a pattern. Nothing, not even the Mistresses, was more important at Knossos than pleasure.

*

The acrobats finished their display, servants cleared away the dishes and brought basins and cloths for the guests to clean their fingers. Asterius rose and offered Pasiphaë his arm. The guests also rose, gathered their monkeys and tame civet cats, and moved into an informal procession behind them. Out of the corner of her eye, Pasiphaë caught a glimpse of Kriti at their head, and felt, more than saw, the nurse at her side.

Asterius led her down a flight of stairs to a long gallery painted with frescoes in bright colours; dancers, birds, priestesses with tall diadems, groups of children carrying flowers, and bulls. Everywhere there were bulls. The light slanted across pavements of orange stone, filling the shaded air with sparks of motes, pollen and dancing insects. The crowd of courtiers in their train chattered, laughter rang out, Pasiphaë's heavy skirts swished, her sandalled feet pattered, but the most intimate sensation of all was the heat of her King's skin beneath her fingers.

The Gallery of Processions opened onto a colonnaded terrace, a space to pause and draw breath before the magnificence of the west court that the people called the Barley Court. It seemed a fortress, large enough to have contained the royal house of Kolchis comfortably. The wall that ran around it was as tall as the fortifications of most cities, and its bronze-bound gates surmounted by gilded bulls' horns, glinting in the late afternoon sun, could have kept an army at bay.

Pasiphaë caught her breath, oblivious of the pressing crowd behind her, deaf to the sound, like a swollen tide rising, of the hundreds of excited townsfolk making their way from the port below to see the dancing. She had seen the Barley Court already, but empty. Now, filling up with a multitude, she realised how vast it was. She was struck again by that first impression of the immensity of Knossos, its buildings stacked like bright caskets one on top of the other, covering the hillside with magnificence.

Asterius took her hesitation for intimidation and pressed her arm reassuringly. 'This is nothing, just clay bricks. Any people can build with clay and strong timbers.'

'It's magnificent,' she whispered.

'The bull-leaping is true magnificence, our creation. The spirit of Knossos runs in the blood that is spilt and not spilt. All of life is in the dance, its joy, excitement, passion and skill. And death too, but it comes in glory and the dancers meet it with illuminated faces.'

Pasiphaë struggled to understand. She had heard of the bull-leaping, spoken of in a vague sort of way as of something splendid and unique, but she had no clear idea of what it was all about. Was it simply a huge sacrifice? A death ritual reduced to public entertainment?

'It's something I've always longed to see,' she lied.

Asterius obviously believed her as he beamed with pleasure. 'With the High Priestess of Potnia Theron to give it her blessing, the dancing today will be sublime. And if the Mistress wills it, there will be no misstep and no blood shed.'

So, death was not the intention, but a mere accident. The Mistresses must have offerings, and sometimes blood must run in the sacrificial basins, just as moon-blood filled the lustral basins. It was the way of the world, of life, death and renewal, though it was hard to be the Mistress of Animals and not feel a shiver of regret when she took a life. Perseis never seemed to think twice about it, and Circe positively enjoyed the thrill of power. They would not have understood her reticence if ever she had confided in either of them. Nobody would. Animals were born to die. They would probably say that dancers were too.

*

The procession moved forward again, through the great gates of bronze-bound timber, beneath the curved horns, to the blaring of bullroarers and trumpets. It left the shallow shade of the walls and spread across the pavement with its flags of polished stone, each one a subtly different hue. Evening clouds were flocking in the blue of the sky, dappling the sunlight that fell on the stone and the paintings that ran around the walls of orange clay.

Images of animals, men, women, children, trees and the waves of the sea repeated themselves, but none more often than the prancing bulls, blue as midnight, and golden dancers, men and women, caught in mid-leap, swinging upon the curved horns, or being caught by waiting dancers. All was movement, rapid and delicate, even the hurtling images of the bulls.

'This will be a special dance,' Asterius said, 'in honour of the Moon Princess. The best dancers will perform, and their bull will respect the wishes of the Mistress and draw no blood.'

Pasiphaë wondered how he could know that. He was not the High Priestess. The Mistresses never spoke to men. But the question floated out of her head.

'They're coming.' Asterius pointed to a doorway in the wall surrounding the court. 'And over there,' he pointed to another gated hole in the brickwork, 'is the bull's entrance.'

Two lines of young men and women marched lightly into the sunlit court, all naked except for a loincloth, many with a talisman or lucky charm around the neck. All were slim, supple and tanned bronze, their hair held back from their faces in tight braids. Their eyes, elongated by kohl, were expressionless.

She watched, absorbing the noise and the swirling scents as Kriti, standing at the altar with its stone horns, officiated at the purification of a team of dancers. It was short, excited, a benediction to Potnia Theron for the safekeeping of the dancers, and the release of two doves with her prayer. The birds flew away together; the omen was a good one. Kriti left the altar, the jars containing wine and oil, the libation still trickling into the stone basin, and took her seat on the dais next to Asterius. At his right hand, Pasiphaë prepared to be astounded.

5

Wedding feast

The crowd flowed into the Barley Court, filling the seats, darting back and forth, hailing friends and changing seats, like finches flocking in the trees. Their movement hadn't settled before the bull entered the arena and the voices, the pointing and gesticulating changed direction. In the spectacle that followed, the leaping flesh-and-blood bodies merged with the painted dancers around the walls, and the roar of the crowd rolled into one with the echo of all the other excited crowds that had punctuated her voyage.

Later, throughout the long evening of her wedding day, long after the white bull, black-saddled and red-eared, the sire of the sacrificial calves perhaps, had been led away, Pasiphaë drew up the memories. Long after the bull-leapers, breathless, their faces shining now with pleasure at the applause and gifts that rained down upon them had left to their own feasting, she recalled the exuberance of their dance.

The wedding feast dragged on, noisy with the chatter of nobles, counsellors and traders vying with one another in praise of the new Queen to ingratiate themselves with Asterius. There was laughter, the jabbering of mock anger when food was tossed to monkeys on chains, when tame civet cats scampered across the tables.

Pasiphaë retreated into her thoughts and saw only bull horns sweeping back and forth, heard the scrape of hooves on stone as he veered and changed direction, teased by the flashing, darting bird-shapes of the dancers. She saw the olive-shiny bodies, long-limbed and supple as serpents, spinning over the cruel points, leaping from the bull's back before he was even aware of where his tormentor had flown. Even the approach of her first night with her husband could not compete in her imagination with the bull-leaping.

When Asterius got to his feet, and the voices loud with strong wine and laughter fell silent, she remembered the reason for her presence at Knossos, for the feast, the celebrations, the bull-dancing. He was announcing the end of the festivities and the beginning of the night. Voices rang out again, joking, and the laughter was coarser. The men shuffled in their seats, stretching legs and rolling their eyes towards the women, who pretended not to notice. Pasiphaë might be Moon Princess of Kolchis and High Priestess of Potnia Theron, but she was still only fifteen years old and had never had a man before.

She had seen men taking women and women taking men. She had seen the servants' furtive couplings and the ritual couplings of priest and priestess. But she had also seen stallions mounting mares, and bulls cows, and she still saw the white and black dappled bull thundering across the Barley Court, his great head tossing, his eyes with only one thought in them. She had not been taught that coupling could be tender. It was part of the price paid for power. She was fifteen, and Asterius was old enough to be her father. Suddenly, the thought taking her by surprise, she found she wanted her mother.

*

Asterius had seen enough bull-leaping to have watched without seeing. His thoughts were full of Minos. He had seen the bobbing of his dark curls at one of the tables, heard his voice growing more raucous as the strong wine rose to his head. He had already prepared himself for a confrontation when Minos got to his feet, a little unsteadily. A wine stain flowered on the white linen of his tunic.

'My thanks, Asterius, for this feast which has been truly regal. And I wish that your last years as King may be full of conjugal happiness. Honestly.' He raised his cup and his followers beat their hands on the table in encouragement. 'Because Princess Kriti won't be long unwed.'

Asterius saw the flash of terror in his daughter's eyes and wanted to put his arms around her, but that, of course, was out of the question. If Minos noticed, he didn't pause in his speech, the words deformed by drink and forced through his flattened nose.

'Follow the oldest tradition and let the Great Mother choose her husband, and you'll be for the dark. Follow the Greek way and sell her to the highest bidder, and you might get an old age. Which is it to be?'

An uneasy silence fell on the tables nearest to the royal couple's. Some pretended not to be listening, feet shuffled and throats were cleared. A voice, louder than was called for, sent a servant to fetch more wine, but all in earshot were hanging on Asterius's reply.

'For one, Minos, who Princess Kriti marries and when is none of your bloody business. For another, today is a day of celebration. Leave death and the Greeks out of it.'

Minos laughed. His teeth were very white in his dark face. 'Celebration of your stay of execution? When Kriti marries, she'll be the new Queen. Lovely as the Lady Pasiphaë is, she's only your wife. I'll put my question another way. Will you adopt the new ways that give power to the King and take it for yourself? Or will you stick to the old ways, that will toss you away when Kriti marries, and die in combat with the King-elect?'

All were listening now and not even trying to hide it. Minos, elated, rocked slightly from side to side. The wine flower on his tunic spread. The silence, too, spread like a sordid rumour, and Asterius's voice dropped into it, a stone into a still pool.

'There is no King-elect and won't be for years, and the death of the old King has not been exacted for generations. Neither fact makes any difference to you, so stop making an ass of yourself.'

Minos spread his legs to steady himself and leaned precariously forward, his beard jutting, level with Asterius's face. 'Oh, but that's just the point. As the heir designated by Europa, and by the laws of both Tyre and Argos that would have her son follow her as King, it *does* make a difference to me. Lycastus accepted that with her dowry, you knew that, and you've gone back on your word.'

'You should water your wine, Minos. Your face has gone the same colour. I've warned you about making yourself look idiotic. Now you're being offensive with it.' Asterius, too, leaned forward. The brows of the two men almost touched. 'I am a Cretan. I have never given my word to a Greek. The ways of Mycenae, Argos, Athens are the ways of warlike barbarians. Princess Kriti will take up her role as High Priestess of the Mother and Queen of Knossos as soon as she is of age, and you, as the son of the Greeks' father god, are free to go where your paternity is more respected.'

The icy silence was broken by some tittering that spread with the infectious ease of relief. But Minos hadn't finished. 'There are more ways than one to seize a birthright. The King doesn't choose his successor. Nor does he know who the Mother will choose, or if her choice will elect to shunt him out of this life.'

The laughter ceased abruptly. Guests looked at one another, questions on their faces. Others exchanged glances of complicity. Asterius hadn't been prepared for such an undisguised declaration of war. Beneath his calm, he sweated, but his thoughts fled to his daughter. Kriti sat with unfocused eyes, her expression frozen in a mask of indifference that perhaps only another girl would have recognised as skilfully concealed terror. Asterius felt terror though, both of Minos the man and of Minos his daughter's half-brother.

Into the silence that followed Minos's statement, Pasiphaë's voice broke. Anger, swelling up from the fount the Mistresses controlled, darted across her vision in black spots like a shoal of gobies.

'Exactly. The Mistresses choose the King. The kingship is not a birthright, not a *gift* from a mortal parent. The Mistresses will choose the next King, and they'll decide when. None of this is in your hands, Minos. To pretend otherwise is blasphemy.'

Minos glared at her. In his eyes, dark and slightly globular, anger slowly melted into hatred and contempt. But before he could gather his wits, a crowd of young men and women, dressed in white tunics and carrying musical instruments or flowers, danced into the room and Minos was, if not forgotten, lost among the gaiety. Some played flutes, there was a kithara or two, but mostly they sang their wedding songs and arranged their dance from its chaotic beginning into formal steps.

This was another crane dance, the boys bowing to the girls, the girls swirling away again. And all the time they laughed. Minos had cast a heavy shadow over the celebrations, but only for Asterius and Pasiphaë. Asterius had expected to go to his marriage bed with Pasiphaë more joyfully than he had gone to Europa's, and Pasiphaë heard only the bellowing of bulls until a softer voice spoke in her ear.

'Time for us to leave the crowds. The night is beginning.'

Asterius held out his arm, and like a mechanical doll, she took it.

6

First night

The boisterous crowd left Pasiphaë at the royal apartment she would share with the King and carried Asterius away with them to the King's Chamber. Her women had filled the apartment with familiarity, their voices, the smells of Kolchis that lingered in their clothes, the perfumes they poured into her bathwater. They washed away the painted goddess, leaving the frightened girl exposed, raw and on the verge of tears. She bit her lip. The thought of her mother was no comfort. Perseis would have patted her hand, told her to be worthy of her heritage and gone back to her potions or whatever else was more important than her second daughter's distress. The flying dancers faded. Only the bull, curved-horned and angry, remained in the pictures behind her eyes.

When everything was tidied away, the women left, leaving only Eritha to prepare Pasiphaë's hair, brushing out the tight tresses, teasing the coils apart and plaiting them loosely again for the night. The rhythm of the brushstrokes was like the pounding of hooves. Eritha tied off the plait, the Barley Court faded, and Pasiphaë was back in the room with its walls brightly painted with flowers and fruit.

'Will you let me give you this talisman, Princess? Leto will stay with you though the rest of the world sleeps.'

She pressed a bronze medallion into Pasiphaë's hand, and her fingers closed around it, as they would have closed around any help offered. She opened her fingers, looked at the lively hooped shape of a marten chasing its tail.

'Will you wear it? She's a good deity to have watching over you, a friend of Eleuthia.'

Eleuthia, the goddess who guides women through childbirth. Pasiphaë would take help from any quarter. 'I'll hang it round my neck with a piece of the thread from the Bull Dance.'

She tried to smile, but the muscles around her mouth wouldn't answer. She wished it were allowed to take the marten to her couch, but that was the kind of thought a child would have had. Eritha brought the marten, just woken from her daytime sleep, and Pasiphaë rubbed her face in the soft, sweet-smelling fur. The little animal placed her paws on Pasiphaë's cheeks and sniffed the unusual perfume. The tears almost came then, but she stifled them. No angry hooves clattered; she heard only the tiny sounds of curious pine marten.

'I never gave her a name,' she confided. 'She was always *the marten of all martens*. From now on, she'll be Leto.'

The marten nuzzled her hair, fascinated by the new smells carried on the Cretan air and the new perfumes in the Cretan water. Pasiphaë stroked the silky ears. It wasn't Perseis she missed; her mother had never shown so much affection. It was this that she wanted, the gentle touch that meant she was loved.

Eritha stopped, hesitated in her tidying away of the brushes and combs. 'I went to the shrine today, the small one next to this apartment, to ask a question. I hope I did no wrong. My mother was a temple servant, on a small island – you won't have heard of it, Antiparos. We were out gathering flowers when the pirates grabbed us... Anyway, Mamá'd picked up a bit about divinations, and she taught me what she knew. I asked the house goddess if we'd be happy here. Me and the girls, I meant.'

Pasiphaë listened, a finger suspended above the marten's head. 'And will you?'

'I don't know exactly, Princess. The signs just said that there'll be a royal child born here, who'd be bright as the evening star. I don't think it was meant for any of us girls.'

Pasiphaë couldn't help smiling, and a thrill of something like hope shimmered in the air. Everything about Asterius indicated a delicacy and attentiveness. But would he make her happy? She had never even considered the possibility. The marten, who must now be called Leto, jumped from her shoulder, chased an insect to the lip of the water basin, skittered and fell in. It seemed to Pasiphaë the funniest thing in the world.

'If the child is as bright as Leto, I'll be happy enough.'

*

The strange room was silent. It was as huge as everywhere else in the palace. Eritha had gone to join the other servants in the Queen's Chamber, and the pine marten had gone on her night prowling. A stone lamp filled with scented oil burned in a corner of the room and the one window framed a bright, starless sky. There would be a full moon, but it sailed another part of the night ocean and Pasiphaë couldn't see it. The moonlight dimmed the stars, though, and there was no sharpness, not even in the sky. All would be soft, she told herself, like the air and the memory of warm fur. In her hopes, Asterius would be soft too, gentle and careful, as if she was a fragile ornament, a newly fledged dove.

She shivered. From another part of the palace, not distant, she heard the laughter and music begin again and the sound of drumming feet. They were coming, escorting the King to his duty. The bright friezes around the walls faded into shadow, odd points of colour picked out by the slender flame light. She touched the amulet round her neck and murmured a prayer to Potnia Theron. It seemed to her fingers that the curled bronze marten wriggled, thick-furred, that blood coursed. Footsteps clattered like the tide rolling in, and Asterius's voice broke into the wordless merriment. She closed her fingers around the bronze medallion.

'Time for everyone to go home to bed.'

More gales of laughter followed and the shrilling of pipes, but she sensed that the ritual was over and there would be no more high-spirited comments. Footsteps receded and the sporadic laughter was gentler. The door opened, and Asterius stood between the red-painted posts.

'The people of Crete love to celebrate,' he said, almost apologetically, as he stepped into the room and closed the door behind him. The coloured frieze of interlocking lozenges that ran along the wall and across the lintel was completed, and Pasiphaë had the sudden impression that the door would never be opened again. She licked dry lips and gathered her courage.

'They have good reason to celebrate today. They have a new Queen.' She didn't mean to sound arrogant. She said it because she didn't know if it was true. Minos and his veiled threats had left a bitter memory.

'They have one who they think will make their King happy.'

'Is he?' she asked, the words tumbling out too fast to call back.

He took her hands and drew her to him. 'He is. The Mistresses chose well for me, and I will try to be worthy of their choice for you.'

Her hands felt small in his, though she was not particularly small. Kolchians were sturdy, robust people and Perseis had never chosen an undersized mate. She was too close to Asterius now, physically and mentally, to judge the space he occupied in the world, but she felt the warmth of his blood, the light grip of his fingers, smelled the perfumed wood oils on his skin. His face was half in shadow, and she couldn't see into the depths of his eyes, which were dark and long-lashed. Athamas would probably have judged him a mediocre specimen, as he did all Cretans. They were too lightly built, too short and spare to make good warriors. But Pasiphaë had seen them dance, heard them sing, and she had seen people for whom war was not the first option. Asterius was of that blood, supple and lithe, and his eyes looked forward to tomorrow, not to past glories and the ending of lives.

'And how is my Queen?' The look of concern reappeared in his eyes. 'It's been a day of many changes… and upsets. I'm sorry about Minos.'

Minos had upset her. She tried to brush away the memory. 'He insulted the Mistresses. It was my duty to be angry. Minos needs to remember his place.'

'He was reminding me of *my* place and that there are other customs that give power to the King. What man offered his life back would not be tempted by his words?'

The words of Pallantides. Another distasteful memory. She didn't know what to say. Old Kings were always replaced by a young King. It was in the nature of things, the tradition that was as old as the earth. Did he expect her to say the Mistresses would never demand his death? Sometimes they did, sometimes not, but if Minos reminded Asterius of the fate of Kings, it was not out of piety or respect for tradition, it was a threat. Whichever Asterius chose, the laws of the Mistresses or the father god, Minos would have it that death was the only outcome.

Asterius seemed to understand her confusion and smiled sadly. 'Let's forget about Minos. I won't have shadows on our first night together.'

His grip on Pasiphaë's hands tightened, and the knot of anxiety in her stomach loosened and fluttered with wings of excitement. As he led her to the bed covered in scented linen, Europa lumbered into her thoughts. She imagined her large and bovine. Minos in female form. She listened for a voice, a sign, but heard nothing. If this had been the Phoenician woman's bed, she had left nothing of herself behind.

Europa ambled away, leaving Pasiphaë alone with the muddle of her thoughts. Duty had led her to this room, this night and a man of whom all she knew was that his hands were gentle. What came next would be what came to all women, and she was a woman, not a wild girl running alone through forests of pine and spruce. She was also a Queen. No man would be her master. She undid her girdle herself and let it fall.

Her dress slid from her shoulders, and she stepped out of it. Asterius drew her to him. Her nipples brushed his chest, tingling. He bent his head. Her lips parted, ready for his mouth on hers.

'The Mistresses will smile on this night's work,' he murmured.

Pasiphaë could say nothing. Her training told her she was in the hands of the Potniai, but they had never been further from her thoughts. She heard the beating of great wings, and it was the sound of Asterius's arms as he enfolded her in a dance she had never been taught. He laid her down on the cool linen and wrapped her in his hot limbs. The rest of her waking was a slow rhythm like the beat of the tympana until even she willed it to quicken, and the window was flooded with the soft light of the full moon.

Asterius took her again while the moon shone and again before the morning, but not like a bull covering a heifer. By the morning, she rose to meet him, like a flower in the first light of the sun, with the dew trembling on its opened petals. Before she fell into a deep dawn sleep, she murmured her thanks to Leto, whose presence she felt watching from the darkest corner of the room.

*

Asterius had woken first and left the bed while she slept. Perhaps to spare her his nakedness. Perhaps because he needed to stretch and show the palace the King had spent a good night. Not that she minded finding herself alone. It gave her time to gather her thoughts, let them unfold undisturbed.

The sky was pale blue with a blush of pink. Birds whistled

somewhere unseen, and muffled sounds of servant activity drifted on the quiet air. At Kolchis, she would have chosen her own tunic and dressed herself. She may or may not have tidied her hair. She would have run barefoot out among the scented garden flowers and forest trees. But now she was a Queen, and she savoured the few moments of being just Pasiphaë before the servants arrived to dress her.

They came in a gaggle, breathless. She saw their faces in the doorway, peering around as if Asterius might be hiding beneath a pile of clothes. Tyro was the first to ask.

'Did you sleep well, Princess?'

Arete jabbed her with her elbow.

'You know what I mean, not *well*, but…'

'Go fetch some hot water, Tyro, and think before you open it again, all right?'

Eune caught Pasiphaë's eye, looked deeply for a sign. When the look of concern turned to a quick smile, Pasiphaë decided she had seen only contentment. Relief, and a surprisingly intense prickle of happiness washed over her.

Eune bent her head to hide her presumption and opened a chest of clothes. 'Do you need something special today, Princess?'

Pasiphaë swung her legs over the side of the bed. 'I hope not.'

'White linen then. Tyro! Where's that water?'

While the women prepared her bath and her clothes, Pasiphaë asked Eritha how Leto had slept.

'Well. I heard her come back to her basket around dawn, when she went into a deep sleep.'

'The goddess was with us both last night then.'

A pair of doves settled on the terrace in a clatter of pinions and a rolling roo-coo-coo.

Eritha looked from the doves to her mistress, her lips parted in surprise. There was no need to speak of the omen, it would have diminished its virtue, but Pasiphaë glowed with pleasure in what it foretold.

*

Stepping out of the lamplit shadows of the Great Shrine into the bright morning sunshine, Asterius heaved a great sigh of well-being. He had asked Inia the Key-Bearer to make a libation in his name to the Mistresses to thank them for the gift they had sent him. From his respectful place in the porch, he had watched her movements, heard her words, smelled the sweet floral honey scents of the libation, and had filled with the same lushness. It was more than satisfaction. It was fulfilment, a deep pleasure. Happiness perhaps, or at least a hope of it.

He stood in the golden light of the portico and breathed in the morning. Knossos was already awake, and a buzz of activity rose from the western palace. A temple servant stepped, skipped almost, from the storeroom with a handful of grain for the birds. Asterius watched as she scattered it across the stone, looked at the sky, the rooftops. In a clatter of pinions, a pair of turtle doves was first to arrive, before even the sparrows. Never had the gentle birds, their tender cloud colours, seemed so beautiful. The feeling of plenitude spread in a broad smile.

PART THREE

The darkness behind the stars

The palace of Knossos that climbed into the sky was full of light and gaiety. But beneath the painted rooms, the flowering abundance of its gardens, the glory of the bull-dancing, dark roots spread. Knossos sprang from ancient darkness, from the time of the Great Mother, before the Mistresses tempered her demands for blood and submission with compassion. The Mistresses understood life and its complexities. The Great Mother knew only life and death, and cared about neither. She gave and took away as indifferently as a sickness chooses or spares its victims. In Kolchis, the Great Mother had slept since time out of mind. In Knossos, she had never relinquished power to the Mistresses.

1

Mistress of Serpents and Bulls

Kriti watched with a cool gaze the bustle of Pasiphaë's cortège as she visited shrine after shrine. When the wedding festivities were finally over, the rituals of her inauguration as High Priestess of Potnia Theron began. Not that that meant much in Knossos. Pasiphaë didn't know that, though. From the stiff way she carried herself, Kriti assumed she thought she was the centre of attention. Kriti, though, knew that the palace had returned to its normal rhythm, and all but the nobles who had overseers for their lands had returned to their country homes and occupations. When the next entertainment was announced, the next sacrifice, they would be back, but Pasiphaë was part of the palace décor now. Nobody would notice her unless she did something interesting or outrageous.

No one noticed Kriti either. Oh, they recognised the girl in the elaborate costume as Princess Kriti, but no one saw the girl inside who cowered whenever Minos stormed upon the scene. They would talk about *the next Queen*, about Princess Kriti, the daughter of Queen Europa, but did anyone notice the Kriti who was transfixed with terror whenever Minos looked at her? Even the wedding feast would have been forgotten by most of the guests, but she remembered. The scene, Minos and his drunken words, ran on and on in her head like an angry river.

Asterius knew what Minos was plotting, but what could he

do? He was only her father, and her mother was dead. There was nothing ahead, nothing she could see that wasn't bathed in blood – sacrifice after sacrifice, culminating in her father's blood. Kesandros? She dared not even dream of him. There was never another face in the blood. Only her own. She wanted to scream at Pasiphaë to open her eyes and understand, but she never spoke. For her father's sake. Instead, she tagged along when Pasiphaë swanned about from one shrine to another, as if any of it mattered. Inia the Key-Bearer would never tell her. Not yet anyway.

Kriti hid her eyes behind a thick line of kohl, and she always wore red, the Poppy Mistress's colour. Only wrapped in the symbols of a goddess did she dare walk the palace, claim the right to be alone. Otherwise, Ananke, her shadow, the one who whispered memories of her mother, little things, fragments, would call her back. Kriti had nothing else. She knew, in an unformed way, that Ananke didn't have any affection for her, but she had Europa's memories and Kriti couldn't bear to let them go. Minos was Ananke's god, and Kriti was caught between the two of them. They were the sickness she felt gnawing her bones. She followed Pasiphaë, the girl not so many years older than she was, like a red shadow. She wasn't sure what she hoped for, a sister to talk to perhaps. She no longer hoped she could be saved.

She had been taken by surprise when Pasiphaë burst in on her spinning lesson and spoke to her, in that strange, sharp, foreign way she had, that Kriti interpreted as imperious.

'I'd like you to take me to the shrine of the house goddess, to pay my respects.'

Kriti saw the words of objection forming on her nurse's lips. She held her breath until Ananke finally flickered her eyelids, giving permission. When they were outside and the door closed, she turned to Pasiphaë eagerly, too excited to hide her enthusiasm. Pasiphaë's eyes, though, were troubled.

'Do you always ask your servants for permission to leave the room, Princess?'

'I don't ask,' Kriti replied quickly. 'But it is only polite to…'

Pasiphaë's frown deepened, and Kriti felt that she had been judged pathetic. Crushed, she was on the point of turning back with some excuse, but she gathered up her courage and her self-respect. Ananke, a servant, bullied her, but she had the weight of a dead mother behind her. Pasiphaë was no more than an ephemeral breeze.

'This way,' she said, and walked briskly towards the western palace.

*

Pasiphaë followed, incomprehension sitting in a slight frown between her brows. She wanted to understand what rule or custom bound Kriti in an almost servile state, but the girl and her thoughts were elusive. At least she was dressed simply, not in her goddess display, with kohl-heavy eyes, always red-clad. The colour had begun to fill Pasiphaë with a dull unease. Kriti said little, a mechanical doll, her gestures betraying nothing of her fears, but occasionally the flash of a girl's eyes appeared behind the mask.

Pasiphaë remembered how she had dreaded accompanying her mother to the ceremonies, the lustral basin full of blood, the metallic smell that the sweet oils never quite covered. She had never had to be dragged to her duties, and if she had, it would have been by her mother or Circe, not a servant. Knossos was full of mysteries, and she tried not to judge Kriti too harshly. She was a child, frail and timid, and her inscrutable eyes always seemed to be watching her.

*

They took the long gallery with its painted people, processing to an invisible destination, with their flowering branches and their accompanying animals. The gallery opened into the royal entrance, where the noise was no longer the murmuring of restrained excitement of Pasiphaë's arrival, but the industrious sounds of metalworkers and carpenters, and the heated exchanges of administrators arguing over taxes and field boundaries. People passed and greeted with respect their little Princess, who would one day be Queen, but Kriti was only interested in how they looked at the girl from the wilds at the back of the Inhospitable Sea who was the King's wife. She decided it was with no more than curiosity.

A series of rooms opened one after the other from the entrance. Beyond the industry of the artisans' workshops and the constant flow of scribes, administrators and their servants about their business, the farther rooms were darker, solemn and silent. Kriti pushed open a door that gave off the central corridor. The room was low, unlit except by lamps high on niches in the walls, and decorated with paintings of mythical beasts. A painted griffin guarded each side of the door, and the only furnishings were two seats in the centre, one large and broad, the other smaller and narrower.

'The Throne Room, where petitions are heard and judgements given.'

The room was low-ceilinged and dark, purposely intimidating. Asterius never insisted she be present when he heard petitions. He couldn't know about the bloody nightmares, she had never told him, but he understood that she had enough to bear. She closed the door quickly and passed to the next doorway.

'And this is the shrine of the Mistress of Serpents.'

Kriti's voice vibrated with the excitement she always felt in the presence of the Serpent Mistress. Awe rather than fear was what dominated. After all, even Minos would not be able to keep her away when his time came. Even Minos would die. They stepped inside and she closed the door, shutting out all sound except the soft sigh of flames. The shrine was windowless, dark, except for the hearth where a fire burned low and sluggish, barely more than embers. It would be kept burning day and night. Above the hearth was a statue, the goddess with snakes in her hands, encircling her arms, waist and breasts. Bronze snakes wound through her hair, glittering in the flame light.

*

'Asasara.'

Kriti pronounced the name with reverence. Pasiphaë bowed her head, in awe of the aspect of the goddess, a personification she had never seen before. The Mistress of Serpents presided over death, the event most dreaded in every household. She could make it peaceful or painful, an agony or sweetly short. In Kolchis, there was just the house snake that lived beneath the hearth at the side of Perseis's shrine, and it was easy to forget whom the snake represented. The house goddess was also Mistress of Serpents, to be kept sweet and, if possible, asleep. There could be no ignoring her power here. Like everything in Knossos, it was exaggerated, amplified.

'Is that where the milk is kept?'

Pasiphaë pointed towards a small doorway opening onto an even darker room. Kriti gave her a sharp look.

'It won't come out. The priestess has already visited it this morning.'

'I'd like to try. The house snake at Aea would never come to me. I'd like to befriend this one.'

Pasiphaë smiled but didn't get a softening in Kriti's hostile expression in exchange. She sighed and went into the storeroom. She felt the girl's eyes following her as she poked about among the jars and boxes, releasing a wave of familiar scents, memories. She closed her eyes and let Kolchis envelop her.

*

Kriti was silent because she had no idea where the milk was kept, and she felt slightly foolish. She had never been shown what was kept in the shrine storeroom and had never thought to ask. Now, following the fluttering movement of Pasiphaë's fingers as they brushed the jars and bottles, light as a butterfly, her own interest stirred. She grew as intrigued as Pasiphaë by the different plants and oils, the scents and powders used in the offerings. She watched the change in Pasiphaë's face when she closed her eyes and inhaled deeply.

'I could almost be back in the palace at Aea, preparing the oils and incense for the monthly offering.'

Her voice had lost the sharp, pointed sound of someone unsure of the language, and it had grown soft, gentle, as she drifted far away, further than Kriti could ever hope to go, to a place she would never see. Pasiphaë seemed to become just a girl again, and Kriti drew closer.

'What's that smell called?' she asked, inhaling too.

'Musk, and this one is cinnamon, this sandalwood and this, my favourite, is frankincense.'

Kriti couldn't hide her surprise and admiration. 'How do you know these things?'

'Because I was taught. You should be taught too. Spinning and weaving aren't occupations for a Queen.'

Kriti didn't need to be told that. Nobody had offered to teach her anything else, though. Ananke had seen to that. 'I'd like to, I think. But apart from the rituals…'

'I'll ask Eritha to teach you. She probably knows as much as I do.'

Kriti smiled cautiously, a brief flutter of a smile. Pasiphaë had found a jug of milk in the cool of the larder and was pouring a little into a bowl. She placed the bowl by the hearth and began to sing. The words were childish, taught her by her nurse, a rhyme to conjure snakes and small animals. Kriti listened in astonishment and gasped as the snake appeared to drink, possibly as surprised as she was. The song continued, soft and rhythmic, low and gentle, and when the snake had finished, it raised its head. Pasiphaë reached out a hand slowly and lifted it, letting the coils wind around her arm. She raised it over her head, waved it back and forth before her face, the snake trailing gracefully and without fear. As the song finished, she set the snake down by the hearth and, slowly, it unwound and slithered back beneath the hearth.

'How did you do that?' Kriti asked in a whisper, the question slipping out before she could stop it. The Princess and High Priestess ought to have known.

'I think Potnia Theron did it, not me. Perhaps this snake doesn't dislike me as much as the one at Aea.'

Pasiphaë was smiling. She hadn't tried to make her feel ridiculous, and Kriti felt a knot loosen in the depths of her belly. She smiled back. 'We say it Pot-*ni*-a *Te*-ron.'

Since her mother died and Ananke had decided her place was in the apartment of the High Priestess of the Poppy Mistress, Kriti had lived in a state of anguish that only the fumes of poppy could numb. She had no company but the silent priestesses, the black-clad nurse and the red-skirted statue. She bathed in blood and the colour of poppies. But through the clouds of cloying scents that brought brief spells of oblivion, she thought she saw a spark of light. The Moon Princess from across the Inhospitable Sea was perhaps only a girl after all.

2

First blood

The first days became first weeks, and the rites that required Pasiphaë's presence dwindled to a trickle. At Aea, there had just been one shrine dedicated to Potnia Theron, and her mother and Circe officiated at all the other rituals. There had never been much to do. She had expected that at Knossos, as High Priestess of the Mistresses, she would be called upon every day for a ritual at one of the many shrines within the palace, and as Queen, to sit in judgement as Perseis and Circe did. There were entertainments, acrobats and feasting, and once, to celebrate the successful wheat harvest, there was bull-leaping. It would be on the tip of her tongue to ask Asterius why there were so few visitors to the shrines; why, though there were countless rooms dedicated to one ritual or another, all were empty. Each time, he would announce some acrobatic display or dancing or games, and the question would go out of her mind.

If the shrines echoed in their sacred silence and the lustral basins lay undisturbed the greater part of the time, the entertainments drew crowds that had to be controlled by the guards. Everything was an excuse for a bull dance, to celebrate the new lambs, the new wine, the last frost, the pig killing, a good barley harvest. There were no end of reasons to celebrate, but the Mistresses, even the Great Mother herself, seemed far from anyone's mind.

The noisy Barley Court was the hub of palace life, where the crowds would gather and applaud. The bull was everywhere, horns rising gold-tipped from rooftops, holding up the eaves of palace halls, in stone symbols on the altars, and in painted images on the walls, but who remembered that the bull was Knossos? Who remembered that the glorious bull-dancing was once religious ritual? Knossos had become a place of wealth and entertainment, easy-going as long as the granaries were full and the land fruitful.

Fights over bets broke out sporadically and thieves drifted like ghosts through the heaving masses, attracted by the vast quantities of gold that changed hands on the outcome of the bull-leaping. Despite her unease that entertainment had upstaged religious ritual, Pasiphaë was invariably captivated by the spectacle of the dancers. Their acrobatic movements were as graceful and agile as courting birds. The bulls seemed to be known to the spectators, who would shout their names, to taunt or praise.

Only once had she seen an accident. A misstep, a stumbling fall, a deft change of direction from the bull, and the sweep of the curved horns had raked the sand and the thigh of the leaper. The Yellow Team was a favourite of the crowd, but the boy was not their best dancer. His death or recovery, though, was important to the punters. The splash of blood on the sand, the trampling hooves, came as a jolt, a shock. She held her breath as the decoy manoeuvres of the other dancers distracted the bull's attention so that their injured teammate could be rushed out of the arena. Hundreds of pairs of eyes followed the limp, limb-dangling body, coolly assessing the damage. She could almost hear the jingling of coins in purses.

Asterius watched with a slight frown of compassion, but already the leaping had begun again, the bull excited by the contact. Pasiphaë rose to her feet, and Asterius's followers sitting on the royal dais glanced at her in curiosity.

'I want to see.'

'The bull-leapers have the best physicians. They'll do their best.'

She wasn't sure why she wanted *to see*, what moved her to think her skills would be greater, but she heard the voice of the Mistress in the bull's snorting.

'Where have they taken him?'

Asterius beckoned to a servant. 'He'll show you.'

He shot her a smile. There was no admonishment in it, only a hint of pride.

*

Eritha was with the serving women behind the dais, and Pasiphaë motioned to her to follow. There were stairs and tunnels, then a long corridor. Through a doorway she saw a shrine with statues of deities lit by votive lamps. The Poppy Mistress with her crimson skirts drew her eye before she looked away. Then came the quarters of the bull-leapers. She was surprised at the splendour of their dining room, the richness of the paintings, the thick carpets on the shining floor. Beyond the kitchens and the pantries was the room where the wounded were tended, clean and airy with daylight from a shaft in the ceiling.

The injured boy, his face pale and beaded with sweat, had been laid on a bed, like an offering on an altar. A man and a woman, both grey-haired, were inspecting the wound. From the way their hands moved together, the way their heads almost touched as they conferred, Pasiphaë guessed they were husband and wife. Both looked up when she entered.

'How bad is it?' she asked, but not as a child, not with the hope she would be told to run away and play. She asked as an adept and bent to peer over the long gash. It was ugly. The physician was tightening an ox sinew around the upper thigh. Pasiphaë pressed the lips of the wound together. Blood seeped but there was no spurting. Either it was too late or the bull had not opened the vein. She looked at the two healers. The woman answered.

'The men who brought him in said it hadn't bled too much.'

'A good sign then. Do you have yarrow, turmeric, goldenrod... solidago?'

'Yarrow and turmeric, but not that last one.'

Pasiphaë sent Eritha to fetch some. 'And the honey too, the special one that Circe prepared.'

*

When the wound was dressed and bound, she went to the shrine to offer a prayer to the Mistresses. A girl was waiting in the doorway, one of the Yellow Team dancers. She had wiped her face, but the kohl had left smuts on her cheeks. She plucked up her courage and spoke.

'Princess, will he live?'

The girl's slender body was naked except for a loincloth, and a white scar curled beneath her left breast. She looked to be Pasiphaë's age, slightly built like Kriti. But where Kriti's limbs were like the shoots of a plant kept in the dark, this girl was like a healthy sapling, supple and tough. Like a reed. Pasiphaë wondered where she came from, with her pale complexion and red-tinted hair. Would he live? Perhaps. If the wound didn't fester. But he might never leap again, and if he did, it might be with a fatal stiffness. Such scars toughened the skin like a rope shrunk by seawater.

'I'll ask the Mistresses for his life. What's his name?'

'Turios.'

'And yours?'

The girl's face brightened. Her name would be included in the prayer for the boy, who was perhaps her lover. 'Here, they call me Lydia. Tell the Mistresses, Lydia will make an offering for him.' She took a gold bracelet from her arm and held it out. 'I'll buy an animal from the temple herds. Will this buy a suitable one, do you think? I've never...' She cast down her eyes and tears flashed among the lashes.

'I'll tell them, and I'll offer too.'

Lydia raised her head, not hiding the tears. She took Pasiphaë's hand and pressed it to her lips, murmuring her thanks, before darting off to the boy's bedside. Pasiphaë searched among the statues for Potnia Theron. There were so many, from the different countries of origin of the bull-leapers, she guessed. Asterius had told her that leapers were chosen from among the slaves who came from all over the Middle Sea. The old leapers were dead, but they had left their gods behind. They had their talismans and their spells bought from wise women, but they also gave gifts to the Mistress of Animals and prayed for a sweet-tempered bull. There were flowers and figs, honey cakes and other sweetmeats before her statue, which was round-bellied, big-breasted, with a broad-winged bird at either side.

Pasiphaë said the words of the prayer, asking for the boy's life, and to give wings to the heels of his dancing team. She listened for a reply and thought she heard it in the splutter of the oil lamps, but the words were mingled with Lydia's tears. So young, yet for all her rapidity and supple limbs, her life was probably almost run. She wondered if Lydia's mother would know when the bull caught her, and would she roar her grief across the sea. If she did, would anyone hear?

3

Mother goddess

In the first weeks after her arrival at Knossos, Pasiphaë and Asterius had not often dined alone. Pasiphaë guessed that Asterius hoped she would find friends among their guests. The most frequent visitors were Kerameia and Antanor and their son Kesandros. She appreciated their company, their relaxed, unaffected conversation. They were true friends of Asterius, with no interest in currying favour. But Kerameia was as old as Perseis, and Kesandros was more or less promised to Kriti, so Pasiphaë looked on him almost as a married man. Until she met Nephele, her closest companions were her serving women, with whom she shared the speech of Kolchis and memories of the land they had left behind.

Nephele was the daughter of a not very notable family from along the coast, not far from Malia where Kerameia had her property. It was Kerameia's idea, the idea of an attentive mother, to introduce her to Pasiphaë. Nephele had been married for a year and had realised very quickly that her choice of husband had been a bad one. She was staying in the family apartments at Knossos while a settlement was made with her husband to end the marriage. Kerameia obviously thought the two girls would be good for one another.

*

Pasiphaë and Nephele stood on the terrace, watching the evening light on the infinite blue of the Middle Sea. The last sun filled Nephele's curls with gold, and coated with gold her slender dancer's arms. She was slight and wiry, like many Cretans, and Pasiphaë felt heavy and slow next to her. She made a mental note to ask where the dancers practised. She needed to recover some of the suppleness she had lost along with her Kolchian hills and forests. Behind them, the conversation of the older people rocked slow and low as the distant waves. Nephele plucked a purple petal from a trailing flower and watched it drift down to the terrace below.

'Knossos is wonderful, but don't you have a longing to get outside the walls sometimes? I don't think I could stand being cooped up here for months on end.'

Pasiphaë tucked away the memory of looking into sunsets from her father's house at Aea and turned to her eagerly. 'I haven't even seen all of the palace yet. Asterius has promised to show me how everything works, but he's been busy with taxes and lawsuits. But yes, I do miss walking. Just walking for no reason, feeling the breeze on my face, listening to the birds.'

Nephele's broad mouth broke into a smile. 'I'll call for you tomorrow morning.'

*

Although it was only the beginning of summer, Pasiphaë found the heat searingly fierce on the island. Few trees shaded the earth, clay baked hard as bricks, and the sea was a glittering mirror, too bright to look upon. She longed to walk beneath forest trees, but even a stroll through olive groves was a pleasure. Athamas insisted on accompanying the two women.

'It's not like Aea here, Mistress. You never know who you'll run into outside the palace. Those peasants up in the hills are a rough-looking bunch, and the port is teeming with sailors from all over the world.'

Nephele suggested they walk out to the fields to the north where the air was cooled a little by the breeze from the sea. They left the palace, not by the grand royal entrance, but a smaller, less used one that descended from the east palace to the gardens around the theatre and, from there, to the pasture and cultivated land.

Pasiphaë took deep breaths of the air, realising how much she had missed the freedom to go where she liked, to simply feel earth, even dry and stony, beneath her feet. Flocks of sheep grazed on the hillsides, and lower down where there was still meadow grass, the royal herds lazed beneath shade trees.

'The white bull will be down there somewhere. I have a longing to see something of Kolchis,' she said on an impulse.

'Won't I do?' Athamas asked with a broad smile. Once she would have bristled at his familiarity, but he had become as Cretan as the natives, as easy-going, and he meant no disrespect.

'You're a sight for sore eyes, Athamas, but you smell like a dancing girl on a night out with her boyfriend. The white bull will remind me of my mother's farms.'

He laughed, as she knew he would.

Nephele pointed. 'That's the royal herd. He won't be far away.'

There were trees at the bottom of the valley, and a shallow stream. Beyond the fold of hills was the sea, and Pasiphaë told herself she could hear it heaving and breaking on the shore. The cows, white or black with patches of red, stood or lay in the shade of the trees, swishing away the flies. Perhaps it had been their buzzing she heard rather than the hiss of foam.

Athamas called out. 'Does this smell high enough for you, Princess?'

'It smells like a farm, and that already reminds me of Kolchis.'

She shaded her eyes and peered between the sun dapples. Athamas had gone to ask one of the herdsmen about the white bull, when she saw him, alone, on the hillside over the other side of the stream. He moved slowly in and out of her line of vision, between the trees and golden streaks of grassland. Athamas brought the herdsman over, a wiry-looking man with a staff. His dogs stayed at their posts on the hillside, not taking their eyes off the cows.

The cattleman bent his head respectfully. 'You come to admire the herd, Lady? They're fine animals.'

'I came to see the bull from Kolchis, but he's wandering over the hill there. I thought I would find him with his cows.'

The herdsman hesitated a moment. 'He'll settle, Lady. We reckon he's still muddled. A bull as was intended for sacrifice is restless. He don't know why he's still in a field and not bones in the ossuary. We call him Belus, being as how he's Poteidan's. He'll settle, though.'

Pasiphaë's good humour left her, and the unease that curled in her belly wriggled. 'He is not Poteidan's! He was a gift to Asterius. If he's restless, it's a sign that he misses Kolchis and his herd. The next time I come, I expect to hear that he's happy with his new herd.'

The herdsman's eyes shifted nervously. 'I meant no offence, Lady. It was Prince Minos as said any bull from across the sea was Poteidan's and it was bad luck to keep him. Belus gets the best of everything, Lady, best pasture, and all the cows if he wants 'em. He'll settle, Lady, don't you worry.'

*

Pasiphaë watched the white bull as he walked heavily, parallel with the stream, his hide brilliant in the sun, like a star. *He's thinking he doesn't belong here either. Not a bull from the sea, simply a bull from Kolchis.* The thought saddened her.

'Is that how they think of me, Nephele?' she asked as they made their way back through the lengthening shadows. 'A heifer to be bred from if the need arises, or sacrificed on the whim of a jealous Prince if it doesn't?'

Nephele tucked her arm beneath her own. 'You shouldn't even ask yourself questions like that! Of course they don't. Minos is a crude brute who has bought any popularity he has. The heart of the people beats with the Mistresses and their Queen. You'll see how they respect you as soon as you take up your regal functions.'

'Asterius wants to spare me the burden. I shall have to insist.'

'You must! Until the Princess Kriti is old enough, you must take her place. Knossos must have a Queen.'

The words echoed back and forth, between Aea and Kolchis. She would insist.

*

She did try.

'I should know how to talk to your advisors, what questions to ask them and what answers to expect. How can I teach Kriti if I don't know myself?'

And Asterius had promised that as soon as he got back from overseeing the sale of some livestock at his property at Phaistos, and paid a visit to Minos's brothers and a few of the noble families, as soon as he had his contracts signed and his trade deals sorted out, she would sit in the Queen's seat in the Throne Room.

'Then while you're away, I shall at least get to know the palace. I'll visit the lower levels where the work is done, the storerooms and magazines. When you return, the working palace will hold no mysteries for me.'

A cloud had passed over Asterius's face, or so it had seemed to Pasiphaë, but in an instant it had gone, and he was smiling. 'That is a good plan. Take Nephele with you. She knows the lower levels scarcely better than you do, but she will be company, and... it's dark down there, a warren.'

Pasiphaë had rarely ventured beyond the part of the palace dominated by the royal apartment, its terraces and flowering courtyards, its fountains and colonnaded galleries. Even Leto, the curious pine marten, chattered anxiously when Pasiphaë tried to take her into unknown meanders of the house, possibly scenting the unfriendly weasels that kept down the mouse population. In fact, Pasiphaë rarely strayed further than the terrace she called the oleander garden, a small, enclosed space shaded mainly by fig and pomegranate trees. But someone had planted oleanders too, and they overflowed from the ceramic pithoi in cascades of pink flowers. The 'garden' faced north, towards the sea, shaded from the most direct sun by the tiered hillside behind and overhanging trees, and a fountain in the centre created an impression of coolness.

The day Asterius left, she went to the oleander garden to sit by the pool and watch Leto chase sun dapples across the red terracotta tiles. Somewhere close, a musician was playing the kithara and singing a melancholy song of lost love, when another, less melodious sound rose up from the level below. Beneath the balcony's pink cascades of oleander and white and yellow honeysuckle, a procession was crossing a terraced courtyard, a sedate procession, silent except for the tympana played by white-robed priestesses. Like a pale serpent, the women wound across the sunlit space and disappeared into the darkness of a gallery at the end of the terrace. At the tail of the procession, two men carried a litter, its contents like a splash of blood amid the snowy garments of the escort. Small hands clutched the bloody billows of her skirts, clenching and unclenching to the pulsing drumbeat, and beneath the diadem of coiled silver snakes, Pasiphaë recognised Kriti.

*

Knossos was layered like the earth and rock it was built upon. Its lower layers collapsed when the Great Mother had expressed her anger and shaken the earth, filled with rubble and left to the darkness. The royal apartments lay above levels of storerooms, and what lay in the lightless levels beneath them was almost forgotten.

These lower levels of the palace, that Pasiphaë could only guess at, had taken on a sinister life. What she had imagined as a silent kingdom of storerooms and granaries beneath the light-filled palace now seemed to hide one of the mysteries that had troubled her ever since she had first seen the child, her stepdaughter, tricked out in the poppy-coloured skirts of death, her lips painted bloody red. She was pleased to be able to call on Nephele to accompany her.

Leto scampered ahead as Pasiphaë and Nephele set off along the richly friezed and frescoed corridors, the rippling-columned galleries between the royal apartments and the great west entrance.

Nephele laughed. 'It makes a change to see such an ordinary little animal in these galleries. You're more likely to see a monkey or a great spotted cat on a lead.'

'Leto isn't an exhibit, nor would I ever make her wear a chain. She belongs only to the goddess and herself.'

The level immediately below the royal apartments bustled with activity. Artisans shouted at servants, sending them running on errands. Scribes and the servants of administrators dashed past importantly, and courtiers with nothing to do but be seen drifted languidly like exotic animals. Accountants and superintendents saluted the Moon Princess respectfully as she passed, the nobles with lingering, equivocal looks.

They passed the entrance to the shrine of Asasara and peered into the next room where a music lesson was in progress. Through another open doorway, a couple of carpenters in leather aprons were sitting amid the angular carcasses of unfinished pieces of furniture, arguing over a game of dice. Sometimes heads were raised at the sound of their footsteps, but mostly their presence didn't interrupt the routine of work.

The hum and chatter was comforting, and there was a soft beauty in the filtered light of the airy, painted rooms. But what intrigued Pasiphaë were the dark, unlit rooms behind, the silence of the floors below. Down short flights of stairs, another world lay, unfrequented except by slaves and servants. These were the storerooms, the treasure houses, set into the hillside, cool underground places, where the great pithoi reigned in their silent splendour.

'Are you sure you want to go down there?' Nephele asked, glancing apprehensively down a stone stair. 'It's just storerooms for food and the rubbish of ages no one wants to throw away.'

'It's the heart of the palace though. The ancient heart that beats through the painted galleries above. We'll just go a little way. Until we terrify ourselves.'

She grinned and Nephele laughed. Leto had already disappeared into the darkness that was not black, but a twilight grey from the light shafts let into the outer walls. This was the realm of the magazines, and Pasiphaë traced the patterns and pictures that decorated the ceramic, while the marten Leto chased mice in the deep shadows. She had known that Knossos was rich, but the extent of the riches surpassed her imaginings. The strangeness almost distracted her from her search, to find the destination of the nameless procession she had seen filing into the shadows beneath the oleander garden.

She thought she knew more or less how to get to the place, the open gallery beneath the oleander garden, where it passed into darkness. This lower level drew and repulsed her at the same time, and the further they descended into its dark meanders, the more she dreaded discovering that the little girl, who was as good as a shade, the ghost of a dead person already, led the rites and prayers of the cult that was the true heart of Knossos.

'Do you really want to go down there? The air feels wrong to me. My skin is crawling.'

Nephele had picked up the animosity of the place, though Pasiphaë had not told her the aim of her search, and it was with a certain relief that she gave in to the mutterings of warning.

'I think I've seen enough pithoi and ceramic jars. We can always come back another time.'

Nephele agreed, though not with enthusiasm. They even set a date to return to explore another deeper level. But the following day Pasiphaë made a discovery that put all thoughts of cellars, dark galleries and Kriti's mysterious cult out of her mind.

4

Changes

Pasiphaë had been a month in Knossos. She was officiating at the libations for the full moon, filling the lustral pool with the blood of priestesses, when she realised she had no blood to contribute, and why that must be. At the end of the ritual, black dots shoaled before her eyes and a wave of nausea washed over her. She swayed, closed her eyes and steadied herself against the stone basin. The smell of women, hot and muggy, in the small sacred space overwhelmed her, and the chanting voices stopped.

Two women moved to her side, their faces full of curiosity. The longing for a mother, anyone, to take her in their arms and tell her that everything would be all right was so strong she wanted to weep. She shook her head, gritted her teeth and finished the ritual. Back in the royal apartment, she ripped off the stiff skirt and diadem and threw herself onto the bed.

When she woke, she sensed the watchful presence of her women. Her eyelids flickered open. The light in the sky was dim and women's faces hung over her, watching in the gloom. Their concerned attentiveness touched her, gave her comfort. Probably more than Perseis would have given her. She sighed and sat up. Her stomach heaved again.

'I think the seed has taken.'

They flocked, hens clucking, full of a joy she didn't share. Not yet anyway. The squirming she felt in her stomach was only in part elation, the rest was fear, of the changes that had begun in her body and what their consequences would be. Speaking the words had given form and solidity to the vague unease. It curled like a serpent next to the seed, as if it would devour it.

*

Asterius returned on a thundery day of sticky summer heat to the news that Pasiphaë was pregnant. His heart beat loud with pride, and he walked wrapped in the cool breath of the sea, wreathed in clouds. He no longer felt the heat that rose from the stone and clay; the world was peace and beauty. Pasiphaë was expecting a child, his child. He knew what they said, that his seed was weak. Only one child and a feeble one at that. He had always suspected that Europa got rid of anything of his that germinated in her belly, that Kriti had been the only shoot that managed to cling to life. This would silence the mockers.

He went first to the King's apartment to wash the dust of the journey from himself, then went straight to his wife. He remembered the faces of those he passed beaming with happiness for him. Perhaps he had simply seen reflections of his own state of mind. Everything *seemed to* smile at him, even the figures in the Gallery of Processions. He waved a green branch with them, and his destination, at least, he desired with all his heart.

*

Pasiphaë was sick. Every smell turned her stomach, even the thought of some smells. She lived on bland gruel and pulses, fruits, bread and oil. Anything else was too strong, made her stomach heave as it had done the first days at sea. She spent the hot hours of the afternoon trying to sleep in the shadowy bedchamber, lulled by the soft *drip-drip* of water on the hot terrace beyond.

She was dozing when Asterius came to her, smelling of the sea and the fresh air of places she would probably never see, a broad smile on his face, and for an instant, she envied his freedom. She had never been so sick and wondered if this was what death felt like. But at the sight of that unequivocal smile, full of tenderness, her heart leapt. She hadn't realised how much she had missed him. He knelt down by the bed and took her limp hand. There was no tingling current, no exuberant animal roar, but there was a feeling of peace and calm and safety. The other feelings, those of a pregnant fifteen-year-old girl who longed for the comfort of the mother she had never had, sank into stillness.

When the tumbling flow of words of his pleasure and happiness slowed, Pasiphaë placed a finger on his lips. 'On the table, there's a list. I had a scribe write it all down. Plants for the sickness.'

'Of course.' The smile didn't change. Did he understand? Could a man understand how she felt? 'I'll send my herbalist with whatever you need.'

She studied his face dispassionately. It had taken no more than a few weeks of sharing his bed for her young girl's fears to be dispelled, for the mystery of intimacy with a husband to have become a simple fact of life. She had come to expect pleasure from those hands, an excitement that she didn't even attempt to control, the wave that rose, the tide rolling. She let it, embraced it, but it went no deeper than the pit of her belly, filled the space that burst up from between her legs that now a child was borrowing.

It was not disappointment, but a feeling of incompletion. Pride in knowing that she was undeniably a woman was tempered with dissatisfaction. For all the magic in Asterius's face, in his hands, she was still Pasiphaë, and she was still running after something more wonderful than red clay and nights of brief pleasure. Sometimes, when she rode the wave, she almost touched it. But when it rolled back, the night and the stars still tasted the same. Sometimes, she feared that only time would change – that she would grow older.

'You'll have to take care of yourself. No exertion. The heat is tiring enough.'

'But I need to move, to change, to see things. These same walls make me dull. Do you want the child to be an idiot?' she snapped, surprising herself, and her nostrils flared as she fought back another wave of nausea. Asterius, though, looked as though she had slapped his face, his eyes wide with uncomprehending hurt.

'I'm sorry,' he murmured. 'I just don't want anything to happen to you.'

Pasiphaë, the sensitive girl, the *High Priestess of Little Furry Things*, was mortified. She had expected him to say, *I didn't want anything to happen to the child.* She took his hand and kissed the tips of his fingers, borrowing a gesture of his that always touched her.

'I didn't mean to seem ungrateful. It's the sickness. Eritha says it will plague me for at least the first couple of months.'

She didn't say that she feared the future, the changes to her body that would make her vulnerable and clumsy. Her fear that the Mistress of Serpents might come for her before she had even lived out her girlhood.

*

The plants she had asked for arrived, and Asterius brought them himself along with the herbalist: a dry, sinewy woman with bright, dark eyes. She described where each plant came from, when it had been gathered and how the roots, flowers or leaves had been prepared. She spoke to Pasiphaë as to an equal, expecting that the High Priestess of Potnia Theron would be at least as skilled as she. Pasiphaë's confidence grew. Was it this she wanted, recognition that she could actually *be* something, *know* something?

Eritha prepared infusions to ease the nausea, pretended it

was a good sign even. She said it meant the child was making itself at home, growing strong. Pasiphaë suspected it just meant that she was pregnant, but the infusions helped, and the sickness became something she could live with.

*

The massive presence of Knossos was gradually becoming less intimidating as Pasiphaë discovered how it functioned. Her friendship with Nephele had given her confidence, overcoming her natural reserve and self-consciousness. She might still speak a Greek unlike the Cretan Greek, and each time she opened her mouth she was reminded that she was different, but the difference had ceased to matter. What still unsettled her was losing the rhythm of rituals that had ordered the days and the seasons in Kolchis. In Knossos, it was clear that the shrines to the Mistresses were peripheral and unimportant places. The only shrine in constant use was the Great Shrine that looked down on the Court of Ceremonies, and she suspected sacrifice and offerings were more a social activity than a religious one. Whatever religious rituals drew the crowds, they were not those dedicated to the Potniai.

The memory of Kriti, carried like a goddess in a litter among her red billows, still tormented her. The slight, timid girl who might never live to marry must officiate as a High Priestess, but in whose cult? She raked through her memories for the answer, sifted the fragments that remained from what Perseis had tried to teach her and found nothing. She added the question to her list of administrative questions for Asterius. For the first days after his return, he had been busy, giving accounts of his meetings to the other members of his house, to the tax officials and the regional governor. When she reminded him that she had duties that couldn't be put aside just because she was pregnant, he agreed to start her initiation, even though she sensed his reluctance.

*

Asterius knew that Pasiphaë was impatient to learn the administrative functions of the Queen, and he was as uneasy as she was about the implications of keeping her ignorant, but he had noticed the sickly tint of her skin, the shadows beneath her eyes, the constant frown on her face. He had seen enough women in the early stages of pregnancy to be uneasy for her, women whose child was never more than blood and matter, women who died in a flood of that blood and matter. He had hoped to ease her into her duties with short sessions of listening to legal requests in the Throne Room. He had not expected that the first place she wanted to visit was the old palace, the deep, dark place full of secrets.

*

'Why do you want to poke about down there in the dark? The old palace was dug out of the hillside, not much better than caves compared with what's been built since. A lot of the old part was damaged when the earth shook. Some of the rooms have fallen in, and they're just full of rubble now. There are only storerooms and cellars below.'

'And shrines.'

His eyes slid away, but he wouldn't lie to her. Asterius was honourable, and he genuinely wanted to please. He gave an affected laugh that didn't fool her in the slightest. She waited for him to go on. Not make her ask.

'Only one shrine. The oldest of all. As old as Knossos.'

And the most important. 'I'd like to see it.'

He nodded, though with reluctance. What else could he do? Wriggle out of it and have her order a servant to take her there? She took his arm and let him believe she leaned on him for support.

To reach the terrace beneath the oleander garden, they took a meandering route. Pasiphaë suspected Asterius was hoping to tire her out before they got anywhere near Kriti's shrine. He set an easy pace, an amble, pointing out the sights, the Undersea Gallery with its frieze of serpents and swordfish, seahorses and squid. They stood in an undecorated yard and watched pairs of young men boxing until Pasiphaë sighed loudly with boredom.

Then there was a gallery hung with arms and painted with scenes of young men and women racing or throwing the javelin. It led to a medicinal garden and Pasiphaë was introduced to a multitude of plants, creepers and climbers, clumps and bushes that flowered in pinks and blues. Her fingers, brushing and crushing, released the oily scents of rosemary and hyssop, savoury and sweet thyme, but she refused to be cajoled into lingering. Asterius glanced at her as they finally left the garden and climbed the steps to a red-columned terrace. 'You look tired.'

He sounded so hopeful, Pasiphaë couldn't help smiling. 'Not yet. I think I know where we are now.'

Beyond, through the red trunks, she saw the glitter of white stone and recognised the great central staircase. They were almost there. Excitement and dread mingled with the sickness in her stomach, but she hurried towards the white glitter, despite the weight of Asterius's reluctance. In the columned shade, the animated talk of a group of men paused. One of them called out Asterius's name, and the whole group made their way across the pavement at a determined pace.

Asterius held up a hand and addressed the man with a short grey beard and the most annoyance in his eyes. 'Not now, Roko. Come to the Throne Room tomorrow and I'll hear your case.'

'You've been saying that for weeks now, Asterius. Meanwhile, I can't get near my olive trees in the top parcel because of his bees! Dromeus isn't a proper beekeeper, he doesn't have the right material, and when he smokes them, they sting everything in sight.'

Another man, shorter, younger, pushed forward. 'The

mountaintop is common land, and if my bees want to feed on the thyme up there, I have every right to let them, whatever he says.'

If Roko replied, it was lost in the shouting from the partisans of both sides. Asterius would have left them to it, but Pasiphaë shook his hand off her arm. This was what she had been waiting for. She almost laughed.

'Be quiet and listen. In Kolchis, this is what we would say was just. Dromeus, your bees have the right to the thyme flowers on the mountain, and you have the right to the honey they make. But they're your responsibility. If they sting Roko's workers, they must pay for it in honey. Settle how much each sting is worth, how many hours work Roko loses because of them, and come back tomorrow and we'll write it down.'

Roko stroked his beard and pulled his nose, weighing up both sides of the bargain. Dromeus opened his mouth to argue, but Pasiphaë silenced him.

'Did you not understand? I have spoken. Judgement is given.'

Dromeus glanced at Asterius, but he was already turning away with Pasiphaë's hand back on his arm. 'The Lady Pasiphaë has spoken. Judgement is given. Work out the details between you and come back tomorrow.'

Asterius had assumed Pasiphaë had no knowledge of judgement, like Kriti, but the light of amusement in her eyes told him otherwise. Perhaps Perseis had begun her instruction. The thought of Kriti, who had been taken from him by the priestesses and turned into something he no longer recognised, pricked his conscience. She ought to be trained to rule, even if… Something more useful than prayers and bloodletting anyway. Pasiphaë claimed his attention though, keen to descend the stair, and he let Kriti sink into the antechamber of his concerns. Her life was not in his hands anyway.

'You gave a wise judgement, for such a…'

'Young girl?' Pasiphaë was learning that Asterius never

meant to hurt her, and she had ceased to hear slights in his words. 'I remember my mother having a similar case to judge.'

'I wondered as much. Let's hope they both abide by your decision.'

Pasiphaë laughed at the memory. 'Bounos didn't. He claimed for damage that was never done, deadly stings that were a complete invention.'

'So, what did your mother do?'

'She turned four bushels of his almonds into bees.' Asterius's eyes opened wide in alarm, and she laughed again. 'No, she didn't. She cancelled the honey debt and made Bounos pay a fine of four bushels of almonds.' Her laughter faded. 'It's what Circe would have done, though. Or turned Bounos into a bee. Or had him drowned in honey. Making a mockery of the Queen's justice must be punished.'

'Of course,' Asterius said. His expression was pensive. 'And the King's justice?'

Pasiphaë thought she knew where the conversation was leading, and she didn't care for it. 'The King doesn't have the power to settle disputes. You had weeks to settle this one and they are still bickering.' It was a reproach, and she saw from his eyes that she had hurt him. She squeezed his arm. 'But it isn't settled yet. I don't know the people here well enough. That's why you have to teach me what kind of justice they'll accept.'

The shade across his features was too deep for her to tell if she was forgiven. She recognised her mother in the casual gesture that meant nothing, a touch, a few empty, condescending words. She hated herself for it, but there was still too much unfamiliar territory between them, the language they spoke not yet quite aligned. She glared at the hand on his arm, suddenly miserable at her inability to ask his forgiveness, or even to show him tenderness, as naturally as she would show Leto.

Asterius seemed to understand her distress and stroked her cheek gently with his finger. She took his hand and kissed each finger, one by one, almost weeping with gratitude.

5

The Poppy Mistress

The sun dripped molten heat down the vast stairwell, and though the older parts of the palace promised dark shadows, there was nothing sinister about the descent. The first steps were flooded with sunlight, and among the pots of fruit trees, medicinal and culinary herbs, the omnipresent thyme and honeysuckle, bees made the air vibrate, and scent hung heavy. Not until the foot of the broad stair did the shade gather and the flowering plants give way to ferns whose fronds curled around the precious drops of night moisture. The smell of damp earth and dew hanging from leaf-tips wrung Pasiphaë's heart with an almost-pain and memories of Kolchis, its forests, rivers and pooled glades.

This lower level of the palace was like the upper, with rooms opening one out of another, galleries and courtyards linking areas with different functions. The main difference was the light: dim, damp and full of the whispering of water. Pasiphaë was ashamed of how she had tried to belittle Asterius, but shame didn't stop her seeing through his ploys to distract her from the real reason behind the excursion. Not that she wasn't curious about the strangely decorated rooms and the contents of the countless boxes and caskets he opened for her inspection.

'They say Europa brought a fortune in her dowry. Is this it?'

They had entered the storerooms where the treasure of gold, silver, polished stones and bolts of silk were kept. Asterius laughed. 'This is the wealth of Crete, trade and alliances, although Europa's gift of cedar wood was very welcome. Not that her countrymen appreciated what we used it for though.' In the half-light, his teeth flashed white. 'More ships. No people build ships the way Cretans build, and none master the waves like us. The mere threat of using our fleet protects us from attack.'

'But the Athenians threatened, didn't they? That's why you made a Greek Princess Queen.'

He looked at her sharply, and she knew he was surprised. 'Trade. Alliances. If you want your trade protecting, you have to pay for it. The Greeks didn't want to. Europa as Queen made them pay up with less fuss.'

He went off into a diversionary tale about some fantasy of the Greeks about a giant defending the coast of Crete. She wasn't listening. The drunken, acrimonious words of Butes Pallantides came back to her. It was natural that weaker peoples should pay tribute for their right not to be enslaved. There was nothing strange or reprehensible in it. Yet Pasiphaë had sensed a deeper malaise behind his words.

'It's time I learned more about *trade and alliances*. There are... gaps in my understanding.'

He nodded, a slight frown barring his forehead. It was on the tip of her tongue to ask what Knossos had done to inspire so much hatred in the Athenians, but the succession of deep, dark rooms had distracted her thoughts, taken them into strange places. She would bring up the subject again later, in the friendly light of the royal level.

Asterius had been leading her round in circles, but they had been diminishing, and she sensed they were at last reaching the centre. His steps slowed on the threshold of yet another gallery with strange, crude wall paintings, unlike the softer, more sophisticated paintings of the higher levels. The gallery was dark, and it smelled ancient, like an unvisited tomb. The wall painting was innocent enough, only flowers, their open faces broad-petalled, black-centred in shades of red. Here and there were yellows, pinks, purples, but mostly they were red, deep and bloody, sombre as the stains on a sacrificial stone. For the first time since she had begun her inspection of the palace, Pasiphaë heard the muttering of the Mistress. She touched the talisman. The bronze was hot. Burning.

'You seem tired, my Princess.'

She was tired, tired of not knowing things, what hid behind the glitter, of being the stand-in for a girl who was going to die and wondering when it would be her turn. And it was true, she had hesitated in the open doorwa; something in the smell, the taste of the air, held her back. But she had come too far to turn away now.

'We can go back as soon as I've seen the shrine. It would be disrespectful if I ignored the ancient deities. It would bring bad luck.'

He said nothing as he turned into the long gallery, but she saw the tightening of his jaw. Dread squirmed. Not like the marten talisman. Like a serpent. She turned her gaze from the unsettling flowers, tried not to listen to the clattering of her sandals or to breathe in the bitter smells of cold incense and ashes. Dead fires. And another smell she couldn't yet identify. She cast her eyes to the pavement. Servants had been there recently, sweeping. The dust tickled her nose. Potnia Theron muttered louder.

They crossed a courtyard, open to the sky, but the walls were high, and the light didn't reach the bottom. She felt like a fish in a well. The still air was heavy with the scent of honeysuckle tumbling from the terrace above, and she knew that it would be entwined with the pink flowers of oleanders. Asterius paused before the doorway.

'The shrine of the Poppy Mistress.'

His voice was pale, colourless. He opened the double doors that swung effortlessly with no grinding of unused hinges, revealing a room half-filled with slanting light and half with deep shadow. Potnia Theron growled with her lion voice as Pasiphaë entered and passed into the arms of a deity older than any she knew, older than Knossos. Asterius hung back, reluctant to cross the threshold, but she had the right, the duty to enter the great domed vastness of the circular shrine. She had never seen such a place, never thought it was possible. Amid the flat-roofed boxes of Knossos its roundness was like an intrusion, a canker. A ripe belly.

The ceiling was painted with stars and the gaping mouths of serpents swallowing the stars. She shivered and lowered her eyes. The small, high windows lit only the middle air. The wall painting, a procession of small naked figures, was dim and dull, figures out of the dead past. The pavement, too, seemed ancient, stone not terracotta-tiled, pitted with deep basins. There was water in the basins, and the water was fresh. No mould dulled the polished stone.

With Theron thudding in her ears, Pasiphaë studied the slightly concave altar, and behind it, rising like a mountain in bell-shaped skirts, the Great Mother. She wore a red bronze wreath of poppy flowers, and the hands of the statue were raised in a blessing or a warning. About the hem of her skirts, jars were placed, shaped like poppy heads, some filled with black seeds, some with a grey powder, and others containing a viscous substance like grey honey. In the centre was a broad bowl with the familiar open-mawed serpents writhing about its rim, full of small bones. She peered closer. Finger bones?

Perhaps it was her state, emotions sharpened by the knowledge of the child growing inside her, or a sign from Potnia Theron, but she saw, in the slight depression of the cold slab, what wasn't there. Asterius had approached silently to stand behind her, his hands placed comfortingly on her shoulders. The stone was a small block, far too small for a bull, not even big enough for a struggling sheep, but just the right size to balance a child's body, bound in the position of an infant curled in its mother's belly.

Black spots swam and the stones howled in distress like

wolves on the hill. Was it a flash of her mother's gift, or did she just see what she suspected in her darkest moods? Ropes held the small body tight, the neck, slender as a lily bending in the wind, exposed to the spear. The air choked with terror and misery. Mothers wept over generations of lost lives. Was she the only one to hear the wailing and the tearing of hair? The shrine was still used; she smelled blood in the air. A poppy petal lay on the altar. Not a petal. She knew, before she touched it with a fingertip, that the red that pooled on the stone was from no flower.

*

Asterius would have turned her about, led her away from the tears and grieving, but it wasn't over. There was more. From one of the small, high windows, a beam of light fell and dragged her gaze with it. Asterius tried again to pull her away, but she had noticed what he had tried to hide. She shrugged off his hands, roughly.

The doorway was small and narrow, barely large enough for a child to pass through. She bent and peered into the shadows. There was no window, but light fell from a circular hole in the roof, and when her eyes adjusted to the gloom, she recognised an ossuary. It was an ossuary such as she was used to seeing at every shrine where sacrifices were made. All offerings to the Mistresses were sacred, even those to Potnia Theron that were left for the wild beasts to consume. If gnawed bones were left behind, they were placed in the ossuary along with the bones of the animals eaten by the priestesses.

She had always sensed tenderness and peace in Potnia Theron's ossuary at Aea. She would take the bones of the dead and place them reverently where nothing more would disturb them. In the calm among the bones, she had felt connected to the *rightness* of the Mistress. There was no *rightness* here. The air was tense and taut, like ropes, vocal cords, bound sinews.

The colourless light that fell through the round roof hole ran across the long leg bones of goats, sheep, calves and smaller bones she couldn't identify.

Behind her, she felt Asterius's breath, sensed his impatience, or perhaps his fear. She peered beyond the beam of cold light into the shadows at the back of the room, drawn by some compulsion, despite the crawling of her skin, and saw. In an alcove apart, she saw the dull, pale glint of human skulls. Small skulls.

She backed out of the doorway. At the contact of Asterius's hands, she choked back a scream. The image of the calf, its blood pumping into the stone basin, mingling with the water, life running away into the earth, filled the back of her eyes. The smell of it made her feel sick. Firmly, Asterius pulled her round to face him and placed both her hands on her still-flat stomach, like placing hands before a child's eyes.

'Come away. This is no place for you.'

'You sacrifice children?' Her voice seemed not her own, too thin, too faint, falling from another world. Asterius steered her away from the dark room, away from the echoing shrine that she suddenly saw could hold hundreds.

'There's a tradition, an ancient one, that the Great Mother demands young lives.'

'In Kolchis, our Mistresses never ask for human life. Never!'

In Kolchis, the Great Mother sleeps.

She felt the darkness pressing against her, compressing her throat so that breathing was harsh, painful. Lights flickered behind her eyes; dark spots swam before them. Potnia Theron roared in a fury in her lion voice and Pasiphaë pressed her hands over her ears, turned from the charnel house and stumbled to the staircase.

The roaring wouldn't stop, but her stomach heaved. She put a hand before her mouth and ran through the dark place into the gallery, turning her eyes from the frieze of children bearing sheaves of poppies to the room of death. The walls opened suddenly and she was outside; the sun had shifted and reached down into the deep well of the courtyard. Above her head, scented white and yellow flowers trailed through pink oleander. She leaned against a ceramic pot, retched and spat the green, bitter-tasting bile, sobbing with pain and compassion. Asterius's hands were there again, on her shoulders, holding her to his chest, smoothing her brow, her hair, as if she were a child. A child.

*

The dark side of the mysteries was something Asterius had learned to ignore. Like most Knossians, he enjoyed the entertainment of religious ritual far more than its sacred aspect. Bulls were sacrificed on the occasions that demanded it, but the people preferred their bulls alive and glorious, in the spectacle of the bull-leaping. Only the cult of the Great Mother, whose sanctuary dominated Mount Iouktas, had much importance. The cult of the Mistresses could not compete with her solemn, bloody rituals. Except for one. The Great Mother had kept the Poppy Mistress with her, the goddess of death and oblivion. She had not been allowed to fade into insignificance. Her cult had grown in importance, and she had changed. No longer a guide and a consolation through the inevitable business of death, she had become death itself, bloody and greedy. Blood and the terror of divine retribution served some human purposes too.

The Key-Bearer had said Kriti must receive instruction in the temple rituals and Asterius had not opposed it. How could he? The priestesses held the power, and his daughter would one day be the Queen. Europa was ailing and didn't care about Mothers and Mistresses, and he, he was just the husband of the Queen.

Asterius stroked Pasiphaë's hair as he would have stroked Kriti's had he been allowed. The Great Mother had demanded his daughter, and no father could have denied her, but he would always see that small, pinched face, the eyes round with uncomprehending fear. Kriti had worn no other since the day of her initiation. Afterwards, Ananke had tried to keep the child in the High Priestess's apartment, but she had run to find him and had clung to him, unable to speak. He had asked then that she be spared, but the Key-Bearer had said it was too late. She had been accepted by the Poppy Mistress. The divination had given the sign.

'The Mistress wills it,' Ananke had said with a strange light in her eyes. Minos willed it too.

*

Later, at night in the bed he shared with Pasiphaë, he asked if she was recovered. He touched her face, but she flinched, as if another brushed her skin with burning fingers.

'Recovered from what? From learning a nasty secret you'd hoped I'd never be curious enough to find out? Or did you think I wouldn't care?'

He stroked her hair. 'There's no secret. In dark times, the Great Mother has always demanded sacrifice.'

'She *did,* because she made life and death. But that was in the beginning. Now it's the Mistresses who watch over birth and dying, making them easier to bear. The Great Mother doesn't care *how* we live, or even if.'

'But the Mistresses can't make death go away, or the fear of death. We hear her too often here, when the mountain on Thera shakes and spouts fire, and the sea rises up and pours through the broken buildings. Her sanctuary isn't in the palace, though. She sleeps, mostly, on Mount Iouktas.'

'The Poppy Mistress is her handmaid, and she's still here, at the heart of the palace, deep in the dark. And she's not the Poppy Mistress I know, the silent woman without a face who takes our hands to lead us through the portal of death. I felt the presence of cold cruelty and the oceans of blood that she's drunk.'

She shivered at the memory and moved closer to Asterius, let him caress her with a soothing hand, as a mother would comfort a sick child.

'She is there, in the darkness, but there's no more human blood shed here. Those are old bones in the ossuary. The child tribute stopped when Lycastus married Europa.'

Pasiphaë's tongue clicked as if something that puzzled her had become clearer. 'What was the tribute Butes Pallantides spoke of, then? The Athenians fear that a new Queen will bring it back.' She rolled on her side to face him. 'But there was fresh blood among the poppies. Why?'

He sighed and carried on stroking her hair. She pushed his hand away.

'I'm not a baby having bad dreams! There was blood on the altar,' she repeated obstinately.

'It would have been an animal. There are no children sacrificed in that shrine, believe me.'

'Where then?'

Her obstinacy would only be satisfied with the truth. 'The sanctuary, Mount Iouktas, as part of the Summer Rites. But only if times are bad, and only slave children have been sacrificed these last years.'

*

Pasiphaë let the words sink in. She heard an apology in Asterius's voice, but she also heard the distress of the cow, her calf bawling. 'What mother would demand a sacrifice of children?'

'No mother that I know of,' he replied softly. 'But it's not up to the King to define the cult of the Great Mother. Only the High Priestess can do that.'

'Kriti could stop it then.'

She heard the sharp intake of breath and knew she had touched a raw nerve.

'Kriti is a child with no authority. Inia, the Key-Bearer, would have put an end to the sacrifices, but there would have been a revolt. The people wouldn't have stood for it. They believe... they have been led to believe that oil and wine and grain aren't enough for the Great Mother. Only blood will satisfy her.'

'They always used to be enough, and they still are in civilised places!'

'Times change. Sometimes men make them change. The Greeks shed blood for the slightest reason, whole herds for something important, and Minos admires the custom. There's an idea taken root that only the blood of children is sweet enough to appease the anger of the Great Mother.'

'And I can guess who planted that idea. How could you let your daughter be used like this?'

It was cruel, she knew, turning the knife in an old wound. She felt some of Circe's fierce anger, some of her mother's cold condemnation. Asterius winced inwardly, she was sure, but she wanted him to tell her that the enemy was Minos. She wanted to tell him that together they could fight him.

'Europa had no time for her daughter and let the temple have her. Kriti was bound to be taught the temple laws anyway, to become a High Priestess.'

'Of the Poppy Mistress, the only one who matters.'

Her voice trembled, on the verge of tears, and Asterius pulled her close, kissed her brow. 'I would have prevented it, but the King has no power. The Queen could have insisted another High Priestess be chosen, but Europa didn't care.' His voice trembled too, and when he spoke again Pasiphaë heard nothing but sadness and regret. 'Yes, Kriti could change the custom, take on the wrath of... the adepts of the Great Mother. But that is not a burden I would willingly place on a child.'

His face was in deep shadow. She saw only the faintest glint of moonlight in his eyes, but his voice was gentle, and she understood that his desire was to protect her. The aching sadness in it was for his daughter, who had always been beyond his help. She felt the heat of his body as a comfort, even in the hot summer night, and in that moment, she wanted his arms about her. Almost timidly, she reached out to him, placed a hand on his cheek, and slowly, Asterius drew her to him, driving away her dark thoughts in the only way he knew.

6

Hopes and omens

Asterius tried to comfort her, and in a way he did, but he couldn't change the fact that the sacrifices continued because they served a purpose. The Great Mother held Crete tightly in her arms, but she demanded a tribute of young lives, taking a few so that the many might live, the priestesses said. The sacrificial victims used to be children from the royal houses of trading partners. It had made Knossos detested and gained a monstrous reputation for the cult of the Mother. Europa's marriage to Lycastus had ended the tribute, but her son, Minos, was itching to bring it back. So far, Inia the Key-Bearer had forbidden it. Perhaps that irked him more than anything. Asterius reported the exchange between the two.

'The bastards, all those piddling little peoples around the Middle Sea, are happy enough to profit from the trade routes we've opened up to exchange their junk for ceramics and oils, spices and jewellery, exotic birds and slaves, timber and gold from the ends of the earth. If Crete builds the ships and takes the risks, they can bloody well pay for the service!' Minos had said.

'They do pay,' Inia had retorted. 'We take a cut of their profits for the shipping. The upkeep of the fleet is our responsibility not theirs. You can't insist they pay for that too, not when their harvests are poor or their flocks are sick.'

'Spoken like a woman, Inia. Threaten to take their children instead and they'll cough up.'

'And if they don't?'

'We relieve them of a few mouths to feed.'

Asterius had sat through this exchange in the Throne Room in silence. Inia's word held far more weight than his after all. He had been disturbed, though, that the Key-Bearer had not silenced Minos when his contempt turned to insult. Perhaps, like him, she had seen approval in too many faces to put her authority to the test. But he could not hide his preoccupation from Pasiphaë.

'We are not pirates! What does Minos mean by threatening to make our trading clients pay in human flesh?'

Asterius hesitated. 'It has happened in the past, that Knossos has taken payment in slaves. But the practice stopped long ago.'

Pasiphaë frowned. 'It must remain a thing of the past. Such a tribute could only lead to war.'

*

War. For Knossos to fight wars, it would need an army, an army would lead to conquests, and to protect its conquests, it would need bigger armies. Conquerors had Kings, not Queens. To Pasiphaë it seemed inevitable that if Minos had his way, the Mistresses would lose Knossos. Despite the tender peace she found with Asterius, she still felt the old unease, sluggish and unformed, like a beast stirring in the mud at the bottom of the sea. She put it down to the growing child.

Now that she had been to the heart of the old palace, she left her discoveries to their darkness. She stayed in the royal levels of the palace, in the light, among the painted flowers and smiling people, and Asterius joined her often in the oleander garden. The summer heat was at its fiercest, the blue of the sky burnished like a mirror, but the evening sun was like honey beneath the trees. Pasiphaë drank in the flower scents, let them drown the pungent, domestic smells of garlic, sweat, onions, hot oil and cheese that made her want to vomit. The infusions Eritha prepared every morning, the ginger root she nibbled before she was even out of bed, helped to keep the nausea at bay.

Asterius took the Queen's place in the Throne Room, letting her sleep or sit among her flowers while he dealt with minor disputes. There was some muttering of discontent among the petitioners, but he insisted the Queen was not to be disturbed.

'You shouldn't pretend that I'm too sick to be pestered by suppliants. Problems don't go away just because the Queen is pregnant.'

She spoke in a bantering tone, but with a hint of seriousness. Asterius simply smiled. 'They don't go away, but they can wait. Most disputes are already covered by the laws, and the rest...'

He waved a hand vaguely. Pasiphaë knew what he meant. She had taken up her duties in the Throne Room and been bored to tears. She had insisted that Kriti also assist. Boring or not, it would be her role later. On her low stool, that she moved deliberately to one side and behind the two thrones, Kriti seemed as insignificant as a small scribe or a favourite hound, no more than an observer. Pasiphaë hoped she was also learning, but often, she really didn't care.

Nausea rolled into the dead calm of the ordinary business of trade, contracts, niggles over clauses, numbers and taxes, and demanded all Pasiphaë's attention. When she wasn't able to hold back the rising bile, she left the Throne Room. In any case, the huge bureaucratic machinery of the Cretan economy turned with no help from royal lawmakers. Her religious duties were so perfunctory, it was unlikely anyone noticed that she skipped most of them.

What she never tired of was studying Asterius, his face, his gestures, listening to his voice, the words and the silences of what he didn't say. Asterius watched her too. She wondered sometimes what he had learned. As a child, she had not been encouraged to have thoughts of her own, much less express them. Perhaps he, too, was learning from her gestures and silences as much as from her words.

He watched her now, as they sat together in the oleander garden, and she knew he was thinking that her chair needed moving further into the shade. His body leaned forward; she saw the tensing of his calf muscles as he prepared to rise. Suddenly he was distracted, raised his eyes to something over her shoulder.

'Look,' he whispered. She turned, cautiously. A pair of turtle doves were perched on the parapet of the terrace. They leaned one against the other, looking out over the palace, down to the port, perhaps gazing as far as the sea. Pasiphaë remembered the sign the Mistress had sent on the day of the wedding, the pair of doves. She smiled.

'Doves dream too,' she said in a quiet voice. The thought of dreams, the achieving of them or their breaking into fragments, no longer made her sad. She would be a mother; she would learn the role of Queen and teach a young girl how to rule. Then she would settle into oblivion like her father Aloeus. She would be happy with what she had. It would be enough. Asterius leaned over the table across the cups and jugs of water and sweet wine, reaching to take the hand she dangled over the arm of her chair. She turned her palm and their fingers entwined. She didn't pull away or accept his attention passively as she would have done once. They were growing together, she thought, like a pair of doves.

The noise of a crowd approaching spoiled the moment, and Asterius frowned. The doves fluttered away as he rose, and Pasiphaë heard the Mistress in the whirring of their feathers. She joined him at the parapet and looked down on a crowd of women clothed in white, followed by men wearing the dark tunics and short hair of servants. Their feet struck no rhythm, there was no music, and no litter carried a goddess. Pasiphaë opened her mouth to ask who and why, when one in the crowd slowed her steps and looked up – a dark-robed woman, grey-haired, thin and stark as a winter tree.

She stepped back, afraid suddenly of the vehemence in the dark eyes.

'It was just Ananke,' Asterius said, as if that would reassure her.

'What were they doing?'

'Preparing the shrine, probably. Ananke supervises the preparations for the ceremonies.' His eyes slid away, fixed on a trailing tendril of pink mallow flowers. 'We're almost at the time of offerings for a good harvest.'

He had no need to say any more. The end of the summer was the time of year Circe loved best. In Kolchis, she would be preparing to make sacrifice to Potnia Athana. Pasiphaë thought with distaste of the fierce light in her sister's face as she wielded the spear, as the blood flowed, and the chanting rose higher than the death rattle of the dying beasts.

*

The heat, between rainstorms, was oppressive. The flowers had faded, the leaves lost their fresh sheen, and Pasiphaë sensed the heavy presence of the Great Mother in the palace. She saw her raised hands in the wall paintings. Her colour leaped out from the cedar columns of the colonnades, the flowered wall paintings. She heard her slow, implacable voice in the end of summer storms that bruised the clouds purple over the pitch-black of the sea.

Pasiphaë rarely ventured out of the palace. Why would she? Everything and everyone came to the royal court, although the faces were changing. Kerameia and her family had gone back to Malia, taking Nephele with them. A settlement had been agreed with her old husband, and she had chosen a new one. She was to be married before the end of the summer. Pasiphaë wondered if she would feel up to travelling to the wedding. When she looked at the implacable sky, brilliant as heated bronze, and bile rose in her throat at a stray smell, a sudden movement, she doubted it.

Beyond the gardens and terraces of Knossos were fields, dry stone and wild mountain, nothing more. But from the terraces piled high and exuberant with cultivated plants, she could see the hillsides beyond the painted and plastered walls, the activity in the fields, the golden barley, the tired gold-green of the vine leaves. She could watch the slow movement of the flocks and pick out the white Kolchian bull as he patrolled his herd.

She visited the white bull again, as she had promised, with Asterius this time. There was less grass in the valley bottom, though the rains had freshened the green, and a couple of cows were preparing to calve. A herdsman took them through the pasture, where only a few cattle still grazed, and to the hillside beyond. On the edge of the oak copse on the hilltop, they could see the white bull covering a heifer. A few bullocks looked on but kept their distance.

'I'd say he's settled, wouldn't you?' Asterius said with a smile.

'He's an asset to the herd, is Belus,' the young herdsman said. 'I don't care what old Kuredju says.'

'What's that?' Asterius asked, curious. Pasiphaë wished he hadn't.

'Oh, some old folk's tale about bad luck, him being Poteidan's, and how he ought 'a been sacrificed. Wait till we see his calves,' he added with a grin, 'then we'll see if he's bad luck or not.'

Asterius laughed with him, but Pasiphaë remembered Minos, and knew that he would not have forgotten his threat either.

7

Summer Rites

The summer was ending, the first of the olives were ready, and it was time for the Mistresses to be asked for a good harvest. There was thunder in the air when Pasiphaë walked at the head of her priestesses to the little courtyard shrine she alone used. It was open to the sky, and in the distance she could see the holy face of Mount Iouktas. She recognised the face of the mountain better than the faces of the priestesses. They all looked more or less identical, with their hair piled in the same fashion, their faces streaked with red and black. There were six of them for this, the most important rite of the year. Six. How many would the Great Mother summon? Sixty? She raised her arms to the sky, weary of the feeling of suffocation beneath the whispering. Nobody cared about the Mistresses, not really, but they feared the Great Mother. And so did Pasiphaë.

She recited the prayers to the Potniai, the prayers she had learned by heart as a child, and it seemed that the cloud lifted slightly, the purple bruising faded to grey-blue. A priestess brought wine, another brought oil, a third a bowl of barley. As she turned, her eye was caught by a movement behind their bending and straightening. More glittering white robes had appeared, clustered thick as a flock of swans about a slender figure in the billowing red skirts of a goddess. Poppy-red skirts.

The skirts rustled angrily, and the bodice revealed Kriti's young girl's breasts. Pasiphaë felt her presence like a harbinger. She pitied the girl, but she was also the Poppy Mistress with death in her hands. Her mouth was suddenly dry as dust, the words of the prayers threatening to slip away, like water into sand. Acolytes brought up a pair of kids, one black, one white. The Mistresses didn't revel in the terror of blood sacrifices, and she had had the kids drink poppy to make them docile. She would not fight babies to death.

Her lips were dry. There was a ripple of movement among the white swans, and she hurried the acolytes, wanting to get it over with before Kriti interfered. Would she dare? The black kid first. Bronze flashed, the hooves kicked spasmodically and blood spurted into the basin. The white kid protested but feebly. The poppy had fuddled its senses, and the blade found the vein in its neck before it was aware of death squatting on the altar.

The basin filled. Oil and wine were poured over the blood. An acolyte skinned the kid, sliced a piece of flesh from its haunch and placed it over the brazier. Some priestesses didn't recoil from eating the flesh raw, but Pasiphaë insisted it was given at least a semblance of cooking. The juices spat, the muscle shrank and singed. She took a piece and brought the knife to her lips, nibbled with her front teeth, lips bared, a small piece, in respect for the life that had been taken. Juice trickled down her chin. She wiped it away with a cloth. The rest of the offering was for Potnia Theron.

As the flames spat, the sky roared with the voice of a lion, and light flashed amid the dark clouds. It was a sign, but Pasiphaë was confused – good sign or bad? White light played in the sky to the south-west, and as she stared, wondering, a voice spoke, close, at her side.

'The sanctuary is touched by heavenly fire. She's angry.'

Kriti pointed, her skirts brushed Pasiphaë's legs, and she flinched from their brittle redness. Lightning, a sheet of flashing brilliance, hung for a brief moment above the peak of Mount Iouktas, and in that moment she saw the sanctuary in silhouette. High on a cairn, a bell-shaped figure raised arms to the sky, before the dark fell again.

'Her child Dias is hungry. He'll eat the entire harvest if he's not fed.' Kriti's voice was flat, toneless. 'The sacrifice to the Great Mother is on the last day of the Summer Rites. Will you come?' The tone was as bland as ever, but the eyes that held Pasiphaë's, dark pools rimmed with black and gold, were full of pleading. 'Please? It'll be my first time. To officiate.'

Pasiphaë forced her fingers to be still and keep away from the pendant of Potnia Theron around her neck. She had no need to touch it; she could feel its heat on her skin, feel the presence of the Mistress in the breathless air. There was incertitude, a pause in the cycle of the earth. All waited for something to turn the wheel, move the moon and stars in their courses, raise and lower the tides, or the world would fall. She could already feel it trembling in the stone beneath her sandalled feet. Kriti waited, her lips pressed tight to stop their quivering. Pasiphaë couldn't refuse.

'Of course. The Mistresses and the Great Mother are sisters. I'll ask for their presence at the ceremony.'

Kriti's crisped features relaxed. She seemed about to express her gratitude, but the black-clad nurse had moved to her mistress's side and her grating voice cut off the formal words before they were spoken.

'Not sisters, Moon Princess. The Great Mother is the One Mother, alone in the sky and on the earth. She has no sisters, only children. Thousands upon thousands of children. The Mistresses are merely nurses of children.'

Full of the presence of the Potniai, Pasiphaë forgot her dread, and her eyebrows rose. 'Who do you think you are, woman, to contradict a High Priestess? And what impudence! In the Mistresses' own shrine, at the offering, claiming they're no better than servants like yourself!' She turned to Kriti. 'She's your responsibility, Princess, but if she were mine, I'd have her whipped.'

Ananke flashed dark eyes full of hatred at her. Kriti's eyes were wide with terror. Compassion fought with anger. If Kriti wanted to be rid of the vulture, she had only to give the word. But only she could give it. Neither Pasiphaë nor Asterius had the authority. Out of the corner of her eye, Pasiphaë saw the white swan priestesses flock about their poppy goddess, as her own priestesses prepared to leave the shrine. She signalled to the musicians to begin. The sweet chords of the kitharai would chase away the malaise cast by the Great Mother. This was not her place after all.

*

The storm didn't break. For the rest of the day, Pasiphaë brooded in the oleander garden, her back to Mount Iouktas and its sanctuary. Asterius was dealing with suppliants, farmers from up in the hills who hadn't heard that hearings were suspended, not even that there was a new Queen. Pasiphaë found she longed to have him with her, not just when the sickness made her feel wretched. When visions of a red-mouthed goddess reared in the dark eyes of Ananke, it was Asterius she longed to confide in, even though he was a man and didn't understand the mysteries.

Asterius was not a god, nor a hero either. He was not a youth of Pasiphaë's age, but a man with wrinkles and creases in the skin of his face. He had lived so much longer than she had and done so much more. Perseis would have said that the things a man does are of no importance, but important or not, he knew many things that she didn't, and ignorance was surely a sign of inferiority.

She had been taught that the King was no more than an accessory of power. He had a function, limited in time, expendable. It hadn't even occurred to Perseis to warn her not to grow attached to what was expendable. It would be like growing attached to a goat's kid vowed to the sacrifice. Yet when she looked at Asterius's sleeping face, or watched his lean, athletic walk as he crossed a room to greet her, she felt a stirring of something like the joy of hearing the first blackbird's song in spring, and how she would wish she could catch it and keep its rippling music for always.

Leto stirred in her lap, scampered round and round before nestling down again. She stroked the small head. Pasiphaë recognised the change in herself. She understood more of the mysteries. She understood her King too, that he was gentle, weak sometimes, ready to compromise, wriggle or prevaricate in order to keep as many people happy as possible. He was just a man, but that was enough.

She listened for his tread, knowing he would look for her on the terrace where oleanders grew. The marten curled on her lap squirmed again, unsettled by the storm in the air and by the malevolent presence of the Great Mother. She was not a friend of the animals, Kriti had made that quite clear when she had sneered at Pasiphaë's squeamishness about killing their young.

'Animals are born to die. If they die honouring the Great Mother, they die happy,' she had said. But Pasiphaë had watched enough young sheep and goats playing their wild games in the meadow to know that death was the last thing they wished for, not in anyone's honour.

She heard footsteps approaching through the gallery, a firm tread. It was Asterius. Her heart lifted, a blackbird rising with fluttering wings. She turned, a smile already on her lips. He looked tired, anxious. The smile died.

*

Asterius came from the Throne Room where he had been surprised to find Minos among the suppliants. Being Minos, the suppliants had all stepped back to give him precedence. He stood with his hands on his hips, his legs planted slightly apart, and Asterius was struck by his ability to make himself look bigger than he actually was. Like a toad, swelling up to intimidate enemies. Even the painted griffons by the door watched.

'I think we would all agree that the most important business today is the Summer Sacrifice. The magazines are all but empty. We can't afford another harvest as bad as last year's.'

Asterius flinched at the untruth and cast about for Eumedes, the regional superintendent. He wasn't surprised to find that Eumedes wasn't present.

'I think you'll find the reserves are healthy, Minos. There were no reports of a bad harvest last year. A bit of blight, some of the pea harvest failed, a few reports of milk fever in the ewes, some cases of foot rot. Nothing out of the ordinary.'

'You call that nothing? You know the cause – the Great Mother was dissatisfied with the sacrifice. Her son went hungry. It's time to show her proper respect and restore the tribute. Only noble blood is good enough, and who here is prepared to offer his own children for the sacrifice?' He looked about the room theatrically. No one met his eye. 'Bring back the tribute.'

Inia the Key-Bearer frowned. She disliked the idea as much as Asterius did. He cleared his throat. 'That has to be the decision of the High Priestess of the Sanctuary.'

Inia stepped forward and turned to face the assembled advisors. 'The tribute was ended years ago because our neighbours had reached the point of taking up arms to oppose it. The Great Mother has not given me any sign that she regrets the end of such sacrifices. She is a mother. She doesn't want war. Bring back the tribute, Minos, and that's what you'll get.'

A murmur of relief ran through the crowd and faces relaxed, but Asterius noticed that the voices openly expressing approval were women's. Many of the men still looked thoughtful, if not tight-lipped. Minos wouldn't dare defy the Key-Bearer, though, nor suggest that he knew better than she what the Great Mother wanted.

'You speak like a mother, Inia, and it's to your credit. But the Great Mother isn't the only consideration. Poteidan mutters, and the signs say he's angry. We ignore the wishes of the Earth-Shaker at our peril.' He looked directly at Asterius. 'You refused him his due after he had delivered your Princess safely, and you kept his white bull for yourself. His priests still hear the rumbling of discontent, you know. You'd be well advised to make amends.'

'Is that a threat, Minos?'

It was Inia who voiced Asterius's thought. He hesitated to provoke his stepson. Not in the Throne Room. Not before so many witnesses.

'Advice, Key-Bearer. To Asterius, not you.'

Asterius gritted his teeth to stop his anger bursting into confrontation. Minos had always been insolent, and insolence used to be frowned upon. Looking around the room, he saw that it was no longer the case. It was only then that he noticed a slight figure among the white-clad priestesses and the butterfly-bright women, a girl dressed in red. Kriti watched him with her large, dark eyes, and their expression reminded him of a sacrificial bull when it realises that death has come and ceases its struggling.

*

When the last of the suppliants had left the Throne Room, Asterius made his way to the terrace filled with oleanders to join Pasiphaë. He found solace in her presence, even if he disliked sharing his concerns with her. Something had grown between them that he was beginning to depend upon. She turned as he approached. Had she been listening out for him? He thought he had smiled, had intended to, but the lingering echoes of Minos's threats must have made it look more like a grimace.

'You look as though someone has been particularly difficult.'

Pasiphaë was rarely duped. He took a deep breath, stretched out his legs and poured himself a drink of honeyed water from the jug.

'Minos. He always uses the Summer Rites as an excuse for a fight. He came to the Throne Room to throw his weight about.'

'Demanding more blood sacrifices?'

'His usual false claim about poor harvests. The Great Mother's son is hungry, apparently.'

Pasiphaë winced. 'It's a barbaric practice, but it's part of your custom. What can you do about it?'

'Me? Nothing.' He hesitated. 'His complaint is that slave children aren't good enough, says it's the Great Mother's right to demand Princes and Princesses.'

'The tribute?'

'He won't get it. Unless a High Priestess demands it. The Key-Bearer won't. She told him so.'

Asterius would have ended the whole cult if he could, cut out the dark root of the Poppy Mistress. If he had asked Inia, she might have ordered it. But what if she didn't, or there was a revolt? Happiness was fragile. It hung by a thread, like the life of a bird. He wanted to taste it first, before Minos opened the gates of war.

'Your daughter asked me to assist at the rites tomorrow at the sanctuary. I said I would.'

His heart clenched. 'Why?'

'She came to the rites for the Mistresses and asked. I couldn't refuse.'

He didn't say that his daughter was drowning and nobody could save her, only perhaps hold her hand at the end. Pasiphaë must surely have seen the darkness that welled up in Kriti's eyes, the black veil that hung about her, the winding cloth preparing to envelop her. He clutched his wife's hand, tightened his fingers about hers. He didn't want to lose her to that darkness too.

'There's no need. The people won't notice which priestesses are present. They want to see a sacrifice, not listen to prayers. And the Great Mother won't care.'

She tried to object but he interrupted, forcing a smile.

'Don't think about it yet. Tomorrow is a day of festivities. There'll be bull-leaping. Three bulls and three teams of dancers.'

*

Asterius left Pasiphaë in the tree shade to find Eumedes – some question about the olive harvest, or the figs, she hadn't really been listening. She was thinking about what he had said, before. How could he, a man, know what the Great Mother thought about anything? He didn't, of course, but that didn't matter. So much of Knossos revolved around perception, what suited, but most of all, entertainment. He was probably right about that. Even the most ancient cult of all was no more than a bloody spectacle, emptied of all religious significance.

His smile had lingered, searching her face for a sign that she had agreed not to get involved in the Great Mother and her mysteries. Not even if Kriti was submerged in it. Drowning. As usual, he had gone, putting off the problem, hoping a few hours of laughter and excitement would give wings to worries, and afterwards, even the memory of them would have flown, leaving no shadow. She couldn't find it in herself to blame him.

8

The Great Mother

The stormy heaviness in the air had not dissipated with the night, and the bull-leaping did little to lift Pasiphaë's sense of oppression. When the dancers entered the Barley Court, she invoked the Mistresses, prayed for good-tempered bulls, for the swiftness of the dancers' feet, but without looking into their faces. She had learned not to look too deeply into those eyes. Death swam in their depths, and the certainty that it would come for them before their youth was over.

The heaving crowd, the bright, swirling colours and excited chatter, the shouting, anger and the fighting when a thief was caught, made her head ache. The smells that trailed behind the vendors of sweetmeats peddling grease and honey, fried meat and sweet cakes turned her stomach. The Barley Court was vast, the movements of animal and dancers too quick for her eyes to follow with comfort. Hundreds watched from the benches around the arena, and hundreds more watched from the openings in the walls that enclosed it.

She put a hand to her brow, closed her eyes, knowing that Asterius was watching. She knew that he was pouring her a cup of perfumed water. His concern was predictable, but it didn't make it less sincere. She opened her eyes and the cup was by her hand on the table.

'Drink. The sun's too hot, and the storm still threatens. Or would you rather leave?'

He would have accompanied her, had servants bring a litter to carry her back to the cool of the apartment, but she shook her head. 'It's only the sun. The headache will go.'

She sipped the water and smiled. It was enough for Asterius's good mood to return. He loved the bull-leaping as much as she did. But for Pasiphaë, the oppression didn't lift. In the concentration of noise and smells and colours, she picked out only mouths shouting, eyes avid for excitement. There was no heart. She placed her hands on her stomach, felt the child, though not physically. The movements were too faint, too deep to stir the skin, but she heard in her head the gentle swish of fishtail, of birdwing. Soon, a hand, fingers would reach out and touch her.

She looked over the heads, down into the court where the dancers taunted death, and hoped the Yellow Team and the girl, Lydia, would not be performing today. Would she be allowed to stay at her lover's bedside? Pasiphaë knew nothing of the etiquette of the bull court, not even the true status of the leapers. Were they slaves or free? Did they have rights? She knew they had no right to life, but then who did? She wrapped her arms around her belly, the swelling so slight it was still easy enough to enfold all of it.

*

When the second bull tired and the dance ended without bloodshed apart from superficial grazes, she got to her feet and placed a hand on Asterius's shoulder. 'I've had enough. The third bull might be the one.'

He knew what she meant, though the courtiers hanging over the wall of the court, throwing money and flowers at the leapers, wouldn't have understood. Even less those who had backed death. 'Shall I come with you?'

He asked because the people liked to see the royal couple. They were one of the reasons the bull-leaping was so popular.

For both to leave, and at such a time of festivity, would cloud the end of the entertainment in disappointment.

'One of us at least ought to stay, and Kriti always speaks the words of closing anyway.' She touched his cheek. 'Besides, there's no need.'

As she left the royal platform, a scream rang out – human, animal, bird? – lost in the clamour of the crowd, and her heart skipped a beat. Ananke, the black crow, appeared in stark relief among the other servants in their bird-grey garb. Pasiphaë felt her presence like the breath of a tomb.

*

The final day of the Summer Rites dawned to rolling drums of thunder. Pasiphaë would have loved to have stayed in bed and pleaded sickness, which was what the girl in Kolchis would have done, had done on many an occasion. In Kolchis there was always a good chance that no one would come to drag her out. Often, she wasn't even missed. In Knossos, no one would dispute the Queen's wish to be left to sleep. And that was exactly why she forced herself to get up. The Great Mother would draw half of the island to witness the sacrifice, and Pasiphaë, if she was ever to call herself Queen, couldn't ignore it.

She had lain awake in the night while Asterius slept the sleep of forgetfulness, struggling with the decision not of whether, but of how she was to appear. Should it be in all the pomp and circumstance of the High Priestess of the Mistresses, as the Moon Princess, or sober and effacing, like a powerful mourner at a royal funeral?

Perseis and Circe wouldn't have thought twice. They would have made sure that no one shone with a greater brilliance, certainly not a child priestess they had decided was stamped with the sign of death. They would have been brilliant, embracing the cult of the Mother. They would have made sure it didn't lose its place in the world of bronze shields and bristling warships. Perhaps if Circe had married Asterius and become Queen at Knossos, she could have sorted out the different Mistresses and kept all their mysteries, each in its own darkness, like the house snake in the dust beneath the hearth. But Pasiphaë wasn't Circe.

'White, Eritha, simple linen, and moonstones. My face too. Theron's pendant is the only jewel I will wear.'

She wore perfumes from Kolchis and sandals with red leather straps. Her dress covered her shoulders and breasts, and over it she wore an ample cloak of Kolchian wool flecked with gold dust, fine and cool, but comfort enough for the dark morning the sky announced. She arranged a fold of it over her hair. She had tried to wrap herself in memories, the familiar, a protection against the unformed dread that squirmed deep down. Yet when she looked in the silver mirror, the face that looked out of it was as lifeless as the polished metal. She might have been the Queen of the Dead.

*

All of the priestesses dedicated to the Mistresses accompanied her, and behind them the serving women for the Queen's personal needs. She clung to the comforting sound of their voices, which almost defeated the twittering of the nascent storm. By the time her litter reached the top of the sacred road, an immense crowd had gathered on the slopes of Mount Iouktas. The sky heaved with billows of grey cloud that piled over the sun's face, sending great pools of shadow like spreading stains across the tired, dusty slopes. Pasiphaë heard the restless voice of the sea in the distance, the breathless murmuring of the people.

She stepped down from her litter and entered the sanctuary in the blinding glitter of precious metals caught in stray beams of sunlight, in the nodding of headdresses. Towering above her head was the bronze statue of the Great Mother, polished like gold, and clad in bell-shaped skirts of poppy red. The Great Mother held up her arms, palms outwards, but Pasiphaë saw no blessing in the gesture, only a warning and a command.

The sanctuary entrance was insignificant, and the sanctuary itself no more imposing that any mountain shrine, a collection of stone buildings, houses for priestesses, guardians, a pen for livestock. Tyro and Arete chatted, their voices an untroubled babble.

'Reminds me of my Auntie Althaea's place. Without the pigs.'

'How d'you know there's no pigs? I can hear summat squealing in one o' those sheds.'

Pasiphaë heard their light laughter, but she listened to something else, and the unease she carried with her wriggled, made its presence felt. They were right, it was more like a farm than a temple. Like all sanctuaries, there was a bathing room for purifications, animal pens, the dwellings of the sanctuary priestess and their servants, storerooms and cellars, but the Mount Iouktas sanctuary sprawled. There were other buildings whose function she couldn't guess, buildings without windows that vibrated with sound.

She led her women away from the windowless sheds and through the shadowy gallery, with its ancient, murky wall painting and the muffled whispers of their footsteps. The gallery opened onto an enclosed court. Above, she saw only sky and the terrible statue of the Great Mother, red-skirted and poppy-wreathed.

Pasiphaë took up her place with her priestesses behind the altar and to one side. Although she wouldn't participate in the rites, the court would see that she respected their traditions, and Kriti would see that she had kept her word. The High Priestess of the Poppy Mistress already stood, immobile, before the altar and despite the diadem and the elaborate piled tresses of her hair, she was still only a girl.

Kriti faced the Great Mother, her back to the seething slopes of Mount Iouktas, but her eyes flickered when

Pasiphaë took up her place. Her head turned a fraction, enough for Pasiphaë to see the wild light in them, like a bird trapped by a predator. She smiled quickly, a mere signal of friendship, and saw it reflected in Kriti's eyes. The wild light softened, but the fear remained. Pasiphaë felt it herself in the brooding light, the red skirts of the effigy, the dark mouths of the windowless huts.

The court had filled with the usual bright colours and chirping of palace noblewomen, and behind, in the space reserved for them, their noble menfolk. As usual, there was excited talk, some voices raised higher than others, then the tympana began to beat, a soft, slow rhythm, a heartbeat, and the murmuring voices fell silent. Only then did Pasiphaë hear the bursts of giggling, rapidly hushed, from inside the sanctuary, Tyro's squealing. Not of pigs though, but the sleepy voices, too loud, of children being put to bed. Put to bed or sent to sleep. Her heart froze, a cold stone, and she clutched her cloak about her, pulled it lower over her brow.

She took no notice of the Great Mother's pantomime, the syringe and auloi that joined with the louder beating of the tympana. She cut out the high, shrill voice of Kriti, the child High Priestess and the lower, older voices of the others. The chanted prayers meant nothing to her. The statue was just a statue, and the Great Mother was buried at the earth's core long since.

Her head beat to the rhythm though, and she raised a hand. Eritha was there in an instant with a cup of water and the powdered plants that dulled the pain. She drank, but the bursts of childish laughter, like martens scampering across a sunlit glade, rang and rippled inside unabated.

She felt the short procession before she saw it. Filing out of one of the windowless buildings, five children stumbled, blinking in the sudden light, with the sweet crumbs of their last extravagant meal still on their lips. They smiled, bellies full for the first time in their short lives, clothed in clean linen, the dirt of slavery scrubbed from them, leaving their skin tender and pink. She looked away. There had been no need to bind them. Even goats had to be led on a halter.

The rhythm of the music picked up, and the sickly scent of incense made her clench her jaw against the nausea. A priestess took the hand of the first child, a girl of four, five years perhaps, and led her to the altar. With a smile, the woman bound the child's hands and ankles with red cords. The girl stirred out of her poppy-induced somnolence, looked about wildly, opened her mouth. A red band of linen choked back the cry, and the child was lifted onto the altar, curled up with her knees up to her chin.

Pasiphaë closed her eyes as the ritual spear was raised, heard only the yelling of the music and the chanting of sixty priestesses, the pounding of the thousands of feet, and hands clapping rhythmically. But she imagined the blade driving into the fragile flesh, the gouts of blood pumping quicker than the beat, then slower, until all had flowed away. She had seen it often enough, the sacrificial animals, their final struggle when they realised, then the hopeless resignation, the blood spurting then failing. Death succeeded death. She didn't count them, didn't open her eyes until the roar of appreciation from the hillside told her it was over. But the worst of the horror was to come.

Kriti was washing in clean water, her arms bloody to the elbows, but against the poppy of her skirts no stains showed, only a darkness, a shadow of death. A priestess stood over the altar where the last of the victims lay still. In her hand flashed a knife such as butchers use. Pasiphaë saw the bared thigh, the skin aglow with the child's only bath, the arc of the blade, slicing through flesh, slicing again, and lifting the dripping sliver of flesh over the brazier.

Pasiphaë's shoulders heaved and Eritha was at her side without having to be called, holding her over the basin, stroking her brow and murmuring sounds full of grief. She put herself between her mistress and the altar so she wouldn't see when the High Priestess lifted the flesh to her red mouth, still pink and bloody. But she heard the sky break with the roar of the Mistresses, fiercer than any lion.

*

Kriti let her arms fall back to her side. She scarcely felt them. They were as numb as the inside of her head. Blood swelled and rolled in through her eye sockets, filling the space behind, but on the swell, drifting away in a white ship, she saw Pasiphaë. If only she could have commanded her feet to move, her tongue to call out, *wait,* she would have followed. But the red skirts clung wet as a butcher's apron and the smooth wood of the spear shaft had burned a red scar into the palm of her hand.

The people roared like the sea, approving, and that should have been all that mattered. The Great Mother had received her offering and perhaps her anger had been diverted. But when she raised her eyes to the bronze face with her bronze locks and fading poppy-flower headdress, she saw implacable, immutable indifference. The Great Mother was a well with no bottom. No matter how much blood was poured into her mouth she would never be sated. Kriti didn't believe she had a son. She didn't believe she was a mother. She didn't believe.

She followed Pasiphaë with eyes full of blood. Would the Moon Princess be a mother? Perhaps she could be a sister. Kriti longed for arms to hold her and smooth her hair, her cheeks where the tears streamed. If only she had had a mother. If only fathers mattered. The only one who Kriti mattered to was Minos, and that was why, when she was allowed to leave the stage, she would chew the poppy gum until darkness fell.

*

Pasiphaë remembered nothing of the return. All was darkness, and darker spots like evil swallows darted across the darkness of her vision. Her nostrils were full of the stink of blood and vomit, even after the women had stripped and bathed her, washed her hair and had her clothes taken away to be burned. They bustled about her, their voices low, exchanges brief. Semele's round face hung before her eyes, an expression of infinite sadness in their gentle depths. Mothers and their enduring sorrow. Pasiphaë wondered how she had lost her children. She had never asked. She closed her eyes tight to stop the tears leaking out.

The day clung to her like a curse. She couldn't pretend she hadn't known what would happen. She knew that slave children would be sacrificed, and she knew that a sacrifice involved killing a living thing that didn't want to die. She couldn't pretend that the horror had taken her unawares. That was what made her sickest of all.

Asterius had been present. All the nobles had turned out for the ceremony. *The people of Crete love to celebrate.* When he came to her, she wouldn't see him until he too had washed and changed his clothes.

'You shouldn't have gone,' was all he said, as if he didn't know why she had to show herself unafraid. She didn't reply.

Later, in his arms, she understood his concern. Her passing malaise was more important to him than any compassion he might have felt for the victims. He held her close, playing her naked flesh with caresses that never failed to make her rise and swell beneath his practised fingers. Pleasure caught her and swept her away in fierce talons, and the blood that ran behind her eyes, the torn flesh, was her own, the time of an embrace. Afterwards, she let him wipe away her tears.

9

Winter

The year turned. After the harvests, there were a few brief weeks of languid summer, and then the storms began in earnest. They had come earlier than usual, the servants said, those whose families lived on the hills, farmers and farmworkers. Tyro and Arete had got friendly with a couple of farmers and reported that the rain had blighted a lot of the grain. There was sickness among the sheep too, they said. Pasiphaë made libations to the Mistresses for the calming of the elements and to drive away the bad luck from the flocks, but whatever she did, no one noticed. Not much was expected of the Mistresses at all, except perhaps at lambing time and the first milk.

At Knossos, business went on as usual. In the Throne Room there were always disputes to settle and new laws to test. Pasiphaë had decided that Kriti should be present, but her blank expression never showed a flicker of interest. Mostly, though, the wheels turned without any oil either of them could add. Most of the business, the counting and taxing of produce, was dealt with by the men and women trained to look after it, and when Pasiphaë left, Kriti sat in the Queen's seat, looking even more like an articulated doll than ever.

Did Pasiphaë hope to leave the memories of death behind, to outwit them and return to her apartment alone? Perhaps, but the ghosts still followed her, and their laughter echoed louder than the whispering of Potnia Theron.

She walked the endless hallways alone, hugging herself and the one growing inside her. *The people must see you, know you, love you,* her mother had said. But no one looked, no one noticed. She missed Nephele, not only a girl of more or less her own age to talk to, but a friend who had reassured her that she had her place at Knossos. Once again, Pasiphaë noticed the sidelong glances, the faint flicker of lips into a smirk when she mispronounced a word. Sometimes she drew her thoughts together, raised her High Priestess face and made her expression say, *I am the voice of the Mistresses. I inspire fear and love. Nothing can devour me.* But often, when the child started to move and grow heavy, she felt only sick, graceless and feeble. And she was afraid. Knossos had so many dark corners but not the friendly dark of Aea. What lived in the dark of the palace was hostile, and it had the face of Kriti's nurse.

Pasiphaë spent hours checking the dried plants in her herbarium, touching, crushing, smelling. She knew them all, but could she be certain of every leaf? Would she smell the poison in a preparation? She threw out all the powders already prepared, keeping only leaves, berries and roots that she prepared herself. The herbs she chewed and the infusions she drank eased the vomiting and later the pulling of ligaments that held her bones together. Some of them cleared her thoughts, others clouded them more with bright gauzy light that made her take to the room with the big marital bed to find solace in its emptiness.

*

'There's mould in one of the granaries,' Asterius confided when she pressed him for the cause of his worried expression.

'I'll sacrifice to Potnia Athana. In Kolchis, she helps with the crops.'

He smiled his gratitude, but it was a strained smile. 'Minos is bellowing again, about the offerings at the Summer Rites. He claims the Great Mother wasn't satisfied. Her child, Dias, is still hungry.'

The memory was bitter, a dark veil of suffering.

'Yet he ate well enough. You should send Minos away. He drove his brothers away, so surely you have the right.'

She didn't say, *I have the right.* She was the Queen only in name.

'As far as Minos and his followers are concerned, *the right* is with the strongest.'

'And you daren't provoke them.'

It wasn't said in reproach, and although Asterius clenched his jaw, his anger was directed at Minos. 'The Greeks are watching for us to start fighting amongst ourselves, and Minos is only too willing to offer them the spectacle.'

So Minos stayed, shouting about weakness, beating his shield in a warlike manner. When he finally left for Thera to supervise the saffron harvest, his arguments remained. When Pasiphaë listened, she heard the voices that agreed, and not just the traders and landowners who looked to their personal commercial gain. The ordinary people too. They were the ones who starved first if there was a poor harvest or the mice got into the granaries. They agreed that the Great Mother demanded princely blood, that Dias was thin on the poor blood of slaves. They muttered about the tribute.

*

She walked the palace alone because Asterius could hardly have insisted she have an escort in her own house. It was vast, but she was still its mistress. She walked without an escort, not even Athamas. What good was the company of a man to a woman with child? Often, she would see the flutter of a girlish form, a timid bird, in a doorway or she would hear the patter of her steps in the gallery behind. She never looked. Never turned her head. She hurried faster, and the fluttering would fade, die. A girl, a child was calling to her, silent as poppies in the wind, but she couldn't bear to listen. Kriti was lost. Perhaps they all were.

PART FOUR

The second star

Asterion began the way all infants begin, in the belly of his mother Pasiphaë, the Moon Princess of Kolchis. His entry into the world was in the spring, when the winter, the long winter of Pasiphaë's confinement, finally ended in the bursting of snowdrops, hyacinths and narcissi. If Asterius was the first star the Mistresses gave her, Asterion was the second, the brightest in her firmament.

1

Asterion

The Barley Court would close for bull-leaping when the first frosts arrived, but Pasiphaë had already grown reluctant to attend. The thought of the growing child, her apprehension about the birth, perhaps, made the excitement, the noise, and the possibility of bloodshed hard to bear. Asterius had been so crestfallen, though, when she told him, that she had relented. For once, the dance was to be dedicated to Potnia Athana.

'To ask that the winter be not too harsh,' he'd said. 'There's already frost on the hills.'

She had agreed, but when she learned the Yellow Team was to be the first out, she almost turned back. There was a bite in the air, a crispness, and the sky was high and clear. Clear except for a flock of crows flapping over the stubbled fields. She shivered and called for a heavier cloak.

There was an anxious atmosphere in the Barley Court. The first bull had broken a horn and had to be taken out. The second one charged in before the last of the boys sanding the pavement had scampered to safety. There was a second hold-up while the court was cleaned again. The crowd muttered, seeing bad omens for their bets. Some punters wanted money back, fights broke out, brawlers were ejected.

Anxiety ran through the leapers too. They snapped at one another, shouted abuse. Lydia danced close to Turios, running out to tease the bull when he looked their way. Pasiphaë saw at once what she was doing. Like a skylark drawing a fox away from her nest, she feinted before the bull, drawing him away from her lover. *He's not fast enough. The old wound has left him with a lag in his left leg. He's going to die.* She wondered what would happen if she stood up and announced the end of the session.

'Why did they let him dance? His wound hampers him.'

The expression in Asterius's eyes told her that he had seen the boy's death too, but there was nothing to be done. 'It's the rule. The whole team must dance.'

The Yellow Team's best leaper shouted something, his face tight with anger. He had spent more time on the bull's back than the rest of them put together. He was tiring. Lydia taunted the bull and dodged away, but the bull's eye had been caught by a closer, slower movement, Turios stumbling. He never caught his step, never had time. The bull hoisted him into the air then shook his head furiously to get rid of the burden.

The boy was still alive when he hit the ground. The team drew off the bull, and Lydia ran to him. The dance went on, but Lydia stood over the twitching body, refusing to move. The bull swung his head about, snorting, his eyes fixed on the girl, and the team danced, shouting at Lydia to get away. She was deaf, and blinded by tears. The bull prepared a charge.

'Stop this! Guards, clear the bull court!' Pasiphaë shouted at the spearmen surrounding the royal dais. They leapt into the arena as the bull-leapers scattered, and encircled the bull that was casting about in confusion. Prodding him with their spears, they got him to turn around, and a final slap on the rump sent him galloping for the tunnel entrance. Pasiphaë watched as Turios was carried out of the arena and the sand boys returned. From the size of the pool of blood, she knew there was little point offering her help.

The next morning, Lydia was found in the bull-leapers' shrine, lying in the lustral basin. Her loosened hair floated about her face, white as a winding sheet. The water was the colour of poppies.

*

Pasiphaë hadn't returned to the bull-leaping. She had left the court with the usual fights breaking out as punters demanded to be given back their bets, amid the mutterings of discontent at the cutting short of the entertainment. From the corner of her eye, she had glimpsed Kriti with her red diadem, standing at the edge of the dais, looking down on the bloody sand, like a widow staring into the raging storm waves after a shipwreck.

Only fury and distress had prevented her noticing the black looks that followed her out. She prayed to the Mistresses, but they sent no sign that their anger had abated. Few faces now showed any warmth or friendship. All seemed to smirk with the smug self-satisfied expressions of the followers of Minos. Winter lay ahead then, and its darkness was already tainted with blood and anger.

*

She spent more time in the Throne Room, flaunting her swollen belly, swollen with promise. She wore the diadem of Potnia Theron and defied the people to deny her authority and status. Asterius would sit at her side, and Kriti would take over when she grew tired, exasperated, or simply bored. So many of the complaints seemed petty, mean, and ought to have been sorted out using simple common sense. She forced herself to accept Kriti's presence. It was her duty, her right, though Pasiphaë was beginning to feel it as bitter provocation. The images of the Summer Rites still haunted her, but so did Kriti's face and the hopeless pleading in her eyes. None of it was her fault – the blood, the thick, seething movement that Minos stirred.

'Kriti should be asked to give a judgement,' she said to

Asterius. 'She watches, but she never speaks. What use is a Queen with no judgement?'

'She is High Priestess. Isn't that enough?'

It wasn't and he knew it, but Pasiphaë understood that Asterius saw responsibility as a burden, and his daughter as too weak to bear it. He saw the darkness, the suffocation of the religious rites as already too much for her slender strength. She replied quietly, gently. Offering him the sweet poppy of hope. 'When she is Queen, the Key-Bearer can take over those duties. She must learn to rule.'

In the Throne Room, Kriti sat at Pasiphaë's side, expressionless and immobile. She never asked a question or ventured an opinion. Afterwards, if Pasiphaë asked what she thought of a particular judgement, she would purse her lips and give a slight shrug.

'The Mother sends the answers to these questions. There is no *opinion,* only what the Mother demands.'

Pasiphaë had been taught that the Mistresses sent signs for the lawgiver to interpret, listening to her inner voice. Perhaps Kriti heard nothing when she stared, stone-faced, into the middle distance, only the beating of the great heart of the earth. Pasiphaë feared she heard not even that, only her life-pulse, throbbing to its end.

The closer her time came, the harder Pasiphaë found it to concentrate on boundary disputes, blight and dog bites, cracked amphorae, cracked ribs, lost sheep. The suppliants looked at her strangely, with apprehension. Asterius tried to convince her to stay in the royal apartments.

'There's no need for you to tire yourself. Anyone can sort out these disputes. I'll send for you if ever something important comes before the court.'

She clung to her duty, as she clung to the armrests of her chair. *The people must see you, know you, love you.* The truth was, she was afraid. She was as afraid to turn her back on the courtiers and nobles as the bull-leapers were to take their eyes off the bull, and for the same reason.

*

Spring came to Knossos while the north wind still blew through the stones of Mount Iouktas. The air was bright and sharp in the mornings. The rains were over and the red clay shone, washed clean. The pains that gripped Pasiphaë's belly like an iron band tightening, keeping her to her bed, came more frequently. Eritha examined her; small, deft fingers probing the passage, measuring, estimating.

One morning, a blackbird sang on a rooftop outside the bedroom. The iron belly-bands tightened as the music rose, and the Mistresses told Pasiphaë, in the words of the song, that the child was ready.

The blackbird sang for the first hours of the morning, and he sang again at the end of the afternoon to the setting sun, and the rising of the star that she carried. Eritha wiped away the beads of sweat, sang soft, nonsensical words to calm her wild breathing and rubbed her belly with diktamo oil to ease the pain. Eune let Eritha give the orders and chivvied the others, bringing more warm cloths, changing basins of water. In an efficient silence they rinsed and washed, sprinkling scented oils to chase away any mischief-making spirits. Doors and windows were open to loosen all the bonds that tied child to mother.

'Holy Mother, can it get any worse?' she gasped. Pain cut off the words and her features crumpled. She panted, hoarse as a thirsty dog, for the long seconds of the contraction.

'Hush, I can feel the head. It won't be long. Breathe, think of the end of the tunnel, the light. You're almost there. Reach out, push out to reach it.'

Pasiphaë was too weary to scream aloud, but she screamed in her head. The pain that tore at her flesh was like a bull butting at a gate. She screamed and saw horns – long, curved – and she bellowed with a cow's tongue. Whatever Eritha was murmuring she couldn't hear over the river-thunder in her head, the roaring of a high wind whipping waves higher than palaces.

Something gave way, something physical, like a tearing. She arched her back, tried to clutch at the talisman around her neck, but her hands wouldn't loosen their grip on the arms of the birthing chair. She gritted her teeth, but the scream, the bellow, found its way out again, again and again. Eritha was saying something in an excited voice, *the head, the head is out,* but the pain didn't stop. It was supposed to stop, the head was the hardest part, they said, *so why is there pain still?* The iron band tightened, tighter and tighter, until she thought it would crush her bones.

Shoulders, shoulders, almost, almost.

The servant's voice came from far away. It didn't matter what she said. Only the pain mattered and the fear that death was waiting. Then, through the red fog, as the cold face of Asasara bent over her, the bellow became a roar of triumph, the tide rushed out and left her, sweeping with it all the pain and even the memory of pain.

'It's here!'

Eritha's voice, the rising tide of the women's crows of triumph, fell into the bliss of no pain, such bliss she just wanted to weep. Eritha held the newborn thing close to Pasiphaë's face, so she could see, before the smeary fruit of her belly was laid on her breast. The child was red and crumpled, covered in blood and birth, muck. A boy. He turned his head slowly, mouth open, not to wail or protest, eyes gummed and narrow, thick black hair. He turned to her, opened his long, murky eyes and smiled. Babies don't smile, she knew that, but her son did, and for that alone, Pasiphaë was joined to him forever.

*

She knew as soon as she saw him the name she would give the child who was a gift of the sky and the sea, the child of the Moon and the Bull. He was fit to light any night, to share the dark sky with any constellation. He reflected what she was learning to feel for his father, but brighter, sharper, like the brilliance of a star.

Asterius was at her side as soon as he heard the shouts of joy. His eyes glittered with pride and emotion as he cut the birth cord. She placed her hand in his, sticky with birth.

'I would like him to have a name like yours. Asterion, my second star.'

He kissed her brow. 'And mine.'

She would always be his first. Perhaps the knowledge came because of the peace that falls after a birth, the relief and fierce happiness that washes away the anguish that preceded it. She looked at her husband's face, the black brows and dark eyes, the lines just beginning to form at the side of the mouth, running into his beard, the lines reaching out from the corners of his eyes that broke up the contours of his face into ripples. She touched his cheek to make him smile and set the ripples in motion. Asterius would never be a warrior. He saw the details, the beating heart. The abstracts of glory and fame, power even, were beyond the line of his vision. And she was glad.

'He's strong, Eritha says. He'll live.'

*

In those first weeks, that was all that seemed to matter. It was only later, when the crumples of his baby face smoothed out, the blotches and blemishes faded, when the black birth hair fell out and new, dark brown hair curled in its place, that anyone noticed that Asterion was not exactly like other babies. His eyes were set too far apart – long, slanting eyes – and his ears were unusually small; his nose, too, was short and broad, the bridge too shallow. And the toes of his feet, his tiny baby feet, parted in an odd way, almost like cloven hooves. Asterius tickled the toes that wouldn't lie straight.

'Whatever he's destined for, it's not to turn heads with his beauty.'

Pasiphaë didn't care. Asterion smiled, and that was infinitely more important than good looks.

*

The news of the Queen's baby was received with joy among the ordinary people, who rejoiced whenever a child was born safely and in good health, and among Asterius's followers. Pasiphaë's disappointment that a difficult pregnancy prevented Nephele making the journey to Knossos was softened by the arrival of Kerameia with her husband, son and a younger daughter, bringing goodwill and gifts. The boy, Kesandros, was courteous, and laughed when Asterion blew bubbles at him. Pasiphaë felt that happiness was tipping the balance in its favour.

*

Kriti learned of the birth of her half-brother with a feeling of apprehension. For the child, she had only curiosity, but she had a longing to be part of a family circle, to be just Kriti, to escape the Poppy Mistress and her exactions. She went to the palace artisans, to the metalworkers, the jewellers and potters, and she found what she wanted in a carpenter's workshop. Among the chairs and tables being turned and decorated, and the more humdrum jobs of repairing platforms and public seating in the Barley Court, an apprentice was whittling at a discarded piece of fruit wood.

*

She took her gift to the royal apartment. On the sill, she hesitated. The murmur of voices, quiet laughter, came from within. Her fingers twisted around the wooden figure she carried, timidity almost stronger than the yearning to join the untroubled people with only gentle thoughts, to be accepted into their affections. Gathering up her courage, she opened the door so carefully the voices didn't pause and no heads turned. Only Pasiphaë, facing the door, noticed and her face broke into a wide smile.

The others turned and made way for her: soft-spoken Antanor, Kerameia, a matronly presence with a cloud of auburn hair, and Kesandros. She caught her breath. Although she would dine with him and his family later, her eyes devoured him, the one Asterius had promised her, the one she prayed the Mistresses would accord her as her King. Kesandros was a flame; he drew her like a moth, and although she might perish if she got too close, she couldn't stay away. She lowered her eyes, terrified he would see the fire in them and despise her for it.

'I'm pleased you're here, Kriti.' Pasiphaë's voice was warm, affectionate even, unless it was love for her baby bubbling over. 'Come and look. Asterion's sleeping.'

Kriti crept closer to the cradle and Pasiphaë pulled back the woollen blanket. It was true, she thought, he was not what you'd call a bonny baby. But if he lived and grew strong, what mother ever asked for more? In the hush, as the others watched for her reaction, Kriti heard the baby's breathing, almost like snoring.

'Like a little bull,' she said, suddenly smiling. 'I've brought something for him, for when he's a bit older.'

She handed the carved bull to Asterius, who admired the workmanship. 'You found a good craftsman. I hope you know his name, so I can show him my gratitude.'

It was so like her father to want everyone to be happy, even the grubby apprentice lad who whittled in a corner of a palace workshop. She wanted to weep. It was happiness, or at least the idea of it, that welled, too strong to be held back.

'I would have loved a toy like that when I was a child.'

The voice of Kesandros, so little heard and so often

dreamed about, was too much. She turned her face and wiped away the tears. But not before Kerameia had seen, and her rather stern features softened into pity. Pity. Kriti's ephemeral happiness fluttered away on black wings. All she wanted was for someone to take her hands and say, *Stay. Be one of ours.* But all they offered was pity. With a sob, she fled from the room.

2

The presentation

These were the best days of the year, when the cold edge had definitively gone from the air, but the summer heat was still weeks away. The Mistresses sent flocks of swallows on the breeze, and Pasiphaë, too, felt as though she had wings. Asterion was strong and healthy. He rarely cried and slept peacefully for long periods. It was time for his mother to be purified after the bloodletting of the birth, and afterwards, to present her son to the people.

The day of the ceremony dawned dull. Grey clouds hurried in from the sea and the air was full of the squabbling of gulls. Asterion was fractious and difficult to feed.

'Colic,' Eritha said. She rubbed him with lemon balm and fennel oils and gave him a cloth dipped in an infusion of camomile to suck. 'Nothing to worry about.'

Pasiphaë tried not to, and Asterion seemed to calm a little, but whatever bad humour had taken him, it didn't leave so easily.

*

Only the priestesses of the Mistresses entered the shrine where Pasiphaë would be purified. They held her robes as she stepped into the basin, recited the prayers. The smell of oils, perfumed and heady, should have cleared her mind of darkness, as the perfumed water of the basin cleansed her body of the memory of birth pangs. Yet even after the priestesses had chanted the prayers to the Mistresses and Pasiphaë was dressed in her robes of Potnia Athana as Mother, white and red with a broad gold belt, the sense of unease persisted. She wondered if a storm was brewing.

Pasiphaë had listened so often in this shrine for the voices of the Mistresses and heard nothing. The day of Asterion's presentation was no different. Their silence was louder than the growling of the storm rolling in from the sea. *Nothing to worry about.* But there was. She saw it in the faces that stared without warmth as she walked with Asterius and the baby between the feathered helmets and swinging arms of their escort. Not hostile, but she suspected the right inflammatory words would fan what she felt smouldering beneath the surface.

The procession to the Great Shrine in the Court of Ceremonies seemed to take forever, the painted gallery to stretch into infinity. The freshening wind lifted the egret plumes of Athamas's casque, the wings of the storm. Asterius walked at her side, practised in keeping all emotion from his features. She had no idea if he heard the signs too, felt the storm though the soles of his feet. Pasiphaë turned when Asterion whimpered, and she saw that Eritha had heard. Her face strained as the bundle in her arms shifted and the child moved his head fretfully from side to side. The storm began to sing.

The Gallery of Processions finally came to an end, and they stepped out beneath the lowering sky. Pasiphaë's spirits shrank. The noise of hundreds of voices, curious and excited, rose from the other side of the walls of the courtyard. The Court of Ceremonies would be packed with the wealth of Knossos and beyond; filling the Barley Court and perched on walls and rooftops, the people would be there like a flock of curious starlings.

The Great Mother's priestesses were already waiting,

surrounding Inia the Key-Bearer. Next to her stood Kriti, small and slender, her hair wreathed in red. Lining the court, filling it with bright movement to make up for the lack of sunlight, were the wealthy and important: governors, landowners, merchants. The unease that murmured in Pasiphaë's ear grew to a wailing warning. Snakes uncoiled in her stomach and the black darts of evil spirits flocked before her eyes.

In a fog, she released ten white doves for Asterion. In a fog, she made the libations of water and wine, honey to sweeten the Mistresses and make them look kindly on her son and grant him continuing health and strength. All about her, like the brittle grating of insects, was the glitter and rustling of rich fabrics. The ritual murmuring of the priestesses rose louder as she took Asterion in her arms, but louder was the sound of the multitude gathered out of sight, and it was like a heaving ocean.

Pasiphaë tried hard to make the prayers she chanted, that the assembled priestesses of the Mistresses and the Great Mother repeated, a paeon of happiness for her son. Almost, she succeeded in conjuring joy and pride out of unease. Almost, she could see the sun gleaming behind the low cloud that threatened rain. Almost, the wind, too, was singing Asterion's praises. But the spell broke and the gleam died.

Kriti stepped forward from among her priestesses and approached the altar with her wreath of fierce red flowers, the dark around her eyes accentuating the pallor of her skin. In her arms she carried a newborn kid.

'May your son be as mighty as the Great Mother's.'

Pasiphaë froze as Kriti placed the kid on the altar. The knife in her hand winked before it slit the tiny throat. A faint bleat was drowned in the pulsing of blood. Pasiphaë felt sick and Asterion hiccoughed, his face creasing as he prepared to cry. Kriti turned to face her, eyes blank, the knife still in her right hand, both hands as red as her dress. In a movement, too quick to anticipate, her left hand reached out and, with her thumb, she traced a bloody mark on Asterion's brow.

'The son belongs to the Mother.'

Pasiphaë snatched her child away from the bone-pale face and the bloody fingers with a sharp cry of anger. She heard the swift intake of breath from the crowd then forgot about them again as Asterion let out a piercing wail of distress, and his body heaved and jerked in convulsions.

She wiped away the bloody mark with her hand and washed the place with clean water. The murmuring of the crowd ceased, and an uneasy silence fell. Kriti watched impassively, as a goddess would watch the acting out of a punishment, while Pasiphaë clutched the child to her breast, trying to still the flailing of his limbs. But he wouldn't be calmed. His face turned red, his little body shuddered, his chest arched, and spittle foamed on his lips.

Eritha slipped from her place in the obscurity of the shrine's storeroom where the servants waited. 'Let me take him.'

Pasiphaë, too terrified to object, handed her the baby and watched as she turned away so the crowd wouldn't see how she held him with his head down, and wiped away the saliva that welled and gurgled in his mouth. So they wouldn't see the stain seeping through the white wool shawl, nor smell the loosened bowels.

'Should I take him back? I've seen this before. I know what to give him.'

Pasiphaë nodded. 'Hurry.'

The mask that was Kriti's face opened and spoke. 'He hasn't been presented. The people must see him first. They're waiting.'

Pasiphaë was aghast. Was she not aware of what had happened? 'Then they must wait.'

Without looking at Kriti again, she led the priestesses in the spring song that ended the ceremony. The strumming of kitharai wove in and out of the fluting of auloi. The musicians in the Barley Court picked up the tune and music drifted over the wall. Dancers entered, plumed and splendid, to dance across the labyrinth. All eyes would be fixed on the raised dais where the royal couple and their son were expected to appear, but would not. Rain spotted the bright pavement. Dark stains.

Pasiphaë laid her hand on Asterius's arm and led the procession away from the bloody altar and into the comforting emptiness of the painted gallery. Along the wall at the back of the Barley Court, boys were perched, peering across the roof of the shrine. It was they who called out the news that the ceremony was over and the royal couple had disappeared. There would be no presentation.

The ripples of disappointment turned to anger, but Pasiphaë heard nothing. By then, she was far away, in the Queen's Dolphin Chamber, watching anxiously as Eritha prepared a potion for her baby.

*

Kriti was oblivious to the noise, oblivious to the breaking storm, the cold rain. She stared after the retreating royal cortège, seeing nothing. Before the ceremony, Ananke had given her poppy to drink to *calm her fears*. When Kriti felt *calmer*, Ananke had told her what she must do to dedicate the child to the Great Mother. Kriti never dared oppose Ananke, never even asked for a reason. Ananke was the eyes and ears of Minos, and Kriti feared Minos more than she feared anything else in the world.

3

Minos returns

The storm of the presentation ceremony signalled a change in the weather. The spring turned cold and windy, summer came late, and the crops were slow ripening. There were fewer lambs than usual, or so the farmers claimed, and the wolves were more daring. Pasiphaë was untroubled by such minor considerations. The palace granaries were full, and there was no want that she could see. Her concerns were with Asterion, who was growing steadily but suffered constantly from snuffles and colds. He often seemed to choke, unable to clear his nose, and she watched him like a hawk, fearful of a repetition of the fit that had taken him at the presentation ceremony.

'He might still get the convulsions,' Eritha said. 'Some children do, but the herbs that I give him will help.'

Every day Eritha had him drink a tiny quantity of hellweed and nettle infusions. Later, when he was able to eat solid foods, she added black cumin oil and the crushed seeds and gum of the balsam tree mixed with a quantity of honey. She had bound his feet to get the toes to grow straight but pronounced his limbs strong enough. Pasiphaë persuaded herself that he would walk when the time came. He had no more convulsions, and she tried not to worry.

She took up her duties in the Throne Room again, trying to recapture the serenity she had felt in the first days after

Asterion's birth. But it was elusive. Something, like a bright bird flashing out of her line of vision, distracted her. Kriti began to speak at the judgements, then to offer judgements of her own. Pasiphaë let her, pleased to retreat, though her mother's words of advice echoed like a warning now, *They must see you, know you, love you.*

Something had changed in the rhythm of her thoughts. She heard the whisperings of the Mistresses only faintly. Always to the fore, louder than any other sound, were the slow, formless babblings of her son. She listened for him all through the night, giving him the breast before he was fully wakened, falling asleep with him snuggled beside her. She felt all that was mysterious and sacred in her role slipping away beneath the weight of his mortal demands. That in itself was a sign, and she feared its consequences.

*

Minos had been away from Knossos since the previous autumn, but the summer brought him back in a clatter of chariots, spears and a train of followers. He had spent October on Thera to keep an eye on the saffron harvest, and the winter keeping an eye on his family. Not that his brothers gave him much trouble. Sarpedon had no ambition and was happy to receive the occasional gifts Minos gave him, of olive groves, sheep or hunting dogs to keep him away from Knossos. Rhadamanthus had gone. To Libya, Sarpedon said, reckoning the Libyans easier to fight for a throne than his brother.

He had heard that Asterius's wife had given birth, and that it was a son. But the child wasn't normal, they said. He was curious to see him, but what had brought him back to Knossos sooner than he had intended was the news that his eldest son Androgeos had had an accident. Broken his leg in a fall. Idyia, the boy's mother, had said the five-year-old had been taunting a bull. He had, in fact, fallen out of a tree when he disturbed a bees' nest, but she knew Minos would prefer a more valorous version of events.

A broken leg, if badly set, could maim the boy for life. Only when he was too far away to help, too late to do any good supposing the surgeon had done a bad job, did Minos realise how much he cared for Androgeos. It was not just pride, but a profound affection that at times made him consider marrying Idyia and legitimating him. Androgeos was headstrong, and at five years old was already showing the determination to be the best, the fastest, the bravest, which would be his downfall. Minos confused arrogance with courage and pointed with pride to the way his son was always at the head of the pack. Androgeos was a natural leader, he told himself and everyone else. If he knew that no other boy was allowed to beat Androgeos because of who his father was, Minos pretended he didn't.

Before leaving his house at Phaistos, Minos had offered a bull to his father Zeus for the boy's safekeeping. On arriving at Knossos, and finding that the bone was not actually broken, he had offered another at the Great Shrine. Overwhelmed by relief that Androgeos would soon be running about again, Minos had been uncharacteristically generous with gifts for the children of his other concubine. In his excitement at his father's attention, red-headed Deukalion, the younger of Minos's three-year-old twins, tugged at his arm to get his attention.

'Papá! Papá! Did you see the bee stings?'

Minos slapped his head.

*

The thought of Deukalion, who Minos was beginning to believe was a cuckoo in the nest, had darkened his mood. It darkened even more when he found Pasiphaë seated next to Asterius in the Throne Room. He almost didn't notice Kriti, crouched on her stool, like a leveret hiding in the long grass, hoping the dog wouldn't see. The sight of her made his blood seethe. This creeping thing they pretended would be the next ruler, and not Androgeos, his bold, courageous boy. He nodded curtly to the throne and glared at the suppliants waiting with their business and their arguments.

'Princess Kriti, Lady Pasiphaë, Lord Asterius, there are urgent matters that need to be discussed.'

It was Pasiphaë who replied. 'At the end of this sitting, you may put them to us, Minos.'

She gave him one of her cool, insulting looks that he longed to wipe from her face with a well-placed slap. He placed his hands on his hips, flexing the muscles of his arms, and turned his most menacing expression on the men and women who were already fluttering anxiously, picking up their pieces of evidence, preparing to leave.

'It's not an idle whim that brings me here, Lady Pasiphaë, but duty. I'm just back from a tour of my properties, and I can tell you, the situation is much as it was last year. Catastrophic. Poor harvests and meagre flocks. The gods are angry, and it doesn't take much wit to guess why.'

Asterius gripped the arms of his chair, but as usual Pasiphaë yapped first. 'Your guess would be?'

Minos ignored her and addressed Asterius. 'The gods are angry. They must be appeased.'

Pasiphaë glared, her nostrils twitching in anger. He almost admired her persistence in defying him. 'Appeased for what? The proper sacrifices have been made.'

'Proper? In the name of the people, I demand that the Summer Rites be celebrated with *proper* respect this year. That means blood, either the blood of a King,' he looked pointedly at Asterius, 'or a King's child.'

'If it's only to spout obscenities, I forbid you to open your mouth in this Throne Room, Minos!'

'You forbid, Pasiphaë? As well as short-changing the Mother? She demands royal blood, not the watery blood of slaves. Bring back the tribute then.'

'Do you want to bring war to Crete, Minos?' Asterius's voice was as pale as his face.

'Who would dare? Our ships rule the Middle Sea and all the trade routes to the east through the Inhospitable Sea. No power can compare to the power of Crete.'

Pasiphaë refused to keep her mouth closed. 'If we demand the children of their noble families they will dare. And who would blame them? The tribute in children's flesh is over, Minos. There's no more to be said.'

'Oh, but there is.' Minos lowered his voice, stepped closer. He looked at Asterius. 'You have offended Poteidan by withholding his sacrifice of the white bull, and he has afflicted your crops and flocks with disease. He has afflicted you with a son who shouldn't have been allowed to live, and a wife with unnatural tastes. They say the Lady Pasiphaë's passion for the bull-leaping isn't just for the dancers—'

'Get out!'

Pasiphaë leaped to her feet, and Minos pointed a finger at her.

'You can't stop the flood with words. There will be blood, whatever you *forbid,* Pasiphaë. The question is, whose will it be?'

*

Minos turned on his heel and stalked out of the Throne Room. Only a few of the administrators had remained to hear his lies, but word would get out. It always did. Black dots, minnows, swam before Pasiphaë's eyes. The child's ghost flashed among them, the sliced and singed flesh, Kriti's blank face as she chewed, blood dribbling down her chin, soaking into the sea of her red skirts.

She tried to invoke Potnia Theron to send a wild beast to tear Minos limb from limb, but the words of the malediction wouldn't come. Bulls bellowed and her mind was blank. The Mistresses were too distant to hear, and there was no magic in her fingers. The only enchantment she found was in Asterion's smile.

*

From that time, although she tried not to think about him, Minos and his ugly insinuations preyed on Pasiphaë's mind. She began to listen to the servants, the whisperings in corners, and she began to hear. The rumours that Minos spread among his followers were fed by the small anecdotes that slipped from the nursery to the kitchens, to the stables and farms. They seeped like fingers of tidal foam into every household of the common people and rocked with mocking laughter the dinner parties of the wealthy.

Pasiphaë didn't attend the Summer Rites, pleaded illness. The ghosts of the previous sacrifice haunted her, and she had no wish to add to them. They filled the dark places of the Dolphin Chamber anyway, waiting to steal her happiness.

She refused to attend the Great Mother's sacrifice, left it to Kriti and her bloody cult, but even slave mothers are mothers. Even slaves grieve. Their cries reached her though she couldn't hear them. Not with her ears. They screamed inside her head, and behind her eyes, spears jabbed like herons' beaks, Kriti's mouth, blood on her teeth.

Asterion screamed aloud. His body shook, and his legs bent, knees jerked up towards his chin. His arms flew out stiffly from his sides and his head rolled from side to side. Pasiphaë screamed too, for Eritha. She was there, scooping him up in an instant, before her name had died in her mistress's mouth. He stopped screaming but his breath came in hoarse, gruff gasps.

Another noise echoed in Pasiphaë's head, shrill and piercing, and it joined the threnody of the slave mothers, the terrified wailing of the half-drugged children. She felt its vibration in her own throat. It was at that moment the milk stopped. Her breasts were dry. The mothers had stolen it for the souls of their children. The people might be forgetting about her, but the ghosts were not.

*

She cried in Asterius's arms that night. He stroked her hair, loosening the tresses. His lips were cool on her brow, then hot like his hands.

'Forget,' he whispered. 'Our son is the child of the Mistresses. They'll protect him.'

He thought Pasiphaë wept only for Asterion. She let him. Would even he, so gentle and considerate, understand that every mother is a mother? He wouldn't see that the choice, this child or that, was impossible. He would accept that children of the people would always be sacrificed before princely children, it was the way of the world. He wasn't haunted by their terror, nor by the grief of their mothers. But he was anxious for his son, and for that she forgave his blindness.

His hands soothed away the barbs and coaxed warmth back into the places grown cold. Her mother's milk had gone and wouldn't be coaxed back, but deep in her belly the place was still fertile. It was that night she was sure, amid screams of distress and terror, of blood and darkness, the seed that grew to be Ariadne was sown. Ariadne, the greatest of all her sorrows.

4

Adoni

The summer ended, autumn slipped into winter, and Pasiphaë watched Asterion grow. Apart from her duties to the Mistresses and in the Throne Room, her life was with her son. The new shoot growing inside would not be a child until long after its birth and there was the hope that it would live. Until then, Pasiphaë thought only of Asterion.

His father was affectionate with him, but there's not much a father can do with a child who can't even walk, and his attentions, though well meaning, were clumsy. Asterion had difficulty sitting up straight; his neck seemed too short and his head too small. His toes still parted in an odd way, though less so than at his birth. He would walk, she was sure. It was his mind she worried about, what went on behind the brow so narrow, what he saw with those eyes of such a strange colour, like river mud, and often vacant.

'He's listening to the gods,' Eritha would say, and wipe away the spittle that dribbled from his mouth. Asterion would blink, like a day-struck owl, and then he would smile. No one who saw him smile could stop themselves smiling back. He was radiant, a small sun. Pasiphaë's son.

*

The spring solstice came around again. Pasiphaë made sacrifice to the Mistresses for the spring sowing and a special sacrifice for Asterion. He was a year old and had still made no attempt to move from the place he was set. She would prop him up against the wall with cushions and show him bright objects, stones and ceramic pictures. He had his toys, small horses and sheep carved in wood, that he manipulated with wonder, holding them up close to his eyes, peering into the grain of the wood, stroking the colours with his strange gaze.

'He sees the spirits of things,' Eritha said. 'He hears the voice of the tree in the carved wood, and perhaps he hears the horse too.'

She meant well, and in a way Pasiphaë believed she was right. When he did move away from his cushions, it was not a baby crawl, but with the gait of a beast on all fours. The servants whispered and she shut out their noise. She wished he would walk and show that he could be like other children too. Sometimes, the strain of wishing was too great and she left the palace by the small east entrance and walked through the groves and copses where she saw only agricultural workers and herders, flocks of small children and the silent sentinels on the hills with their dogs. More than ever, she missed having a companion. She missed Nephele. But Nephele was dead – she and the child she had been carrying, a small corpse inside her for months, her wise women said.

On the best pasture in the valley bottom, she would see the Kolchian bull that had been named Belus, and he would always salute her with a toss of his proud head. She would sit beneath a tree while the baby grew and squirmed, and her mouth filled with bile. In the open air it wasn't so bad. The cows lying beneath the shade trees watched her, chewing and possibly sympathising. She appreciated their stolid company more than the frivolous gaiety of the palace people.

*

It was in the days before midsummer, the solstice and the longest day, and Pasiphaë felt her time approaching. She enjoyed the beauty of the last flower-scented days before the air was stripped of everything but heat, and she had her couch brought onto the terrace overhung by olive trees and cascades of lavender. She watched the hillsides moving beneath the flocks, the white bull from Kolchis with his harem, listened for the distant rise and fall of waves.

Leto the marten played around her feet, and Asterion watched, his lips parted in delight, his little hands reaching out to touch her as she flicked past chasing pine cones. Perhaps she was obeying the call of the Mistresses, an order whispered to her by Potnia Theron, but she bounded onto the chair next to Asterion's pile of cushions and dangled her luxuriant, irresistibly silky tail, just out of reach of his exploring fingers.

The breeze dropped, the olive leaves hung in silvery stillness, the sun paused in his flight, and Pasiphaë held her breath. In all the world, only Leto's tail moved, an invitation, and Asterion's hand grasped the leg of the chair. His bulky little body heaved. She saw the muscles of his shoulders clench, his feet take his weight, push. Both hands pulled, and with a gasp of pleasure, he stood like a man. He reached out a hand so gently to touch the animal, her magical sleekness, that his mother's pride swelled. It burst the waters where the new child swam, and she felt the kick, squirm, heave – *annoyance, anger?* – that preceded the tightening of the iron band about her belly. The baby was coming, but Asterion would walk!

*

Pasiphaë sat on the birthing chair and watched blue and silver dolphins dancing around the walls while Eritha rubbed her distended belly with oils. She took deep breaths of the heady smells and prepared for hours of torment. She knew what to expect and gritted her teeth, but the second birth was easier. The pains that started in earnest in the morning with the birds still singing, were over before the sun had reached its zenith. The baby burst out of her dark hiding place like a fish, a trout, slippery and quick.

'A girl child! The people will be pleased.'

Eune dashed to the door. Asterius wouldn't be far away. 'Asterius! Your daughter is born!'

He filled the doorway, eager to see, to know that all was well. He glanced at Eritha inspecting the baby, cleaning the orifices, preparing her to accept the world of air and light, and went straight to Pasiphaë. She held out her hand and he clasped it tight, his face glowing with happiness and relief. Her own relief was more like an emptying than a fulfilment.

'Did you see her?'

He smiled. 'She's perfect. It's time to cut the cord, give her her own life.'

Eritha showed him the right place to cut, the silver knife glittered, and the baby was parted from her mother. Though the physical bond was severed, the invisible bond between mother and daughter would grow naturally, if the Mistresses were willing. Gently, Asterius gathered up the baby. Already, the child's limbs were thrashing and her face was crumpled in anger. Tyro took her from him to the bath Arete had prepared to wash away the birth muck. Eune held her for a moment, considering the furious little face.

'That's how to start out in life, flower. Kick it and shout at it. Make the bastard listen.'

'She's a dote though, isn't she?'

'A Queen if ever.'

The women agreed with Eune, and passed the baby from one to the other, cooing and clucking over their chick. Semele placed the baby in Pasiphaë's arms and took a last look, her face bent close, round and gentle as the moon. She touched the baby's head with a finger that trembled.

'No fear of bad miasmas and water fever taking this one.'

Another mother the Mistresses had forgotten. Pasiphaë turned away, not wanting to share such sorrow, not now. She watched her child struggling with life, making it listen. Her women smiled at the baby's piercing cries, Asterius laughed in pride, but she remembered Asterion's placid, awestruck expression. She placed the nipple in the tiny mouth and she suckled greedily. Pasiphaë put her arms around her, almost without thinking. She was her daughter after all, her child, and one day, she would be Queen.

In that quiet time after the birth, she forgot that Kriti still lived and ruled in her bloody shadows. Later, when she did remember, she recalled the pale, lifeless girl in the seeing that Perseis claimed was Kriti. Perhaps they were not the same. She had only her mother's words describing the face of the dead girl. Slight, pale-faced, dark-haired girls look very similar in death after all. She put the vision out of her mind. She didn't wish Kriti an early death.

The girl-child struggled with the nipple, pulling and tugging, and Pasiphaë almost laughed. What a lioness she was! She stroked the damp, sticky head. 'There's no milk yet, little one. Soon though, pull, demand, and it'll come.'

Eritha took the child away to give her some honeyed water to suck, and Pasiphaë let her thoughts drift into quiet waters as the servants bathed her and helped her to her bed. There were too many thoughts to sleep. She drank the fennel infusion that Eritha brought to bring down the milk and recaptured some of the peace and plenitude she had felt when Asterion was born.

She had known Asterion's name immediately. It had always been in her heart. The girl-child, though, she would let Asterius name. Pasiphaë had sensed a detachment, a separation even before the cord was cut, and although the child was a lioness, Potnia Theron had not roared for her. Perhaps she hadn't listened hard enough.

*

When the ten days had passed and Asasara had not claimed the child's life, she was given a name. Asterius chose it from ancient pieces of his tongue. She would be a true child of Knossos, he said. The name, Ariadne, meant *most holy* and even then, when she was just a tiny, angry red thing, Pasiphaë feared that it would draw the pitiless gaze of the Great Mother. Would she claim her? The thought ran like ice in her blood. She looked at her child and couldn't think of her as *most holy*. She called her Adoni because it meant *dragon-fighter,* and she looked like one who would fight anything, even dragons.

Adoni fought her mother from the start. The birth-blood flowed for so long, Pasiphaë was pale as a winding sheet and had no strength to rise and take pleasure in the early summer. Eritha gave her infusions of yarrow and ginger to strengthen her blood and stop the flow. The baby raged at the breast.

'She doesn't like the taste. Perhaps I shouldn't add ginger—'

'No,' Pasiphaë snapped. 'It's not for her to decide what's best for her mother.'

So, she drank what wisdom advised, and there was even more blood – in the milk, from the baby's ferocious suckling. Feeding Adoni was a torture. She was a dragon, Pasiphaë told herself, not a dragon-fighter. She clenched her teeth and fought back.

*

Kriti visited, as timid as she had been when she first came to see Asterion. She looked older now, physically changing, but her eyes were the same. Lost and slightly unfocused. Pasiphaë wondered if she, like Asterion, was watching things no one else could see. There was a distance between them that seemed impossible to bridge. Too much blood, too many tears flowed in that particular breach. But Pasiphaë tried, and showed the girl what gentleness she could find.

Kriti approached the cradle with her small, rapid steps, like a blackbird, and peeped at the small face, frowning even in sleep. Pasiphaë watched her warily.

'I have something for her,' she said, and placed her gift at the foot of the cradle. It was a doll made of cloth, and its skirts were bright poppy red. When she left, Pasiphaë tossed it into the hearth and watched until it had fallen into ash.

*

Meanwhile, summer unfolded and Asterion grew almost adventurous. His feet were released from their swaddling, and his toes, still slightly splayed, were not beautiful, but they held him anchored to the ground and he learned to move his feet one after the other without falling. Leto scampered before him, always just out of reach, seeming to enjoy the game of outmanoeuvring the ungainly human child. Asterion stumbled after her, laughing when her tail swished across his face. He had still not spoken aloud though Pasiphaë heard his voice in her head, a gentle, wordless murmuring like a forest brook.

He was fascinated by the baby and would watch her sleeping with the same intensity some watched the bull-leaping. When she was awake, he would reach into her cradle, hold out a finger and gurgle with laughter when she put it in her mouth. There were always women around the newborn's cradle, watching for signs that Asasara was calling her to give her to death, and burning incense to placate the Mistress of Serpents. Sometimes they would shoo Asterion away, afraid of his strangeness, afraid that he would cast some misfortune on his sister.

Pasiphaë visited the snake goddess' shrine with offerings for the snake beneath the hearth. In Kolchis, there had been no danger from the house snake. Perseis had made little mystery of the fact that the venom was removed periodically, though she still made her daughters swallow disgusting potions just in case they were ever bitten when the snake was in a venomous state. Although it never obeyed Pasiphaë, it was a placid creature and let itself be worn as a necklace by Circe without ever protesting. The house snake of Knossos, though, had grown furtive and timid with Pasiphaë, and the statue of Asasara that dominated the dimly lit shrine had blood on her hands and in her eyes. Pasiphaë wondered each time if her gifts were enough to make the goddess look away from her children. The statue gave no sign one way or the other.

*

The Dolphin Chamber was full of women preparing baths, cleaning clothes, washing out swaddling bands and preparing oils. Pasiphaë had taken a chair out onto a terrace where honeysuckle grew, to sit in the shade and watch the light on the hillsides, the glitter that came from the sea. Adoni was sleeping and Asterion was playing with Leto. She let her thoughts float away to the brilliance of that early summer, to the summers of Kolchis and the forest shade where jays and woodpeckers broke the green silence. She let the anchor stone go and floated. How long, she didn't know, but it was the hiccoughing baby cry that preceded a full-blown bawl that dragged her back to Knossos.

She listened, hoping one of the women would hear. But when she heard no footsteps, only the baby's gasping sobs growing louder, she leaned forward to pull herself to her feet. The sobbing stopped. She heard a contented sigh and then silence. She sank back into the cushions. Adoni slept.

It was later, when the sun had shifted and the shade moved, that Pasiphaë went into the chamber and found them, Asterion and Adoni, curled up together on the floor, Asterion holding his sister in his arms, Adoni's hand on her brother's cheek. The curved space between Asterion's round, naked belly and the bundle of linen that swaddled Adoni was filled with the sleek sinuosity of the pine marten. As Pasiphaë's shadow fell over him, Asterion opened his eyes slowly and murmured sleepily.

'Ad-am-am-á.'

A weight lifted. The Mistresses were watching over them after all.

*

Asterius watched his son tapping pieces of wood together and laughing at the sound.

'We'll present them both,' Pasiphaë said. Unease clouded her husband's expression, but she insisted. 'Asterion's strong now, he can walk, he's learning to talk. He won't... be afraid this time.'

The concerned frown didn't ease from Asterius's brow, not until Asterion raised his head and smiled. His face was a sun, a spring morning sun. It radiated warmth and tenderness. No one could be the object of that smile and be untouched by its beauty. Asterion bent and ran his fingers through his son's dark curly hair. It was long enough to hide the odd shape of his ears and draw attention from his small, wide-set eyes. Pasiphaë could see the thought forming in Asterius's head – he would pass.

'Show me how you can walk, Asterion.'

He held out his hands and Asterion took them in his gentle grip. It was still a struggle for him to get to his feet, but once there, he stood firm.

Asterius tried to let go of his hands. 'Show me, Asterion. Walk for Papá.' He smiled and his eyes creased. The creases were getting deeper, Pasiphaë thought, all of a sudden, and the thought frightened her. Raven's feet, they said. Was he in the sights of the raven already? 'Let go of my hands and walk.'

Asterion shook his head and held on tight. He shuffled forward until his feet touched his father's. Only then did he let go, to wrap his arms around Asterius's legs. He raised his face in triumph. 'Ap-ap-á,' he said, and laughed.

Asterius bent down and picked up his son. He held him up before his face, and Pasiphaë thought she saw the glitter of tears in the corners of his eyes. He kissed Asterion's brow and seemed about to speak, but a baby wail from the room beyond distracted him.

'Ariadne!'

He set Asterion down without another word. Pasiphaë heard him in the next room clucking over the crying child, not daring to pick her up. Asterion waddled after him. Pasiphaë followed, watched her son peer into the cradle and point. 'Ad-da-do.'

The small room lit up with sunlight and laughter. Pasiphaë went to Asterius and put her arm about his waist. He put an arm around her shoulders and pulled her closer. She remembered that moment, a star of a moment that would always shine bright and clear. She was the Mistress, filled up with happiness, full and round as the largest pithos, enfolding all of her brood in her embrace. She remembered that moment as the happiest in her life.

5

A walk with bulls

As the summer drew to its breathless close, Asterion began to walk with confidence, and Pasiphaë experienced it as a liberation. Since his birth, an obscure feeling of dread had prevented her leaving him behind in the palace. She felt no such fear about leaving Ariadne with her nurses. The baby would wake, demand and sleep again no matter who was with her. Pasiphaë felt the need to walk out beneath the sky, beyond the palace walls. She had received some disturbing news from Circe and wanted to mull over the implications.

She had sent a messenger to Aea to announce Ariadne's birth to her mother and sister. The messenger had returned with the news that there was no longer a Queen in the royal house. With her younger daughter settled at Knossos, Perseis had retired to her island house, to her sisters and the other mysteries of the sea, leaving the throne of Kolchis to Circe. According to the message, signed by Aeëtes, Circe had been chased away by her husband Agrius and his supporters when she tried to force him into a noose in the oak grove. Aeëtes had in turn chased out Agrius and had taken the King's place until his daughter Medea should be old enough to rule.

Pasiphaë had always suspected Agrius would turn on the custom, and she considered Circe an idiot for trying to insist on his death. Now Kolchis was in the balance, and Pasiphaë feared the consequences for Knossos if it, too, left the lap of the Mistresses.

With Asterion trotting by her side, she left, one golden morning, by the small east entrance. The path led through gardens and the theatre that, when it was not in use, was as peaceful as a ruin and full of the sound of birds and insects. Asterion ran around the area where the actors played out their stories, whooping and stumbling, holding high the carved bull that Kriti had left in his cradle. Dust rose beneath his clomping tread and his face radiated happiness, even when he tripped and fell.

Pasiphaë took his hand and they followed the path to the farmland, certain that they would meet no palace courtiers and few farmworkers. They were in the brief period of hot hush when the harvests were in and the stubble had not yet been burned. The stalks were full of pigeons and crows, a ripple of feathers that enchanted Asterion. Descending the hillside, they came to the last bit of green, the pastures along the stream in the valley bottom where the royal herd grazed. The cows lay beneath the trees or cropped the grass further up beyond the shade.

Asterion held his toy high and yelled, 'Drupa!' – pointing at the cows that watched him impassively, their jaws working methodically. Suddenly, he stopped, and his mouth fell open, an O of astonishment. He held up the carved bull, gazed at it for a moment then, squinting slightly, stared beyond the trees, murmuring, 'Drupa.' The white bull appeared, ambling down to the stream. He barely acknowledged his herd, confident that none of the young bulls would defy his authority, confident in his superiority. Asterion tugged Pasiphaë's hand, dragging her towards the stream.

The bull raised his head and snorted, but not at Pasiphaë and Asterion. There was movement along the treeline, and voices, of two men in conversation, rose from the shade. When they stepped into the sunlight, Pasiphaë halted, recognising the stocky figure with elaborately curled hair, the nose broken in a boxing match, or so he said, the dark, malicious eyes, and the loose-lipped mouth. The feeling of dread squirmed and snarled.

'Pasiphaë, Princess! How strange to find you here. Or perhaps not. You're on the same mission as myself, I suppose.' Without waiting for a reply, Minos went on. 'I was looking for a bull.'

Leaving the herdsman behind, he walked towards her, a knowing smirk on his face. Asterion tightened his grip on her hand. She steadied her voice.

'And I was showing my son the fields he has only seen from behind the palace walls.'

She would have walked by, left him with a brief nod of the head, but he barred the path.

'I want a bull to sacrifice for my new daughter. Inia has seen that she will be the wife of a hero and a King. Belus would make a fine offering.'

She struggled to keep calm. Minos's presence disturbed her; animosity hung around him like the smell of a terrified animal. 'My best wishes to your daughter, Minos, but the white bull is not yours to choose. He was a gift to Asterion. Take one of his sons if you like. He has plenty.'

'Unlike Asterius. He has only this one.' Minos stared at Asterion, the simper becoming a grimace of distaste. Pasiphaë clung to the little hand, aware of something stirring in his blood. She hoped it wasn't fear.

'Drupa!' Asterion shouted in his deep, husky voice, and held up the carved bull like a talisman. Did he expect Minos to shrink away in terror? 'Drupa says no!'

Minos raised his eyebrows and turned to Pasiphaë, smirk and grimace gone, and cold contempt in his eyes. 'My apologies, Princess. I shouldn't have mentioned the Kolchian bull before your son. It was inept of me.'

'Asterion is reminding you that his father's property is not yours. It was inept to have suggested you had any rights over his herds. Now, if you'll excuse us, we'll finish our walk.'

She walked, Asterion clutching her hand, towards the valley bottom, along the path that led eventually to the port and the sea. She didn't hurry, nor did she turn her head, but she felt Minos staring after her, like a spear-thrust in her back. The shade fell over them like a gentle mantle, and Asterion peered through the branches, Minos forgotten, she hoped. In the sunlight, higher up the pasture now that he had drunk, the white bull stood, watching.

'Drupa!' Asterion called joyfully, waving the wooden toy. The while bull bellowed in reply, and Pasiphaë would have laughed had not the squirming dread reminded her that no one was truly free of destiny.

*

Minos watched the young woman and her ill-made son scuttle away and thought of his own son who was the stuff of Kings. He thought of his daughter who was predicted a famous future and of the injustice that fell on men if they didn't fight against it. Asterius was of no account, had no weight in the matter at all. His days were numbered and he knew it. This girl from Kolchis, though, she thought she had rights, that her children had rights. He wondered if she ever thought of the true Queen at all.

He certainly did. Kriti, his half-sister, might be weak and sickly, but she would inherit the throne. Again, there was no justice in it, but what was justice but a malleable thing, that any man with self-respect would take and make into something that worked for him and his interests? The girl and the child had stumbled into the shadows where they would stay if he had his way. His eyes narrowed as he let his gaze turn inward. He saw Androgeos, his bright-eyed son, leading his band of the wealthiest sons of Knossos. He saw his line, the sons and daughters who would perpetuate it, and the house of Knossos ruling without contest the entire Middle Sea.

It was a glorious prospect, and if it meant defending his

power with spears and fortifications, wasn't that only what the Father expected? Minos rocked back and forth, heel to toe, toe to heel, feeling the bucking boards of a warship beneath his feet, the waves that ruled the world. The white bull bellowed, but that wouldn't save him. The future belonged to Minos, the Father and his sons. The Key-Bearer, Inia, had seen as much in his new daughter Phaedra's fate.

He smiled, coming back to the present. The Kolchian Princess was no longer in sight, and the herdsman had approached, timidly. It was time to choose that bull.

6

The second presentation

Asterion and Ariadne were presented together. It was high summer, the barley was almost ripe, the meadows parched, and there was a lethargy in the air that throbbed with the song of the cicadas. Pasiphaë longed for shade and hugged the shadows of the interior, the cool of walled courtyards where fountains played. The celebrations would chase away the summer torpor; there would be bull-leaping and feasting, and the people would finally be satisfied that there could be pleasure and happiness without the sacrifice of children.

She called a council of domestic administrators to plan the ceremony and was surprised to see a sprinkling of courtiers among them, courtiers she associated more with bull-dancing and lavish feasting than with the dull details of seating arrangements in a shrine. She assumed the presentation would be at Knossos, in the Court of Ceremonies. The nobles would watch from the galleries and the people would fill the Barley Court, to be shown the royal children at the end of the ceremony.

A quiet voice at her side, Kriti's, was raised in objection. 'The Barley Court's too small. The whole of Knossos will be present, the port of Amnisos, all the outlying villages. Too few will see, and they won't like it. If the harvest is poor again, they'll blame you for not respecting the tradition.'

Kriti spoke directly to Pasiphaë, the tone of her voice

steady and unmodulated, like a speech she had learned by heart. Pasiphaë was reminded of the very first words she had spoken to welcome her to Knossos. The voice was firmer now, but her face was, if anything, paler, her eyes just as dark and expressionless. Her short speech was greeted with approval by the nobles. The administrators made no comment. They couldn't afford to, Pasiphaë thought, with a ripple of unease.

'The sanctuary on Mount Iouktas is the only suitable place.'

The room filled with murmuring. With its low ceiling and dead forest of pillars, it felt oppressive, stifling with humanity. Pasiphaë studied the crowd more closely. The women present were Kriti's priestesses, and there were priests of Poteidan among them. The courtiers nodding in approval she recognised as followers of Minos. In their faces she saw cold indifference or animosity. *See you, know you, love you.* Though Minos was absent, she saw his hand in this. He had no need to show his face; he would reap the prize, and Pasiphaë wondered how the Great Mother and her cult fitted into his plan.

Pasiphaë didn't look at Asterius, wouldn't ask his advice or permission. She turned instead to Eumedes, the district governor, a rosy-cheeked man, who recorded the harvests and imports, the taxes paid and the quantities of the reserves in the palace magazines.

'How many people will be present? An estimate, Eumedes.'

'If half the population that we would expect to feed in case of famine were to leave their work to be present, Lady, there will be fifty thousand souls to see the royal children. I don't count the slaves, nor the rural population. We have no means of knowing how many of them there are.'

The calculation was simple. Kriti, or whoever whispered to her, was right. The Barley Court and the Court of Ceremonies could hold only a fraction of that number, so most would be disappointed. And Pasiphaë would take the blame. She made her decision immediately. She wouldn't have anyone thinking she had been forced into it.

'We'll use the sanctuary. It will, of course, have to be purified first.'

She would brave the high place and the presence of the Great Mother, but she would not do it with the ghosts of sacrificial victims fluttering about her face.

*

'Why would she even care if the common people weren't present at the ceremony? She shows little enough interest in the workings of government and her future duties. Who has put these words into her mouth, and why?'

Pasiphaë and Asterius were alone in the royal apartment, in the royal bed. Knossos was quiet, and only the murmur of the night breeze from the sea disturbed the silence. Asterius squirmed. Not literally, but Pasiphaë could see the conflict in his face. Kriti was his daughter after all.

'She's the High Priestess. Anything that affects her duties is important to her, and Mount Iouktas is the logical place for the presentation. There was none for Asterion, the people will be expecting a celebration this time.'

He turned to her, his eyes dark and still in the shadows, but was there reproach in them? And for what? That Asterion was delicate, that the sanctuary was full of horrors, or that she had failed in her duty by being sensitive to such things?

'The people will have their celebration,' she replied coldly. 'But I will make the offering.'

'Of course.' He touched her face, so lightly, a butterfly touch. 'Don't think badly of the girl. She has nothing but her role. She never knew a mother.'

'She had Ananke instead.'

He was gentle, attentive, but Pasiphaë wouldn't be mollified. Would she have given her infant daughter to the black crow, let her child be shaped as a tool for Minos, given her to the rottenness creeping into the roots of the palace? She sighed. How could she blame him when the Mistresses were silent, even for her? Though the palace was full of light, scented flowers, dancing, Pasiphaë felt and feared the creeping darkness. The Serpent and the Poppy, sword and spear of the Great Mother, cast a shadow, and the people cared only for their pleasures. Circe told her, so long ago, when she was still a child in Kolchis, that her duty was to save Crete for the Mistresses. When she looked at Kriti and the smug, self-satisfied faces of the courtiers, she wondered if she had already failed.

*

The day dawned, hot and still, the air dry with grass stalks and chaff from the first of the winnowing. Pasiphaë looked for a sign and saw a sky scattered with noisy flocks of swallows, listened, and heard only Asterion's babbling as Eritha bathed and dressed him. She took that as an omen and was content. She had grown to dread the huge gatherings, the atmosphere of gaiety that offended her, the lack of solemnity. The air smelled of sweetmeats offered by vendors, dried fruits and pastries. How often did any of them make an offering at one of the shrines? Perhaps when they had a special boon to ask, a death to avoid, a debt.

Once her breasts were bound lightly to catch leaking milk, she had her women dress her as the Moon Princess, her diadem, her hair piled in dark coils and her neck hung with golden lions and a silver hawk. She would be majestic, queenly, sacred. She would not be a figure of derision. Nor would her children. Asterion wore a necklace of golden bees, his sandals tightly strapped so his odd toes were less noticeable. Adoni was swaddled in linen and wrapped in a shawl of the finest wool worked with gold thread. They would have a guard chosen from the tallest of the palace soldiers, and Athamas would be at their head. She worked methodically at the details because the greater picture escaped her, flew out of her control. She would have cursed the onlookers who dared to mock if she had known the right words.

Eune held up the silver mirror.

'There! Is that a goddess or what?'

'I hope that lot out there appreciate what they've been given.'

'Like bloody hell, they do,' Tyro muttered. She and Arete had lovers; they knew what was said about her in the farms, among the ordinary folk.

She turned as Asterius entered the Queen's apartment. Dolphins leapt in painted joy around his head, and the sunlight caught their sleek blue bodies, turning them into flesh-and-blood creatures of the sea. She said a silent prayer to Potnia Theron and heard the splash of seawater. Asterius offered her his arm, and together they led the procession of their household to the west entrance.

She had been expecting a crowd, but what she saw was a sea. With Adoni in her arms, she took her place in the first litter and pulled the curtains closed. She had not had to speak to the people, but they were there, the eyes of thousands peering, trying to catch a glimpse of the children. The rumours, of course. It was not a benevolent curiosity; they wanted to see a freak of nature. She turned and caught a last glimpse of Asterion in the chair behind, before Asterius also pulled the curtain closed. The sun was excuse enough.

The royal road wound south, stone-paved, and the carriers were sure-footed. They would reach the sanctuary before the shambling crowd burdened by the heat, their children and the effort of keeping their best clothes out of the dust. When the royal couple were carried, it would have been discourteous for anyone else to make use of a chair. All walked, even the nobles, in the heat and the dust of the harvesting. It was the expectation of something worth seeing, Pasiphaë thought bitterly, that drew them in the wake of the litters, not piety or devotion.

Adoni squirmed in annoyance, at the heat, the curtains, or

just out of habit. Her mother bounced her up and down until she smiled, gurgled, forgot to cry. Pasiphaë pulled back the curtain, showed the baby the passing scenery; stones, sheep, olive groves. Adoni blinked, not bored. She was quick. Her dark eyes were bright, darted here and there, noticing. Her gaze reached further than Asterion's ever did. Even now he was slow to focus as if dragged from a daydream. Pasiphaë tired of the scenery long before her daughter, still fighting against her closing lids, fell asleep.

At the sanctuary entrance, the litters were set down, disturbing a flock of finches feeding on the yellow flowers gone to seed that grew among the stones. The sun was high, and the portico, thick cedar-columned, beckoned with shade. But within, the doors were all opened wide, and in a golden square of light, figures could be seen already gathered in the courtyard of the shrine, the white of their robes glittering with a fierce brilliance.

The heat of the sun died and Pasiphaë shivered. Even with Adoni in her arms and her two stars at her side, it was getting harder and harder to confront the cold cast by the shadow of the Great Mother. *Her son Dias is hungry.* Kriti's words lurked in the dark corners, and here, in the domain of the Mother, they danced, chanting a threnody. Pasiphaë felt the shadow of the Great Mother in her bones, and as she walked towards the bright courtyard, she heard the sucking, hissing of her voice in the rooms on either hand. She refused to look at the paintings, the processions and the red poppy flowers, but their death songs echoed in her ears, and Adoni squirmed restlessly.

She took a deep breath on the sill, before stepping out onto the bare stone, with only the overarching sky above, and the effigy of the Great Mother, raising her arms to claim it all. Her shadow lay shrunken by the high sun, a snake's sloughed skin, but it would grow as the night drew nearer and all shadows lengthened.

Pasiphaë's steps slowed. Asterius placed a hand on her arm

and moved to her side, Asterion clinging tightly to his other hand. The High Priestess standing beneath the effigy made no objection to the presence of a man in the sacred place. It was only Kriti beneath the diadem after all, a slender girl beneath the elaborate skirts. Pasiphaë stared up at the Great Mother, dressed as Poppy Mistress with red bell skirts, at the bronze coils of her hair, and she gave no sign of displeasure either. No one else would dare object. Only Kriti had the rank and she seemed withdrawn, as if the role of High Priestess had palled or grown too heavy to bear.

Pasiphaë prayed to the Mistresses that the ceremony would not be held up. Already she felt the heat, the expectancy of the crowd, and the restlessness of the children. She wanted to be gone, out of the baleful gaze of the too-bright sky, gone before the shadows touched them.

Eritha held Adoni during her mother's purification, when she bathed in the basin of the shrine, in the cool darkness. The ritual words were pronounced, and water washed away the memory of pain. She dried herself and poured scented oil on her hands, cleansing all traces of the smell of blood. Potnia Theron whispered in the running water. Or was it Asterion's voice, murmuring his familiar soothing words? It had become difficult to follow the tangled threads of voices.

Pasiphaë took Adoni back in her arms, and Asterius led his son reluctantly to the altar. The child bent his head, his thick curls falling into his eyes, apparently absorbed in his feet. With dread Pasiphaë climbed the stone stair, each step bringing her closer to the summit of the mountain, where there would be nothing but the sky above, and nothing to protect her from the gaze of the multitude gathered on the slopes around the sanctuary.

Asterion slowed their progress, dragging on his father's hand and stomping with both feet on each step as if threatening to budge no further. They climbed in silence, between the ranks of white-clad priestesses, beneath the red skirts of the Poppy Mistress. Pasiphaë had asked for music, musicians to make a celebration of the ordeal, but no one had given them the order to play.

They reached the altar, only the statue closer now to the sky. Pasiphaë stood higher than the sanctuary walls, and gazed out on the mountain, its scrubby grass and stones hidden beneath a sea of watchers. She looked down and, with a shiver, realised their eyes were raised not to the Great Mother, but to her. Then she turned to Kriti, and her own terror subsided. The girl had grown taller and no longer looked like a doll, out of place among the women, but she was pale as death. The whites of her eyes were an unhealthy yellow and glazed, like those of a sacrificial animal when the last flicker of life is leaving. She had grown, but closer to her death. And she knew it.

There was a wave like a swelling tide of murmured voices, some gentle laughter and cooing noises at the sight of the swaddled child. Adoni wriggled, turning her head from side to side. Asterion kept his head bent. Pasiphaë watched Kriti, wondering at the glitter in her usually dull eyes and what it meant. This was a presentation to the people, not a sacrifice to the Great Mother, but did she know? Pasiphaë glanced up at the bronze-haired statue. Did she care?

Kriti led the prayers, the invocation of Potnia Eleuthia who had guided Pasiphaë through two births and assured the well-being of her children. Pasiphaë and the priestesses chanted the responses, a single syrinx wove a gentle melody about the words. Asterion listened to the rise and fall of the notes, his mouth open in absorption, and Pasiphaë began to relax. It would soon be over.

Temple servants placed two cages full of doves on the altar, and Kriti opened the first, for Asterion. He raised his head as the birds jostled in a flutter of white feathers to get out, fly. His eyes followed them as they took to the sky, a smile of wonder on his face. The second flock was for Ariadne, who paid no attention, but Asterion clapped and made happy gurgling noises. There was no blood, no death. No mother cried out in anguish. The birds flew high, and made a single flock, white against blue. The crowd cheered. The Great Mother looked straight ahead, seeing nothing. A flock of doves would be of no interest to her.

Pasiphaë's heart beat at a normal rate again, and she heard the high, shrill twitter of swallows. The Mother had given no sign, and her shadow lengthened away from the altar. The air was heavy with expectation. Asterion would be first. His father held him high, turning in a circle so all could see. The child's eyes opened wide in surprise and incomprehension. So many people!

'People of Knossos, people of Crete, behold the son of the Moon Princess and the Bull King. Prince Asterion.'

Asterius's voice fell into the expectant silence, and for the length of a deep breath it remained unbroken, until the crowd burst into wild applause and the trumpets brayed. Jubilation had quickly replaced disappointment that the freak of nature was just a child. Then Pasiphaë held up Adoni.

'People of Knossos, people of Crete, behold the daughter of the Moon Princess and the Bull King. The Princess Ariadne.'

This time there was no hesitation. Adoni had barely time to give out a lusty cry of hunger, before the cheering began. Pasiphaë let out her breath, and her heart pounded with relief that the ordeal was over.

She had triumphed too soon. A fluttering caught at the tail of her eye. A priestess had left the ranks – not a priestess, a black-clad woman. Ananke scuttled to Pasiphaë's side, a black spider, and held up a shawl that smelled of temples, incense, darkness and blood. And it was bright poppy red.

'The goddess gown for the Princess,' Kriti said in her toneless voice as Pasiphaë flinched away from both shawl and black crone. Ananke hovered, the red square outstretched to envelop Adoni, who was now choking with anger. Pasiphaë pushed the ancient thing, reeking of sacrifice, away from the baby. She had forgotten Asterion. The crowd had not. Still held high on his father's shoulder, he threw back his head and bellowed, a cry of terror and horror. Ananke flapped the red shawl again, her eyes on the howling child. His cry of distress roared out across the mountainside, filling the ears of the watchers, avid for the spectacle he was giving.

'Take it away!'

Pasiphaë snatched the shawl out of Ananke's hands. She would have thrown it into the fire had she dared. Worse even than the blood of a calf was this ancient fabric impregnated with the blood and oils of sacrifice. It had lain in a casket in the bloody shrine year upon year, while death and loss and grieving seeped into its weave. Asterion writhed and kicked off his sandals, revealing the strange formation of his toes, like cloven hooves. His face was a rictus of terror, his mouth a round O, the mouth of a bronze salpinx, and the crowd listened to the animal-like sound that came from it in horrified fascination.

Asterius held him tight and whispered into his son's ear, calming him enough for the struggling to stop, the bellowing to cease. From a distance, would it have looked like play? He smiled, a broad, teeth-flashing smile, though his eyes were full of concern, and shouted. 'Hear how your Bull Prince roars!'

There was some cheering and stamping of feet and handclapping, but from afar, from those who had not seen, whom the rumour had not yet reached. Asterion's face, though, was congested, and before he could roar again, Pasiphaë nodded to the musicians and dancers below to begin. In the few instants before the bright music rang out, she heard the amazed voices, the words that rustled like a fire fanned by the wind – *It's true! The child is half bull!*

Bound tight in her linen bands, Adoni struggled, her head turning, crumpled and red with the anger bubbling in her throat. She cried her baby cries, but the sound was drowned out by the music.

*

In the privacy of the litter, Pasiphaë gave Adoni the breast to stop her crying. She trembled uncontrollably. Where were the Mistresses? Had they not heard the prayers? Was Mistress Eleuthia not pleased with the doves? No blood had been spilled, so Ananke had brought blood, ancient and bitter. Asterion tasted it, his eyes were filled with it. Eritha said he listened to the voices of the essence of things, trees, animals. Did he hear the pleading for mercy, the screams of terror in the red shroud? Did he hear the mothers tearing their hair? Adoni pulled pitilessly at her breast and black darts flew across Pasiphaë's vision – not swallows, but arrows. She heard no comforting voice of Potnia Theron. The air was still. Empty.

7

Kriti

There was bull-leaping with the palace dancers in the Barley Court for those influential enough to have a seat. The people organised their own entertainment in a field outside the palace. When the light grew softer in the evening and the heat less intense, there would be feasting, lasting long after nightfall, and torches would mirror the stars in the dark sky. Custom obliged the Queen to attend the bull-leaping, so Kriti's presence would have been enough, but Pasiphaë dared not stay away. She could not let herself be forgotten.

She rumpled her son's hair, which was a little damp, and smiled at the sucking sounds he made. His lips were sticky with honey and his breath smelled faintly of balsam and cumin. Adoni would probably wake again and demand feeding, but Asterion, after his bouts of terror and Eritha's potion, would sleep heavily until he was woken in the morning.

'Send for me if he...'

Eritha nodded. Pasiphaë had no need to spell out what Asterion might do. She trusted Eritha. She was one of the few. Leaving the royal apartment, Pasiphaë descended to the long gallery that led to the Barley Court. The frescoes were bright, and they usually raised her spirits, but she looked at the procession, the musicians, the servants waving branches, the children holding hands and dancing, and wondered why there was no painting of their destination.

*

Kriti had disrobed in haste and slipped away from her priestesses, ordering a chair to carry her back to the palace. Ananke, full as a tick with venom, was too pleased with the effect of her *gift* to notice. Kriti fled back to Knossos and waited for Pasiphaë, clinging like a shadow in the Gallery of Processions. The poppy left a thick taste in her mouth and still drifted like fog in her head, but there were fears it couldn't numb, and she had to tell someone.

Pasiphaë had turned into the gallery, but she obviously hadn't seen her, too absorbed in her thoughts. Kriti stepped into the light, trembling with anxiety, but she had to speak. When Pasiphaë finally noticed her, her eyes had widened in surprise. The effect of the poppy was receding, leaving Kriti raw, and Pasiphaë's reaction hurt. Had she really expected understanding though? Kriti was aware that she was being manipulated, and through dint of being told, believed she had no will of her own. But she also knew that, despite what Ananke said, Pasiphaë was not the enemy.

'Princess, may I speak to you? Please?'

Pasiphaë's surprised expression softened. Was there a glimmer of understanding there?

'Can we talk here? Or would you rather go somewhere more private?'

There was no one in the gallery but there were voices from the rooms before the west entrance, artisans with work that couldn't be left, furnaces, kilns, ovens that had to be watched, kitchen servants preparing food for the feasting. Kriti knew where they wouldn't be disturbed.

'There'll be no one in Asasara's shrine.'

She hurried ahead, her skirts fluttering. She had not had time to get rid of all her elaborate jewellery, and she felt its weight, too heavy for her slender bones. She pushed open the door painted with serpents. There was no one inside. There rarely was, and today everyone had something better to do.

The light was dim, falling from a light shaft in the ceiling. The paintings were dull red. The smell of ashes hung in the air.

The serpent goddess ought to be neutral. Her role was to protect the house, listen to petitions to keep sickness and death away. Often, though, she chose not to hear and let death run like fire through the painted apartments. Kriti doubted she cared anything at all for those who lived in them. She hurried through the shrine and into the preparation room. What she had to say, she would keep from the goddess too.

'I've had my first blood.' The words came out stark and blunt with no preamble. 'Ananke said she wouldn't tell anyone, but I don't trust her.'

'Why should no one know? It's something to celebrate. You're a woman now.'

Did Pasiphaë really expect her to be bursting with pride? Didn't she realise what becoming a woman would mean for her? A flood of despair tugged at the slender thread of hope.

'All women marry, and for a Queen it's also a duty. You must make an offering to the Mistresses. Asterius told me who he hopes they will choose for your King.'

She didn't understand. Her father *hoped*. That's all he could do. There would be no *choosing*. Pasiphaë couldn't know who *intended* to be her husband.

'The Mistresses have no power over Minos.'

Pasiphaë's eyes flashed with anger. 'Minos is no more than a man. The Mistresses won't allow—'

'Allow?' Her voice was shrill. She was on the verge of tears. 'Not even the Great Mother can stop Minos. Do you think I haven't prayed to her every day to strike him dead? Minos will be King by marrying… the Queen! I've seen it. Ananke read me the signs.'

The mention of Ananke's name sent Pasiphaë into a fury. 'Ananke is a witch, a sorceress, bound through some twisted affection to Minos. Of course she'll tell you horror stories! Give your permission to have her banished. She's a poison!

Minos is your brother! The Mistresses would never accept such a marriage.'

'The Mistresses have no power here, not anymore.' The words fell from her mouth like stones, but she knew she was right. 'Such marriages have always existed, and Minos knows it. I'll die rather than marry him.'

Pasiphaë's expression was of horror, revulsion, but Kriti saw what perhaps the older woman had not intended to show, that she had lost hope in the power of the Mistresses too.

'Asterius won't allow it. Let me speak to him.'

Asterius. Her father had no more power that a dry stalk in the wind. No one had.

'Give me something for the bleeding. Your servant taught me a lot about plants and I know what I need. But I have no store of my own. Ananke says herbal lore is wickedness. Please.'

Her fingers twisted the front of her skirt between nervous fingers. She looked into Pasiphaë's eyes, searching for the glimmer of understanding. There was so much blood behind her eyes, she feared Pasiphaë would see only the effigy of a priestess. Then her heart leaped – she had seen it, the spark. Pity or kindness, friendship, it didn't matter.

'I can let you have raspberry leaves and yarrow and ginger.'

She clutched eagerly at Pasiphaë's words. 'And lady's mantle if you have some. And red clover.'

'I'll get Eritha to prepare them. It would be... prudent if you came yourself to collect them.'

Pasiphaë had begun to understand. Her voice was gentle, so gentle Kriti wanted to weep. Kriti nodded, too relieved to speak her thanks properly. She would stop the blood, put off her destiny for a while. But the fear of Minos still gnawed at her bones, and she had an overwhelming longing, a need for something to drown it in oblivion. Only poppy could dull the terrors and give her a darkness full of dreams.

She watched Pasiphaë leave, then hurried away in her turn,

leaving Asasara to her blind contemplation in the gloom of her shrine.

*

Pasiphaë left the lugubrious place, relieved to be back in the light of the Gallery of Processions. Kriti's eyes followed her, the paint around them brighter than the pupils that were dull-dark, like a pool within a cave. The dull, dark force embodied by Minos and Ananke would have it that she and Kriti were enemies. Yet when she recalled the horror of that moment of sacrifice, the white teeth clenched about the bloody flesh, all she could see was a child without a mother.

Behind Kriti's timorous figure hung the face of Minos, and of the two, Pasiphaë was lucid enough to know which was the more dangerous.

*

She sat with Asterius on the royal dais while the crowd cheered and clapped at the dash and excitement of the bull-leaping. She was present, but her gaze was inward. The sanded pavement was scuffed into dusty clouds. Bare feet flew, hooves clattered. She flinched at each cry, expecting the red spurt of blood. Blood. It was life, so easily spilled, giving life, letting it flow away. She reached out to Asterius and placed a hand on his. He turned to her and smiled. His body was still firm, but his face looked old. The creases were deeper and there was an air of weariness about him. For the first time, Pasiphaë noticed the grey threads in his hair.

She had not given much thought to the choosing of the King, the measuring of life by custom not nature. Few creatures that walked beneath the sun lived until they died peacefully in the sleep of old age. No animal, no bird, no slave. The labourers died in the fields, of festering cuts, animal bites, kicks, falls. How many women and girls died on the painful road of bringing to birth? And the King. Why should the King escape the rule? Was his time not to be counted?

She looked at his face, the lines, creases, the fall of his hair, the way it curled over his ear, the tendons tightening in his neck when he shouted in excitement. The King was bound to die, but he was a man too. Her thoughts raced, formed a plan. They would retire to one of the smaller houses, far away, like Europa's sons Sarpedon and Rhadamanthus did when Minos turned on them. Like her own father had done. Asterius would become just a man and leave the throne to Kriti as was her right, let her choose her King.

She won't live long enough to marry.

Perseis had been wrong about that, at any rate. She hadn't seen Circe's downfall either, had she? Pasiphaë wouldn't listen to any more predictions that might or might not come true. She would seize her own destiny. She glimpsed a future shining bright blue as the sea, and the words were on her lips, bubbling over like spring water.

A cry of fear, a gasp and a moment's silence shattered her thoughts. Asterius leapt to his feet. The arena was a flock of birds, sparrows twittering at a hawk in their midst, and the speckled bull snorted, his horns red with a dancer's blood. The dream dashed on the rocks. Life ended for everyone. The dancer was born with his bull's name on his heart. Asterius, like all the Bull Kings, had his successor's name written on his. Kriti's husband was not obliged to spare him the King's death.

*

Amnisos was alight, and torches set the hillsides aglow in celebration of the presentation of the royal children. Even the royal road was a moving sea of revellers and hucksters, lit by braziers. Over all hung the smoky, fatty smell of roasting meat, now that the improvised bull-teasing, boxing matches and foot racing had given way to feasting. The people of Crete like to enjoy themselves, Asterius had said. Pasiphaë preferred to see them take their pleasures in feasting and gambling, dancing and athletics rather than in gossip and idle chatter.

The great dining room that looked out over the Barley Court was full of the wealthy traders and shipwrights of Amnisos, the nobles of Knossos, Phaistos, Malia and Zakros. There were kinsmen of Asterius, and even Sarpedon was there. Pasiphaë hoped it meant that Minos had left again. She gazed about the hall, looking for friendly faces, but there were too many unknowns, and few were very interested in a provisional Queen. They were profiting from the occasion to make deals, broker contracts, discuss barley blight and the cost of silver ore.

Pasiphaë ate without attention, picking here and there with less discernment than a jay. She was thinking of the peace and quiet of the royal apartment, the sleeping children, the quiet rustling of the serving women, and longing to be able to leave. A fluttering of black fabrics, the self-important bustle of an ageing woman elbowing past the diners, caught her attention. A lull formed in the conversations. She had heard the same at sea. It presaged a gale.

'My Lord, Lady.' The woman in black, the crow-crone Ananke, pushed to the fore and stood proudly before the raised platform. 'I am the bearer of good news. An event which is *truly* worthy of celebration.' She leaned on the word and glanced around to gauge the effect. 'The Princess Kriti has had her first blood! We have a new Queen to follow our beloved Europa.'

The lull became a silence. All eyes searched for the absent Kriti then turned to Pasiphaë. It was up to her to say something.

'That is a private matter concerning the Princess Kriti alone. And it's certainly not a servant's place to spread tittle-tattle at the royal table.'

Ananke's eyes flashed, her face alight with a feverish glow. 'Not *tittle-tattle,* Lady Pasiphaë. Proof!'

With a flourish, she held up a linen sheet so all could

see the dark red smear in the centre. The viper, the traitor! Pasiphaë's first thought was for the girl she had betrayed, then she looked about again for Minos. This piece of theatre was intended for him, the only one who would not find such a display distasteful. As she cast her eyes over the astonished crowd, she found him, the man getting to his feet, stocky, with a broken nose, dark curls held back by a gold circlet. Minos. His purple cloak was bordered with gold, and his bare arms and legs were thick with hair. He moved without grace up to the dais, his face twisted in a grimace of pleasure.

'Where is your daughter, Asterius, so that we can all drink to her health and her womanhood? Were you intending to keep this news from us?'

Only then did Pasiphaë look at Asterius. His face was white, his jaw clenched on the words of anger she was certain were choking him.'

'*This news,* as Lady Pasiphaë said, is private, to be announced when the Princess Kriti decides. If she isn't here, it's because her duties have tired her. She takes them seriously. Unlike her brother.'

'Half-brother.' Minos gave a sly, sidelong glance to the nearest diners. 'Zeus was my father, not you.'

Pasiphaë sensed the ground slipping, heard the buzzing of intrigue in her ears. The guests, too much wine drunk, too much meat eaten, were avid for more entertainment. The ground was slipping and with it her grasp on happiness.

Asterius remained seated, gripping the arms of his chair with whitened knuckles. 'There will be a time and a place to discuss a husband for Princess Kriti, and it will be with Kriti herself, not now, not here.'

Minos turned again to grin at the diners seated closest to the royal table. 'Of course. You'll need time to organise the celebrations. And the suitors.'

'The Mistresses will send the King, Minos, in their own good time! The Princess is not a cow to be sold at the fair to the highest bidder!'

Pasiphaë knew her voice was shrill with anger and that it amused Minos, but she could see his game and it disgusted her. Asterius, too, and his disgust was even greater.

'Lady Pasiphaë is right. There is no obligation for Kriti to marry yet.'

'Then ask the Oracle at Amnisos. Let's see if *the Mistresses* know who her King will be.'

There was a murmuring of approval that became cheering and applause. Calls of 'Princess Kriti' and 'the Queen' rang out, feet stamped and dishes clattered. Among the red-faced feasters stamping and shouting, three faces remained pensive and uneasy – Antanor, the shipowner from Malia, Kerameia, whose wealth was in vineyards, and their son Kesandros. Pasiphaë glanced at Asterius and saw in his face the seeds of despair.

*

Pasiphaë and Asterius retired early. There were no calls from the guests for them to stay. Antanor and his family had already left. Only when they were within the walls of the royal apartments, the door closed on the rest of the palace, did Pasiphaë return to the dark brew that Minos was stirring.

'You said the divination has already brought up Kesandros' name for Kriti. Ask again. Let everyone see that she isn't meant to marry Minos.'

Asterius was standing on the terrace, looking up at a sky where there were no stars. Pasiphaë went to him and took his arm, made him look at her. He shook his head. 'No names. Just signs, symbols. We tend to get the answers we suggest to the priestess.'

Pasiphaë was shocked. No vision, no certitude then? Asterius glanced at her quickly and turned away.

'If we have an official, public divination, Minos will buy the answer he wants or interpret it the way he wants. Inia saw the port of Malia, and Kesandros is from Malia. Minos has property there too. She saw ships and vineyards. Who doesn't have those? She saw red hair—'

'There you are! Nobody could accuse Minos of having red hair!'

'He'll say it was the red gold of a crown.'

'But Inia will insist that—'

Asterius took her hands. 'Do you think Minos is so stupid, or fair, or pious that he'd let the Key-Bearer be the only seer? He'll pack the shrine at Amnisos with his priests. They'll make their own divinations at the same time. He'll get the answer he wants, don't worry, and he'll make sure the whole world knows that he has been chosen.'

Asterius went to bed in silence, to empty his head of unwelcome thoughts and sleep. Adoni, though, was hungry. While Pasiphaë fed her, she asked Eritha after Asterion.

'He slept all evening. You'd never have known he'd been upset at all.'

'And Princess Kriti?'

'She came for the herbs you said, what I'd have prescribed for a woman losing too much blood. All except for the sweet clover. She's a quick learner, keen, but it baffles me why she wanted that.'

'She's maybe not quite as clever as she thinks. She must have meant red clover. You'd better take her some tomorrow. And make sure she doesn't mix them up.'

8

The confrontation

The days that followed were hot and stormy. Pasiphaë kept to the Dolphin Chamber, watched Asterion for signs of a relapse and sent Eritha to Kriti with a packet of red clover. The servant came back out of breath and with a worried expression.

'There's guards on Princess Kriti's door. Wouldn't let me in.'

'Tyro, go fetch Athamas for me. They won't keep him out.'

'I'd like to see 'em flamin' try! He'd wring their necks for 'em, one in each hand.'

This was what she feared, the closing of the trap. In front of her women she showed no fear, laughed when Tyro squeezed Athamas's biceps, but she saw unease in his eyes, and wondered how long she could count on his loyalty.

'Take a squad of men and make sure Eritha delivers her message. If that crone Ananke is with the Princess, bring her to me.'

For the moment, her orders were respected, her threats carried some weight, and it was not long before Ananke flapped into the room, shaking off the men escorting her. Pasiphaë noticed that none of them touched her, as if they, too, felt the venom in her presence.

'Princess Kriti is unwell. She shouldn't be left alone.'

'Since you've screeched Princess Kriti's womanhood to the rooftops, you've only got yourself to blame if you're out of a job. She needs women servants now not a nursemaid. But the house at Phaistos does need a housekeeper. You'll go there.'

Ananke's eyes flashed then narrowed with cunning. 'I was promised a place in the royal household as long as I lived. Only one of the royal line of Knossos has the right to dismiss me.'

Pasiphaë was weary of the woman. She was a servant, nothing more. 'The house at Phaistos *is* the royal household. You'll leave as soon as arrangements for your transport have been made.' She beckoned to Arete and Tyro. 'Go to Princess Kriti's apartment and see she has what she needs. Stay with her until I send for you.'

Ananke glared after the two girls. 'Prince Minos will be displeased.'

Pasiphaë could take no more of her. 'Princess Pasiphaë *is* displeased. Athamas, take her to collect her belongings and then to the servants' quarters. She can wait there until her removal to Phaistos.'

The woman's cunning expression didn't change. 'Minos will hear of this. And Princess Kriti won't thank you for interfering in her household either.'

She turned away before she could be dismissed. In a white fury, Pasiphaë called up all she remembered of Circe's incantations and threw them at the crow's back. Ananke stopped on the sill and Pasiphaë half expected to see her crumple and fall. Instead, she turned, slowly, deliberately, and on her narrow face the cunning expression had spread to become one of smug, thin-lipped triumph.

Athamas, too, had seen, and fear flickered in his eyes. For the first time, Pasiphaë noticed how he had changed. Except for his physique, there was no difference between him and the Cretans. Kolchis had slipped into the past, and she was alone.

*

Asterius was in the Throne Room wrestling with one of the interminable boundary disputes that formed the daily business of the court, when Pasiphaë entered and took the seat by his side, the larger, broader seat, designed for the generous forms of Potnia Athana. She sat, expressionless, while the law men droned on, reading out precedents. A glance at her face told him she was upset. He brought the hearing to a rapid conclusion, despite the protests of the two litigants.

'I'm afraid,' she said when the room was cleared, and they were alone except for the painted griffons at either side of the closed doors. 'I'm afraid for your daughter.' She took his hands. 'And I'm afraid for you, too.'

Asterius looked deep into her eyes. She understood what was coming, and he longed to comfort her and tell her he would fight it, but he couldn't. It was the law, the bedrock that Crete was built upon. He would not try to outwit fate.

'When Kriti marries, she will make a King. There can't be two Kings at one time.'

'But she doesn't have to marry! Not… yet!' Not Minos, was what she meant. She had understood it all then. 'What about your followers? Where are they all? Where is Antanor and his son?'

'Gone,' he replied, bluntly. He wouldn't give her false hope. 'Minos has driven away all those who aren't in his camp. He's powerful. Few dare to defy him.'

He didn't need to tell her this, she knew, but perhaps she had thought, hoped, that Kerameia and Antanor were stronger, more courageous than the rest. They were courageous, but not foolhardy. Minos didn't issue threats openly, but cattle died, barns caught fire, children fell down wells, quite inexplicably. The Cretans were not a military people. They gave so little thought to armies and defence it should not have surprised her they gave no thought at all to protecting themselves from their own.

'Come,' he said, getting to his feet, still holding her hands. 'We still have time together.'

*

Together, still King and Queen, they walked back to the royal apartment and closed the door of the bedchamber. Asterius undid the girdle of Pasiphaë's dress and let it slip from her shoulders. She shivered as she had done the first time, perhaps because this would be one of the last. His hands, so gentle, drew her to him and pressed her against his chest. She clung to him as tears wet his shoulder, ignoring the milk pain of her hardened nipples, and pulled him to the bed.

It was not yet midday, but it felt like midnight or the end of the world. She had learned to find intense pleasure in his caresses, but she was only now aware of how much more than pleasure there was in their oneness. Only now when she knew it must end. The separation hung so black and ominous that it filled all of her thoughts, a dark sea. She didn't wonder what would happen to her afterwards, without her King.

*

The black banner shook the darkness in its folds over the next feast. Pasiphaë had had Eritha spread the rumour among the servants that Kriti's first bleeding had been due to an accidental poisoning, hoping the incident would be forgotten. She had reckoned without Ananke's power to do harm. There were innumerable problems with getting her away from Knossos. First, she fell sick and took to her bed. Then the mules she was assigned were found to be lame, then a messenger arrived with the news that the earth had trembled at Phaistos and many of the buildings had been damaged. They needed workmen not housekeepers. Ananke was just a servant, but she was the spider in the web and the web was Minos.

Bribery was easy. Only the most loyal and well-considered servants were above it, and in the huge, rambling household that was the palace of Knossos, no chain was without a weak link. It was probably one of the laundry slaves who got hold of the bloody bed linen. Kriti's next flow had been too strong to stop it altogether, and a mere spotting was enough for Minos and his followers to cry victory.

*

It came at the Summer Rites. The thunder began to rumble as soon as the procession left Knossos, and by the time it reached Mount Iouktas, the wind had joined its roar to the song of the storm. The clouds, charcoal grey, seemed to touch the Great Mother's upraised hands, her bronze locks, flickering like flames in the strange, intermittent sunlight. Asterius had pleaded with Pasiphaë to stay away.

'Mount Iouktas has become an accursed place. Listen to the sky! If the Great Mother is angry, she's capable of shaking the earth until the palace falls. She's done it before.'

'Kriti's obliged to go, and she has more to fear than I do.' She was touched by the concern in his eyes. 'She shouldn't have to face this alone.'

He looked away, and she knew he was torn between what custom told him was right, and the nagging of his heart. He loved his daughter, and Pasiphaë's heart, too, was torn, though not over Kriti. Custom would make her Queen and at least gave her the right to choose her King. Custom had no use for the old one.

'We're all alone with our destinies.'

Tears made his voice hoarse. She reached out to take his hand, but the reflex came too late. Asterius had risen and turned to leave, to prepare himself for what would be his ordeal too.

*

Pasiphaë and Asterius walked together, letting the litters follow. They had no reason to hide, and despite the solemnity and splendour of their escort, it was obvious that the crowd, moving up the lower slopes of the mountain alongside the royal road, were not particularly interested in either the Moon Princess or the man who could soon be a lifeless carcass. The air was heavy. Pasiphaë heard it twittering. Not with the conversational chattering of feeding birds, but the malicious clacking of idle tongues. Feet raised the end of summer dust, pebbles skittered, and overhead crows flapped, scanning the stubbled fields. Black against black. The sky was angry. Dias? Was the Divine Son hungry? That was what Kriti would have said. Pasiphaë closed her mind to the watery blood trickling down her chin.

She listened for the voice of the Mistresses – soothing, or angry, either would have done. There was nothing but the clashing of the clouds and the tiny scraping sound of sandals, the irritation when small stones worked their way inside. Asterius was listening too. His face, all his senses were alert, alive. She caught his eye and he smiled. He was absorbing all the life he could, storing it for later, for afterwards.

The sanctuary loomed, a rocky excrescence, its pinnacle the forked effigy with piled hair and raised arms. The Great Mother. *She has no power.* The Mistresses dropped the thought into Pasiphaë's head. She glanced at Asterius. The Great Mother with the face of the Poppy Mistress had no hold over him either. It was not she who shed the blood; she had no voice to demand it. Her priestesses held the power in their chanting voices, the men and women like Minos and Ananke who revelled in the shedding of blood. Not Kriti. She was one of those the rites had broken.

'She won't live, you know.' Pasiphaë almost said *either*. Asterius heard the unspoken word but still smiled.

'She'll walk with me. At the other side of death, I'll be allowed to watch over her.'

And what about me? The niggling pain of the stones of the road digging into the soles of her feet was all that held her in that moment. *What about me, when you're gone?* Tears welled and ran down her face. The clouds clucked and rumbled. The Poppy Mistress had no deathly sleep for her.

*

Musicians took up position at the sanctuary entrance, scattering finches from the scrubby bushes. Pasiphaë wondered if they were the same ones, and whether they had their children with them. Birds and animals kept their children by them until they could make their own way. Why did men not do the same? Why did women agree to let them go? She would have asked Potnia Theron, but she couldn't feel her presence. Perhaps she was watching over the flock of finches, guiding them to a better feeding ground.

Her thoughts were idle, but they prevented her pondering the future, the bleak, black future she read in the lowering clouds. She had no need of a divination to tell her that death was coming. How many would die was the only imponderable.

'Take my arm,' Asterius whispered, drawing her back to earth and the present. Together they entered the dark doorway, knowing they would not come out the same.

She left Asterius with the men in the gallery that looked onto the courtyard of the shrine and took her place with the noblewomen. She wore the robes of Moon Princess, not High Priestess, having no wish to be a celebrant. She stood to the fore amid the rustling of rich dress fabrics, the sound of dead oak leaves in the winter wind. Circe said oak leaves remembered the voices of the dead. She wouldn't have been afraid to listen, but Pasiphaë practised the only talent her mother had ever been able to nurture in her, the art of escape. Her eyes slipped out of focus and she folded over the soft inner shell of her ears. Her hands hung by her side, numb, and she closed the narrow caves of her nose, let nothing enter. Her tongue slumbered in her mouth, a familiar presence, telling her nothing.

The Great Mother waved her arms over Pasiphaë's head,

but she couldn't see her. She shouted with the voice of the storm, but Pasiphaë heard nothing. She filled basin after basin with the thick blood of children, but its taste didn't stick to Pasiphaë's tongue, nor its smell fill the inside of her head.

When the dead had been taken away and the last prayers recited, the salpinges bellowed beneath the sanctuary walls and the tympana took up a marching rhythm. The wind was gusting wildly, blowing bursts of music over the wall, and the sound of high spirits rose, as the crowd eased the stiffness out of their limbs in the first dance movements before the procession made its way back down to Knossos.

Gradually, Pasiphaë came back to the world, the hilltop buffeted by the wind and the stench of blood. The nobles at either side of her were moving, flowing towards the dark doorway and the painted poppy room, along the gallery with the painting of children dancing, drawn to more excitement outside. She was right, nobody was the least interested in the Moon Princess, and the knowledge filled her with fear. She let herself be carried along, pleased to be leaving the shrine. She would wait for Kriti when she emerged with her priestesses, let her see that she walked at her side.

The dignified crowd poured out of the sanctuary in a whisper of fabrics and low voices, and she was caught up by the wild sky. It swept down to the mountain slopes, brushing a rough hand over the gathering, trembling the trees in the olive groves. Her skin shivered and she rubbed her arms to bring back the warmth. Her eyes searched for Asterius, but they were drawn inexorably to the group directly before the sanctuary gates, inspecting each woman and man who passed through them.

In the midst of the armed men in Greek-style greaves, breastplate and helmet was Minos: purple-clad, gold-circleted Minos. Behind him, in his shadow, a shadow herself, was the crow, Ananke, and in her hands, she clutched a rag. Pasiphaë knew what it was. Her nostrils flooded with the rank smell of blood. Minos gave her a triumphant look and held out his hand.

'Don't leave, Pasiphaë, not yet.'

What choice did she have? The road was like a swollen river blocked with fallen trees and boulders. Her litter was somewhere behind the mass of curious spectators, and the lowering sky was howling with storm rain waiting to burst. A movement, a wave of warmth, and she sensed Asterius before she saw him. In a moment their hands were joined, and their thoughts too. *Kriti. He's waiting for Kriti.*

The royal guardsmen had formed a barrier around Asterius and Pasiphaë, keeping back the curious. Athamas was at their head, but even he seemed shadowy, insubstantial in the storm light of that terrible afternoon. Pasiphaë recognised nothing of Kolchis in him any more. His dress was Cretan, and she caught the glitter of gold about his neck and arms, even his waist. He wore the ornaments he had once despised, the perfumes too. The sea had risen, and all she had to hold on to was a man, a mortal man.

'Princess Kriti!'

The roar of Minos's voice rose about the murmuring of the crowd, even above the rumble of the storm. White robes fluttered down to the sanctuary gates, and among them, one red-robed figure, Kriti, slight and frail, her diadem too heavy for the slender bones of her neck. She brought the smell of the slaughterhouse with her, and in the folds of her dress, the last pitiful cries of children. Her eyes, usually so blank, were open wide in shock.

*

Kriti heard Minos before she saw him and missed her step. But the flow of priestesses filling the gates behind would not be stopped, and she was carried stiffly towards her half-brother. She could do nothing else; he would have taken her arm and stopped her had she tried to pass him by.

The shocked silence in her head began to fill with an undercurrent of murmuring, like the flow of the tide, the voices of the common people, the servants and the farming folk gathered outside the sanctuary. *At last, we will have a Queen, the Great Mother has spoken, a new King, the harvest, the blight, a better season, next year, next year, a new Queen, King, the Mother, her son is hungry, the tribute, the tribute.*

'The tribute, the tribute, the tribute!'

This was what Minos wanted, though Kriti had never understood why. That he wanted to be King was what mattered to her. He smiled at the crowd, raised his hands as if to coax the sound louder. A salpinx brayed, then another, the bone trumpets of the sanctuary, a whole troop of them, aggressive as soldiers, and the foot stamping began. Minos gestured for silence and the braying stopped, the stamping dwindled.

'Princess Kriti, High Priestess of the Great Mother, has offered sacrifice in gratitude for the harvest, and to ask that it stay sound and healthy in the granaries and storehouses. This is the prayer we send her every year, but each year, the harvest is less.' He paused, waiting for the murmuring of agreement. 'The Divine Son is still hungry. The sacrifice is not enough for the Great Mother. She demands richer blood, the blood of Princes. For too long, she has been offered nothing but the watery blood of slaves.' The murmuring grew, louder than the gusting wind. 'But now we have a new Queen and will have a new King. The old ways will return!'

His words chilled Kriti to the bone, but when Ananke stepped forward, the chill turned to terror. The crow-black nurse raised her arms to exhibit the ghostly white of a linen sheet, and the dark red stain in its centre. 'The Queen's first blood!'

The crone cackle split the air, and Kriti cringed in horror. She had thought she could hide her womanhood, but she was no match for practised intriguers.

'The Queen!'

The crowd roared, and Kriti clutched her stomach as the fear and humiliation at the violation turned to nausea. The crowd roared as if her first blood could change the sky, the earth, the world. She looked for no sign from the Mistresses. They were silent. This was the sacred mountain, the sanctuary of the Great Mother, and the Great Mother demanded her, heart and soul. Beneath the shadow of the bronze arms, Kriti felt as fragile as eggshell. A harsh word, an angry gesture, and she would break.

Minos raised his square, indelicate paws, and she would have run if there had been anywhere on the bare mountainside to hide. He beamed, triumphant.

'Today belongs to the Summer Rites, but tomorrow will be dedicated to the new Queen.'

*

Pasiphaë watched helplessly. She had never been more than a scene in the picture, and Asterius had diminished to a shadow of the décor. Minos – the broad, glossy Minos – had taken centre stage, and there was nothing that anyone could do about it.

PART FIVE

The first star sets

Storm clouds wreathed Mount Iouktas, and the bellow of the salpinges was like the swell of the sea. Martial music roared and echoed in the sea cave at Amnisos and rolled through the deeps to the mainland where there were ears to hear, armies eager for war, spear tips thirsty for blood and men hungry for gain. Minos invoked the Great Mother but what answered his call was a force not even the bloody-mouthed Mother could withstand.

1

The embassy

The storm finally broke as they flew, Pasiphaë and Asterius, back to Knossos. They flew as a defeated army flies, as the countryfolk fly before an invader, as a flock of sparrows flies when the marten pounces. The Summer Rites were only just begun, and the people demanded their share of the celebrations. The storm would not last, and when the sky had blown clear, the bull-leaping would begin in the Barley Court. The bull-running would stampede up and down the royal road and the streets of the port. There would be boxing and wrestling and foot races, none of which the royal couple would be required to watch. They were for the people, and the people had already forgotten Pasiphaë, the woman who had lain with a bull and given birth to a monster.

The rumours had sickened her at first, but she had grown deadened to them. She saw her dull acceptance reflected in Kriti's eyes. They were not so different. Kriti's absence was not indifference, it was a barrier against the pain.

Kriti was allowed only a brief respite, to change out of her priestess garb and into a dress suitable for a Queen, before she was exhibited again on the dais of the Barley Court. It was she who said the prayer to Potnia Theron to whisper mercy to the bull and spare the dancers. It was her name the people called, even those beyond the walls and out of sight.

Pasiphaë felt something slipping out of her grasp; not

power, that had already gone. She had not even been able to have Ananke dismissed. It was not happiness either, but the essence of life. The leaping dancers, the sweating bull, the excited shouting were as unreal as the life of fish in a pool, in another element.

She sat with Asterius, surrounded by nobles who talked across them as though they weren't there. They waved their arms, laughed, and smiled obsequiously in the direction of Minos, who stood by the wall of the court, looking down at the spectacle, shouting like a docker at the bull and leapers indiscriminately. He expanded to fill the side of the court. It was he who drew the eye, not the bull-leapers. They were vowed to death after all, but Minos, everyone knew, Minos would be King.

The celebrations went on long after nightfall, and the royal couple were obliged to stay until the feasting was over. In the frenzied joy-taking, Pasiphaë heard a confused plea for a kind of security. Voices were not raised to praise the good harvest, the healthy animals and children born, but in a plea that the next harvests, next year's child, would be better.

'The harvest this year was good,' she said, though Asterius gazed without seeing across the crowded tables. 'I went over the accounts with Eumedes. There was no more barley lost to blight than usual, and the wheat harvest was small but sound. The ewes were mostly full and we lost not too many lambs in the early spring.'

Asterius gave a weary shrug of his shoulders and sighed. 'It doesn't matter what the district governor says, the tally of the granaries he can produce. The people believe the Great Mother is angry with them and that there's only one way to divert her anger. No noble Cretan family would agree to sacrifice its children, so we must take the children of our enemies.'

'We have trading partners, not enemies,' Pasiphaë said bitterly.

'Partners who don't always honour their contracts.' He

sighed again. 'The truth is, we might have the best fleet, control all the trade routes and have the whole of the Cyclades in our orbit, but when a district decides it doesn't want to pay its full tribute, what threat can we make?' Pasiphaë was going to say something uninformed about warships, but he shook his head. 'A fleet without an equivalent military force is simply a fleet of cargo vessels. We have no military. We don't even build defences. Our people dance and feast and enjoy themselves. They're not warriors. Bureaucrats and merchants, but not soldiers.'

'And that's why we make trade deals not enemies,' she repeated stubbornly.

'They will be enemies when we take their Princes and Princesses.'

His voice was flat, matter-of-fact, and he was right. But fear of war, famine, disaster were distant, intangible. All that really touched Pasiphaë was what would happen to Asterius, their children and herself. She looked, in vain, at the faces shiny with grease, glittering in the torchlight, for those who had once been courteous and respectful, but those who were not Minos's partisans, who were not in debt to him for favours, promotions, contracts, loans, had been chased from the court. She looked for one face in particular, daring to hope. He wasn't there. Asterius didn't even allow himself the luxury of hope.

'Kesandros won't come, not now.'

'Then send for him. He can still change fate. The Mistresses choose the King through the wishes of the Queen. You know who she has chosen. Let him come.'

Her voice, she could hear it ringing in her head, was full of passion. Asterius pressed her hand, but he didn't reply. If he wouldn't do it, then she would. Kesandros wouldn't demand the full price of Asterius. That custom had fallen out of usage long ago. But it was still practised on the mainland where sons were impatient to sit in their fathers' seats. *My father's people*, Minos claimed. Minos would show Asterius no mercy. Kriti must have Kesandros. He was young, straight-limbed and he had a sensitive face. He would be kind to Kriti. In time, he might even come to love her.

Kriti sat at her own table, close enough for Pasiphaë to be able to watch her. She ate nothing. Picked up pieces of food and put them down without touching them. Her eyes were huge and empty. Pasiphaë guessed that the poppy allowed her spirit to wander, to leave her body and walk outside in the silence and the absence of the world. But it left her body in this world. Pasiphaë's heart contracted with pity, and she made up her mind, left the table, the feast. Nobody would notice that she had gone anyway. Asterius followed her with his eyes but stayed at his place, and as she passed into the quiet of the royal entrance, his gaze turned back to stare, unseeing, over the heads of the laughing feasters.

*

Once in the apartment, she sent for Athamas. 'I want you to take ship for Malia on the first tide. Go to Antanor's house and give a message to his son Kesandros. Tell him Princess Kriti is now Queen, and the Mistresses have chosen him to be her King. Tell him to come quickly and accept the honour.'

Athamas had become a Cretan; he understood what was at stake as well as any. It was only then, at that moment of finishing her message, that she asked herself what Athamas thought. Whose camp was he in? She looked away, not wishing to see if the answer in his eyes was one she would not like.

*

Pasiphaë fed Adoni and sang to Asterion, a song her nurse in Kolchis used to sing to her, until he fell asleep. She could sing the same song over and over, the same melody on a handful of notes, and he would listen with the same rapt expression on his face, his small, impenetrable eyes fixed on something she couldn't see.

'Am-am-á,' he whispered, and sighed into sleep, still smiling. She kissed his brow and went to the bedchamber to wait for Asterius.

It was much later when he finally came to his bed. She heard the clatter of guards outside the door and knew that he was afraid. His tread was heavy, uncertain, and when he unpinned his cloak and threw it onto a chair he staggered slightly. She could smell the wine, thick, sweet and strong, and her heart wept for him. Even the lamplight, golden and warm, couldn't soften his drawn features. She went to him and wrapped her arms about him. He seemed to melt, merge with her flesh, and she sensed that he had given himself into the hands of fate. She was not ready to give in, though. Not yet.

*

They didn't speak until afterwards, when they had loved furiously, as if it was their last time. For all they knew, it was. Asterius lay in Pasiphaë's arms. She stroked his face, combing back his hair with her fingers. Beneath her touch he trembled, a leaf in the wind, and she wondered if she would find tears in his eyes when he turned his face to her.

'I've sent for Kesandros. He'll listen to the voice of the Mistresses. He'll come.'

The trembling ceased, but although something seemed to leave his body, like a wounded bird flying from the huntsman's bag, she knew Asterius wouldn't allow himself to hope.

'If he comes, Minos will kill him.'

His voice was heavy, full of sadness. Pasiphaë wanted to shake him, tell him he was wrong. Custom would prevail. 'If he comes as a pretender to the kingship, it's you he'll have to fight, not Minos.'

He turned on his side then and faced her. There was a

glitter in his eyes, but not of hope. 'And you believe that Minos will let him get so far?'

She saw Minos, his broad, brutal face leering behind her eyes, his square, blunt hands that twisted, a neck, a limb, and his thick tongue mocked her. But she still refused to believe.

'We'll protect him. He already has the protection of the Mistresses.'

Asterius kissed her on the brow, then on the mouth, with passion, and they came together again, squeezing out the pain and the grieving for a future that was slipping from their grasp.

*

Leto and the morning sun woke Pasiphaë. The sheet was tangled up with Asterius's flung limbs. She let him sleep, picked up the curled marten and carried her through to the small room where the children slept. Asterion was on his back, breathing laboriously, his forehead sticky with sweat. She swept back his curls and breathed onto his brow. A small smile twitched the corners of his mouth. She placed Leto in the crook of his arm and the arm curved around as the little animal turned about herself, curling back into a sleeping position. She left them, marten and child, curled together, and washed in the tepid water that flowed into the basin of the bathing room.

The storm of the previous day had washed the sky clear. It would be a beautiful day. She took it as an omen that the anger of the Great Mother's day was over, and Kriti's day would be calm and serene. Kesandros would come and he would stop Minos and his dark plotting. She stepped out onto the terrace and watched the morning light pour across the hillside to the west where the white shapes of sheep moved, and lower down, where the grass was lusher, a herd of cattle. In his own field, pacing along the boundary fence, was the white bull from Kolchis. If she went among the herd, she would be able to pick out his offspring. She took the time to say a prayer to Potnia

Theron, and to Athana to guide the ship from Malia safely to port. If Kesandros accepted his destiny, he would arrive on the morning tide.

When she was dressed, Pasiphaë went to speak to Kriti. If there was hope, she deserved to know about it. She took no one with her, though she still had a horror of the old part of the palace with the shrine to the Poppy Mistress, where the High Priestess had her apartment. The ghosts of that time before the tribute, when child sacrifice was made to the Red Lady, lingered in the stones, even in the bright splashes of paint on the walls. She hurried through the central courtyard, at such an early hour meeting only servants and slaves, and the scribes and artisans beginning the day's work.

The morning air was cool, but as she ran down the stair to the level beneath, the cool grew damp, the cool of earth and stone that never sees the sun. So much blood had soaked this earth, so many last cries were smothered here, the earth filling so many dead mouths. The old palace had once been as bright as the new, but since the last time the earth had shaken, the paintings had not been renewed and pithoi and amphorae stood or lay or were buried in most of the rooms. Crete's treasure house, Asterius had said, but there was more than wealth in those dark rooms.

She hurried along the Poppy Gallery that led past the shrine to the apartment marked with the Great Mother's sign, flanked by the images of two lionesses. She should have expected what she found. As well as two painted lionesses, two armed men guarded Kriti's door. Their crossed spears, she guessed, were as much to keep Kriti in as unwanted visitors out. In the thick, heavy atmosphere of the place, it was so hard to keep believing that Asterius was wrong, that Minos could be defeated.

*

Kriti was to be recognised as the new Queen in the Court of Ceremonies, and an army of servants was filling it with bowls of petals, pots of flowers, green branches and scented oils. The basins would be filled with fresh water, and jars of oil, wine and honey had already been brought to the altar for the libations. Asterius and Pasiphaë stayed in their apartment, preparing themselves and Asterion. Pasiphaë told herself that nothing would happen today. This was the Queen's day, devoted to her praise, games, feasting and dancing in her honour. There would be a dance through the labyrinth, music and festivities. There would be no death today. Not even a sacrifice. The blood shed was the Queen's, her womanhood, no other.

They prepared themselves for the ceremonies and waited for news from Amnisos. A messenger was to run up from the port when Kesandros' ship docked; an escort was already waiting to accompany him. Pasiphaë refused to believe he wouldn't come. Asterius leaned on the parapet of the terrace and stared down towards the port, invisible in the fold of the hills. His shoulders sagged, his hands worked, cracking his knuckles, the lock of grey quite visible in the hair that hung to his shoulders. Suddenly he straightened and turned, his face alight. He pointed.

'Look. The same pair. The Mistress has sent a sign.'

A pair of turtle doves settled in an oleander, their pale greys and creams set among the brilliant rose-red blooms. Pasiphaë wanted to believe that they were special, *their* doves, not just two birds looking for berries. She listened to the sky, pretended she heard the whispered voice of Potnia Theron, and returned his smile.

A small hand tugged at her dress. Asterion's strange little face looked up, his eyes the indeterminate green-brown of shiny river mud or winter willow leaves, unblinking as a bird's.

'Am-am-á, not sandals.' He raised one foot and shook it, wobbling unsteadily. 'Hurts. Adoni don't.'

Pasiphaë smiled and bent down, took his face in her hands, searching those flat planes for something of the sharply chiselled features of Asterius, and found nothing, only the same gentle light in his eyes. She almost wept at the realisation. That was the most important, the inside, and when did gentleness ever stem a tide of cruelty?

'Adoni doesn't need to wear sandals, Asterion. Her feet can't walk yet.' She showed him her own gold-strapped feet. 'Mamá wears sandals like yours.'

'Feet walk. Not sandals,' he said with surprising logic, and pointed at Asterius. 'Feet walk. Ap-ap-á feet walk. Walk, walk, walk away.'

When Asterius turned, there were tears in his eyes, and she knew that the doves were no more than birds and no one had sent them.

The sound of running feet broke into her misery. A messenger, his chest heaving with exertion, sweat beading his face, waited in the doorway for permission to speak. She called, her voice loud with excitement. 'Asterius!'

He stepped in from the terrace, his face drawn, the muscles working to maintain a neutral expression. 'The ship has docked?'

The messenger nodded. 'The ship bearing the emissary Athamas has returned, and he has brought Kesandros, Antanor's son with him.'

In the silence that followed, Pasiphaë's ears filled with the sound of her blood pulsing, heart pounding. Such longing she had withheld, flowed out in a long, slow stream of relief. The merest change in the muscles around Asterius's eyes betrayed his own relief. He dismissed the messenger and took her hands. Neither spoke, but their eyes shared a glimmer of hope.

2

Erythros

Salpinges sounded, boomed their deep hoarse roar, as the procession of dignitaries reached the Court of Ceremonies. The Court would be full, but the dais would be empty. Nobody would take a seat before the King and the Moon Princess. Whatever Minos intended, custom would prevail to the end. The royal couple left their apartment, Asterion walking between them. He had wanted to bring Leto and threatened to cry when he was told no, but Pasiphaë placated him with a painted wooden bull, Drupa, his favourite, the one Kriti had given him. Eritha followed with Adoni in her arms, and Athamas at the head of their personal guard flanked the little procession.

Much as she longed to question Athamas about Kesandros, how many men he had brought with him, whether he had spoken of his intentions, it was, of course, impossible. All she knew was that the young man had been met by his father's men and escorted to their house in the hills. She prayed to the Mistresses that he would do his duty.

As they left the gallery and stood at the head of the staircase, the braying of the salpinges died away. Auloi and syringes fluted a melody, and the voices of Kriti's priestesses took it up. The courtyard below ebbed and flowed with the white foam of their dresses, and on the fringes, the brilliant patterned and hooped skirts of courtiers. Pasiphaë held her head high, but her heart was heavy. Such a clear blue sky, soft sun, yet she felt no warmth in it. A dozen different scents rose, thick, sweet and overpowering, and she thought of the preparation of corpses.

She began the descent. Asterion tugged at her hand, stumbling, and his father caught him. He had dropped his toy and she heard the wheezing, huffing noise that preceded a wail. Asterius scooped it up and handed it back. The snuffling stopped. They exchanged glances. Worrying about a child, watching him for signs of a fit, was a small distraction from the turning of the wheel. The King's season turned as all did, as spring flowers followed the frosts, as blossom fell, and the summer sun parched, shrivelling the green to winter dullness again. The grey in Asterius's hair glinted in the sun, but he was not old. Not old enough to die unaided.

Asterius took up his place on the royal dais, and the other seats filled behind him; skirts rustled impatiently, voices too loud. He greeted some, but there was no contact, no one touched his hand. Minos was the last to take his place. He made sure Pasiphaë and Asterius saw him, stalking before the dais like a master of ceremonies. Which, Pasiphaë supposed, he was. When she saw that Asterion was settled on the ground next to his father's chair, she walked across the pavement, the coloured stone slabs that marked out the labyrinth dances, and climbed to the altar, to take her place as High Priestess of the Mistresses.

Minos finally took his seat and the music struck up again with a new tune, and a new chant. The purification began, the washing of Kriti's hands in the basin, the anointing of her hair, then Pasiphaë, as officiant, placed the Queen's diadem on her head and Kriti raised her hands in imitation of the Great Mother. She could not meet Pasiphaë's eyes, but the beads of sweat at her temples gave her fear away, like bronze tears melting.

The crowd standing around the court cheered; scores more perched in the windows around the courtyard cheered and tossed flowers. As Queen, Kriti made libations of honey and wine to the Great Mother and the Mistresses and released a pair of doves, symbolic of the new Queen and the King who would come to her. Pasiphaë was perhaps the only one to notice how her fingers fumbled with the catch of the doves' cage, but the priestesses standing behind the altar certainly saw how the second dove did not want to fly, how the new Queen had to reach inside the wicker cage and pull it out in a flurry of beating wings and lost feathers.

When the two birds were finally in the air, Pasiphaë spoke the prayer to all the Mistresses. 'Behold, Mothers of the Earth and Sky, the Queen, Kriti of Knossos, Princess of Crete, and High Priestess of the Great Mother. In your bounty, send her a worthy King that she might bear strong daughters and a great son like the mighty Potnia.'

She turned to the watching crowd and raised her arms as Kriti had done, as the statue of the Great Mother, the mountain goddess, did in her summit sanctuary, and the people roared, chanting the name, *Kriti, Kriti, Kriti.* In response, the dancers – white swans or egrets – flocked onto the dancing pavement, to dance the story of the new Queen. With a cascade of flute notes, the dancing birds, in a swirl of white skirts, covered the coloured stone of the steps. The melody was joined by the sweet strumming of kitharai and the sinuous movements of male dancers, their oiled brown skin gleaming otter-sleek. Tympana beat an increasingly intense rhythm until it pounded rapid as pulsing blood, and the crowd tapped hands and feet, urging the dancers faster, encouraging them to touch, hold and embrace.

The rhythm rose to an impossible cadence, the bird dancers met, joined and, as the music crashed and subsided, sank to the ground in voluptuous exhaustion. The crowd cheered enthusiastically, and Pasiphaë watched Kriti. She was not watching the dancers, and she was oblivious to those hanging in the openings of the many windows. Her eyes flicked over the faces heaving in and out of sight on the edge of the courtyard, drawn to the royal dais and the burly figure in a seat just behind her father's, his legs sprawled insolently, his chin resting on one hand, a mocking expression in his eyes.

Pasiphaë saw what passed between them, the fear in Kriti's eyes and Minos's contemptuous dismissal of her plea. Suddenly, the air charged with excitement, and Kriti's lips parted, her expression changed to astonished disbelief. Voices rose in cheers of encouragement as a tall young man entered the court from the Gallery of Processions.

He was cloaked in purple and gold – proud, then – and he carried a spear. The red cast to his auburn hair glowed fiery in the sun. Pasiphaë heard the murmur of his nickname, *Erythros*, that fiery hair had earned him, and her face broke into a smile of joy and relief. Kesandros had grown to manhood in the year and more since he had been absent from the palace. This man would make a good King, Pasiphaë judged, and he would not exact the tribute of death.

From the corner of her eye, she caught the slight movement among the seated figures on the royal dais as Asterius leaned forward, gripping the arms of his seat. It was Minos who drew the eye of the crowd as he sprang to his feet, and Pasiphaë could only hope it was in anger and surprise. He said nothing. How could he? Kesandros had not stated his intent yet. The priestesses around the altar murmured. Was this a breach of protocol or did they welcome it? Pasiphaë didn't know enough of the custom of Knossos to be sure. If a handsome pretender had arrived at Aea at the presentation of the Queen, it would have been seen as a gift from the Mistresses. She would have welcomed him with open arms.

Kesandros had reached the altar, and in a simple gesture of deference, knelt before it, his head bowed. For a moment Kriti appeared stunned, fuddled by poppy fumes or too happy to speak. When she found her voice, the words of welcome tumbled out like spring water. She wanted to believe in this story, as much as Pasiphaë did. The Mistresses willed it; they both clung to that certitude.

*

'What brings you here, this first day of the rule of the new Queen?' Incredulity made Kriti stumble over the words. Happiness too; it tied her tongue.

The reply rang out clear and steady in the hushed silence. 'I come at the behest of the Potniai, to become the new King.'

She studied his face, wondering if it was ambition that had decided him or piety. There was no love in his eyes. How could there be? The excited conversations they had had were only in her imagination. They had never exchanged more than common courtesies. But there was a softness in his face, as if he would be willing to give his affection. She could barely contain her emotions. Already she was dancing the Bull Dance with her King. She turned to her priestesses.

'Bring water to wash away the impurities of his past life, honey to give him strength in the combat and wine to drink to his royal future.'

Acolytes hurried with jars of water and honey, and another placed a dish on the altar. Kriti couldn't take her eyes from Kesandros' face. She had forgotten everything else. Her fears had flown with the doves. Perhaps the reluctant bird had been struggling with Kesandros' doubts, or with the clash of his and Minos's desires. Either way, the bird had taken wing and so had her hopes.

A priestess poured a little water into her cupped hands and she sprinkled it onto Kesandros' head bowed over the stone basin, then poured a libation of honey for the Mistresses and invited him to rise. Inia, the Key-Bearer, picked up the dish of wine already poured, ready for the pretender, and offered it to Kesandros. Kriti, happiness bursting through the fog of poppy that calmed her terrors, barely registered the Key-Bearer at her side. When she spoke, her voice trembled, on the brink of too much joy.

'Drink to your future, that the strength of your arm will make it a glorious one.'

The words were merely symbols, not a call to murder. Not any longer. She had no thought of demanding the life of the old King, and she was sure Kesandros wouldn't demand it either. He drained the cup and handed it back to her. Their fingers touched, and she felt the hot blood rise to her cheeks. Her eyelids fluttered with pleasure and she smiled.

Minos had still not spoken, and after his first brusque movement, had returned to his place. It was the turn of her father, the old King to rise now, and take up the challenge. Once, the challenge would have been the high point of the ritual, more highly awaited than any other part. Blood would be shed, and a man would die. It was honest entertainment, and no blame was to be had in its enjoyment, because the Mistresses willed it, and it was the custom. Was. But no longer. Kriti, for the first time since she could remember, felt truly happy.

*

A servant ran up with the Bull King mask and spear. Asterius put the horned helmet on his head, undid his belt and let his kilt drop to the floor. Clad only in a loin guard and the bull mask, he took the spear and leapt down from the dais. Eritha grabbed Asterion to stop him following.

'If you want the kingship, you must take it.'

His voice was solemn, but his step was light, eager. Pasiphaë wished she could see his face, the glitter of amusement she imagined in his eyes. Kesandros tossed aside his cloak and kilt, picked up his spear. The two men danced the Dance of the Kings, their feet following a pattern, their spears feinting and weaving in a ritual. She knew the lines of Asterius's body so well, the muscles, how they knitted together, the hunting scar on his left thigh. He danced like a young man. *Not old! Not old enough.*

She wondered if Kriti was thinking about the old custom, abandoned not so very long ago, imagining the spear taking her father's life. Did she care, as long as the outcome was that she had Kesandros as King? The dance was coming to a conclusion. Women danced around the pavement's edge beating tambourines, repeating the beat of the tympana and the clashing bells of the koudounia; the crowd clapped and chanted the names of Kriti and Erythros.

The climax came when the two men reached the centre of the labyrinth. There was a final clash of weapons and Asterius fell down on one knee. Pasiphaë's heart contracted as Kesandros' spear dipped, but it was only to flip away the Bull mask. Tossing the spear to one side, he took up the mask in both hands and turned in a circle so all could see. Her heart beat again, pounding like a charging bull, and the crowd cheered as he placed the symbol of kingship on his head and over his face. Kriti's eyes glittered. It was done, they said. She was safe, the nightmare over.

But the Mistresses were looking elsewhere, and Kesandros' triumphant display faltered, his legs bent strangely, his hands went to his throat then fell limply to his side. He staggered and fell. The bull mask clattered to one side as his knees flexed up to his chest then stretched again, rigid. His back arced and his fingers tore at his throat. Pasiphaë's own hands rose to her throat. Her eyes flew to Kriti and she saw the horrified expression, the dawning of a terrible realisation as the girl's gaze went from the man struggling against his death to the empty wine dish. Pasiphaë turned to Minos, saw his faintly amused expression, then she ran to Asterius.

Women fluttered around Kesandros, forcing some liquid between his frothing lips, trying to make him vomit. But it was too late. When he did retch and spew out the contents of his stomach there was black blood in it, then more, brighter red until all he was throwing up was blood. Poison. But who had done it? Minos? But he hadn't known Kesandros would be the pretender. He had been poised to challenge Asterius himself.

'The Great Mother has spoken.' Minos had left his seat and strolled nonchalantly into the middle of the pavement. 'Kesandros was not her choice. Let's see who her favour *has* fallen upon.'

The crowd roared in confusion, though only the common people who hung in the window spaces. The courtiers were silent, moving back from the edge of the dancing court. Minos picked up Kesandros's spear.

'This time, Asterius, you will meet the Great Mother's choice.'

Pasiphaë looked to Kriti to stop it, but she seemed frozen with shock. She put herself between Minos and Asterius. 'No, Minos. There has been one Bull Dance, there will not be another. Not until the shrine has been purified and offerings made. A man is dying.'

'The Mistresses struck him down,' he said laconically, 'or else the new Queen poisoned him.' Pasiphaë heard the gasp and Kriti hid her face in her hands. She could have killed Minos then, but the Mistresses had denied her the power they gave Circe. He hefted the spear. 'Get out of the way, Pasiphaë. You have no place here.'

Slaves were carrying Kesandros out of the courtyard. Kriti followed with her eyes, but it was her duty to stay until the end. Asterius put a hand on Pasiphaë's shoulder and squeezed it.

'Go to our child, my love. Don't let him fret.'

'When I've dealt with the man, I'll deal with the monster,' Minos said, and his lips stretched over his teeth in an ugly grin.

Asterius pushed her firmly to one side and lifted his spear. 'The only monster here is named Minos, and the Mistresses forbid him to harm the Queen's brother.' He turned to Pasiphaë, his teeth still clenched in hatred. 'Go!' His voice was white with fury. 'Don't let him see.'

With the numbness of despair in her heart, she returned to the dais and took Asterion in her arms. He snuffled, 'Am-am-á, Am-am-á,' and she pressed his face to her breast, but she couldn't leave Asterius, even though he was already marked for death. Minos was younger, heavier, he had the goddess and most of the court on his side, and he intended to exact the full tribute from the old King.

The spears rose and twisted in the air, sweeping like staves, aiming for the legs, the arms. Each tried to turn the other into the sun, to snatch small advantages. Neither man was a warrior. Neither had much skill at arms, but Pasiphaë could see that Asterius was not really trying. Even when his spear blade opened Minos's right forearm, he seemed to take no fresh strength from it, as if the blow had been accidental, pure luck. Minos was enraged, his strokes grew more chaotic, he slashed and raked, like a thief beating back a guard dog.

Minos's lack of skill made no difference in the end. A blow to the shin, Asterius stumbled, and Minos was on him with all his weight, driving his spear into his neck. Blood, poppy red, pumped onto the pale, glittering stones of the labyrinth, like a sacrificial bull. There were pigeons cooing on the roof of the gallery. Asterion's hands gripped the front of his mother's dress. In the shocked silence, before the crowd could decide whether to cheer or cry out in anger, he threw back his head and howled.

3

Funeral rites

Kriti had gone. Pasiphaë didn't know when. She had servants bring Asterius back to the royal apartment. No one else stepped forward to do it, none of his former followers. The wound was clean, not ragged. The lifeblood had drained away, nonetheless. His face was calm, sad but resigned. He had not wanted to die, but it was his duty. He was a King. His life had always been in the hands of the Mistresses.

She carried Asterion, who refused to let go of her dress but hung there like a young, still-blind animal. The court must have been full of people, but she remembered nothing afterwards. Memory was a blur, as her vision was then, clouded with tears. Semele and Eune took Asterion, cooing and singing to him while Eritha made up a potion to send him to sleep, a gentle poppy. He would wake again. Pasiphaë wouldn't take anything. There was little enough time she had left to spend with Asterius. She wanted to be awake for all of it.

Her eyes saw through a veil of tears, her own and those of her women. All their own sorrows, their lost loves, homes, merged in a liquid stream with Pasiphaë's. There was no difference between them, no hierarchy of suffering. Eune's sharp, critical eyes glittered, and Tyro and Arete sniffed and wiped their noses constantly. Semele's hands fluttered, longing to hold her, even though she knew, better than them all, that there is no comfort for some sorrows.

They laid Asterius on the bed where Pasiphaë would never sleep with him again, and the women helped her clean his body of all the blood and sand, the dirt of combat. The skin was still warm, but beneath it was cooling. The fire inside would not burn again until she joined him in the afterlife.

His larnax was waiting for him. He had shown it to her months before, and she had admired the wave designs around it. 'For my final voyage,' he'd said and laughed. She had asked what gift he would like her to put in it, and he'd asked for one of Asterion's wooden bulls, and to be perfumed with the scents that she used. 'So that I will have your presence with me forever. And don't let them take away the thread bracelet.' He had worn it since the wedding.

All these scenes and words came back to her in a rush, like a great warm wave, so immense and full of sadness she couldn't bear it. Perhaps Eritha had slipped poppy into her drink after all, because at some point of the night, the images stopped, and she slipped into blissful oblivion.

*

Eritha woke her the next morning, and she found that she had been laid on a small bed next to Asterius. Leto was curled in the crook of her arm, and she wept the first tears of the day into her soft fur. Asterion was tearful and Adoni too cried from the moment she woke, demanding her share of attention. There was so much to do that day, preparing, organising, arranging, and she was to remember nothing of it, only Asterion dragging at her skirts and Adoni's plaintive cries whenever she was put down.

Word had been sent to Malia, and Antanor and Kerameia came to take their son's body home. Pasiphaë didn't know what Minos told them, she wasn't present, but whatever it was, they didn't believe it. She spoke to them both, the solemn, grey-bearded man and Kerameia, red-haired as her son, with eyes as grey and empty as a winter sea. She told them how sorry she was, but she could accept no guilt. The Mistresses had called Kesandros, and he had answered the call.

'It wasn't the Mistresses who gave him poison to drink,' Kerameia said bitterly. Her husband put a warning hand on her arm. What could they say? What could anyone do? They suspected Minos but had no proof. And Pasiphaë had her own sorrows. 'We were received by the Queen. The name of Kesandros was written on her heart. His death wasn't meant to be.' Her voice cracked and there was a pause as she recovered herself. 'She won't be long behind her King. The boy will have his Queen's company soon.'

Nobody referred to Minos as King. His name was offered at the tip of the tongue, scarcely touching the lips, like the taste of something rotten.

*

The funeral was to take place immediately. The days were hot, and Minos had a wedding to think about. The old King was to be hurried away as quickly as propriety permitted. Asterius came from a Knossian family; their tombs were in the hills to the west of the city overlooking the sea. Custom had it that a funeral was a cause for celebration, but what event was not, in Crete? There would be feasting and entertainments at the tomb, and Asterius would be bid farewell in an atmosphere of gaiety. Pasiphaë, though, was filled with dread, at the endless procession of faces, some wearing a false sorrow, others openly jubilatory.

She wore the panoply of High Priestess. She wouldn't let Minos forget who she was, and Asterion was dressed in the gold and purple of a Prince. She let herself be prepared while her mind floated elsewhere. No anchor stone weighed her to Knossos. She had no happiness now, only duties to the Mistresses and to her daughter. The only light in the gloom was Asterion, and she clung to his small hand as tightly as he clung to hers. The hardest part of that terrible morning was watching him say goodbye to his father.

She took him to the shrine, the small shrine dedicated to the Potniai close to the royal apartment, that she had had lit with a hundred lamps. The larnax stood beneath the small bronze statue of Potnia Athana, who opened her generous arms amid a ring of lamps that bathed the clay casket in a warm orange glow. She had brought a basket of his toys, and Asterion had been playing quietly. Sometimes, in the game, he would make one of the wooden figures shout or bellow or laugh, and he would put a finger to his lips. 'Shush, Ap-ap-á sleeping.'

Pasiphaë watched him weaving his stories with their simple lines and comforting conclusions, where fathers lived forever and little sisters and pine martens never grew older. In his story, Asterius slept because he had a long journey ahead, and that was what kept sorrow from overwhelming him. She watched as he ran his finger along the decorations in the glaze of the larnax, the wiggly wave lines, or serpents, or dolphins. Whatever took his fancy. He raised his face, the face they said was vacant, simple, but she knew was wise and gentle, and it knew how to smile.

'Will you give Papá one of your toys to take with him on the journey? He said he would like one.'

Obediently, he crouched down and stood his favourites in review on the cold stone pavement. After much thought, he picked up the white bull with red ears and horns. 'Asti will give Drupa to Ap-ap-á. He's the King of the bulls.'

He raised his favourite toy for his mother to admire, the smile wider, his eyes inviting her approval. He had never said such a long phrase. She lifted him up, he leaned into the larnax, and she helped him settle the wooden bull among the stiff tangle of Asterius's hands.

'There,' he said, satisfied. 'Ap-ap-á and Drupa. Two Kings.'

Pasiphaë led him away before they closed the lid.

*

The road to the family tombs was dusty, a mere cart track, and after the rites, the celebrations were interminable.

Asterion had been left behind for fear of the effects of the long, emotional day. Kriti was not present, and Pasiphaë was alone amid a crowd of unknown relatives and courtiers whose motives she distrusted. The litter brought her back to Knossos by torchlight, rocking on the uneven road like a ship in the night. She slept in the Queen's apartment, among dancing dolphins, supposing it to be for the last time. She was not the Queen, never had been. The new Queen would find it a more cheerful place than her old rooms in the dark of the old palace. The thought was not without bitterness.

Eritha had brought her a sleeping draught and she was grateful for it. Despite the exhaustion brought by grief and the strain of watching others enjoying themselves, the pictures in her head would not be still. There were so many memories she was terrified would be lost: the way Asterius looked at her with one eyebrow slightly raised, the brush of his lips when he whispered in her ear, the touch of his long, gentle fingers as they stroked her like a silky animal. She let them crowd and call until she wanted to weep with so much lost happiness that she had not recognised until now for what it was.

*

She woke to lamplight that made the painted dolphins leap, and the sensation of being alone. She would have gone back to sleep and slept until all the grief was over, but it was not permitted. She had duties as a royal consort, a mother and a High Priestess. Minos would want his marriage celebrating, his union with his half-sister, to begin his reign. Nobody could have been under any illusion that he intended to respect tradition and bend the knee to the Queen. All those ingratiating followers would be eager to see their favourite installed to gather in their winnings.

In the long predawn darkness, Pasiphaë began to wonder about the triangle of Kriti, Kesandros and Minos, and why it was Kesandros who was dead. But even the darkness was not sacred, even the closed door of the Dolphin Chamber could not keep out the world.

'Lady Pasiphaë! Princess Kri— the Queen, sends for you.'

Eritha had closed the door on a rustling, murmuring crowd, and Pasiphaë had to rein back the anger that rose to her lips, to scream that she was not at her beck and call. The servant saw the fury in her mistress's eyes and dropped to her knees.

'The Queen's women came to me asking advice. None of them knows anything of herb lore, and they knew that I... I've seen her, Lady, and I think she's taken poison.'

*

Had she felt concerned about Kriti, or did her grieving leave no room for any more pain? The events of that terrible night were wrapped in such a fog of suffering that afterwards, she couldn't remember. She dressed quickly and was escorted by a gaggle of Kriti's women to her dark apartment. There were no guards placed on the door this time, only the lionesses with their bland stare. No one would have dared enter uninvited, not even Minos, not now that Kriti was Queen. Pasiphaë looked around quickly, half expecting to see Ananke, suspicion already falling in that quarter, but the Key-Bearer was at Kriti's bedside. She would have kept the black crow away.

The room was dim, lit by lamps and the grey light of dawn, cold and distant, that fell from a shaft. The air was thick with fumes, incense burning and the sweet, sickly smell of perfumed honey, the trick to make bitter herbs palatable. Kriti vomited blood. Blood ran from her nose and her stomach cramped in agony.

The women stood back from the sickbed in the shadows, beyond the poisonous vapours of her breath, and Pasiphaë saw that there were men, too, by the bedside. One was Eumedes, the short, rosy-cheeked man with a deceptively childlike expression, who was district governor of the Knossos area, and Asterius's most trusted advisor. Sitting on a low stool, she recognised Klymenos, the chief scribe, the one who inscribed the legal cases in the records. He had a wax tablet on his lap, and another, already full of words Pasiphaë couldn't read, lay on the floor beside him.

'The Queen is making her last wishes known, before witnesses. She believes it would be prudent,' Eumedes whispered, giving Pasiphaë a knowing look. 'She has made her half-sister Ariadne her heir, and has put her half-brother Asterion under the protection of Asasara and the Great Mother, with you, Lady Pasiphaë, as the regent of both children.'

Pasiphaë looked at the pale face, the cracked lips labouring to form the words, the blood running, the brow wrinkled in pain, and she was ashamed. Kriti stood between the posts of the last and first door, in despair and suffering, yet she was thinking of others. She had been distant, but that was because she lived in the realm of the poppy, and Pasiphaë knew what drove her to that kind of detachment. It had been cruel of her to pretend she didn't understand.

When the lips were still, Kriti's eyelids flickered in dismissal, and Klymenos picked up his tablets and moved aside. He stood next to the governor by the door and Pasiphaë thanked them for carrying out her last request.

'She would have made a wise Queen,' Eumedes said. His voice was grave and, Pasiphaë thought, tinged with genuine sadness. She touched his hand, and the two men left. She knelt beside the bed, took Kriti's wrist. The pulse was racing.

'Kriti, it's Pasiphaë. Can you hear me?' The girl's eyelids fluttered and she turned her head a fraction. Her face was like wax, melting in the lamplight's glow, melting her eyes. The whites were bloody. 'Tell me, what did you take? If it was the sweet clover, there might still be time. Eritha might still be able to prepare an antidote.'

She asked, but it was too late for questions. The girl already looked like a corpse, and Pasiphaë had a fleeting glimpse of a dead girl, her face floating among pink petals in a still pool.

*

Kriti flickered her eyelids in assent, it was easier than nodding. There had been oleander too, but she had misjudged the quantities of both. Too little. For Minos, she had prepared enough to kill a bull. For Minos. From a great distance, she heard Pasiphaë's voice calling for water infused with camomile and wild ginger. She wouldn't drink. What would be the point? She held Pasiphaë's gaze until she was certain that she had understood she didn't want that kind of help.

'Like Kesandros. Was it you then? Why?'

Kriti's bowels knotted so violently she gasped. Liquid gurgled over her tongue. Bitter bile. Her eyes veiled with blood and Pasiphaë appeared tinged with pink. She moved her lips but no sound came; she was failing, fading. One last effort. She would not leave such a lie behind. 'Not Kesandros! For Minos. I thought… never even hoped…'

Bloody tears ran and ran from her eyes, her mouth and between her legs. She was a torrent of sorrow. But she saw that Pasiphaë had heard and understood. After the terror of Minos, she had come so close to happiness. Despite the pain in her belly, she could still recall the pure joy she had felt when her red-haired Erythros marched into the Court of Ceremonies and challenged the King. At the sight of her hero, Minos and the poison prepared for him had fled from her thoughts. She had never been quick and clever. Always obedient, never been taught to think. She had been so unused to happiness, it had muddled her thoughts. Happiness had been her undoing.

All that was left now was a release from pain and grief. She trusted Pasiphaë to understand and forgive.

*

Pasiphaë's heart, that she thought had turned to stone, contracted with pity. She touched Kriti's cheek and wiped away the bloody tears.

'I couldn't believe it was your doing. Go, to a happier place, Kriti. Your Erythros will be waiting impatiently for you.' She kissed the girl's brow, tasting sweat and death, and whispered to Eritha. 'Make her a poppy drink. Strong enough to deaden the pain, the worst pain.'

Eritha would know what she meant.

*

Pasiphaë stayed with Kriti until she slept and her pulse slowed. She stayed until Minos stormed into the silence, his anger setting the shadows flying and the heavy air quivering. She had been wrong about Minos. Respect and custom could not keep him out of the Queen's bedchamber. He would dare anything where only women were concerned. He glared at them all, serving women and temple women, who had gathered around the bed. He looked through Pasiphaë as though she had no substance.

'Why was I not told?'

Inia, the Key-Bearer of the sanctuary, bringing more incense to burn by Kriti's bed, answered in a toneless voice. 'That the Queen is ill? You knew that. There's no change, nothing more to tell.'

He pushed past the crowding women and peered into Kriti's face. She looked peaceful, her breathing quiet.

'I wouldn't breathe in the vapours, Minos,' Inia said. He looked at her, questioningly. 'She's been poisoned, like Kesandros. The same poison.'

Pasiphaë held her breath, wondering if Inia would dare accuse him. Minos was only a King, and soon he would be without a Queen, a nobody, and he would get no help in his ambitions from the temple women. He turned his head, as if noticing Pasiphaë for the first time, and she wondered if he would charge her with the crime. But he had no proof, not even a motive. She looked away.

Minos left. She knew he had great plans, but she was too burdened with grief to imagine what they might be. Her thoughts scattered like a flock of sparrows. What he had done was already more than she could bear.

4

More rites

By the morning, Kriti was dead. The endless ceremonies and festivities that should have only begun with the presentation of the new Queen were abruptly ended. Even Pasiphaë heard echoes of discontent in the mutterings of the servants and the palace officials. There were to have been games and dancing, feasting and a mass marriage ceremony for all the sixteen-year-old farm boys whose mothers had found brides for them. Now, all that was planned was another funeral, and even the Cretans didn't see Kriti's death as anything to celebrate.

Her own women weren't thinking of missed entertainments. Tyro's eyes were red again.

'Well, it never rains but it pours, dun't it?'

'Poor wee lass. What were her women thinking of, to let her do such a thing?'

Eune's sharp eyes were tinged with anger. 'An' you'd be just rarin' to be wed to your brother, I suppose? Sometimes, Arete…'

Pasiphaë saw how they all looked at one another. Semele kissed an amulet she wore around her neck, and Eritha glanced at the closed door. Fear was growing among those at the heart of the drama. The storm wasn't over, and the doubt was growing that the Mistresses had even noticed.

Pasiphaë had been to see the dead girl arranged for burial. The royal pottery had a stock of larnakes in readiness for royal deaths, and Kriti's was decorated with lionesses, the supple lines of their bodies weaving in and out of the waves, and serpents symbolising her last voyage. Pasiphaë's gift was Leto's pendant. The goddess had been good to her and guided her twice through the near-death of childbirth. She prayed she would guide Kriti safely to her Erythros.

Kriti was to be buried in the same tomb as Asterius, next to her great-aunt Queen Keraso. Pasiphaë prepared for the ordeal of the dusty road again, to have the unhealed wounds torn open. Once again, she was dressed, painted, robed and decorated like an effigy, and helped into the litter. Her movements were stiff, her body behaving as though it no longer belonged to her, as it didn't. Asterius had taken part of her with him, and the other half longed to follow.

She thought she remembered nothing of Asterius's funeral except her own grief, the moving muscles in the back of the slave carrying her litter chair, the feel of the fabric beneath her twisted fingers. But the sights of particular trees, strangely-shaped rocks, the way the light fell across a particular oak copse, brought back details of that other journey, stamped them firmly in her memory, a procession of images she feared would haunt her sleep every night of her life.

Kriti's last journey had brought streams of glittering nobility from the palace and sober, uncomprehending knots and clots of countryfolk. Pasiphaë let her mind drift away from funeral rites. Although Kriti and the tragic waste of her death had touched her in the end, it caused no greater pain. She had already drowned in it. Grief filled her throat, her eyes and ears, every chamber of her thoughts. And the black tide was still rising. She heard the muttering voices of the people directed at the sky, the customs, the foreigners who were causing the spring hunger, the mouldy animal fodder. The anger of the Mother was so great, they said, she had not been content with the old King's life. She had taken the new King too, and worst of all, the Queen. To Pasiphaë, their voices fell like waves on a distant shore. The Great Mother had taken Asterius, the life and love she had never expected. Nothing else had any weight in the world.

*

Asterius was in a place built to look like a grand house, but where only the dead dwelled. There was a clay box that bore his seal, but Pasiphaë's husband, the man she had grown to love, was not there. He waited for her somewhere beyond her reach. All the tomb contained was sorrow. She called for her litter as soon as Kriti's funeral rites were accomplished and left the crowd to their desultory celebrations. No one had any real heart for it. The Queen was dead, and what use was a King without a Queen? The problem of the succession didn't concern Pasiphaë. She would retire with her children, and when Adoni reached womanhood, she would be Queen. What happened in the interim seemed to affect a different world, not the one she lived in.

*

The road to Knossos was just as rocky and dusty as it had been for the start of Asterius's last journey, the orchards just as full of pigeons, but the sky was dull. Autumn had arrived and winter would come. That was all she knew with certitude, and she had lost any curiosity she had had for the details. It was Athamas who noticed the stir in the palace, as he walked by her side through the majestic west entrance and along the Gallery of Processions. There was the usual bustle of activity, of scribes running back and forth with the tools of their trade, artisans' apprentices running errands, the kitchen slaves fetching and carrying, but the intensity was different. Pasiphaë sensed an urgency as if something, a threat, drove the activity.

Athamas stopped an elderly scribe hurrying past and asked what was the news.

'The King Minos is to marry,' he said, and disappeared into one of the administrative rooms. Pasiphaë sensed only the usual profound distaste when she heard that name spoken, grief leaving no room for curiosity.

She left Athamas at the door of the Queen's apartment that Kriti would never need now and found it full of the same sense of industry as the suites of rooms in the west entrance. The heady scents of perfume being prepared, berries and essences being ground, powders combined, cosmetics, hair and body cleansers, and the expansive smell of fabrics unfolded and liberated from chests of cedar wood and sandalwood. Only Eritha stood in a pool of stillness. Ominous stillness.

'There's been a messenger.' She hesitated slightly. 'From King Minos.' Pasiphaë felt as though the ground had slipped from beneath her feet and she was falling into even deeper depths of sorrow. 'The King has been chosen, he said, and the next Queen. Her mother must be his wife. He said tomorrow, Princess. Everything was already prepared for a wedding before Kriti, the Queen…'

Everything except Pasiphaë. The dancers and musicians had been ordered, the feast, the temples provided with incense, oils and lamps. Only Pasiphaë was unprepared, had no argument ready, no followers paid to back her decision to choose a new husband or not. She was Pasiphaë, Moon Princess of Kolchis, and in Knossos that meant very little.

'Bring me Eumedes.'

He would know the precedents, what the law was. She would let Eumedes think in her place. Her own thoughts were devoured by that single monstrous demand with the grinning face of Minos.

*

The rosy-cheeked man, whose eyes seemed less kindly in the light of day, raised his hands helplessly. 'It will be fifteen years perhaps before the Princess Ariadne can rule. We have a King, but no Queen.'

'Then let me be regent until then, as Queen Kriti asked.'

Eumedes looked quickly over his shoulder then around the room, at the servants and armed men in the doorway. 'A word in private, Lady,' he murmured.

Pasiphaë led him through the bathing and robing room to the small shrine behind and closed the door. The expression in Eumedes's face softened. All she saw now was sympathy. Commiseration.

'Minos alone has no legal right to the throne, but he's the richest man in Crete, and that gives him immense power. He has more followers, more income, more ships, more allies than any other family head. The one thing he can't buy is the custom and the law. Yes, Queen Kriti designated her heir, and as long as you live, you are the Queen in her stead.'

'So, I shall be Queen.'

He sighed. 'And Minos? The throne was in his grasp. He defeated the old King in combat, chosen by the Mistresses to succeed him, only for his Queen to die. Think carefully, Pasiphaë. Minos is the King of a dead Queen, and an old King has no more importance than last season's fashion in tame civet cats. If he is to remain King, he must marry the Queen, or the Queen's regent. Do you think he will allow you to refuse and live? Your children are young, Lady. Without you, do you think they would live much longer?'

She turned to the statuette, the small goddess glittering in the light of the votive lamps. She listened as hard as she was able, but all she heard was the governor's heavy breathing. The Mistresses were silent, keeping their counsel to themselves. She wouldn't weep, not in front of Eumedes, but again, she felt her feet slipping over the edge. He patted her arm in a familiar gesture.

'Marry him and let them live, Lady.'

She had no choice.

*

There would be no dance led by the Queen to entangle her Bull King. The Bull King was already self-proclaimed, and he had chosen a mate from his herd. Pasiphaë was led out from the Dolphin Chamber, a guard before, a guard behind. Even the presence of Athamas could not alter the feeling that she had no more choice in the matter than a sacrificial offering.

Athamas led the way to the terrace overlooking the Court of Ceremonies. She looked at the sky, listened to the blustering clouds. The winds were getting wilder now as the autumn closed in. Only the olive harvest was still going on. Few workers were needed now in the fields; most would be gathered to watch the entertainments. But there was no great vibration of expectation, no sense of a silent crowd waiting for the moment to burst into gaiety. The wind blew, tugged at her headdress. She shivered and her bare arms prickled with gooseflesh.

There were faces. Hundreds of faces, curious, bored, indifferent, but none shone with friendship. Pasiphaë had no friends at Knossos, and no followers to smile because they had been paid. She looked at the sky, hoped it would rain. A small flock of gulls glided over the court before veering off back towards the sea. She hoped for a sign, but not doves this time. She hoped for an eagle and a swift death. For herself? She turned the talons of the thought to hatred of Minos.

He was there, at the far edge of the dancing pavement. All paths of the labyrinth led to the centre, inexorable fate. He stood like a rock where Asterius had been a tree, and Pasiphaë knew he thought she would break on his weight and solidity. But she was a wave like her mother. She heard Perseis whispering to her that the wave never broke, it parted and returned, and each time it hit the rock it washed a little of it away. Nothing resisted the force of the waves, not reefs and not Minos.

5

Another death

Pasiphaë descended the stair and danced the Sun Dance. She had no ball of thread; Minos would never have accepted that, and in any case, she had no desire to bind him to her. She danced as though she was alone, dancing for the sun, and the black rock washed by the tide was nothing more than an ephemeral bystander. She heard his name chanted, *Minos, Minos, Minos,* but the voices were of his followers, who were bought and could be bought again. Such people had no loyalty and no value. Sometimes, though, the wind carried her name, and she smiled. She had bought no one. Those who called her name gave their loyalty willingly. Minos was rich, but he didn't own everything.

Only when she reached the middle of the labyrinth did Minos catch her. His square fingers grasped her arm, pulling her to him. He wore the bull mask. She hadn't even noticed. It changed little; his face was always bestial. She saw the glitter of his eyes behind the mask as the mouth opened, spoke.

'Your time of ruling a weakling is over. You'll dance to a different tune now.'

His words grated over her skin like a rasp, but she had not expected words of tenderness or even of respect.

'I will do my duty as the mother of the next Queen.'

The grin didn't falter. She doubted he even listened to what she said. Listening, except to rumours and sycophants, was not something Minos did. He pulled her closer, his arm around her waist. She heard the crowd clapping and cheering but with little enthusiasm, and distantly, more distant than the memory of another dance in another life. All Pasiphaë felt was his hot, panting breath on her face. She turned her head as his mouth lunged, his dry lips lost in the coils of her hair.

Without releasing his grip, he marched her up the steps to the altar and raised his hand for silence. She heard pigeons cooing sadly on the gallery roof and wondered if it was the same pair who had watched Asterius die. The crowd was silent, and no great wave of joy flowed over the watchers, merely a dull resignation. The young couple, Kriti and her Erythros, still danced for them.

*

Minos gazed over the crowd and his chest swelled with pride. 'I, Minos, son of the Great Father Zeus, who took the life of the old King, take also his wife for mine.' He raised his hand and pointed at the statue of the Great Mother, smaller than the giantess that dominated Mount Iouktas, and in his nasal voice, raw with forcing, bellowed ancient words that Asterius would never have uttered. 'Behold! Mighty Potnia has borne a great son!'

He had twisted the words to a new meaning, away from the Potnia, casting the glory onto his own person. Who else, after his mother, had ever sung Minos's praises? The reaction of the crowd was as slow as water rising, not the great swell Minos had expected. Applause was sporadic. His triumph was clouded with the familiar feeling of being passed over.

'The times are changing. The years of humiliation are over. You have a new King, and I, Minos, promise to lead Knossos back to glory.'

The nobles at the front of the crowd, his indebted followers, applauded enthusiastically, but unease rose in a murmur and some louder voices from the further ranks. 'But the Queen? What about the Queen?'

Minos didn't even consider Pasiphaë. His mother had been the last Queen. He glared angrily at the frowning faces, but there was always a Queen, and nothing he could say about new Kings and new power and new glory could change that. Not yet at any rate. He ground his teeth.

'The Queen!' Pasiphaë's voice broke into his anger, the sound taking him by surprise. He had almost forgotten her existence. 'The young Queen Kriti named her heir. Her name is written on a tablet in the room of records. Her name is Ariadne, sister of Queen Kriti and grand-niece of Queen Keraso.'

As if her light, hesitant voice had untied a knot, loosed a stopper, opened a fountain, the tension broke and voices rose, first here and there, then as a great single cry, 'Ariadne, Ariadne, Ariadne!'

She smiled, but not at the crowd. Minos followed her gaze to the royal dais. The bull-boy Asterion stood quietly between two nurses while another stepped forward with the baby, too big now for swaddling bands, in a long dress of white linen bordered with gold. Eumedes appeared at her side, short and avuncular, beaming at all around him, and the child was held high for the watchers in the Court of Ceremonies to see. *Ariadne.* The watchers perched in the windows relayed the news to the crowd in the Barley Court beyond, who passed the word to those outside on the west terrace, who shouted to the hundreds gathered outside expectantly.

'Ariadne!' The name rang out across the hills, bouncing back and forth to Amnisos, echoing in the sea-cave shrine and rolling through the deeps. The whole world of the Middle Sea heard it. Asterion clapped his hands, shouting, 'A-do-ni, A-do-ni!' His mother smiled, and it looked not so much a sign of happiness as a grin of victory.

*

Minos snorted behind his bull mask, but his followers were powerless to stop the shouting. He was forced to wait until it died before he spoke again, his voice cold and bitter. 'You have the name of the future Queen, but until she becomes a woman, you have a King. And your King will begin his reign with a purification.'

This was a part of the ceremony Pasiphaë had not expected, an improvisation of Minos. Improvised perhaps, but its organisation would be perfect. The chill wind blew colder, blew away the sadly cooing pigeons. Minos glanced at her and his eyes glittered.

'There must be a purge of the stain on the house of Knossos, the unnatural child, fathered by the Kolchian bull. Dias is hungry for princely blood!'

Pasiphaë froze, unable to speak, to order her thoughts. His words were too monstrous to make sense. But two guards were already on the dais and had snatched Asterion from his nurses. She felt his numbed limbs as her own, heard the scattered thoughts that rang nonsensically inside his head. Then his legs flailed, his arms, fists. Asterion had barely mastered the skills of walking and speech, but he was strong, and when he was afraid, he grew wild. The guards hurried their struggling burden across the labyrinth. With Asterion's rising wail, the voice of the crowd rose in anger.

'Look at what Pasiphaë's union with the bull produced! This should never have been allowed to live.'

She ran to the guards – *don't let him have a fit, don't let him have a fit* – her women with her, and tried to take Asterion from them. He reached out his arms, and her women beat the guards with their fists, screaming abuse. From the crowd, more women's voices joined with theirs. The air rang with the cry, 'Let him go!'

Pasiphaë's voice rose to a shriek. 'Give him to me! Give me my son!' *Look at me, Asterion, look, don't be afraid, don't have a fit, don't have a fit.*

The guards pushed her away without looking at her and

took Asterion to Minos, who stood before the altar. Priestesses looked at one another in shocked incomprehension, but there were priests of Poteidan among them who stared ahead blandly, waiting for their orders. Minos called to a couple of acolytes to bring a cord to tie the child's hands and feet. The voice of the crowd was inside Pasiphaë's head, a roaring of pure anger. She flew at the guards, tearing at their faces, the arms that held her child, while she held his gaze, never letting him go. *Don't let him have a fit, not a fit.*

A priestess left the group behind the altar: Inia the Key-Bearer, with her diadem of High Priestess. 'This is impossible, Minos. The child is the brother of the Queen, and he is touched by the goddess. Harm him and you'll bring down the wrath of the Great Mother.'

'Leave the child!' the crowd shouted, and then, 'Leave the Prince! The Prince! The Prince!'

Minos persisted stubbornly. 'The affront to the gods must be purged.'

Inia refused to back down, and her voice carried to the crowd pressing closer, flowing over the pavement. 'There is no blood sacrifice necessary, Minos. You have shed the blood of the old King. Custom calls for no more.'

'In times of need, the Mother must be placated with blood, and our need is great. Famine threatens if this harvest spoils like the last and our subject peoples refuse their agreed tribute.'

Minos was lying. The harvest hadn't spoiled, but the lie that he had spread had taken root. Most people half believed it, and all feared famine. But not enough yet to sacrifice their Prince. Minos looked across a sea of hostility. Pasiphaë heard nothing but defiance in the voice of the crowd. Asterion was not the only withheld sacrifice, though.

'Asterius denied Poteidan the white bull, which was his by right. His greed has brought us nothing but misfortune and the god's anger. That affront too must be cleansed.'

Minos switched his angry gaze from the wriggling child to the white bull standing on unsteady legs behind the altar.

Attention shifted, and the guard's grip relaxed. Pasiphaë snatched Asterion from his arms as the white bull, the gift of Kolchis to Asterius, was brought up to the altar. He had been given poppy and his head nodded slowly, his feet dragged. Asterion's trembling stopped, his fear almost forgotten at the magical sight. He pointed in delight. 'Drupa!'

'There is no need to shed blood, Minos.' The words came out higher than Pasiphaë intended. Almost a shriek of pain. 'A libation is enough for the Mistresses.'

'Dias is hungry. Wine and honey are not enough.'

He turned his back on her and the servants dragged Belus-Drupa up the last step. They bound his legs together and he toppled to the ground with a grunt, and as they pulled his head over the basin, his eye caught Pasiphaë's. She covered Asterion's face with her hand and took him away. The crowd parted to let them pass, and the low murmuring of sympathy drowned the white bull's last strangled bellow as his throat filled with blood.

*

Pasiphaë slept that night in the royal apartment, in the bed she had shared with Asterius, but before she slept, she was used by Minos as he used the lowliest of his women. His presence, his smell, the brutal touch of his square fingers, the ugly words he poured into her ear would have broken her had she not already been broken by grief. Minos couldn't find where she hid, in the labyrinth inside. She filled it with leaping dolphins and Asterion's smile. Adoni had her place in it, a sleeping Adoni with clenched fists. She bathed the place in the kindness and gentleness Asterius had shown her and washed it in the warm tears that lapped her memories like an unquenchable sea.

*

Minos took his wife with fury and vengeance. He would have killed her if he had dared. She deserved no less a punishment for what she had done.

'You poisoned Kesandros to save the skin of your King, but Kriti you poisoned out of ambition,' he hissed in her ear as she lay, rigid and unyielding beneath him. 'She gave you her trust, and you gave her death.'

He thrust, making her gasp with pain, but he couldn't make her cry out. She turned away from him and closed her eyes so he wouldn't see the guilt he was sure burned in their depths. Minos believed he had felt a sincere affection for his half-sister and imagined that he would never have caused her pain. He didn't delve too deeply into why she had been so terrified of him. The fear of all young girls for their first man, he told himself. Minos had never searched Kriti's eyes in the way he peered into Pasiphaë's. Kriti had never given him any reason to.

He had had no choice but to marry the mother of the next Queen if he was to remain King. But as King, he intended to stamp out the line of women. He had no lack of sons already. He would see Androgeos King, Phaedra married to a Greek Prince, and he would bring all of the Middle Sea into the orbit of Knossos. Not through trade agreements but fear. He would make them respect the might of Crete. The people would see he was right, and the child Ariadne was so far from the throne they would have forgotten her existence long before she was old enough to sit on it.

While Minos dreamed of grandeur, Pasiphaë opened her eyes and mocked. He punished her the only way allowed him.

*

Pasiphaë looked at Minos and saw a brute, as much beast as man. She saw something else too – a weakness, a lack of confidence that made him demand, crush, hurt, that made him buy rather than make friends. He saw no other way to be obeyed. Was that what Europa taught him, she wondered, to treat the world as his enemy?

'If I poisoned Kesandros and Kriti, are you not afraid for yourself, Minos?' she mocked, wanting only to hurt the one who had killed Asterius needlessly. His eyes, belligerent and lost, narrowed. Of course he was. Even after he had had all her herb store burned, he still feared her.

'I've heard the stories about your witch of a sister, Pasiphaë, and your niece Medea, and your mother. I'd be a fool to trust you.'

'Then let me go. Let me take my children out of your way, out of your sight. Custom doesn't require that the King live with the Queen.'

He only shook his heavy head and grinned, though his eyes remained uncertain. 'Not yet. The people still think they want a Queen. You'll give them your presence, and perhaps even another Prince. With luck, his birth will kill you.'

So, he took her night after night for all of that dark winter that she never left the palace. His tongue filled her with the foul taste of things long dead that even honey could not take away. Her only respite was in blood. The days when her blood flowed, sacred and poppy red, she rejoiced and bathed in the shrine where the Potniai watched but never spoke.

'Your seed will never take in this womb, Minos,' she whispered in his ear before he slept, after each rough taking. A vow, a small victory. He paid no heed. Minos never listened, but the words lingered inside his skull. She wondered at his stupidity. Did he think Pasiphaë, daughter of Perseis and sister of Circe, didn't have the means to rid herself of his unwanted get? The means to turn her womb into a sink of poison grew in the fields all around the palace. Eritha brought her poisoned bouquets and he suspected nothing.

At the end of the winter, when the milk rose in the ewes and the first seed was ploughed into the earth, when the new grass grew in the meadows and the birds nested in every crevice, on every ledge of pillars, sills and beams, Minos admitted defeat.

That last morning, when she showed him the red blood that meant yet another cycle had turned unfertilised, he told her to leave.

She had expected to be vilified and charged with sorcery, but he had simply seemed relieved. As soon as she had had her belongings moved into the Dolphin Chamber, he had brought his concubines to the royal bed. Pasiphaë ought to have felt relief too, but the Dolphin Chamber was still within the prison of the royal apartments, and she could not rid herself of the suspicion that Minos still had a use for her.

6

The Hall of the Double Axe

From that day, Pasiphaë rarely left the palace. She extended the Queen's apartments to include a shrine that ran to the outer wall and put the labrys seal above all the doors. She renamed it the Hall of the Double Axe, and nobody would dare enter who was not invited. She cleared two magazines of their pithoi, opened a shaft to let in the light and had one painted with lionesses and water birds, the other with bulls. She refreshed the paint of the frescoes in the Dolphin Chamber and had the window enlarged and extended to a small terrace, so that she could look across the great staircase down into the Court of Ceremonies and watch the life of the palace without being touched by it. At the eastern end of the Hall of the Double Axe, she had another, larger terrace built out so that she could sit outside, as if she were among the hills where the flocks grazed and the light of the sea glittered. It didn't give her happiness, that had flown forever, but it was a sort of peace.

She lived there quietly with Asterion, Adoni, her women and personal guards. At first, she took Asterion out to see the herds, and to walk down the road to the place where an olive tree bent its back to the wind from the sea. There the road dropped, and you could see the port of Amnisos and the glittering sea that lapped its feet. They would talk to the herdsmen and Asterion would ask after Drupa and shout his name to the cows and sheep. Pasiphaë would exchange glances with the men who understood, and they would rumple the little Prince's hair and tell him Drupa was over the hill visiting another herd. It puzzled Asterion, and it upset Pasiphaë too, reminding her that all she had left of Kolchis was a pine marten.

One day, a day of bright flowers and the memory of dew still in the grass, Asterion asked the wrong herdsman. 'Asti wants Drupa.' He tugged the arm of the herdsman, one Pasiphaë didn't know, a young man with impatient eyes. 'Drupa's lost! Find him for Asti.'

'Who's Drupa?' he asked, though all the herdsmen knew the name Asterion had given the white bull.

She felt the storm coming from the irritation in his eyes.

'Drupa's the King of the bulls, the whitest and biggest.' He looked up at the herdsman fiercely, defying him to claim he still didn't know Drupa.

The herdsman pointed with his stick to a bull trotting back and forth inside an enclosure. 'See him? The black bull with a white head? That's Thunder, the King of the herd. The old white one's dead.'

Athamas had to carry Asterion back to the palace, thrashing and screaming, all the grief for all the deaths bursting the bonds of his small child's reason. Athamas brought him inside through the small east entrance, along the dark, narrow corridor that wound among countless magazines and storerooms. His cries echoed through the lower levels, drawing the idle curious to the stair as they hurried to the regal floor. Nobody would dare harm Asterion but that didn't prevent them believing him to be unnatural. Pasiphaë wished, for the hundredth time, that she had Circe's skill in inflicting pain and humiliation.

*

Eritha gave Asterion his remedy, and eventually he slept. That was the first time Pasiphaë asked the servant to make her a poppy drink.

*

The great storm of that winter destroyed the last opposition to the return of the tribute. The storm made the sound of a great bull bellowing in the sea-cave shrine at Amnisos, and Minos declared that Dias was hungry. He had whipped up the people to a frenzy against the laxity that had done away with the royal child sacrifices, and Inia, the Key-Bearer, had been forced to officiate at the sacrifice of the son of a bankrupt merchant, banished from Knossos after an outburst against Minos's raised taxes.

But the storm had not abated. If anything, it grew more violent. The sea broke the mole at Amnisos and the fishing fleet was wrecked. Inia called all the priestesses from all the cults to make another offering, and Pasiphaë could not ignore the call. The sky itself thrashed in fury, and she had no doubt that some evil was in preparation, but she couldn't stay away.

Lightning played about the bronze locks of the statue, and even so far from the port, the growling of the unchained sea would be heard. Minos had sent his followers among the crowd of desperate fishing and farming folk gathered before the sanctuary to start a clamour for more blood. Their cries joined with the howling of the gale, and when it had reached near-hysteria, Minos, usurping the power of the Key-Bearer, appeared beneath the statute of the Great Mother and called out, as if addressing the sky, for a sacrifice.

'A princely sacrifice calls for a Prince!'

His voice was snatched away by the gale, but among those sheltering beneath the sanctuary wall, enough heard and repeated the cry. 'A Prince! A Prince!'

'We have a Prince of royal blood, a sacrifice long withheld. Will we give the Great Mother her due now?'

'A Prince! A Prince!'

Pasiphaë cringed beneath the weight of the sky, the horror repeated again and again behind her eyes, and saw with the clarity of terror her own child bound on the bloody altar. A thousand faces were turned to her, and she had nowhere to hide.

'Well, Pasiphaë?' Minos's voice rolled round and round inside her head.

'No! You won't have him!' The storm, the clamouring crowd, the thought of so much blood and Asterion's smile was more than she could bear. She sobbed. 'Never!' But her voice was drowned in a torrent of rain.

Minos stalked through the sanctuary to where she shivered in her water-heavy robes. 'The Prince or the tribute. Choose. And quickly.'

She cast about, saw nothing through the streaming rain, the sea of black cloud. She felt no compassion anywhere in the cold world. 'The tribute,' she whispered.

'Louder!'

'The tribute!' she screamed again and again until Inia took her by the arm and led her inside the shrine.

Beyond the walls, the crowd still chanted, but it was changing. 'A Prince! A Prince!' was becoming 'A Greek Prince! A Greek Prince! The tribute! The tribute!'

It was to the baying for blood that Pasiphaë was carried back to Knossos, behind the drawn curtains of the litter, with her face in her hands.

*

In the palace, in his room with the bull paintings, Asterion heard the battering of the storm and curled in a corner, his toys gathered in his arms. With the help of Semele and Eune, Pasiphaë managed to get him to bed, then collapsed on her own bed, barely conscious, to drink the poppy prepared for her. She slept as the storm grew in strength, the wind rose higher. She slept even when, in the dead of night, Asterion began to howl. At first it was the wail of a frightened child, but as if his whimpering had called up the fury bellowing in the sea cave, his cries grew to fill the room, then the apartments, until the east wing of the palace vibrated with his distress.

By the morning, the sea and the storm had subsided, and in the port the people counted the dead and missing, and began the task of rebuilding their ships. Minos declared that the Great Mother had calmed Poteidan's anger thanks to the promised return of the tribute and the sacrifice of Greek Princes. By the time Pasiphaë woke, there could be no going back.

PART SIX

The empty sky

The world was changing and what was broken could not be mended. There had always been sorrow, mothers had always wept for lost children, but it seemed to Pasiphaë that the Great Mother's thirst for blood and tears grew the more she drank, as if it would never be slaked. Her skies were empty, and at night only one star remained, big and bright. She hoped, as all mothers do, that its light would shine long after her own was snuffed out.

1

Daedalus, the first Greek

In those first quiet years of Pasiphaë's cloistered existence, both Asterion and Ariadne grew, though where Ariadne grew sharp and quick, Asterion hunched over his slowness, his gentleness, as though he would rather hide away out of sight. Ariadne ran and climbed, stole her mother's face paints to make pictures on the floor, played in the sacred basin and chased Leto until she refused to leave her hiding place beneath Asterion's bed. Pasiphaë decided it was time she began to learn. It would not do for her to be as ignorant as Kriti had been. Minos would crush an ignorant girl, incapable of governing. So, when she was in her eighth year, Ariadne was given into the hands of Eumedes and Inia for instruction.

It was at that time, when the tribute of noble youths and children had been exacted for several years, that a Greek craftsman came to Knossos looking for asylum. Minos took him in because he had been banished from Athens for murdering his nephew. Minos liked to have people in his power. Giving Daedalus refuge got him an artist for nothing, and it showed the Athenians how little he esteemed them.

Daedalus was a master craftsman with magic in his fingers. His talents could have been used to the greater glory of Crete, but Minos chose to have him make toys. It was likely Minos intended his commissions to be demeaning. He enjoyed belittling the people around him. And Daedalus considered himself aggrieved. His hooded eyes glowed with resentment like a chained dog's.

Pasiphaë hated Daedalus from the first time he came to the Dolphin Chamber followed by a flock of servants carrying boxes full of his precious creations. The first thing she noticed was the scar, ugly and livid, that ran from his left temple down to his ear, a parting gift from the angry crowd at his ignominious banishment from Athens. He was old, at least as old as superintendent Alkeus, who was as grey and lined as the tablets he worked with in the records rooms. Unlike Alkeus, the eyes of Daedalus glittered with arrogance. He presented himself stiffly then flicked a hand at the servants, waving them into the chamber. Pasiphaë heard Asterion's heavy breath behind her.

'Who is he, Am-am-á? What's in the boxes? For Asti or Adoni?'

He was used to his sister being sent gifts. She went out in the world of the court, met nobles and noble children. From Eumedes, she learned to make marks on wax tablets that others could understand, how to count and assess and how to judge people. Inia taught her the temple wisdom, the prayers to the Mistresses, the rites and rituals, how to listen for signs, and how to make wise decisions. Later, she would teach her divination. Pasiphaë taught her what she knew of calling on the Mistresses, the winds and the animals, but she had never mastered many talents, and they shrank in the immensity of the palace that breathed with its own powers.

'They're gifts for both of you, I expect,' she replied, looking at the dry, sinewy man with resentment and supressed ambition in his eyes.

'The King ordered magical toys for the royal children. All of them.' He looked with undisguised contempt at Asterion, who stood at Pasiphaë's side, an arm around her waist, unsmiling, even at the promise of a new toy. He was ten years old and should have been playing with swords and javelins, going to the gymnasium to box and wrestle, learning to be an athlete or a musician, to judge a good grain, the quality of cloth, the worth of the saffron harvest. Instead, he kept to the Hall of the Double Axe, content to live within the orbit of his mother and her women, among their comforting scents and rituals, with his toys.

Daedalus had the servants open the boxes and himself took out a wooden horse with articulated legs and a head that nodded. He held it out of Asterion's reach until he had shown off everything the toy could do. Asterion forgot his suspicion and took the horse in his small, careful fingers, absorbed in its lines and the way it worked. Pasiphaë turned at the clatter of a child's sandals as Ariadne arrived, running from whatever occupation she had been about. She leaned over her brother's shoulder, poked the horse then looked at Daedalus with the expression Pasiphaë knew so well: winning, polite and determined.

'I know you,' she said. 'You're laying a new labyrinth for the dancing floor in the Court of Ceremonies. The colours are pretty. Can you make some stones with lions on them?'

Daedalus gave a thin, unconvincing smile, possibly not liking to be reminded that he, the builder and designer of great works of art, was reduced to stone-cutting and the entertainment of children.

'The King chose the design, Princess. There are no lions. But I have made you something more suitable for a Princess than wild beasts.'

He spoke patronisingly, and Ariadne was sharp. She heard it, and her eyes narrowed in annoyance. Daedalus bent down to another box and took out a doll, a woman with embroidered skirts over a body that bent this way and that. Ariadne put out her hands to take it, but the old man kept it from her until he had shown her all the wonders it could perform. Like Asterion's horse, the doll could walk and sit and move its head from side to side.

'How does she speak?'

Pasiphaë tried hard not to smile as the haughty expression

on the Greek's face faltered. 'Only the gods can give human speech to a machine, Princess.'

Asterion raised his head. 'Asti can make Sabazios talk. This is Sabazios.' He held up the horse. 'Listen.' He wrinkled his nose and made a series of snorting noises. 'He said, *Sabazios is hungry.*'

Ariadne laughed. 'If Asterion can make a horse talk, it can't be so difficult.'

Daedalus frowned and unpacked the rest of the mechanical wonders with only a perfunctory explanation. Pasiphaë thanked him, pleased to see him go, leaving the servants to collect up the boxes and packaging.

*

She put Daedalus out of her mind. His story was an ugly one. Although she knew men capable of all kinds of wickedness, she could not imagine how a grown man could be so jealous of the skill of a boy, his sister's son, that he would murder him. Daedalus carried a coldness with him that told her he was not protected by any deity. His own cunning and ambition had kept him from harm so far. Adoni, though, felt no such repulsion. In fact, she seemed intrigued by the very cunning that chilled her mother's blood. She was lithe and athletic, spare like her father and supple, but Pasiphaë heard Perseis in the way she spoke and saw Circe in the calculating look in her eyes.

*

'Adoni's dancing again. Look how her feet fly! Swallow-feet,' Asterion said one day not long after the visit from Daedalus. He was on the terrace outside the Dolphin Chamber, watching the bustle on the great staircase, and in the Court of Ceremonies, where a group of girls were dancing a bird dance. Pasiphaë glanced down and saw Ariadne leave the group. She was easy to spot. Smaller than most of them, she carried herself like a Queen and walked everywhere with determination and her head held high. On the edge of the court, in front of the Great Shrine, Daedalus was supervising a group of masons. Ariadne spoke to him then ran up the steps to the shrine. Without hesitating, she climbed the steeper flight to the shrine roof.

'Ooh, ooh! Adoni is being naughty,' Asterion said with a chuckle.

At the top, she beckoned to Daedalus to follow, which he did grudgingly. She waved her hand over the landscape she could see from her vantage point, the hillside to the west of the palace where the herds would be grazing. She pointed and turned to Daedalus with a question. He replied and Ariadne let her hand drop to her side, slowly, as if deep in thought. Daedalus turned abruptly and hurried back to his stoneworkers. Pasiphaë heaved a sigh of relief. Given his history, watching Daedalus with a child on top of a building was unnerving.

Later, at table for the evening meal, Ariadne gave her mother a strange look.

'This morning, I asked the Athenian to make a toy for Asterion. I told him I wanted him to make a bull, like the King bull. When I showed him Thunder, he asked me was that the bull that fathered my brother.'

She said no more, but Pasiphaë could see that Ariadne had heard the smutty laughter, the whispered stories, and accepted that they might be true. Pasiphaë wanted to weep. The hurt that an eight-year-old child was prepared to believe that her mother let herself be used like a cow in a field, went too deep for reason. Asterion must have sensed her distress because he left his seat and put his arms around her neck, but Pasiphaë drowned in remorse, with no idea of whom she had angered, what she had done wrong. She lost any hope that the days would grow a little less dark. Instead, their claws grew longer, reaching into the night, snatching away her sleep. She no longer asked Eritha to make her an occasional poppy draught. She made her own.

2

The palace of men

Pasiphaë heard little of the noise of the world in her apartments sealed with the double axe. Minos led the dance now and the world was changing. He brought his concubines into the royal apartment, and his sons by various women were given places at court. She knew them by sight, the sons, and one of the daughters, the youngest. The women changed often, and Minos always seemed to have a different one on his arm. Androgeos, the eldest son, must have taken after his mother because he was tall, and his hair was fair for a Cretan. He took after Minos in his arrogance, but Eumedes said he showed no interest in the working of government and never set foot in the Throne Room.

There were twins too, slightly younger than Androgeos: Katreos who was short and square like his father, and Deukalion who had fiery red hair. Minos disliked the redhead and denied he could be his son. Pasiphaë decided it had nothing to do with the colour of his hair, but because he was likeable and popular.

Ariadne began to spend more time in the company of the sons and daughters of noble families than she did in the Hall of the Double Axe. When she was twelve years old, in preparation for her womanhood, she was given a room off the Great Shrine, where she lived. Her visits to her mother's apartments were sporadic and, Pasiphaë sensed, reluctant, out of a sense of duty. Inia had taught her respect, and Eumedes had taught her the law, but neither could teach her to unhear what she had heard about her mother or unsee what she thought she saw in her brother's features.

She danced often on the new pavement of the labyrinth, and Asterion and Pasiphaë would watch from the window as she led the youths in the intricate steps of some Cretan elemental dance. It was from these noble children that Ariadne learned the court gossip and the rumoured plans of King Minos.

*

'Look, Am-am-á! Adoni Swallow-feet's dancing with Deuka again. Look at Poppy-head bow to the birds.'

He chuckled to himself and drummed his fingers on the wall of the terrace in an attempt to follow the beat of the tympanum. Though he had grown rapidly in the months since he turned fourteen, his fingers and hands had remained small and childlike. He had a thick neck, his head set down on his broad shoulders like a small boulder, and he often appeared stooped, his shoulders and chest overdeveloped for his short legs. His face had lost none of the wonder in all that moved around him that he had had since he was born, and his strangely shaped eyes, though still a vague colour, were as untroubled as ever. Wise, Eritha had said, not empty. He couldn't dance or play music or even keep a rhythm. He forgot things he had been told a few moments before and remembered things told him when he could barely walk. But he looked into the heart of things, knew their spirit, and he loved with all his being, unreservedly.

The dance broke up and Asterion nodded to himself. 'Now Adoni is angry. You'll see in a moment.'

*

For the first time in more than a week, Ariadne decided to visit her mother's apartments, and burst into the Dolphin

Chamber as only an adolescent girl with a sense of righteous grievance can.

'Do you know what the truth is in this story, Mamá? What Deukalion told me about his father?'

'That he's a bull too?' Asterion asked innocently.

Adoni clicked her tongue impatiently. 'Minos doesn't intend to step down when I reach womanhood. He says that the times are turning to war, and Knossos needs a strong man at the helm!'

'No, I haven't heard the story, but it doesn't surprise me. Minos has never hidden his ambition.'

'A strong man? Minos is flabbier than a beached porpoise!'

'And smellier than when Eune dropped Mamá's perfumes and they all broke!'

'Shut up, Asterion. You're not funny.'

Pasiphaë smiled to herself at her fury of a daughter, her flashing eyes as she tossed her head with its cloud of dark hair. Ariadne was dark-eyed and dark-haired, but it was a soft dark, not black like Pasiphaë's thick locks, though her skin was as dark, not golden olive like her father's had been. She had the body of a dancer, and her mind was as swift and sure as her feet, the quick mind of a lawgiver. Too quick sometimes, but if it could be tempered with a sense of justice, she would make a good Queen.

'Minos likes shouting about war and the Greek menace. It frightens the people. And it's true, if he keeps driving up taxes and levies, the Greeks will revolt—'

'He takes their princely children if they don't pay,' Ariadne interrupted. 'That's worked so far.'

'So far. You wait until the Hellenes organise themselves, build their own fleet. They're warriors. Their sons are sticking spears into one another as soon as they can walk.'

Ariadne frowned. 'That still doesn't mean he can overturn the custom and keep the Queen from her throne. Wait until I have my first blood. We'll see if the people want a Queen or a warmonger.'

Ariadne was right in a way. The Cretans would always choose entertainment over war, and so far, the Greeks had pulled back from outright refusal to pay the tributes, even handing over a few unimportant royal children. Pasiphaë weighed them up, Ariadne and Minos, and was inclined to believe that her daughter was quite equal to Minos and his puffed-up toad-like blustering.

3

Medea

With Pasiphaë's retreat from any public functions came a certain peace. Not happiness. That had fled when Asterius was taken from her, but the noises in her head, the giggling of small children beneath the black skies of Mount Iouktas, the gurgling of blood, the mindless roar of excited crowds, were calming to mere whispers. Her worries were those of a mother, for Asterion when she was no longer there to protect him, and for Ariadne, that her headstrong nature could lead her into trouble.

Any attempt she made to talk to her daughter met with a wall of silence. Ariadne preferred the advice of the friends who praised her beauty, her dancing, her quick wit, her spirit. She had no wish to be warned about dangers she refused to believe existed. Minos stayed clear of Pasiphaë, her apartments and her children, and Ariadne assumed it was out of fearful deference. Her reply, when Minos's ambition was mentioned, invariably began with, *When I am Queen*. Pasiphaë began to doubt her daughter's famed cleverness.

Pasiphaë rarely ventured beyond the palace walls. The Knossos she had known had gone, happy times replaced by ugly memories. As for the world beyond, it had receded into the past, its memories softened with time, too painfully gentle to recall. But the world continued to turn, and though she never left Knossos, she could not stop Kolchis and Aea coming to her. Her childhood home arrived in a theatrical manner, one spring day when the first fluff had appeared on Asterion's chin, and Ariadne was a long-legged adolescent.

Eritha put her head round the door to the Dolphin Chamber. 'Lady, the lads at the granaries found this person wandering around the Barley Court, said she was looking for you. They had your guards bring her up here.'

Pasiphaë started. The childish apprehension she felt when she was *looked for* had never left her, and since the death of Asterius, it had sinister implications. 'Who is she?'

Eritha raised her hands in a shrug. 'Didn't give her name. Just a young woman with a little kid in her arms. Dark like you.'

Eritha seemed not to see a threat, so she nodded. 'Let her come in.'

The woman sailed into the chamber and flung back the hood of her cloak revealing a thick cloud of black hair. The child in her arms turned his head. His eyes, fearful at first, lit up when they caught sight of the dolphins.

'Pasiphaë! You can't imagine how glad I am to see you!'

The quick dark eyes, suddenly familiar, flitted around the room, settling finally on Asterion, crouched over some game, too absorbed to have noticed the visitor.

'My son, Asterion. What brings you here, Medea?'

She didn't mean to be cold. She simply dreaded change. News always seemed to be bad. Medea dropped into a chair and set the child down on the floor. He hid his head in her lap, and she stroked his hair. 'It's all right, Medus. No more ships and travelling for a while. Aunt Pasiphaë will look after us.' She cast a bright – and, Pasiphaë thought, rather calculating – smile in her direction. 'Won't you?'

'Perhaps you'd better tell me why you need looking after. I have had no news from Kolchis since Circe sent word that she had been banished and that Aeëtes was keeping the throne warm for you. Would I be right in assuming he didn't?'

Medea sighed heavily and ran her fingers through her hair.

She grimaced. 'I feel disgusting. Ships. Yes, you'd be right, though it wasn't all Father's fault. I made a stupid decision and I've paid for it, a dozen times over.' She paused for effect. 'You remember when those sailors were washed up at Aea? Looking for fleeces from golden sheep? Well, they came back. I was fourteen and thought I knew everything. Circe encouraged me, but you know that.' Again, the rather calculating smile. 'Father thought he could trade with them, or rather hoodwink them. They were only Greeks after all. They still believed in the golden fleece story, and Father went along with it.'

The door opened quietly and Ariadne crept in. Pasiphaë put her finger to her lips, and she sat down to listen. Medea glanced at her with interest before continuing.

'He sold them a few fleeces, newly washed. You remember how they glittered in the sun from the little flecks of gold in the river? The idiots were thrilled to bits and keen to get back home to show off what a goldmine they'd discovered. I wasn't really paying attention. I couldn't take my eyes off the captain of their ship. He was so handsome! He really was. Then. He told me his father was a King, and proposed marriage, to unite Kolchis and Iolchos. But then I did something stupid.'

Pasiphaë raised her eyebrows, but not in surprise.

'I told Jason that it wasn't certain I would ever be Queen. You remember my brother Absyrtus? He had started bragging that Father intended that he would be King. I didn't really believe it, and I only told Jason because I was playing for time. I'd barely clapped eyes on him and he was proposing marriage!' She heaved another great sigh. 'Ah well, we all make mistakes. I was very young, and how was I to know that Jason would kill him like that?'

'Because he was a Greek? Killing the opposition is what they do.'

'He threatened to tell Father that *I* had done it out of jealousy.'

Pasiphaë glanced at Ariadne. She was drinking in Medea's

words, her mouth slightly open. 'Don't tell me. You accepted to marry him, ran away to Iolchos with him, and he dumped you when he discovered the fleeces weren't actually golden?'

Medea clicked her tongue and frowned. 'The bastard. The lying son of a mangy bitch. There wasn't a truthful bone in his body. He wasn't a Prince, the King was his uncle, he had dozens of sons, and he hated Jason. Jason thought his uncle would be impressed by an alliance with Kolchis. His uncle was about as impressed as if he'd suggested an alliance with a dead cow. So, Jason did what he knew best. He killed the old man. When he started on his sons, they objected, and we had to flee to Corinth. That was where he dumped me for a King's daughter.'

'So, you picked up your child and you left?'

Medea shook her head, letting the thick locks hide her eyes. The glitter in them was not calculation this time, but tears. 'Medus isn't his. Jason killed our sons before his marriage. That was the bargain with the bride's father. What you just said, about Greeks killing off the competition. The lying, bloodthirsty rat killed my beautiful boys.'

'You're Medea!' Ariadne burst out. 'In the story I heard it was *you* killed your sons.'

Medea turned on her, the genuine tears in her eyes glittering with hatred. 'Lies! So, they've spread even here, where I thought the Mistresses still ruled.'

Ariadne lowered her eyes. 'I'm sorry. It was Daedalus, a Greek, told it me.'

Medea snorted. 'They're all the same. All liars, ambitious and bloodthirsty as weasels. And none worse than that runty bastard, Theseus, who turned his father against me.'

Medea threw herself against the back of the chair and closed her eyes. A tear worked its way from the corner of her eye and ran down her cheek. Pasiphaë couldn't tell if it was a tear of sorrow or of anger.

'You'll have to explain, but later. Let me call for some food, and a bath perhaps. Would Medus like to sleep first?' She smiled at the child, who shook his head. 'Would you like to play with Asterion then? He has lots of toys, even a wooden horse that walks.' Hearing his name, Asterion looked up. 'Asterion, Medus would like to see Drupa and all the other animals.'

Asterion smiled and waved. 'Hurry up. They're just setting off, going on a procession to the sea. To collect shells and pebbles.'

As Medus trotted over, Medea gave Pasiphaë a questioning look.

'Don't worry. Asterion is very gentle. Just like his father was.'

*

Medea unburdened herself of a story which Pasiphaë, even though she still couldn't warm to her niece, admitted was tragic. After being hounded out of Iolchos, Medea was chased from Corinth. Jason hadn't given her much choice. Before she left, though, she poisoned his bride-to-be. She would rather have poisoned Jason, but he was too wily to let her near him. She took a ship to Athens, because the Athenians hated Corinth, and threw herself on King Aegeus's mercy. Aegeus was so taken with her, he married her.

It seemed she had at last found some kind of security. Aegeus wasn't in the first flush of youth, but he was a reasonably kindly man and his appetites were undemanding. He was wifeless and, he said, childless. Medea remedied both lacks in his life, and the birth of Medus helped with the nightmares that had grown unbearable since the murder of her boys. Aegeus doted on Medus and appeared grateful for the potions and cataplasms his wife prepared to help with his old man's complaints. Medea truly believed he cared more about his wife and son that anyone else on earth. She didn't know about the fantasy he had kept hidden for decades. She found out the day a dusty, irritable young man marched up to the royal house from the Isthmus road.

Medea had accompanied Aegeus to greet the visitor, a short man with an arrogant but unintelligent look about him.

'Who is she?' the unprepossessing individual asked.

Aegeus frowned. '*She* is my wife, the Lady Medea, and *you* will show her due respect.'

Aegeus didn't know then that the unprepossessing individual was his son, fruit of his youthful wild oats. Later, though, they exchanged some secret signs that their gods love to sprinkle into stories, and all was revealed. Medea had lived among the Greeks long enough to know what that meant. If Theseus, for such was the bastard's name, had searched out his father, it was for the sole and unique purpose of claiming his throne. The only question was, would he wait until the old man died?

All Medea could think about was Medus and children hacked into unrecognisable lumps of bleeding flesh. The nightmares flashed like migraines behind her eyes even in daylight, and she struggled to stop the screaming. Alcimenes and Tisander, her boys. She felt every one of their wounds, the gratuitous horror that seemed to be Jason's hallmark. She refused to allow another Greek to treat Medus the same way.

*

Theseus settled in. He made himself at home in the royal apartments and would have liked to keep Medea out of the room when he spoke to his father, always on the same theme: himself, the innocent victim of a careless father and useless mother. It was a litany of his heroic and bloody journey to make himself known to his father. The tales went on for days, a tedious account of one heroic murder after another, one region after another liberated from the cursed rule of the Mother and the Mistresses, all told in his monotonous voice. Medea almost yawned once or twice but Aegeus was slack-jawed in admiration. Then he got on to the subject of his mother, as if she was the legitimate wife and Medea was some harlot dragged out of a cheap port-side brothel. Aegeus squirmed, but it was obvious he was besotted by the little dunghill cock.

On the third day, she had had enough. In the middle of a blow-by-blow account of how Theseus delivered a region from a fearsome and gigantic bandit, she left the room and came back with a tray, three cups and jugs of wine and water.

'We have been so absorbed by the account of your journey, we have forgotten our manners, Theseus. Please, drink a welcome cup with us.'

A refusal would have been churlish, even for Theseus, so Medea poured the wine. One cup, she moved to one side for herself, in the second she'd slipped enough poison to fell an ox, and to the third, she added water, as Aegeus usually drank his wine watered. She held the third cup out to him. Theseus, rudely, took it for himself.

'I never drink unwatered wine.'

He handed instead the cup with the poison to his father. Aegeus smiled indulgently and raised it to his lips. Medea couldn't let him drink it, and with a cry, slapped the poisoned cup out of his hands.

Theseus, suspicious as a peasant, snatched it up and sniffed the dregs. 'Poison!'

Aegeus looked confused, his family bliss shattered. 'I don't believe it.'

Theseus offered him the cup. 'You trust her that much?'

Of course, Aegeus wouldn't touch it.

Theseus turned to her with a complacent smirk that reminded her of Jason and yelled, 'Guards!' Two of them burst into the room. 'Take this murderess to her room and keep her there until justice is done.'

'Don't touch me,' Medea hissed in her best enchantress voice, and raised her hand. The trick never failed. The guards cringed back against the wall as if she'd impaled them, and she flew to her apartment. She cast blinding spells on all who crossed her path, using ground pepper that she always carried, just in case. There was no time to do more than throw her jewels into a bag, and there was only one thing she valued.

Medus was sleeping in his cot. She picked him up and settled him on her shoulder. He curled up, his head nuzzling her neck. He didn't even wake. No guard stopped them at the gate. A woman in a grey cloak, a sleeping child in her arms – who would even have noticed? Down in the port she took the first ship leaving, a cargo to Lemnos. At Lemnos, she remembered Pasiphaë.

*

'He's coming, mark my words. It's all Theseus talks about, liberating the world from the rule of the Mother. He's made it his sacred mission, that and proving his virility. He dislikes most people and hates all women. He hadn't a single kind word to say about his own mother, having to bring him up alone because Aegeus didn't know he had a son. She'd only ever been a one-night fling to cheer himself up. Theseus simply resented that he'd missed out on being brought up a little Prince.'

'And how's he going to get here to *liberate* us?' Ariadne asked sarcastically. 'Swim?'

Medea gave her a withering look. 'He'll find a way, even if he has to steal your own ships to do it. You Cretans are complacent, arrogant, and you have no idea how much the Greeks hate you. It's a warning, Princess Ariadne. Don't take them for fools.'

*

Medea and Medus stayed in the safety of the Double Axe for a week before Medea grew restless. 'I can't stay here forever, and I can't go back to Aea, obviously. But I want to go *home*.'

'Circe would take you in.'

Medea shrugged. 'She might. But she's grown strange,

living alone with just her magic for company. I wouldn't want her to fly into a fury with Medus over something silly and turn him into a pig. She's quite capable.' Pasiphaë couldn't disagree. 'No, I think we'll take our chance with the plains people, the horse people. You'd like that wouldn't you, Medus? To live with the ponies?'

Medus held up Sabazios, the wooden horse Asterion had given him, and nodded.

'There's a wild people I know of, to the north of Kolchis, just waiting for a ruler to unite them and give them a name. We'll go there.' She turned to Pasiphaë and took her hands. 'We didn't get on when we were younger, but the world's changed. We've had to adapt, lose our certainties. Just don't let the Greeks in, and make sure your girl never gets the stupid ideas that I had.'

She left the next day on a cargo bound for the shores of the Inhospitable Sea, taking her son with her on another adventure. Pasiphaë wished her well. She almost envied her.

4

Queen's blood

Medea left, and on the back of a spring gale, the second Greek arrived at Knossos. Ikarus was the son of Daedalus, the Athenian, got on a slave woman. Ikarus immediately struck up a friendship with Androgeos and was admitted into his band of followers. The youths called themselves the Heracleidae after a Greek hero who was honoured, as far as Pasiphaë understood the stories, for the number of Kings he had killed and women he had raped.

Androgeos and his Heracleidae rampaged across the countryside, taking farm girls and killing labourers as it pleased them. Minos did nothing to curb his son's crimes; in fact seemed to approve of them. The only time he denied Androgeos anything was when he declared his intention to leap the bulls at the next celebration.

'I wish he'd let him,' Ariadne said, her lips curling in contempt. 'Androgeos can run and throw javelins, but he knows as much about bull-leaping as Asterion does about precedents in law and how to calculate taxes. Deukalion says an old cow could run him through and he'd just stand there and let her, but those arse-lickers of his pack tell him he'd be the best bull-leaper that ever lived.'

According to Ariadne, Androgeos and Ikaros were as alike as two peas in a pod, their arrogance equalled only by their stupidity. Both were obsessed with showing off their virile skills. The Athenian games, she said, were meant for cretins like them.

Ariadne saw an idiot; Pasiphaë saw just another ambitious young man. There were so many of them, and the atmosphere within the palace encouraged them to take command in spheres that the priestesses had once ordered, ignoring the daily rites and monthly women's rites, and ordering extravagant sacrifices to Poteidan, now called Poseidon, followed by feasting for the whole population. At such a rhythm, Eumedes worried that the palace reserves could be wiped out should the next harvest be mediocre.

When Minos proposed more celebrations and sacrifices instead of the modest spring rites with libations to Potnia Athana, Ariadne spoke against it with the priestesses. But the Throne Room was packed with followers of Minos and their sons, Androgeos's troupe, and the women's objections were cast aside. It was in this climate that Ariadne burst into the Hall of the Double Axe one peaceful afternoon, brandishing a blood-smeared piece of linen.

'Look!' she shrieked with excitement. 'My first blood! We'll see how Minos proposes to ignore it.'

Minos proposed to do just that. Ignore it. The Princess Ariadne would have her first bleeding celebrated in the Great Shrine, but there would be no women's dance, the Mistresses would send no pretenders to depose the old King, because Minos had already decided whom his stepdaughter would marry.

*

'Mamá! You must have known about this! Why didn't you tell me? I will never marry Androgeos. I'll kill him first!'

Ariadne's face was white with fury, and the worm in Pasiphaë's stomach squirmed. She should have predicted this. She shook her head. 'Minos never tells me anything.'

'Adoni can't marry Andro. He can't dance. Not like

Poppy-head. Perhaps you can box instead of dance.' Asterion beamed, and his little eyes twinkled at his joke. 'Or Andro could bull-leap for you. Poppy-head says he thinks he is the best bull-leaper of all.'

Ariadne's furious glare died, and her eyes slipped out of focus. A faint furrow of calculation appeared between her brows. When she spoke again, her voice was cold, distant. 'This nightmare is your fault, Mother. You lost all respect and your reputation before I was even born, but the Mistresses have given me the wit to think for myself. I will have my rights, by making Androgeos's dreams come true.'

The words were like slap in the face with a cold, hard hand. A faint smile spread over Ariadne's lips, and she left, not trusting Pasiphaë with the details. She thought herself far beyond her mother in intelligence and the ways of the world. She was bright and sharp, quick to learn and forgot nothing, but she had not learned compassion or sensitivity. If she noticed she had cut her mother to the quick, she felt no remorse.

*

Pasiphaë kept to her Dolphin Chamber for days. There was nothing in her head but the pounding hammer of grief. She longed to have Asterius back, to hold him in her arms again. Ariadne's insult would not have been so hard to bear then, but Asterius had gone and so had the voices of the Mistresses. Even Asterion had retreated into one of his dark moods when he allowed no one near him. The air bellowed with distress that could find no expression but in fury. In waves of fists, it would break against the walls of his room. Later, she would hear the sobbing that meant it was over, and she would find him hunched in a corner, cradling in bloody-knuckled hands some broken toy.

While Asterion raged, nothing broke the silence that shrouded her, no murmuring of counsel or consolation from the Mistresses. Even her weeping was confined to the dark chambers inside her head. It was the silence more than anything that drove her to ask the Key-Bearer for a divination. Although she prayed to the Mistresses and poured libations of the best wine to them, they refused to speak to her. She had lost their ear and had never had the ear of the palace to know what this *plan* of Ariadne's was. Pasiphaë wanted to know if it was carrying her towards disaster.

Inia agreed to ask Eleuthia, at her shrine in the cave at Amnisos. Eleuthia, midwife of the Divine Child, would surely see Ariadne's fate. There was a brisk wind when Pasiphaë set out, the litter swaying like a small craft on the sea. It was a time of flourishing green, unfurling leaves and the last blossom in the orchards. The new lambs and kids played in the rocky pastures and the air was tossed with swallows. Yet sorrow had never lain upon Pasiphaë so heavily. The bright bustle of the port, the stevedores scuttling back and forth to the ships tied up along the mole with bales and amphorae, boxes and jars, only deepened it. She smelled salt and fish, tar and blood, heard the raised voices of the buying and selling of the catch, the shriek of gulls and the laughter of women without the cares of dead husbands and lost children. The sounds and smells brought back memories of her only sea journey, and tears pricked in her eyes for all that had been before her then, that was now gone forever.

The path turned away from the port, following the line of the coast. Eleuthia's shrine was in a cave hollowed out by the pounding of the waves in the sheer seaward cliff. At high tide, access to the shrine was through a stair cut into a blowhole. The litter bearers left Pasiphaë at the top of the stair, her heart pounding at the idea of entering such a holy place, listening to the goddess whispering with the voice of the waves.

She descended into echoing darkness lit only by the fire glow of the sacred flame and the reflection of light on moving water. Inia's presence was a fluttering of light and shadow at the altar, where a stone statue of Eleuthia stood, her arms open in welcome. Even the jars in the form of poppy heads held no menace. Pasiphaë knew their meaning and what they held and hoped it would give Inia a vision of Ariadne's future. Nothing stirred, the sigh of wavelets the only sound, and the still, cold air hung heavy with the thick smell of poppy. The smoke from the gum heating in a dish rose around Inia's stern face, softening her features.

Pasiphaë poured wine from the jar carved with poppies and waves, into the stone basin that emptied into the lapping waves where salt and sweet waters met. She stood close enough to Inia to hear her whispered words and breathe in the fragrant smoke. It had become one of her rare sources of solace in the dark days after Asterius. Only poppy sleep soothed when Asterion closed himself in the meanders of his strange mind and not even she dared speak to him for fear of provoking the violent emotion that took control of his body.

The air quivered and the statue moved, her poppy-wreathed head bent, or seemed to bend, swaying in the sweet-scented smoke. Inia tossed gum into the flames beneath the tripod and the smell thickened. Pasiphaë breathed in deeply and tried to grasp the images that formed, but they were too quick, faceless, with hooves to carry them away before she knew. All she saw was a sea, dimpled with hoof marks, thick as honey. She breathed out, raised tired eyes to Inia's face. Her eyes were wide, and Pasiphaë knew she had seen what lay beyond the dimpled hoof prints.

'Has Eleuthia spoken? Has she shown you?'

Inia tipped the smoking poppy into the fire. 'I saw nothing. Only blood. An ocean of blood.'

5

Deukalion

'Well, that's that. They've gone.'

Ariadne flounced into the Dolphin Chamber as if nothing had happened. Her eyes glittered and Pasiphaë knew that she was so full of something that even her mother was worth telling. She played her game. 'Who's gone?'

Ariadne laughed and twirled around, her muscled dancer's legs flashing pale as leaping river fish through the slits in her skirts. 'The boys, men, the team for the games at Athens. And Androgeos with his sycophantic troupe of sheep. Including Ikarus.'

Minos refused to let Androgeos try his luck with the bulls, but Pasiphaë knew he was keen to show off his favourite son. The Athenians were proud of their athletic skills and Minos liked the idea of sending a team led by Androgeos to their next games.

'Minos thinks challenging the Athenians and beating them will bring great honour to Crete. Deukalion thinks it'll get Androgeos killed.'

Ariadne's eyes shone, and Pasiphaë wondered if she knew more than she was letting on.

*

Pasiphaë perhaps hadn't shown sufficient curiosity, but Ariadne told her nothing more. Pasiphaë saw blood in her eyes and although she told herself it was her woman's blood that had still not been honoured as it should, she feared it was more than that. Whenever she left the Hall of the Double Axe and wandered the corridors and galleries around the Court of Ceremonies, she heard the buzz of conversation, snatches of exchanges, but she understood little. Voices faded when she grew close, and in any case, names and places meant nothing to her. She had been away from the life of the palace for too long.

It was from a surprising visit from Deukalion that she learned more than Ariadne had ever told her. Eritha opened the door to a tall youth with a shock of red hair, framed by leaping blue dolphins, the image so bright, so full of life, that Pasiphaë smiled before he had even presented himself.

'Lady Pasiphaë, I hope I'm not disturbing you…'

'Not much disturbs me anymore, and never a visitor.'

'Then… I'm Deukalion. Perhaps you've heard of me from Princess Ariadne? Can I come in? I have to ask…'

Whatever had been holding him up, courage or courtesy seemed to give way, and he fell down on his knees, bending his head, as a child would to beg his mother's blessing, or a subject before his Queen. The gesture moved and confused her. She touched his head and made him get up. His voice was quick and bright like Ariadne's but there was no sharpness in it. His eyes were a golden green, his looks were striking and pleasing, and Pasiphaë found herself hoping that the surface was a reflection of what lay inside. She led him into the hall and called for another chair. They sat by the great window that looked east upon hills and flocks, living things, not dead painted clay. He gathered up his courage and his courtesy.

'I wanted to ask you if Princess Ariadne had spoken to you.'

'Spoken about what in particular?' She couldn't say that Ariadne told her nothing about anything. He paused and twisted his fingers in his lap, his bare feet shuffled.

'About marrying Androgeos. Surely she can't be in agreement!'

Pasiphaë was unsure how much Ariadne would want her to tell Deukalion, but the boy seemed so distressed and sincere.

'If your father has not succeeded in changing the custom, and Ariadne is still allowed to marry the King the Mistresses choose for her, she will pray it isn't your brother.'

Deukalion's eyes lightened a little, but they were still clouded with doubt. 'Ariadne *says* she despises all of them, my brother's troupe and the Greek he confides in, but she can't keep away from them. She can't be interested in that contemptible little shit, can she?'

'Ikarus? I think she feels much the same way about him as she feels about Androgeos.'

Doubt turned to hope. Deukalion asked eagerly, 'And she never talks about him, not in a *positive* way?'

Pasiphaë almost smiled. 'His name crops up when she talks about the games at Athens. She seems to find it amusing that Androgeos and all his friends have gone.'

'Amusing? It stinks to high heaven.' He raised his eyes to hers and they were full of concern. 'Ariadne spends so much time with Ikarus. She's plotting something with him, she must be, and if it's not marriage... She won't tell me what, says it's a secret, but I'm certain it's something to do with what she calls *her rights*, and it'll end badly. How can she trust a Greek?'

His voice had risen in anger and fear. Fear for Ariadne. She couldn't tell him that her daughter's destiny was bathed in blood. She refused to believe it herself.

'Ariadne's a match for Ikarus, if he's as stupid as she describes him.'

'Ikarus couldn't plot his way through a labyrinth! It'll be his father behind it, that snake-eyed Greek! He hates us, despises us, and resents being made to work for Minos for his keep.'

Pasiphaë had no love for Daedalus and thought that he

ought to have been grateful to Minos for giving him asylum in the palace. 'I don't understand. Daedalus must take whatever he's offered.'

Deukalion gave her a dark look. 'Perhaps he's found someone to offer him what he wants.' He sighed, his hands falling open in a tired gesture. 'I've tried to find out what's going on but Ariadne won't confide in... anyone. She seems to have no close friends.' Pasiphaë listened, let him talk. 'The trouble is, Ariadne cares more about *her rights* than...' His expression softened, grew tender. 'If the Mistresses were to choose me, if she were to ask them, I would gladly be her King. I've told her but she just smiles and dances away. I wonder if she doesn't despise me as much as she does Androgeos.'

'Ariadne despises a lot of people, but she's never led me to believe she thinks badly of you.'

She had never said anything in his favour either. Ariadne wasn't like that. Deukalion could obviously have talked about Ariadne for hours, but he was interrupted. Asterion had been drawn by the sound of voices.

'Hello, Poppy-head.'

Deukalion's eyes opened wide in surprise, and he leapt to his feet, recoiling slightly in fear. Asterion was big, not especially tall, but broad and strong. Beneath a narrow, dark-curled brow, his eyes were small, strangely slanted and murky, his nose broad and flat, with flaring nostrils. His head seemed too small for his great shoulders, and he stooped as though beneath the weight of the mass of muscle. His legs were short and he walked awkwardly. His feet had never grown straight and his toes were splayed, cleft. Pasiphaë tried to see Asterion as others saw him, as Deukalion was seeing him, but all she saw was a baby with a gummy smile.

'We watch you dancing, don't we, Am-am-á? You dance well, but you can't catch Adoni Swallow-feet. Poor Poppy-head.' Then he laughed, and his laughter was like the gurgling of a baby. 'Have you come to play with me?' He held out his hand. 'I'll take you to Asti's room. There are bull pictures. You can play with Drupa if you like. He's my best toy.'

Pasiphaë watched Deukalion anxiously, wondering if he would decide that he had stayed long enough. But the apprehension faded from his face and he smiled. 'I'd love to see Drupa.' And he took Asterion's hand.

She watched them leave the room, Asterion with his shambling gait, Deukalion supple and graceful at his side, and the wave of happiness that flowed over her was so unexpected and so strong it was as painful as sorrow.

*

Deukalion came to the Hall of the Double Axe often after that, and Asterion was overjoyed to have a friend. Sometimes Semele brought her daughter to play with him, and there were Eune's two boys, but not often. The women had work to do, and they couldn't be watching children at the same time. Unlike Ariadne, he had no contact with the children of the nobles and spent most of his time alone.

The women fussed over Deukalion and made the same kind of remarks to one another they would have made when they were young girls leaving Kolchis all those years ago. They were older now, married, all except Eritha, and their rather earthy remarks were tempered by maternal feelings. They had children after all. Semele's moon face was placid now, the old sorrows faded.

'He's a good lad, that one. Steady. If Ariadne's any sense…'

'If.'

'She's *clever* all right, too clever by half, some might say.'

'And she's a sight too full of herself. If I'd had a lad like that come courting me when I was her age…'

'We all know what you'd 'a done, Arete, spare us the details.'

'Go on, you'd 'a been the same Tyro, an' you, Eune.'

Semele sighed. 'It breaks my heart the way those green eyes of his go when he says her name, poor flower.'

'Aye well, it's not mopin' and sighin' that's going to win him any points with our Ariadne.'

The voices lowered into the gentle clucking of hens. Pasiphaë wasn't meant to hear when her women talked about Ariadne, so she pretended she hadn't. If they said what they thought, it was because she had never beaten honesty out of them. Circe wouldn't have stood for it, but, well, she wasn't Circe, was she?

She welcomed Deukalion's company as much as Asterion did, even if she was under no illusion about what drew him to the Hall of the Double Axe. He came to talk about Ariadne, to make himself agreeable to her mother, as if she might have an influence over her. But he was gentle with Asterion, kindly. He brought him presents of carved pieces of wood, seashells and pebbles. And he was patient, sitting with the great baby and playing with his herd of wooden cattle and Ariadne's dolls that she had cast aside years before. He even offered to take Asterion to watch the boxing in the gymnasium, but Asterion had shaken his head sadly and told him that the outside wasn't good for him.

'We'll practise on the Court of Ceremonies then,' Deukalion had said. When he smiled his eyes disappeared into narrow green slits behind his curled golden lashes. 'You can watch from your mamá's Dolphin Chamber, and I'll wave to you.'

He did too, and Asterion crowed with delight. The women watched with maternal pride, and when some of the athletes stared with a too insistent curiosity and made snide comments, they nudged one another.

'Did you see how Deukalion put that little gobshite in his place?'

'He's a loyal lad. He'll not have any of their lordships poking fun at our Asterion.'

'Is Deuka telling them why Asti can't come to play?'

'He is that, flower, an' he's telling that thick gawn that he'll knock his teeth down his throat if he asks again.'

Asterion gurgled his contented baby gurgle and waved to his friend. It was a happy afternoon, or as close to *happy* as ever afternoons came since Minos ruled. Pasiphaë watched Deukalion, imagining what it would be like to have such a son. She would have spoken for him to Ariadne, braved her temper if she accused her of interfering in her affairs, but she never had the opportunity. In all the long weeks that the ships that carried the team to Athens were gone, Ariadne did not come to the Dolphin Chamber once.

6

Games

Pasiphaë heard the news from the games. Androgeos was, apparently, taking all the prizes, and Minos glowed with pride. The offering to Poseidon's three sea goddess daughters would be dedicated to Androgeos and his safe and glorious return. Minos himself would officiate as High Priest of Poseidon, and a bull, a splendid one, would be sacrificed. There was, of course, no talk of Ariadne's official presentation as Queen. That, she supposed, would take place when Androgeos returned covered in honours, in the hope that the celebrations, and the announcement of his marriage to Ariadne, would make the people forget that they even had a Queen.

Ariadne was being ignored. She prowled, out of sorts and on edge. On the day of the sacrifice, she had been by turns good-humoured, indulging Asterion when he wanted her to play dolls with him, and snapping at the servants over a mislaid paintbrush. Priests and priestesses from the shrine at Amnisos thronged the stairs before the Great Shrine, but Pasiphaë hadn't joined them. In fact, nobody had thought to ask her. From the window of the Dolphin Chamber, she watched the crowd that filled the Court of Ceremonies. She watched, but with an ear turned to the Bull Room where Asterion was playing. She heard Ariadne's squeal of surprise before she noticed Minos.

*

The bull, drugged and tethered to his iron ring at the altar, awaited the knife with a resigned expression. Minos gazed at the expectant crowd, the wealth of Knossos gathered about his feet, priests, priestesses and merchants. Beyond the walls of the court, the great sea of the people watched too, all one with him in his pride and joy. At his side, his precious youngest daughter Phaedra officiated as High Priestess of the Serpent Mistress. A relatively minor cult, but she was young yet. He was hoping for great things from Phaedra.

His heart swelled with pride in what he had achieved, but more than pride in himself, Minos was full of Androgeos, the son who would follow him. He would bring him home in a blaze of glory and prizes, and he would present him to the people as the next King. Ariadne, her *rights*, custom itself, didn't even cross the threshold of his thoughts.

It was into a dream of dynasty and grandeur that the messenger from Athens arrived with the news that Androgeos was dead. The ceremony stopped; the music fell silent. A cry went up, a wail of horror that became the bellowing of a hundred bulls. The messenger's words clanged back and forth inside Minos's head, and he realised that the bellowing came from his own throat. With a sob, as the tears broke, he plunged the priest's spear into the struggling bull's neck with all his force. It was not a bull he saw coughing to death in its blood, but the whole of Athens.

*

Ariadne watched and listened with her entire body, leaning over the parapet, her lips parted, brow furrowed with concentration. Minos was bellowing something, then he finished the sacrifice. Blood flowed and he left in a flurry of purple and gold.

'Go down and find out what the crowd are saying,' she

ordered Eune. 'If the news is what I think it is,' she said to her mother, 'Minos is going to be very angry.'

Her parted lips curled into a grin of victory.

*

Whatever Ariadne discovered, she didn't tell Pasiphaë. It was Deukalion who told her the details as he had heard them from the messenger.

'Ikarus had been telling the Athenians stories about the bull-leaping, how dangerous it is and only the bravest attempt it. Of course, they wanted a display, and of course, Androgeos was only too willing, with Ikarus egging him on, telling anyone who'd listen about his skill and courage.'

Pasiphaë was appalled. The bull-leapers were special, they devoted their lives to dancing with the bull. They were experts, yet they didn't live long once their reactions slowed.

'But Androgeos never trained as a bull-leaper!'

Deukalion raised his hands and shoulders in incomprehension. 'But he's always been stupid, and he's always believed Ikarus's flattery.'

'So, he tried to leap a bull he didn't know, without any training and without a team to back him up, and the bull got him?'

'Worse than that. It was Ikarus chose the bull and prodded it until it was thoroughly enraged. He passed it off as making the dance a bit more interesting. How the Athenians must have laughed! Ikarus apparently danced around, claiming to be drawing off the bull, but he was simply goading it. Androgeos didn't have a chance.'

'But why would Ikarus do that? Androgeos was his friend, wasn't he?'

Deukalion shook his head slowly. 'I knew something murky was going on. I never guessed—'

The boy's voice caught in a sob and he began to tremble. Pasiphaë sent Eritha to make him a calming drink.

'Minos will have Ikarus's hide for this.'

Deukalion swallowed, recovering himself. 'Ikarus has gone, last seen boarding a fast ship to Sicily. King Aegeus of Athens will pay. Ikarus is an Athenian after all. Minos is demanding a heavy tribute in goods and slaves, including the life of Aegeus's son, Prince Theseus, in revenge.'

That explained why Minos had had Daedalus locked up. If Ikarus wasn't caught, his father would die. It was too much to unravel, too tangled. Daedalus could rot in prison for all Pasiphaë cared. She was more concerned by the part her daughter had played. Was this the blood that Inia saw, or only the first small waves?

'I must go, Lady.' Deukalion got to his feet, his jaw working with the effort of keeping back the tears. 'My father is giving his orders, commanding the fleet. I must be there if he has a role for me.'

He wouldn't, they both knew that. He said it wistfully, knowing that Minos would only notice him if he was his last surviving son. He deserved a better father than Minos, but whoever gets what he deserves?

*

Theseus furrowed his brow, trying to understand. Aegeus had accepted the demands of the Cretans without a murmur, and they were monstrous. The country people would starve if they handed over such a quantity of grain and livestock. What shocked Theseus, though, was the tribute of a hundred young men, no girls this time, from noble families, including the King's own son in retribution for the death of one idiotic Knossan. Aegeus stood there with an expression of infinite sadness on his face, as if that made it all right.

'You can't be serious!' Theseus stormed, and Aegeus motioned to the servants to leave the room. 'I saw what happened! It was that fool Ikarus who got his Prince killed.

Maybe he had a grudge or owed him money, I don't know, but it was none of our doing.'

Never had a royal Prince been sent to feed the Knossan monster. There had always been a margin for bribery or substitution. The idea was preposterous! Theseus glared at his father, seeing senility in the face that now reflected only the familiar paternal doting. He rarely tried to discover what lay beneath the surface of an expression, having not much use for the subtleties of human nature.

'You're already a hero here, but this is your chance to become a legend, boy, the hero who killed the Minotaur and liberated the Hellenes from the Cretan oppressor.'

Theseus's green eyes narrowed. 'How?'

'Well, you get on the Cretan ship, they take you to Knossos, you and your companions go into the palace, and you take it.'

The simple smile on his father's face broadened. Theseus would have liked to wipe it off with the flat of his hand. 'Just like that?'

Aegeus frowned slightly, as if he was beginning to think his son obtuse. 'With Minos and his fleet either chasing Ikarus or blocking our ports until all the tribute is paid, Knossos will be as defenceless as a twelve-year-old virgin. You're surely a match for a half-man. And think of the prize!'

Theseus let it sink in. The prize, a kingdom handed to him on a plate. It seemed too good to be true. 'And when Minos captures Ikarus, and with the entire Cretan fleet after him, he's bound to, and quickly, where does that leave me?'

'Minos won't capture him. This wasn't some fortuitous accident, you know, Androgeos and the bull, Ikarus winding him up and escaping. It was all planned. Ikarus has a safe port, Kamikos in Sicily. That wild woman who rules there is more likely to call for a week of feasting in his honour than hand him over to Minos, who she loathes. He'll be held up there quite long enough for you to do what's necessary.'

'Like single-handedly capturing a huge city?'

Aegeus gave him a look almost of exasperation. 'The girl

will be waiting for you, Ikarus said, to make you the King, in return for getting rid of Minos for her. That is part of the plan too. And don't forget to give Daedalus whatever he asks.'

'Why? I shall be doing the fighting, and his son is taking all the risks.'

'That was the bargain, his reward for thinking up the plan, freedom to go where he likes, even return to Athens if he thinks that's where his *genius* will be acknowledged. Ikarus just does what his father tells him.'

And what else was he, Theseus, doing, except his father's bidding? He looked at Aegeus and tried to pierce the laughing light in his eyes. Was this a warning, this story of the father using the son for his own ends? For the first time it occurred to him that the old man might be wilier than he appeared. Theseus had fought hard to convince King Aegeus and his people that he was Aegeus's son and saw most men as rivals and enemies. What if the plan was to get rid of him? Had Aegeus really forgiven him for the business with Medea and her whelp? The old man was quite capable of marrying another slut while he was away waging war on Knossos, and getting another son. The smile on his father's face seemed suddenly less senile, more cunning.

Theseus made his decision. He would conquer Knossos, Crete, marry their Queen if that was the quickest way of settling it, and bring their riches into the orbit of Athens. He began to make a tally of the young men he would make sure were selected for the tribute, already seeing them marching through the unguarded city, cutting down the effeminate men, raping the women. He smiled as the future began to take shape. He would take the riches of Knossos for Athens and its King. And he did not mean Aegeus.

7

The last of Minos

The palace was a chaos of commotion, its usual lively bustle swollen to an angry roar. Pasiphaë seemed to hear bulls bellowing in the deep darkness of the magazines beneath her feet. Even the courtiers had left their languid attitudes at home and hurried from one social or business appointment to another like commanders on a battlefield.

She left the Hall of the Double Axe to look for Ariadne. Asterion was quiet in the Bull Room. He had his women like soft, comforting bird shadows around him. Athamas posted guards on the outer door and watched over Pasiphaë's household himself from the inside. Asterion knew him well enough not to be alarmed by his presence. Inia's words, slurred as if in a dream, echoed inside her head, and the vision the priestess described had painted itself on the walls behind her eyes. She was afraid, and not just for her daughter, but for what she had unleashed upon the world.

In the long galleries, even the painted people hurried, and their faces seemed set and determined. They had lost their gaiety, the children with the waving flowers, the dolphins and smiling sea creatures. No one stopped to greet the former Moon Princess. She wore a light scarf over her head and shoulders, and the only paint she wore was on her lips, a bright splash in her grey face. She listened for a sign, but there were no echoes, not even from the Great Shrine. Perhaps the ghost of the bull was stretching its legs, but the Mistresses were silent.

She found Ariadne with her priestesses in the shrine of the Poppy Mistress, the darkness ablaze with lamps and the air heavy with the smell of burning gum. The monthly rites were finishing, the basin red with blood, and the sound of water flowing was suddenly menacing, like the hollow growl of a caged beast. Pasiphaë waited on the sill. Beyond the upraised arms of the Mistress was a dark door that led to the room full of bones, some chewed by animals, others not. The sound of their distress, animal and human, washed like a tide in those shadows. She could go no closer.

She waited, emptying her mind to fly in a mild sky above soft clouds, weaving the only magic she had ever really learned. The empty sky was the place she flew to more and more often, when even the dolphins were of no comfort, and Asterion's mood was dark and his movements disjointed, like one of Daedalus's dolls. She waited until Ariadne had washed and disrobed and led her priestesses to their apartments that looked down on the eastern hill slopes, beneath the Hall of the Double Axe.

'Adoni, I have to speak to you.'

Pasiphaë almost asked permission. Ariadne seemed so much more imposing than she was, than she had ever been. The girl's glazed eyes took a moment to focus and recognise her mother. She left the flock, took Pasiphaë's hands and kissed her cheek. Pasiphaë smelled the gum on her skin and in the folds of her dress, in her hair. The smile on her face was distant, and Pasiphaë knew she was still under the influence of the Poppy Mistress.

'Of course. I can guess what you want to know.'

The smile remained distant, inward-looking. As was Ariadne herself.

*

The apartment where Kriti had been lodged, imprisoned in Pasiphaë's memory, had been dim and windowless, with only a shaft to let in daylight. Now it was bathed in colour. A floral frieze ran around all four walls and the furniture was a pale gold-coloured wood, the seats painted red and gold. The ceiling was like looking up at the floor of the sea, a green wash, scattered with a glorious pattern of complicated shells, extraordinary fish and water plants, lilies and irises, leaping dolphins and dancing seals. It was almost two years since Pasiphaë had set foot in the room, and Ariadne had transformed the place, which had not been refreshed since ancient times.

'How beautiful,' she murmured.

'The ceiling is the sea, beneath our feet is the sky.' Ariadne giggled and swept an arm to encompass the floor, the blue-painted tiles with, here and there, a white bird, gull, egret, a dove with spread wings. 'I had it made. It was my idea.' Even the lingering fumes of poppy couldn't dampen her pride. Pasiphaë should have been proud too, but she heard the ring of disaster in it, like the reckless spirit that leads to the edge of the cliff and the fall beyond.

They sat, and Pasiphaë asked her what would happen now, as if she expected Ariadne to know, as if she was responsible for the turning upside down of Knossos, the murder in a distant land that had tossed the fleet on the seas. Ariadne's smile broadened, and the light in her eyes glittered, focused. She was once again the girl who would have her rights.

'Has Minos gone yet?' she asked. 'I expect he's like a raging bull, taking fire and the sword to the entire Middle Sea. Theseus will be here before Minos even has time to get over his seasickness.'

'Theseus?'

Her eyes took on a dreamy look. 'Prince Theseus, son of old Aegeus, a hero such as the world has never seen. Daedalus told me.'

'The Theseus who called your cousin Medea a sorceress and chased her from her home and husband? That Theseus?'

The dreamy look turned to laughter. Ariadne wasn't listening. 'The Theseus who will defend my right to the throne. Not that Minos is likely to come back from chasing Ikarus anyway. The royal house at Kamikos in Sicily is loyal to the Mistresses, and Minos is the last person they'll help out. More likely rip out his liver for deposing the rightful Queen. But supposing he does, he'll find a hero waiting for him.'

Pasiphaë snorted incredulously. 'It's only in the stories Daedalus and his Greeks tell, that one *hero* alone brings down kingdoms and seizes thrones.'

'He won't be alone. Do you think Minos only has friends, followers and sycophants? The palace is full of arms and plenty of men who'll follow a true war leader. Theseus will lead them, purge Knossos of my enemies, and in return for winning back my throne, I'll marry him.'

Her face radiated a fierce glee, like an eagle's must when it spies a newborn kid. More than any of her tale, this final flourish froze Pasiphaë's blood.

'You've trusted one Greek in a plot that could cost you your life, another to spin a yarn to make it work, and you've pledged yourself to a third? I thought you were wiser than that.'

Ariadne's grin of triumph faltered slightly but she tossed her head. 'With Theseus to fight for my claim, I can't fail. I intend to be Queen, Mamá, and I shall make Theseus my King. Let me be the judge of my ability to control him. He's only a Greek after all,' she ended sarcastically.

Pasiphaë remembered Circe's prediction. The old ways were under threat. So many places had already fallen. Circe herself had been chased from Kolchis, and great Knossos was teetering on the brink. What if Minos wasn't killed? And even if he was, what if his followers refused to accept a Queen, if one of his sons made a counterclaim, if she had been mistaken about Deukalion's ambition? So many ifs. And nothing she could do about any of it.

*

Pasiphaë made her way back up from the darkness of the shrine and its aura of blood, seeing and hearing nothing. Her world had shrunk even smaller. Ariadne was outside it now; she had chosen an armed camp. Pasiphaë's duty was to Asterion. He greeted her with his usual smile of wonder, as if she had been absent for weeks, and hugged her in his great arms.

'Amas watched with Asti, the people being busy,' he said. 'We saw Poppy-head too. No dancing today, though, Amas said. Too busy.'

'Athamas is right, there'll be no dancing today. Perhaps Deukalion will come to see us later, though.'

'Unless he's too busy,' Asterion said, and huffed his hoarse, snorting laugh. Together, they watched the preparations for Minos's last voyage, and Pasiphaë sent a silent prayer to the Mistresses that he would not want to take Deukalion with him.

8

Theseus

The fleet sailed for Sicily, leaving only a small garrison of armed men at Amnisos, and the palace guards. Pasiphaë watched the troops of farm boys, sailors and fishermen assembling in the Barley Court before marching down to the ships at Amnios. Minos was everywhere, striding on his short, muscular legs, bellowing orders and rhetoric of encouragement. Firing their blood, he would have called it. She supposed he was hoping the Queen at Kamikos would refuse to hand Ikarus over, to give him an excuse to wallow in the blood of her people.

When he wasn't shouting at his raw recruits as if they were hardened hoplites, he was invoking the gods. His gods. His last act before embarking was to make yet another sacrifice, this time to Poseidon for the success of his voyage. She caught sight of him as he came out of the Great Shrine. He hesitated, looked about him as if he had forgotten where he was. He wiped a hand across his eyes and raised his face. It was stricken, wild. Anger, she supposed. That it might be grief didn't occur to her.

She and Asterion watched him leave in a war chariot flanked by his personal guard. The memory he left was a colourful one. Asterion had never seen a chariot before and was full of questions, more about the horses that drew it than the contraption itself, which baffled him as to its function.

'Is King Minos sick, his feet hurt?' he asked. 'Asti's feet hurt too.'

He looked at his misshapen toes, lost in speculation about the shape of Minos's feet and why he wouldn't walk like everyone else. The braying of the salpinges, that at first had made him croon with delight, then imitate, began to distress him. Pasiphaë tried to distract his attention.

'Drupa's herd might be frightened by the noise. Let's go inside to comfort them.'

Appealing to Asterion's kindness always worked, and in a few moments, he had forgotten the noise of trumpets and drums and was absorbed in the world of cattle and horses, where the King bull was always Drupa and the King horse Sabazios. Pasiphaë wondered how long it would be before he asked Deukalion to give him a chariot to play with.

*

'Sabazios says he would like a chariot.' At the sound of Deukalion's voice, Asterion had lumbered out of his room, a wooden horse in his hand. 'This is Sabazios.' He held up the horse and smiled expectantly.

Deukalion smiled back, but distractedly. His green-gold eyes were troubled. 'Hello, Sabazios. I know you already. I'll see what I can do, Asterion.'

Pasiphaë led him to a seat, but he couldn't sit still and paced incessantly to the window and back again, his attention always wandering to what was going on outside, listening for a change in the low hum of activity.

'Father's gone and left my brother, Katreos, in charge. He had no post for me.' The words sounded bitter, but he shrugged and turned the thin line of his mouth to a smile. 'He has enough men with him to capture one foolish Greek, and who wants to sit in a port blockade watching cargo being loaded?'

'I've spoken to Ariadne,' Pasiphaë said, cautiously. 'She doesn't think Minos will be welcome in Sicily.'

'She's right. The new Queen has already protested about the higher tributes.'

'She also told me that the old King Aegeus is sending his only son with the tribute. A King agreeing to send his son to his death?'

Deukalion listened with only half an ear, as if the fate of the Athenian Prince didn't much interest him. 'He wasn't given the choice. The ship should be here tomorrow.' He turned to Pasiphaë then, his eyes wide and frank and full of a young man's suffering. 'Have you news of Ariadne though? I never see her. She's stopped practising with the other dancers, never visits the music rooms or the gymnasium. She hides away with her priestesses, making offerings and libations, but for what? Why has she withdrawn from the court?'

Pasiphaë heard his real question: *Why has she turned away from me?* And she couldn't tell him the truth. 'She doesn't confide in me. I wish she did. But it would be in character for her to be praying for a storm to wreck Minos's ship.'

He gave a wry smile and nodded. It was in character. Pasiphaë longed to reveal Ariadne's plan to Deukalion, but what could he have done without betraying the girl he loved? The Mistresses, if they even cared, had declined to advise her on the matter.

*

The last verses of the story came not the next day, nor the day after. Storms held up the ships leaving Athens, and there could be no news from Sicily for at least a week. The priestesses of the Great Shrine were constantly solicited by the families of the men gone with Minos, making offerings for their success. Few thought it necessary to offer for their safety. The Cretan fleet was the greatest in the world, that it carried only sailors and a handful of soldiers didn't seem to matter.

The ordinary people saw nothing reprehensible in being the most powerful, but many of the governors and superintendents who had advised Asterius warned Minos of the dangers of treating trading partners as subjects and exerting heavier and heavier taxes. Pasiphaë remembered being present at one council meeting, in the early days when she was still paraded at his side. Eumedes had pointed out the obvious, that a country with no army would be ill-advised to provoke countries who believed in nothing but warfare. Minos had simply laughed.

'None of them would dare lift a finger against us. They have their toy soldiers, but where are their ships? Crete controls the tide of trade. Crete *is* the tide of trade. Without us, they wouldn't even have pots to piss in. They'd have nothing but their bickering and tribal quarrels.'

Pasiphaë saw the sense in Eumedes' warning and knew that Ariadne was playing with fire. She waited with apprehension for the Greek Prince to arrive. Ariadne was bringing the wolf into the sheepfold, and the shepherd with his dogs was too far away to even hear the cries of his flock.

*

The threads were drawing together like a spider enveloping its prey, so quickly Pasiphaë had scarcely time to be afraid, to wonder how life was to be lived afterwards. The sea storms that had been felt in Knossos merely as pleasant cool breezes to stir the heavy summer air, finally ceased. One morning, the tide brought in the ships from Athens. A messenger arrived panting in the great west entrance, looking for Katreos. The news spread in minutes, and although Pasiphaë dreaded the idea of the crowds, she couldn't stay away knowing that, whatever happened, her daughter had set it in motion.

Again, she left Athamas in the Hall of the Double Axe, fearful more for Asterion than herself. The royal road was crowded as everyone hurried down to Amnisos, and rather than drawing attention to herself by calling for a litter, she joined them. It had been so long since she had walked anywhere outside the walls of the palace, beneath the broad sky, and she basked in the ephemeral feeling of freedom. She stopped on the edge of the town, before the road plunged down to the harbour, and let the crowd, eager to get as close as possible to the docks, flow around her.

The first ship was manoeuvring into its berth, manned by Androgeos's followers and carrying the larnax containing his remains. The crowd on the mole, gathered to welcome the Prince home, chanted enthusiastically, anticipating the lavish feasting and festivities of his funeral. The second ship, carrying the Athenian Prince and the hundred men of the tribute, hung back at a respectful distance.

When the larnax and the weeping procession of family mourners had set off on the royal road back to the palace, the crowd turned its attention to the disembarking of the prisoners. There was much curiosity, little animosity. Androgeos had been detested by the ordinary people. Pasiphaë had seen Katreos, dressed in a golden kilt and a heavy gold neck chain, at the head of his household, but she couldn't see Ariadne. She had assumed she would want to see her Prince arrive, but of course, Ariadne would be preparing for what came afterwards.

A group of armed men waited to escort the prisoners, their heavy belts and helmets glittering in the sun. Pasiphaë watched the sky but there was no sign, no soaring eagles, not even crows. Perhaps it wasn't yet time. She waited for the Greeks to march past, not knowing what she expected to see, chained hands, cowed expressions? Or was she hoping that the Prince in whom Ariadne had placed her trust had a glimmer of the goodness she saw in Deukalion?

*

Theseus squinted in the light, too bright after the dark of the hold, but he held his head high as he led his companions of the tribute from the port to the city of Knossos. As ordeals go, the voyage had not been a tough one. The prisoners had been well fed, they had not been chained, and they had even been allowed up on deck. For quite long enough, in his opinion. The sight of waves and nothing but waves had unsettled Theseus more than he would admit. The Cretans had paid them scarcely any attention at all. The insult was palpable, and Theseus would happily have massacred every one of them, but his fear of the sea was stronger even than his pride. His companions, sons of nobles, the best blood of Athens, didn't know one end of an oar from the other. An unsung, unwitnessed death at sea was not how he intended to leave this life.

He glared at the handful of guards detailed to escort the prisoners. Another insult that would be wiped away in blood. He registered, without much interest, the fat flocks grazing in the pastures at either hand, and focused on the city on the hill. He saw no defences, no walls, no spear points glinting along the top. Only cascades of flowers, gilded horns, painted pillars and balconies. Crowds had come to peer at them, as if they were exotic animals, and so many women, unaccompanied, heads and shoulders uncovered, painted faces. One, grey in her dark hair, a red gash of a mouth, stared at him unashamedly. He stared past her, contempt and disgust mingling.

Perhaps it was his unimpressed expression, the faint sneer forming on his lips, that the guard marching next to him noticed. He nudged him, pointed with his spear at the coloured boxes piled into the sky.

'See? Knossos. Knossos palace. You ever seen anything more wonderful?'

Theseus couldn't prevent his eyes widening in astonishment. His mouth was dry, no words came. No, of course he hadn't. It was a marvel! Cascades of flowers from undefended terraces. His eyes narrowed, calculating the manifest weaknesses. His father, credit where it was due, had been right. It was more than just possible. It would be child's play.

*

The line of prisoners walking between ranks of the palace guards drew close enough for Pasiphaë to see their leader. She took him, mistakenly, to be no more than a boy. It was his stature that misled her, short but muscular. His hair was the colour of dead leaves, a deer's winter coat. He walked proudly, his head held high, his eyes on the palace that climbed the hill before him. He walked past, looked through Pasiphaë – she was just a woman, too old to be worth a glance. Then she saw his eyes widen in wonder just as hers had done, when he realised the town was a palace, the biggest palace he had ever seen. She watched his face, listened for a voice in her head to whisper, *yes, yes,* but there was silence, and the wonder left his eyes. They grew furtive, cunning, and her heart sank.

Bringing up the rear of the file, a guard, captain, wearing a helmet with the boar-tusk emblem of Minos's household, turned his head as he passed. His eyes met Pasiphaë's, and she recognised that arresting green-gold, the thick curled lashes. His eyes too were full of apprehension and a deep sadness.

*

She walked back to the palace, listening to the animated chatter around her, the speculations about what was to become of the prisoners, where they were to be kept and for how long. The most likely place to hold them seemed to be in one of the grain pits in the Barley Court. The harvest wasn't in yet, and there would be at least one completely empty. Pasiphaë wondered if such a makeshift prison would hold the ambition she had seen in the eyes of the Greek Prince.

The palace was emptying of Minos's household and those of his followers, the nobles, the wealthy and all who had not sensed that their King's time was over. She heard the laughter in the throats of a flock of crows, saw the end in the still, bone-white ranks of priestesses, waiting to bless the remains of

Prince Androgeos before he was carried to the family tomb. She could see the place, as big as a rich trader's house with its portico and cedar-wood pillars, looking down on the palace from a hill to the west. The procession, glittering and chattering, was gathering. She could hear the music, before she reached the west entrance, beginning a threnody for the dead.

The wealthy and noble families would follow the larnax, vying with one another in their show of luxurious pomp. The sun glittered on spear points and helmets, small armies of personal guards. Pasiphaë knew the boar-tusk helmets of Minos, the golden crest of his brother Sarpedon, the horse tails of Kerkios the shipbuilder. Feathers, tails and coloured fans, the emblems of all the best noble families, were gathered to accompany Androgeos. All had sent ships and sons with Minos on his mission of vengeance, but most importantly, empty cargoes to be filled with gain and profit. Pasiphaë thought that Androgeos would probably have loved to be at the centre of such a display. Such a shame he'd got himself killed instead and opened the gates to Crete's enemies. The crows that sat among the bull-horned corniches of the porch agreed. She heard their mockery.

The escorted prisoners were taken up the western staircase to the great entrance, to show them the might and glory of Knossos, no doubt to make them tremble. The blindness of vanity. Nothing in the Greek Prince's eyes suggested he was given to trembling before a pile of clay walls and painted wood columns. Pasiphaë wondered that he was still only a Prince. The man behind those eyes did not look like one who would wait patiently for his father's death before claiming his throne.

Deukalion hadn't followed the prisoners. Pasiphaë could see him with Sarpedon and Katreos, the men waiting to escort Androgeos's larnax. His hands waved in exasperation, pointing at the Athenians, the massed guards, denouncing the folly of leaving Knossos defenceless just to escort a boy who was already dead. She knew also that Katreos would be more concerned with his own protection than that of the palace, and too imbued with his own importance to forego leading an army, even if it was only as far as a tomb.

She left the throng gazing in admiration at the spectacle of the wealthy preening themselves, and made her way to the east entrance, through the silence of the empty theatre and the gardens that surrounded it. Here, the birds sang without competition from the bronze braying of trumpets, and she longed for complete silence. She took the gallery with its painted lilies and irises, a froth of white, gold and pale blue, to the stair that climbed to the royal level, to the cool, shaded apartment guarded by the seal of the labrys, where she still thought she would be safe.

She greeted Athamas, who was standing at the door, spear in hand. His lips parted in a smile. He moved aside, a little stiffly, not as supple as he used to be, and she noticed for the first time his black hair was threaded with silver. Kolchis was slipping into the past with their youthful selves. She longed for silence, and the lush green forest memories that only poppy could bring now. She longed for the stilling of the trembling of her hands, the grieving that filled the walls and the air she breathed. She almost called for Eritha to prepare her a strong dose, to let her sleep, but there was Asterion.

He was waiting in the hall, sitting hunched over a game he was playing with coloured pebbles among the inlaid seashells of the terrace pavement. When the door opened, he smiled and came to greet her, gathering her in his great arms as if it had been years. However much she longed for poppy dreams of green forests, she didn't dare leave Asterion in the apartment of clay walls and seashell pavements. Not when his sister walked in blood about the palace.

*

The air was full of swifts and swallows, but their bright twittering couldn't dispel the sense of dread. Perhaps she should have spoken to the Mistresses, made a libation of honey, brought them gifts of flowers, offered a precious coloured stone that Asterion had given her. Perhaps. She knew what *would* happen. Perhaps she should have sought out Ariadne and asked her *how*. But she stayed in her apartments, listening to the swallows and Asterion's low babble of talk.

When they had eaten, Pasiphaë wiped Asterion's face and hands, and he went back to his private game where coloured stones had voices and souls and the pavement was a great sea. She listened for a sign, but the swallows told her nothing. Then the door opened. Athamas let in Deukalion, still in his military apparel, breastplate and helmet, his eyes still anxious. He knelt briefly.

'I just wanted to check that you had a guard at the door to your apartments, Lady. There's not really anything to worry about. The prisoners are well guarded, but...'

'I know, Deukalion. I saw the others leave.'

If an enemy were to attack Knossos, it would be tonight.

She took his hands. 'Guard them well. And beware of treachery.'

She could see resignation in his eyes. He tried to smile. 'I will have eyes everywhere.'

Dusk was fading and the stars were appearing one by one. The torches on the hillside would be lit by now, the funeral games over and the dancing and feasting beginning. She would hear the music from the window in the Dolphin Chamber.

'The old storerooms behind your apartment, Lady, and the ones below, do you know your way around them? Could you show me them, to see if they would be... suitable?'

To hide in, was what he meant. Pasiphaë had already thought of it, but to make a serious investigation would have been to admit of the necessity. She called for lamps, and while they were waiting, Asterion appeared.

'Hello, Poppy-head. It's too late to play. It's almost dark. Bedtime.'

Deukalion forced a smile and took Asterion's stumpy

hands in his. 'We're going to look for some secret places. Will you come too?'

Asterion's mouth opened in surprise then curled into a great crescent-moon grin as he looked at his mother.

'Find your sandals then. There'll be sharp bits on the floor.'

The first of the storerooms were small, mere cubicles with thick walls to support the floor above. They were still in use, full of pithoi and amphorae sunk into the earth, containing grain, oil and wine, Pasiphaë's personal stores. Asterion had poked around in them often enough with Leto, hunting mice. The marten followed. Leto was old, almost blind, but she was still interested in the evening smells. Asterion wandered, peeping with the same inquisitiveness as Leto behind the ceramic jars, tracing patterns with his finger, wanting to know what was in this one and that one. Pasiphaë could sense Deukalion's rising impatience and hurried Asterion along, though he grumbled and dragged his feet.

The reserves came to an end at a door that opened onto a staircase with treads of planed tree trunks. Pasiphaë went first, and Deukalion held Asterion's arm in case he stumbled. At the bottom was another door and, beyond, rooms that were hollows piled with rubble and broken things, debris from the earthquakes. Here and there an unfilled crack snaked across the path and Asterion played at leaping chasms. The air was chill and had an ancient taste to it. In the floor of the last room built into the rock of the hillside, was a trapdoor. Deukalion lifted the ring and heaved it open, revealing a circular room, an old grain pit perhaps.

'This would be a good place,' he said. 'Dry. And the trap isn't too heavy.'

He didn't have to say any more. In the ancient silence, Pasiphaë could hear the running of water in one of the many pipes taking sewage and used water down to the sea. There was no other sound. Asterion, too, listened and whimpered. She took his hand. It was cold. 'We'll need blankets and a ladder, and some water and food.'

She had decided. The water muttered, and the pit echoed sounds from the other pit in the Barley Court where prisoners were hunched, waiting. Deukalion hesitated, probably seeing the time slipping by, not wanting to get involved in unimportant domestic arrangements. She waved him away.

'I'll see to that. Go and find Ariadne.'

His expression changed; his eyes glittered. In his head, he was already running to the depths of the east wing, tracking down the one who had his heart. Deukalion would imagine what he wanted. Pasiphaë had her own reasons for wanting him to keep watch on her daughter.

9

The second star falls

Deukalion left after having a word with Athamas. Pasiphaë had her women take blankets and carpets down to the old grain pit.

'He'll take his death down in that hole!'

'You're surely not going to let the child sleep in a grain pit, are you?'

Pasiphaë would normally have been amused by their concern, but she had caught Deukalion's anxiety.

'Just do it, Arete. He'll take no harm from it if he has warm enough blankets.'

Eritha tapped Arete's arm. 'Don't fuss, nor you, Tyro. I'll stay with him. He sleeps like a boulder as soon as he lies down anyway.'

Eritha had never taken a husband. 'Where would I find the time?' she'd said. 'I have this great baby to look after. That's enough for any woman.'

Asterion took her hand and beamed at her, his wide, gummy grin. 'Asti's going to sleep in the secret place with Eritha, Rete, and you're not to tell anyone about it. Not even soldiers. Deuka said.'

Arete looked at her in surprise mingled with worry. Pasiphaë nodded. 'No one.'

'There's trouble, isn't there, Princess?'

Semele knew. She sensed it. Pasiphaë hesitated. Should

she send them all home? They had homes after all. But it was late, they'd have to find their way across the stony fields in the dark. And she knew they wouldn't leave her anyway.

'There are Greek prisoners in the palace and Deukalion's being very cautious. You know what he's like. He's a worrier.'

'He's a good lad. Thoughtful. But they're locked up safe, in't they? It's just, Eune's lads are here, an' I've got Sima with me today. Mother-in-law's sick and there was no one to watch her.'

'They're locked up, but most of the guards went with Katreos to the funeral. He's just being cautious. But take Sima home. It might be best.'

Semele seemed to hesitate. She looked out of the window at the hills sleeping in darkness. 'If there's going to be wild men rampaging, we're as safe here as anywhere, I reckon.'

Pasiphaë saw the future in Semele's eyes and turned away. 'Asterion, get your warm cloak, the winter one with the fur lining.'

*

They went down to the *secret place*, past the familiar reserves, down the dark stair and past the ruins. Eritha came with them, bringing Leto in her basket. Asterion had insisted. He made *whoo whoo* noises into the rooms where no one ever went, to frighten himself. Once the trap was closed behind them, the only sound was running water, and once Asterion had grown used to it, it served as a lullaby. Leto, though, was uneasy and left her basket to curl up with her big man-child.

Pasiphaë watched him fall asleep, astonished as always at how he slipped from wakefulness to unconsciousness almost instantly. He shuffled himself into a comfortable position, one arm crooked so Leto could curl up against his shoulder. She heard him murmur, *Am-am-á,* sigh gently then begin to snore. Eritha glanced at her mistress. Asterion slept with his mouth open and his snoring was as loud as a bull's.

The trapdoor fitted well, but it was not particularly thick. Pasiphaë would soon find out if it was thick enough.

She had decided to go back to her apartments, to avert suspicion should anyone come. Empty apartments were not usually guarded. Nothing had been said, but there had been no need. It was what always happened when a dynasty was overthrown, the heirs were eliminated. Would the Greeks consider Asterion a potential threat? Their reputation was a bloody one. Like weasels in squirrels' nests, they killed until they couldn't raise their sword arms for weariness.

Before she lowered the trapdoor, she looked down at her sleeping son, prompted by some innate sense to capture that peaceful image and store it away in a room inside her head where it could never be changed. It was not the Mistresses who whispered to her, they had been silent for too long, it was simply the instinct of a mother.

*

All was quiet in the Dolphin Chamber where Pasiphaë slept, but the Barley Court rustled with movement, no louder than autumn leaves stirred by the wind. Ariadne watched from the steps of the Great Shrine as the motley crew of servants with a grudge, discontented mothers' sons, slaves promised their freedom, heaved open the great circular door of the barley bin where the Greek prisoners were kept.

She had never felt so excited in her life. This was what she was meant for, to lead, to command. She would only have those about her who were as strong as she was. Strong and clever. It had been clever of Daedalus to understand that the event most likely to make Minos lose his reason entirely would be the murder of his favourite son. It suited her admirably too. Daedalus was the kind of advisor she would value when she was Queen. She laughed silently when she thought of Deukalion, his kindness and gentleness. Where had it got him? His father despised him and she didn't admire him either.

Ariadne exulted. Before even he climbed out of the barley bin, she had decided that Theseus was the man for her. She didn't deny that Deukalion was brave. He would risk his life for a cause, for something he held dear, but he would never risk his life to snatch a prize. Not like Theseus. That was what she admired, or thought she did. Audacity, the striving for glory, pride. She saw him, standing bareheaded at the foot of the steps, and she stepped out of the shadows of the portico into the moonlight so he would see her. He climbed to meet her. She held out her hands.

'Welcome, Prince Theseus.'

He cut her short. 'Where are the guards?'

He didn't take her hands. She was surprised at the gesture. A flicker of annoyance clipped her reply. 'There are no guards, only a handful. They're probably asleep anyway.'

He looked across the court, let his gaze rove across the rooftops, the columns, the tiers and tiers of sleeping splendour, then back to the Barley Court. Armed men flowed across the pavement to gather in the shadows. She watched his face, how he grinned, thinking of victory probably. And her?

'Are you as rude as this with every Queen who offers you a kingdom?'

He turned as if seeing her for the first time. 'So, you are Ariadne? The woman who's betraying her King and her brother?'

His eyes dropped from her face to her breasts, exposed to show her rank, priestess and goddess, to impress. It was not awe she saw in his eyes, though. Confused, she stammered the beginning of a reply, but Theseus didn't wait to hear it.

'I thought you were a whore.'

He took her hands, though this time they weren't offered, took them roughly, pulling her after him beneath the portico, into the shadows of the shrine.

Ariadne's breath came in sharp bursts of excitement and

alarm. He shouldn't be there, not a man, not armed. She, being a Knossian, being a Princess, a Queen in all but name, a priestess, couldn't imagine what he wanted. When he pushed her to the floor and fumbled with her skirts, when she felt the cold terracotta beneath her, his hard hands between her thighs, it was as though her thoughts were suspended, frozen. Her mind was a black starless sky. He was inside her before she knew, before she could scream, and when he thrust and the scream began, his mouth swallowed it and spat it out. 'Quiet!'

Her thoughts jangled broken into tiny sharp pieces, and they settled in her belly and between her legs where the pain was. But she didn't scream. It would be the end of everything if she screamed. Perhaps it already was. Instead of screaming, she sobbed.

*

When he had finished, he pulled her to her feet. 'The pact is sealed. You belong to me. Now take me to the monster.'

She could barely speak because of the thick, viscous tide of shame, pain and disappointment that filled her mouth with bitterness, her ears with mocking laughter. Through the gloom she knew the Mistresses were watching her and the man she had brought to profane the sacred place. 'Monster?'

'The Minotaur.' He spoke sharply. 'The son of Pasiphaë and the bull. Where?'

'Asterion lives with Mother. What do you want him for?'

'To destroy the monster that devours Greek children, to cleanse the world of the horror of your blood tribute. Now move it, quick. Even your womanish soldiers won't sleep forever.'

Ariadne didn't know what that had to do with Asterion, but her fears were for herself. She stood on the precipice. She was meant to rule, she was sure of it, but amid the clamour of her thoughts, one was growing louder – Theseus cared nothing for her beliefs or her rights. He took her hand firmly, as if she were a naughty child.

'Quick.'

Outside, the Barley Court was empty, and in the guardroom, the only sound was the choking cough of blood bubbling in opened throats.

*

Pasiphaë leapt from bed as the din began outside the door to the Dolphin Chamber. She wrapped a shawl around her shoulders and picked up the knife she had left by the bed. Shouting, the clash of metal on metal, the thud and scuffle of fighting ceased, and the door was flung open. She knew it would be him, the Greek. Theseus stood panting in the doorway. The body of Athamas lay slumped on the ground behind him. Black darts, crows, vicious-beaked, swept across her vision and the taste of blood filled her mouth. She clenched the knife so hard she couldn't feel it.

'Where is he, the monster?'

The voice was precise, imperious. A little fighting cock, she thought, with an ocean of blood on his hands. She turned her sorrow for Athamas to fury, contempt, to keep back the tears. 'Look in the mirror, Greek.'

He strode into the room as if she hadn't spoken. When he was within reach, she lashed out at him, but she had never been taught how to fight, and he knocked the knife away contemptuously, as if she had been a child attacking him with a stick. He pushed her to one side and she saw a figure in the doorway hesitate, flutter, then step over Athamas's body.

'No, Theseus! Stop!'

Pasiphaë's grief hardened into pure anger. Theseus didn't even turn his head at Ariadne's voice, just grabbed Pasiphaë's arm. 'Where is the bull-man, woman?'

The servants clustered in the doorway of their room, ruffled and startled out of sleep – Eune, eyes narrowed and flashing; Tyro and Arete bewildered; Semele, pale, fearful; and small children's faces. Two of the small faces darted away and Eune shouted, 'Run, Pinu, Tiduni! Run home!'

Theseus turned, hesitated, and another child raced into the room.

'No, Sima!'

The child flew, but not fast enough. Theseus let Pasiphaë go and snatched at the girl's hair as she passed. She shrieked as he reeled her in and put a knife to her neck.

'Tell me where the monster is, or you die.' He spoke to the girl, not Pasiphaë. A servant was more likely to tell than the mother. His voice rose to a shout. 'Where?'

Semele ran forward two steps, her eyes on the knife. 'She doesn't understand Greek, let her go! There's no *monster* here.'

Ariadne fluttered into the room, wringing her hands. 'You have no right! There must be no blood shed here!'

Little idiot. Stupid, selfish, arrogant little idiot.

She didn't touch him, didn't get close to that blade already black with blood. His arm jerked back, pulling the blade across the child's throat, but his furious eyes never left Ariadne's. He let the child go, and she fell, gasping then choking on her blood. Semele screamed and he grabbed her by the throat as she leapt forward. 'Where is her son?'

She pointed to Asterion's room. 'Through there.'

He pushed her away and she bent, snatched up Pasiphaë's knife, and with a shriek of fury and grief, lunged at his back. But Ariadne – sharp, quick, clever Ariadne – had anticipated the blow and snatched at her arm, holding her back. Pasiphaë saw not fingers but talons. She stared into her daughter's face and saw nothing that she recognised. She didn't see the desperation. Ariadne's eyes were covered in a veil of blood.

Theseus slashed at Asterion's bed, and stood, panting, in the doorway. The women flocked around Semele where she sat on the floor, cradling her daughter in her arms, rocking back and forth, moaning. Only Ariadne was left standing, apart, like Asasara. Pasiphaë had no fear of death. When Theseus turned his cold anger to her, she didn't move. He could cut her throat and that would be the end. It would almost be a relief. His hand, dark with blood, reached for her. Then Asterion roared. His terror rolled through the empty storerooms, up the dark stair and bounced against the plump bellies of the pithoi in the reserve. The furious eyes flickered, the head turned, and Theseus had only to follow the sound of Asterion's distress.

Pasiphaë struck Ariadne hard in the face. 'You are no daughter of mine, nor of Asterius. May wolf-headed demons take you and your murdering Greek!'

Ariadne stared, wide-eyed with shock, a hand to her cheek. Pasiphaë saw then the disarray of her dress, the stains on the front, and she felt nothing but contempt. She felt nothing when Deukalion appeared in the doorway. His eyes were empty. He didn't even look at Ariadne but followed Theseus into the darkness. Asterion's bellowing grew louder as doors were opened and not closed again. Pasiphaë took a lamp and ran after him.

*

Was it the weight of her mother's hand on her cheek that shook Ariadne so, or the weight of Theseus and his unloving hands between her thighs? Both, no doubt, but it was in that moment of clarity, of light that blazed in her head when her mother struck her, that she recognised she deserved the curse flung in her face. Salt in the wound, it stung, worse than shame. Theseus would not make her Queen. He had given her as much as he was going to. The rest, he would take.

The ringing of her mother's sandals on distant stone flags echoed in her head, but shame wouldn't let her follow. Hopes of redemption turned to feathers and flew away, as time sped and what she had started was accomplished. But her obsessive thoughts remained, like flies trapped in honey. Once Minos was dead, she would be Queen. With Theseus as her King, who would dare defy her? No one among the rabble of Minos's followers. And afterwards?

Even in those moments of pure pain, Ariadne's mind leapt from one possibility to another, her swift, sure feet finding the stepping stones in the torrent. She would let Theseus think he could be a King such as the Greeks had. That had always been his intention. She realised that now. Her thoughts flowed freer, swift and sure. She would show him otherwise. She would think of a way.

Somewhere, in the bowels of the palace, a woman screamed. In Ariadne's head, a gruff, gentle voice chuckled, *Look at Adoni Swallow-feet, Am-am-á.* And the torrent broke its banks as the tears came at last, in an unstoppable flood.

*

Theseus crashed through the dark, stumbling on the uneven floor and pieces of rubble, knocking into doorposts and broken pithoi. Deukalion had almost caught up with him when Theseus reached the empty room ringing with Asterion's wild cries. He wrenched open the trap and leapt inside.

Asterion's bellowing stopped as curiosity prevailed over fear. Pasiphaë slithered down the final steps as Deukalion dropped through the trap after Theseus. She ran to the edge, saw Asterion's face light up.

'Hello, Poppy-head. Who is—'

Theseus. She saw the spear, the careless thrust. Asterion screamed in pain and terror, his hands flung wide, in terror of the pain springing, a red blossom, from his chest.

Deukalion jumped over the jumble of toys and mattresses, and Pasiphaë slid down the ladder. Asterion stumbled towards her, his eyes rolling in terror. 'Am-am-á!'

Deukalion's spear arm swung back, but Theseus pushed Asterion between them, and the spear poised, motionless. Theseus struck a second time, and Asterion's eyes bulged. He fell on his face, his small square fingers reaching out.

Pasiphaë dropped down by his side, and his fingers curled around hers. She heard a muffled *Am-am-á*, a sigh, and then there was nothing but screaming.

She saw Eritha's open mouth as she tried to back away from the two men fighting. She saw her double over when a swung spear raked across her belly. She saw Leto's little mouth clacking open and closed with terror until Theseus stamped on her blind head. She saw Deukalion stumble backwards over Asterion's fallen bulk, Theseus lunge, his spear plunge into Deukalion's throat, the green-gold eyes widen with pain, mouth open on his last breath. But the screaming continued, because it was Pasiphaë's, hers the only throat left to scream injustice to the heavens.

10

The end of the world

The sea glittered bright as unshed tears. They were not Pasiphaë's tears, though. Her eyes were dry. She had used up all her sorrow. She remembered asking once, long ago, what mother would ask for the blood of a child. The answer was clear now – any mother, as long as the child was not her own. The world was full of blood and no pity. Yet every mother's tears sound the same. Perhaps that was why the world had grown twisted. Nobody listened to the weeping. Certainly not the Mistresses. They were dead, or at least they gave Pasiphaë no sign.

*

There was no light left in the world, and the doves were gone long since. She had been given two stars to hold and both now were dark and dead, and not all the weeping in all the world could bring them back.

*

Pasiphaë went to the sea often these latter days and wondered what it would be like to be a dolphin and swim back to Kolchis. Circe had gone, and she had had no news of her mother for so long, she supposed she must be dead, but the royal house at

Aea would still be there, quiet, among the green forest trees full of birdsong. She had been happy then, she remembered, in the forest quiet. She had never been intended for greatness. Perhaps no one is. None of that mattered, though. Nothing mattered now that the stars were dead.

*

Her women stayed with her, Eune, Tyro, Arete and gentle Semele, silent now in her sorrow, but all the others were gone. They told her that Ariadne had rummaged among her boxes in the Dolphin Chamber for the ball of Kolchian thread to dance the marriage dance with Theseus. He had indulged her, called her Queen of Crete, then took her on a ship to Athens. On Naxos, they say, he abandoned her or killed her, unless she abandoned him or killed herself, or she was sacrificed to a Greek god, or she ran off with him, or she escaped and sailed to the ends of the earth. On the winged swallow-feet of a dancer, Ariadne's story flew, veiled in ambiguities. Whatever her destiny, she was gone.

You drew up a sea of sorrows, daughter. Perhaps you drowned in it.

*

Theseus had left Pasiphaë alive because women were not threats. In his world, they were tools to be used, bartered and passed on from one man to another, but not threats. Men made the stories, not women, and Daedalus, when he went back to Athens, told hers: Pasiphaë, the monster who coupled with bulls. So, Theseus left Pasiphaë in her apartments, her room with the leaping dolphins and the room with the running bulls. Asterion's room.

*

She still had the last Drupa, and sometimes, if she had taken enough poppy to let her sleep, to chase away the blood dreams and let her walk in the green forests of childhood, Drupa talked to her about Asterion, how his small hands were gentle, and his smile lit up their lives.